## LOVE PLAY

His lips nibbled at her ear and his hands moved with sure possession over her body as he aroused a desperate need in her. His fingers loosened her hair and it fell like a halo around her on the pillow.

She reached up and pulled him back when his lips left hers, and kissed him longingly. She needed him so! While her lips were so pleasurably occupied, her hands opened his shirt and slid over the coarse hairs on his chest. Physical sensations seemed to consume her. It was so good to feel this way again.

*Other Avon Books by*
**Andrea Edwards**

NOW COMES THE SPRING

*Coming Soon*

ALL TOO SOON

---

Avon Books are available at special quantity discounts for bulk purchases for sales promotions, premiums, fund raising or educational use. Special books, or book excerpts, can also be created to fit specific needs.

For details write or telephone the office of the Director of Special Markets, Avon Books, Dept. FP, 1790 Broadway, New York, New York 10019, 212-399-1357.

# POWER PLAY

## ANDREA EDWARDS

**AVON**
PUBLISHERS OF BARD, CAMELOT, DISCUS AND FLARE BOOKS

POWER PLAY is an original publication of Avon Books.
This work has never before appeared in book form. This
work is a novel. Any similarity to actual persons or events
is purely coincidental.


AVON BOOKS
A division of
The Hearst Corporation
1790 Broadway
New York, New York 10019

Copyright © 1984 by EAN Associates
Published by arrangement with the authors
Library of Congress Catalog Card Number: 84-91073
ISBN: 0-380-87692-2

All rights reserved, which includes the right to
reproduce this book or portions thereof in any form
whatsoever except as provided by the U. S. Copyright Law.
For information address Carol Mann Literary Agency,
168 Pacific Street, Brooklyn, New York 11201

First Avon Printing, July, 1984

AVON TRADEMARK REG. U. S. PAT. OFF. AND IN
OTHER COUNTRIES, MARCA REGISTRADA, HECHO EN
U. S. A.

Printed in the U. S. A.

WFH 10 9 8 7 6 5 4 3 2 1

Special thanks to
Nancy, Joan and Mary

# CHAPTER ONE

Antonia James closed the folder before her with a satisfied sigh and placed it carefully on top of the thirteen others on her desk. A small smile lifted the corners of her mouth as her fingertips ran along the edge of the files. They were hers, all hers, she thought as a thrill of pleasure raced along her spine.

After four years of work for Henderson, Bradley and Smythe, she had been made a manager and these were the fourteen clients that she and her team of accountants would serve. It was a pots-and-pans territory, where all new managers started, but if she made it there, she could make it anywhere. And Toni knew she was going to make it.

When she had come to Chicago after getting her MBA from the University of Michigan, her goal had been a partnership in a public accounting firm by her mid-thirties. Now, at twenty-seven, she was a little ahead of her schedule and still as hungry as ever. She closed her eyes for a moment, savoring her triumph. She had fought her way up one more rung of the ladder and now the top could be seen through the clouds.

As Toni picked up the file folders, the solitaire diamond on her left hand caught her eye. Her sense of victory was heightened by a glow of affection. How lucky she was that Bob not only understood her ambitions, but shared them. He would be just as pleased as she was about her promotion, and the five-thousand-dollar raise. She mustn't overlook that, she thought with a smile. That lakefront condominium that they wanted to buy after their wedding next month was a bit closer now.

"Hey, are you working all weekend?"

Toni looked up to see Simon Bradley, her boss, watching her from the doorway.

"Isn't that what managers are supposed to do?" she laughed, and slipped the folders into a drawer of her desk. "Or is that privilege reserved for partners?"

"No, even partners get Memorial Day weekend off."

Toni locked her desk and took one last look around her office to make sure that no sensitive material was left out. It was a tiny little cubbyhole with black steel, general-issue furniture, but she couldn't suppress her smile of satisfaction. Even an inside office with no windows was still better than the bullpen.

Simon smiled as he watched her. "The fight to keep this is a lot tougher than the fight to get it."

"I'm not planning to keep it," she informed him. "Before too long, I'm going to trade it in for a corner one with a view of Grant Park."

"Well, you can always try," he chuckled as they walked down the hallway with its stark white walls. The sound of their footsteps was muted by the deep carpeting. "After all, you've proven to be a good swimmer so far."

Toni laughed at his reference to the firm's "promote or out" policy. "True, I've come up for air in every pond you've thrown me into so far. Aren't you tired of looking for bigger and deeper ponds?"

"Oh, I still have a few more up my sleeve," he promised. They stopped at a small alcove where he took a light brown raincoat off one wooden hanger and hung it over his arm. "And, when we find the one that's too deep for you, I promise to dispose of your body quietly."

Toni laughed again as she got her raincoat, a slightly more feminine version of Simon's. "Dream on. I'm not going to sink, no matter where you put me. I am a force to be reckoned with."

Simon nodded. "That's what I'm counting on," he admitted quietly, then turned to go. "Have a good weekend."

"You too," she called after him, knowing hers was going to be fabulous. How could it fail to be? Bob was back home and she had the best news ever.

With her coat over one arm and her briefcase in her other, she hurried down the hall and into the ladies' lounge. She was due to meet Bob at Kon-Tiki Ports for a drink and then they would go on to Morton's for a steak dinner, like they did each Friday, and she wanted to look her best.

Her auburn hair was released from its confining pins and fell in gentle waves onto her shoulders. She brushed it briskly until it shone and then replaced some of the pins to keep it back from her face. A little mascara was applied to the thick eyelashes that framed her green eyes, blusher to her cheeks and deep red lipstick to her lips. Then she was ready to meet Bob.

Toni hurried out of the building and down Michigan Avenue, barely noticing the light rain that was falling. Even when a cab raced through a puddle as it rounded a turn, she didn't feel the water splashing her legs. She was walking on air, flying along, as she hurried to meet her love. Her heart was racing at the thought of seeing him again. How had she ever been silly enough to think that marriage was not for her and that a career alone could be fulfilling? Just because her mother had had a string of disastrous marriages didn't mean that she would too. After all, Bob was different. He wasn't looking for a maid, and she wasn't looking for security. No, Bob's love had erased all those sensible plans for a solitary life she had made on the drive from Niles, Michigan, to Chicago when she had started her first job.

Toni thought briefly of the disappointing love affairs she'd had in college and grad school, and how her emotions at the time paled when compared to the real thing. No wonder she had thought marriage was not worth the price, for none of those other men had stirred her heart the way Bob did. He was so perfect in every way: a terrific lover and a good fellow accountant. She wished Simon had not sent him out of town this past week, so he could have been in the office when her promotion was announced. How he would have loved to share in her triumph! It was amazing how many jerks really believed that men have careers but women have jobs. Bob was one in a million, and she certainly appreciated him.

Kon-Tiki Ports was like a trip to Polynesia, even though it was located in the Radisson Hotel on Michigan Avenue. The maitre d' greeted Toni at the end of a darkly paneled hallway and led her across the deck of the *White Cloud II*, the ship used in the movie *Around the World in Eighty*

*Days.* On the other side, they crossed the wooden gangways to the small clusters of tables. Like islands, the tables were surrounded by streams, trickling waterfalls, and high-growing plants.

The maitre d' stopped at Bob's table. He held out the other king's chair for her before handing her a drink menu and slipping silently away. The high rounded backs of the rattan chairs further enhanced the sense of privacy and feeling of isolation that the decor suggested.

"Hi, darling." She smiled quietly and leaned over to kiss his lips. "How was your trip?" She tried to keep her question light, although she knew that her eyes were glowing. The brisk walk up Michigan Avenue had exhilarated her.

"Rotten," he snapped, then shook his head apologetically. "Let's not talk about work. We're together and have three whole days free, so let's just forget that the office even exists." His lips touched hers in a plea for understanding as his hands began a lingering caress across her back that left Toni slightly embarrassed. She wasn't comfortable with such public displays of affection.

"Bob!" She gently pushed his hands away in protest, trying not to be disappointed that Bob's words and mood were keeping her from sharing her news. "Bob, I want to tell you something."

Putting his fingertips gently over her mouth, he stopped her words with a shake of his head. "Let's just talk about us for a change." His voice was low and seductive. "Where shall we go for our honeymoon?"

Toni sighed with resignation as Bob lowered his hand. Well, her news could wait until later. "I thought we had decided on Las Vegas."

Bob nodded. "I know we talked about it, but somehow it just seems wrong for a honeymoon. I was trying to think of someplace quieter, where we could be alone." He looked at her meaningfully as an Oriental waiter dressed in a white nautical uniform came over to their table.

Toni turned toward the waiter, her insides in turmoil from having to repress her excitement; the tall, smooth, pineappley Tahitian she had planned would help right now. But, before she could speak, Bob brusquely ordered a martini for himself and a gin and tonic for her.

A gin and tonic? she thought. She could have a gin and tonic anywhere.

After the waiter had left, Toni looked at Bob in surprise, trying not to sound impatient or angry. "What was that for? Aren't I allowed to order for myself anymore?"

"Did you mind?" He took her hand, suddenly contrite. "It's just that you never let me do things for you . . ."

"Hey, I remember letting you dry the dishes last week," Toni teased him gently.

"Oh, come on, Toni," he snapped. "You're not at the office now. You can cut out the great liberated-lady act."

She felt a rush of irritation but forced a smile on her face. Bob liked to feel that he was taking care of her. Why couldn't she let him without putting up a fuss? Did it really matter what she had to drink? It was such a little thing to argue about. Toni took a deep breath and clasped her hands tightly together under the table. "I really missed you," she said appeasingly. "I just don't feel whole when you're gone."

She could almost see Bob's anger disappear. "Then let me take you to the right sort of place for our honeymoon." He rubbed his thumb on the inside of her elbow.

"But Las Vegas wasn't my choice. I wanted to go someplace quieter."

Bob nodded with an intimate smile. "So that's what we'll do. After dinner, we can get some ideas from a travel agency and take them back to my apartment to study. We'll find a place that's just what you want. Making you happy is all that's important to me."

Bob's solicitous manner was slightly confusing. Not that he wasn't always considerate, but this selfless eagerness to please was something new. It made her feel warm and loved, and eased some of her tension. Occasionally playing the weak and helpless woman for him really was a small price to pay, she told herself, and gulped her gin and tonic. Once she felt its relaxing effect begin, she reached across the table to squeeze his hand tightly. "I certainly do love you."

Bob reached over to kiss her again. "That's the kind of talk I like to hear."

"Some of these places look great," Toni called to Bob. She had taken her jacket and shoes off, and was curled up on the leather couch that filled most of his tiny living room.

Bob's apartment was quite small. The kitchen where he was pouring their brandy was no more than an alcove. He didn't mind, though. Goethe Street was along the Gold Coast on Chicago's near north side and a great address, as he had told her several times. Neither did it matter to him that he could get an apartment twice as large for the same cost or less just a few miles away. This was *the* area to live, and the condominium he wanted was around the corner on Lake Shore Drive.

Toni was not as impressed by addresses as Bob, but she was happy to help him achieve his dreams. It would be part of what they did for each other in marriage. He would help her break out of her middle-class mind-set and learn to appreciate the luxuries that together they would be able to afford. She would, in turn, help him break out of his routine and show him the vast array of things Chicago offered. They would try all kinds of restaurants, go roller skating in the park, see local theater productions . . .

"I'll tell you what really looks great," he said, suddenly sitting down at her side. After putting the drinks on the small table in front of the sofa, he took the brochure from her hands, tossed it next to the brandies without so much as a glance, and pulled her into his arms. "You do. God, how I've missed you." His lips found hers and he kissed her hungrily until Toni pulled away with a satisfied sigh.

"My, that was some welcome."

"Do you know, I almost skipped last night's meeting and came home yesterday?" Bob unbuttoned her white blouse and kissed the hollow of her neck. "Hmmm, very nice," he murmured huskily, seeing her delicate ivory lace bra. Her breasts seemed to glow inside it. He bent down to kiss the valley between them.

Toni's eyes closed as the pleasure of his touch grew. "How would you have explained that to Simon?"

His fingers had continued to unbutton, his lips lingering along her throat, but he stopped at her words. "Nothing's as important to me as you, certainly not some damn meeting." He sounded angry that she should doubt him.

"Now I know what you are planning." She reached up, bringing his head back down to hers. "You hope you'll get fired so I can support you."

"Sure." He parted her lips with his tongue while his

hands, feeling warm and insistent against her skin, slid inside her blouse to loosen her bra.

Toni sighed as his fingers brushed against the fullness of her breasts and his caress roused a fever in her blood. His lips moved to take the place of his hands and the fever grew.

Somehow she was lying on the sofa with Bob leaning across her, when his hands stopped suddenly. Her eyes flew open in surprise. He had not moved, but his face was serious.

"Darling, will you do something for me?" His voice was soft and seductive.

"Sure," Toni said, relieved when his hands went back to stoking her fires. "But I'm not into kinky."

He laughed softly, and kissed her lips with slow, definite possession. Then he moved back and looked down into her half-closed eyes. "Tell Simon that you don't want that new job."

"What?"

Bob ignored her startled cry and bent down to nuzzle the sensitive area around her ear. "Tell him you don't want it."

Toni sat up, shoving him away. "I don't think that's funny."

"It's not meant to be." His hand gently smoothed the hair back from her face. "I just hate to see you being used."

"I don't know what you're talking about." Pushing his hand away, she stood up and moved around the sofa.

Bob rose to his feet slowly. His eyes were sad. "Didn't you wonder why you got that promotion?"

Toni frowned. "I earned it. Why shouldn't I have gotten it?" She started to cross her arms, but realized her disheveled condition. With more anger than embarrassment, she pulled her lacy bra into place and hooked the thin strap of elastic in the back. Then she buttoned her blouse.

"Oh, Toni." His sigh was one of pity. "Do you really believe that? A number of people were quite surprised at your appointment."

"So?" She felt at a disadvantage without her shoes on.

"So, can't you guess what some people are saying?"

She remained silent.

"Some people said that you earned it for overtime on your back."

7

A brief flicker of anger flashed through her eyes. "That's a rather tired insult. If you really want to shock me, you'll have to come up with something original. Something that almost every woman hasn't heard each time she won an award or honor."

He took a step toward her. "Oh, I knew it wasn't true. And I told that to those busybodies at the office. But the fact that you were given the job to satisfy some equal opportunity quota isn't much better."

"That's not too original either. Especially since you know very well the government doesn't pay much attention to little firms like ours."

"No, but Simon always did like to be in on the latest fads."

Toni gave him a cold look as she walked around the sofa and slipped into her shoes. She wouldn't listen to this at the office, so why should she listen to it here?

Bob sighed, coming over to take her hand, but his touch had become abhorrent and she avoided him.

"I was afraid that you would take it this way, but I felt I had to tell you." His eyes were sadly knowing.

Toni was not fooled. "How kind of you! And which part was your own personal touch? The equal opportunity quota?"

"Oh, darling, how can you ask that? You know I'm only thinking of what's best for you. Didn't you think it was strange that you were chosen ahead of so many others?" He pleaded for her understanding.

Unfortunately, she understood well enough to see through his protective-fiancé act. She walked over to where she had left her jacket, pushing her hair back when it fell into her face. His timing had been perfect, she acknowledged. With her body aching for his, she was torn apart by his insults. Had he been counting on that?

"Why don't I ask Simon if what you say is true?" she suggested cynically.

Bob was shocked and took a few steps toward her. "What good will that do? Do you really think he'll admit that they're just using you?"

"How can you be so sure that they are?" Toni argued. "How do you know I didn't get it because of my ability?"

He turned away with a shrug. His brandy was next to him and he picked it up, his back to her all the while. "I

8

happen to know someone else was meant to get the job," he admitted reluctantly, staring into the liquid in his glass.

Toni's eyes narrowed. "Who?"

"Does it really matter?"

"Who?"

As Bob sipped his drink, everything became clear to her. "You thought you were going to get it. You're jealous because I got the promotion, not you."

He started at her words. "I'm not jealous," he snapped, spinning around to face her. "You make it sound like some lovers' quarrel. I was promised that job, and I don't intend to be cheated out of it."

"And who promised it to you?"

"Your precious Mr. Simon Canfield Bradley, that's who. He promised me the next audit manager position that opened up. Why do you think I left Price Waterhouse? I had a good future with them."

"Did you?" Toni scoffed, remembering things she had shrugged aside earlier. "You were there for four years and you still hadn't made senior."

"I explained that to you." He became livid with rage. "My managing partner had it in for me. It didn't matter how good I was at my job, he would never let me move ahead." He took a deep calming breath. "Besides, that has nothing to do with this."

She just shook her head. "Maybe it does. How can you be so certain that I didn't truly earn this promotion over you? Do you really think I am that bad an accountant?" Her voice taunted him defiantly. "After all, I made senior in two years."

Bob looked away, visibly fighting to get control of himself. With an exasperated sigh, he turned back to her. "For God's sake, Toni, don't make a federal case out of it. Just tell Simon you don't want it, and we'll be done with this."

"So you can have it instead."

"If you really loved me, you'd do it."

"That's almost funny," she said quietly. "I was just thinking that if you loved me, you wouldn't be asking me to do this. You'd want to earn your own promotions, not get them by default."

Her words set fire to Bob's still-smoldering temper. "I have earned it, damn you! I won't stand by and have some idiot partner who wants to do the 'in' thing steal it from me!" He stopped for a moment and eyed her unpleasantly. "Or maybe I was wrong. Simon always did take a strangely close interest in your career."

His meaning was very clear to her, but when she said nothing, he went on. "Or wasn't it just Simon? Maybe old Mr. Henderson and Don Smythe were in the fun, too. Somebody must have been laying you, because you aren't much of an accountant."

Toni stared at him for a long moment, her eyes reflecting a mixture of animal anger and agony over the death of all her dreams of love. "What happened to all those flowery speeches you made over dinner? Were they just an act?"

"Hey"—he shrugged contemptuously—"isn't love all just an act? I gave you what you wanted to hear and you were supposed to give me what I wanted."

"If that's all love really is, then I think I can do without it." She turned toward the door.

"Can you?" The smirking contempt in his voice made Toni feel sick to her stomach. "Didn't you moan about how empty your life was before we met? Do you really want to go back to that?" He followed her slowly, his voice losing some of its anger as his self-assurance grew. "You can't play the macho career girl and still be treated like a woman, you know. And that's what you really want. Your sexy underwear under the damn nun suits proves that." He leaned against the wall in the narrow hallway, his arms crossed as he gazed at her body. The look in his eyes was insulting.

Toni took a deep, unsteady breath as her shaking hands picked up her raincoat. Her chest felt as if it were being crushed by some huge weight. Had her heart really broken or had she merely stopped breathing?

"You won't hold out for long," he mocked. "Your work'll never be your whole life again. You want a man's hands on you more than you want that promotion." He watched as she put her coat on and buttoned it up. "Think about it, and call me on Sunday."

Toni carefully tied her belt and smoothed down the ends. Then she pulled the diamond ring from her left hand and laid it on the table near the door. "Go to hell," she said, amazed that her voice sounded so steady and composed.

She let herself out the door and closed it gently behind

her, as if that gentleness could ease the unbearable pain in her heart. Her anger had already been replaced by sorrow. What had happened to that beautiful love that she thought had been hers? How could Bob have killed it like that?

With slow, careful steps, she walked down the narrow staircase, through the entryway, and out onto the sidewalk. The day seemed to have been unending. Exhausted, she had to force her feet to keep moving. How could Bob have betrayed their love? she kept asking herself, but the only possible answer was as painful as the question. He had never really loved her. An intolerable sense of loss enveloped her.

Toni automatically walked toward the lights of the Ambassador East Hotel. She had stopped in front of it, trying to focus her thoughts, when a tall, elderly black man in a brown uniform walked up to her.

"Are you all right, miss?"

Toni stared blankly at him.

"Are you all right?" he repeated. "Can I get you something?"

She realized she must look as terrible as she felt and tried to smile. "I would like to get home," she said, suddenly wanting nothing more than the privacy of her own apartment. "Can you get me a taxi?"

"Sure. Why don't you sit inside and wait?"

Toni shook her head and sat on the edge of a nearby concrete planter. The nakedness of her left hand caught her attention. How empty it looked! With a trembling finger she gently rubbed the white streak where her ring had been. That was all that was left of her love—a faint scar that would fade quickly in the summer sun.

She closed her eyes and put her knuckles to her mouth, fighting back the tears. If only the hurt would disappear as fast!

"It turned out to be a beautiful night."

Toni opened her eyes. The doorman was back, and watching her with kindness. She fought the temptation to cry at his gentle smile, and looked around her.

"I hadn't even noticed that the rain had stopped," she admitted.

"Not only that," he said, looking up above him. "It's cleared up. The stars are coming out."

Toni looked up too, but the lights of the city were too

bright, and the stars were invisible to her. She shook her head with a smile at the old gentleman as a taxi pulled up in front of the hotel.

The doorman walked over to it with her and opened the door. "Those stars are there," he told her quietly. "You just have to keep looking so you can make your wish on the first one you see."

"Sure," Toni agreed weakly as she climbed in the cab. She suddenly realized that she had no tip ready to thank the man for his thoughtfulness, and fumbled in her case.

Reading her mind, he put his hand over hers and shook his head. "No, you just find that star and make your wish. I don't need anything."

"Thank you," she whispered, tears rushing to her eyes again.

The doorman closed the taxi door, and she gave the driver her address. Then she leaned back against the seat, staring out the side window. It hardly mattered whether she saw her star or not; her wish was going to come true. She would make certain it did. Never never again would she stray from those goals she had set while in school. Marriage and commitments were not for her. She would not let love and all its pain get close to her again.

# CHAPTER TWO

Sam Morici paced about his small office nervously. He was sixty-two years old and had money enough to burn, or throw away on a stupid two-week vacation in southern France. Mid-America Supply, the little restaurant supply house that he had started over thirty years ago, had grown beyond his expectations. So when was he going to be able to relax and enjoy it?

He reached the door of the room and peered out into the general office area. Everyone seemed to be busy working even though it was a Friday afternoon in mid-June and they all probably would rather be outside soaking up some sun. That's what Frances had wanted him to do: stay home and relax by the pool, even though he had done nothing but relax for the last two weeks. She couldn't see any reason why he had to go in to the office.

"It survived the whole time we were gone," she had pointed out. "Don't you think it can last another weekend without you?" Thank God he hadn't listened to her!

Mrs. Flores, the executive secretary and informal head of the clerical staff, saw him standing in the doorway and paused in her typing. "Can I get you some coffee, Mr. Morici?"

He nodded curtly. "But what I really want is Ramsey. Haven't you found him yet?"

"He got my message back in the warehouse," she assured him soothingly, rising to her feet. "He knows that you want to see him, so I'm sure he'll be here soon. He must have been detained by someone."

Sure, Sam thought. Ramsey was probably busting his ass to get there. He watched Mrs. Flores go for his coffee, absently appreciating her calm, efficient manner. She was

13

in her late forties and had been the perfect secretary for all the years he had known her. There was none of that liberation junk. She knew her place and stayed there. Not like some others. The worries returned and he went back into his office.

Sam could feel himself sweating. Damn air conditioning must be on the fritz again. Or more likely, it was a power problem. They'd had a lot of electrical problems in the building this spring. The old place was sound enough, he knew, even though it was about seventy years old, but it was starting to cost more and more to keep up. The plumbing had had to be replaced six years ago, the roof four, and now the wiring.

Hell, it was hotter in here than outside. Or was it all in his head? He knew he had to learn to cool it, but it was hard with that jerk Guy Ramsey around. He was a two-bit street punk. Strutting around the place like he owned it. He didn't, though, Sam reminded himself; it was his. His and his partners'.

Sam clenched his jaws as he thought of the silent partners he'd let in when he'd needed a little cash years back. After that he had been richer than he had ever dreamed, but with all that gold came a little dirt.

His pacings brought him back to the door and he glanced over at an office just down from his. The door was open but it was dark inside. He wondered how Jon was. Maybe he'd be back from his rounds before Sam left and they'd have some time to talk. It seemed like they never really talked anymore. Not since Jon joined the firm last year.

Sam sighed. Maybe it had been a mistake to have his son come work with him, but this place would be his one day. His and the partners'. That was the problem, he knew. Just how did he explain the partners to Jon?

Sam looked up to see Guy Ramsey strolling toward him, and a more immediate problem wiped the other from his mind.

Tall and handsome, Guy was overflowing with confidence. As Sam watched, he stopped several times to flirt with a girl or slap a man on the back. He acted like he was running for mayor, Sam thought angrily.

"Hey, El Presidente," Guy boomed out jovially when he caught sight of Sam in the doorway. "I hear you're looking for me."

"Could we go into my office, please?"

Guy continued smiling. "Right on, guv'nor," he replied with a salute.

Sam slammed the office door shut once they were both inside and walked over to his desk, his eyes blazing. "I don't need your comic act out in the bullpen."

Guy's affability was tossed aside like an overcoat. "What do you want?" he snapped.

Sam was thrown off guard. Damn bastard. One of these days he was going to put his foot down and Guy would be out. After all, he owned 51 percent of the company, and was the president. He didn't have to put up with Guy.

As he stared into the coal-black eyes though, some of his bravado slipped away. There were many rumors about Guy Ramsey, but Sam himself had seen the young Puerto Rican warehouseman Ramsey had left covered with blood. His mistake had been cutting Ramsey off in the parking lot, something Guy had seen as a personal affront. That picture lingering in his mind, Sam swallowed nervously a few times before starting to speak. "Well—"

A gentle tap on the door interrupted them and Mrs. Flores stepped in. "Here's your coffee, Mr. Morici. Can I get you anything, Mr. Ramsey?"

Sam curtly thanked her, while Guy shook his head. She pulled a withering leaf from the plant on Sam's desk before moving soundlessly toward the door.

"What the hell are you doing about our new audit manager, Ramsey?"

"What's there to do?"

Sam gulped at his coffee and made a grimace. Frances was right. He was going to have to cut down on this garbage. Not only did it look like it came out of a septic tank, but it was beginning to taste like it. On top of that, it set his nerves on edge.

"Don't play games with me. You know we have some rather unique accounting requirements."

"No fooling." Guy snickered.

"God damn it, Ramsey!" Sam slammed his fist to the desk. "I've told you a hundred times I don't want any trouble."

He watched Guy draw on his cigar, knowing Ramsey'd like to see him have another cardiac. Right here and right now.

The cigar came out of his mouth and Sam was favored with a cold stare. "I told you when I came here, Morici, I would take care of the books. Everything's under control." He was cool and confident.

Sam pulled a handkerchief from his pocket and mopped his brow. "Lou wants to know if there are going to be any problems with the new audit manager."

Guy glared disgustedly at him. "What the hell did you tell him for? You know that I handle all operational matters with Lou."

That showed how stupid Ramsey was! Sam thought with disgust. How could he have told Lou? Sent him a postcard? Sam went back to his original worry. "Well, will there be any problems with the new audit manager?"

"Hell no. It's just some little broadie a few years out of college. Her virgin veil probably ain't even broke yet."

"Have you talked to her?"

"No, I haven't talked to her. What for? Should I clue her in on everything?" Smiling contentedly and blowing his cigar smoke toward the ceiling, Guy continued. "Look, Morici, we do it like we always did. We cooperate with all her requests, just control what data we give her. No problem. Besides, she's got at least ten other accounts. It ain't like this is General Motors with everybody watching."

"Yeah? Well, things had better stay under control or else."

Without taking the cigar from his mouth, Guy sneered. "Or else what? You can't do nothin' and we both know it."


"Sorry that I never made it to Star Communications this morning, George," Toni apologized. She put her briefcase down on the long work table at Mid-America Supply and pulled a chair out to sit down facing him. It had been a long Friday already, and it wasn't over yet.

George Manning was one of the accountants on her team. He was nearly the same age, but certainly lacked her drive and push and needed almost constant direction and supervision. That was what she had planned to provide this morning at Star.

"I got stuck on the phone with Peoria, and then had to run down to Federal to settle some things there. With Carlson still sick, that place is in a mess! No one has the right experience." She wearily pushed back a few loose strands of her dark red hair.

George nodded. "Going from private ownership to public is always a lot of work. I'm surprised that Simon gave the account to you."

"Why shouldn't he have? I can do it."

"Hey!" George raised his hands in mock surrender. "Don't be so touchy! I just meant that it was a lot to throw at you when you were new to the job."

Pacified slightly, Toni opened her briefcase and began sorting through some papers. "Did you go through those files yet?"

"No. Rosie hasn't brought them in, but she ought to have them by now. Maybe I'd better go see what she's doing."

Toni watched with narrowed eyes as George left the room to check with the young accounting clerk who had been assigned to help them. He was certainly casual about getting those files, but then he was casual about everything from his appearance on up. His suits always had a faintly rumpled look to them, as if they were at least one size too large for his short, pudgy body, and his copper-toned hair never seemed to stay neatly combed. Had he been this lackadaisical for Martin? she wondered. Or was he playing games, thinking she was an easy mark just because she was a woman? She thought she had put enough pressure on her team in the past three weeks to dispel any such misconception.

Suddenly impatient with her thoughts, Toni got to her feet. She grabbed a few coins from the wallet she kept in her briefcase and left the room. She had to stop being so sensitive, she scolded herself sharply as she walked down the hall to the coffee pot in the lunchroom. What difference did it make what George or any of them thought of her if they performed their jobs? She had to take a more professional attitude toward her managerial responsibilities and stop seeing antifeminists around every corner.

Since Bob's derision, though, she had been suspicious of every remark, no matter how innocent. Working like a dog, she was determined to prove them all wrong. She was going to be the best damn audit manager they had ever seen. People would not wonder how she had gotten the job, but why she had not gotten it sooner.

She picked up a white Styrofoam cup and filled it with coffee. It didn't matter that the long hours she spent working were taking their toll, she told herself, tossing a quarter into the change box. So she was a bit drawn and had lost weight. Once things were under control she would go back to her running and be back in shape in a few weeks. She was also not concerned with her reputation as a slave driver, even though Simon had had to tell her to ease up on the troops. She knew she was doing an outstanding job and that Simon and all the firm's other managing partners had agreed.

The thing that she could not explain to anyone was that she welcomed the long hours. The heavy work load kept her busy so that there was no time left to weep over Bob. Actually, it left her no time for any kind of socializing, but she didn't miss it. In time, she supposed, she would drift into some light, casual affairs, but they would be strictly for fun and would never interfere with her career.

George was still gone when Toni returned with her coffee, and she glanced around the empty room. Mid-America Supply was one of their smaller clients, and for their occasional visits, she and George were relegated to this seldom-used meeting room. Its pale green walls were bare, with no pictures and only one venetian-blinded window, a light switch, and two outlets. In the center of the room was a standard six-foot work table surrounded by four molded plastic chairs in a bright orange. A file cabinet reposed in a corner near the door, and on its top lay a beige phone. It was an impersonal room, yet typical of the places she worked in.

She walked across the room with her cup of coffee and sat down in one of the chairs, glancing at her watch impatiently. If George didn't bring those files soon, she was going to build a fire under him.

Just as she was about to get some matches, George came back into the room.

"Get lost?" she snapped.

George shook his head in disgust as he tossed some folders onto the table. "I couldn't find Rosie at first, and then when I did, she didn't have the files anyway. Seems Mr. Ramsey didn't give her the necessary approval."

"But you got them after all?" She reached over and picked up the first folder and began to page through the contents. A frown came to her face and she quickly flipped through the other files. "These can't be their five largest suppliers. I doubt that these would even be in the top half. Did you specifically ask for the top five?"

George shrugged. "Yeah, I did, but I told you, Rosie didn't have approval on those. The office manager finally said that I should just take these."

Toni looked at him in astonishment. "But you should have insisted on—"

"Look, Toni, Martin always accepted what they turned over."

"Martin is no longer audit manager. I am," Toni reminded him tersely. "We have a responsibility to do a proper audit, and that does not include reviewing files selected by some damn clerk."

"But they don't care," George replied with a slight whine.

"I do."

George licked his lips under her stern gaze. Toni rose to her feet. "I'll get this straightened out myself."

She didn't mind some compromise, but George had certainly picked up some bad habits under Martin. She sighed. Well, he had better be ready to change.

Down the hallway from their workroom was a large office area, and behind that was the warehouse space where Mid-America Supply stored the restaurant equipment and supplies that they sold. Toni went down into the large open office and looked around her. Her lips tightened. Rosie was not at her desk. Since she was nineteen, unmarried, and getting desperate, she must be chasing some stray pair of pants.

Rather than waste time looking for the clerk, Toni went over to the row of small offices along the far wall where Guy Ramsey had his office along with other managers of the firm. Mrs. Flores looked up from her work as Toni approached; a warm smile came over her face.

"Miss James, how are you today?" she asked. Her faint Spanish accent seemed to add a musical quality to her voice. "How nice to see you again. Is there something I can do for you?"

Toni put the files she had been carrying onto Mrs. Flores's desk. "It's these files," she explained with no hint of her earlier frustration and anger. "They aren't the ones Mr. Manning asked for when he was in last week."

Mrs. Flores picked them up with a sigh. "I knew they weren't, but I was hoping you could use them. Mr. Ramsey was in a meeting with Mr. Morici and couldn't be disturbed."

Toni smiled back slightly, fighting the temptation to point out that they had had the list for more than a week, so why had they waited until the last moment to check it out with the controller? Instead, she glanced around, and noted that most of the offices were dark.

"Is he free now?"

"Well, Mr. Morici left a little while ago, so that meeting is over, but I'm not certain just where Mr. Ramsey went. He is in the building; that I know."

"Thank you. If he comes back, would you tell him that I would like to see him?"

Mrs. Flores nodded and went back to her transcription, but as Toni walked away, the older woman stopped her. "Oh, Miss James, I do believe that I saw him with the younger Mr. Morici. Perhaps they went for some coffee."

"I'll look there. Thank you for your help."

Toni walked back down the hallway she had just come along, not particularly anxious to confront Guy Ramsey. Even though he was in his middle thirties, good-looking, and seemed to ooze charm and self-assurance, she did not trust him. His clothes were expensive and well tailored, the Brooks Brothers' image of conservatism and unspoken authority, yet the man inside them was far from that. The fact that he was crude and unpolished did not bother her, but the fact that he so obviously did not respect her did.

At their first meeting Ramsey had dominated the conversation, spouting opinions on everything from accounting controls to trade relations with Japan. Mixed with his pronouncements had been crude jokes and double-entendre remarks. She had kept her temper under control by thinking of a cartoon she had seen in a *Salesman's Coloring Book* while in graduate school. The caption had read: "See the man. He is dirty, ugly, obnoxious and he stinks. He is my customer and I like him."

With a deep breath, she went into the lunchroom.

Jon Morici was bored and irritated. He had spent another whole day smiling at restaurant managers and trying to convince them that they really wanted to buy a more expensive quality of paper napkin. He certainly had an earth-shattering responsibility resting on his shoulders.

He tried to push the impatience and annoyance from his mind, and sank into the soft leather chair in his office. His father needed his help and that should be what counted, not the trivial irritations of the job. After all, look at all the old man had done for him. Vacations all over the world. Yale for his architectural engineering degree. Harvard Graduate School of Business. So what if this job hardly made use of his design skills? This was his father's business, which he had built into a large, successful firm, and one day it would be all his.

The thought was so depressing that Jon jumped to his feet and wandered from his tiny office. This wasn't what he wanted to do with his life, he wanted to cry out in frustration. He wanted to get back to his architectural and design work, but how could he? He couldn't tell his father that he hated this business when it had been his father's whole life. There was no way, he knew; not after his father had had that heart attack last year and the doctor had warned him to slow down or he'd have another one. No, this was where he was stuck and he had better make the best of it.

If he could just get more into the managerial side of it, he thought. Things might be more interesting if he could do some real work instead of attending civic luncheons and wining and dining their larger clients. Maybe he'd try another talk when his father got back from vacation. This time he wouldn't let himself get pushed off onto some other issue. He would demand more responsibility, so that his father could take it easy like his doctor had ordered him.

"Jon! Hey, I'm glad you got in early today!"

Jon was surprised to see his father standing in the doorway of his office. "I thought you weren't due back until next Monday."

"So, I missed the place," his father laughed. "Come on in for a minute. I've got a surprise for you."

Jon went past him into Sam's office. It was the same size as his own, but the plants on the desk and the framed snapshots on the wall gave it a more lived-in look. It wasn't a place his father came to once or twice a week to return calls and process orders. No, it was more like his home. It was a part of him.

The collection of photos of himself and his mother, some sitting in a place of honor on his father's desk and some on the wall, awoke the nagging sense of guilt that seemed ever present these days.

Jon turned toward his father to avoid his thoughts. "So how was France?" he asked, noticing the lines of worry that his father's new tan could not hide. Hell! What a trap he was in!

"It was okay." His father shrugged. "Your mother thought the food was terrific, but you know me, I don't like ta eat nothin' I can't pronounce." Jon smiled as his father went on. "But that's not my surprise. I made you reservations tonight at the Ninety-Fifth, and the dinner's on me."

"What are you talking about?" Jon asked with a frown.

"Isn't tonight the night you're taking out Steve Gendler's daughter?"

Damn! He had forgotten about that date his father had roped him into. "Yeah, so it is," he muttered with little enthusiasm. "You know, Dad, I wish you wouldn't get me into these things."

"This won't be like those others," his father promised. "Steve's a great guy. You'll like his daughter, I know."

Sure, Jon thought morosely. Just like the other ones he'd been stuck with.

"And if he buys that new kitchen equipment that he was looking at, you'll like the nice little bonus in your paycheck," Sam said with a laugh. "Doesn't seem quite fair, now that I think about it. You're getting two bonuses out of the deal. Seems like the lady's company ought to be enough."

Jon smiled slightly as his father's hearty laugh boomed across the room. Actually he'd be delighted to do without both the lady and the bonus, and feel like he owned himself again.

"Well, I promised your mother that I wouldn't stay long, so I'd better be going," his father said. "Come up for dinner over the weekend, why don't you? Your mother's anxious to see you."

Jon nodded and walked with his father to the door. The vacation didn't seem to have helped him, he thought as he watched the older man leave the building. He looked just as tired and worried as ever. Why wouldn't he share some of the responsibilities?

Jon began to walk down the hallway toward the lunchroom, when another man approached him.

"Getting some coffee?" Guy asked. "Sure would rather have a shot of whiskey right now."

Jon turned toward the other man and shrugged. Guy was his father's right-hand man, but that didn't mean that Jon liked or trusted him. Nonetheless, he could think of no real reason to refuse to have a cup of coffee with him.

"Now here comes a nice piece of ass," Guy snickered as they carried their cups of coffee to a table.

Jon looked up and saw a neatly dressed young woman in the lunchroom doorway. Her navy blue suit could not hide her trim figure or the shapely legs that emerged beneath it. The deep auburn of her hair hinted of a fire smoldering beneath.

"Wouldn't you like to—" Guy's coarse whisper changed as the woman approached them. "Why, Miss James!" he cried, his voice and manner courteous. "You're just what I needed! I was getting tired of Jon's ugly face."

Jon took a sip of his coffee, not surprised that Guy made no effort to introduce them.

"Mr. Ramsey—" the woman began.

"Guy! The name's Guy. Come on, sweetheart, you're part of our big happy family here."

She smiled politely and made a slight bow with her head, but Jon sensed that she had not been won over by Guy's charm. "Okay, Guy! We have a problem here that I would like to discuss with you."

Guy smiled expansively before looking at Jon with a snicker. "Hey, I need a club to keep them off." He turned back to the woman and, still smiling, he said, "My place or your place?"

"Since we're already here at your *office, Guy,* I see no reason to make the long trip downtown to my *office.* I think we can adequately handle our *business* right here."

Jon almost burst out laughing at the flicker of surprise that flashed across Guy's face. This lady certainly had his number.

Guy's smile remained unchanged, though, as he turned again to Jon. "She's a cool one, isn't she, Jon? I wonder if they stick them in a freezer before they give them a diploma."

"I wouldn't know," Jon replied, giving the lady an encouraging smile, but her eyes were on Guy.

"Your company is paying for the accounting services of my team, Mr. Ramsey, so I don't think it's fair to joke around on your company's time. If we could go to your office, we could solve the problems that are impeding my team's progress. Then we can go back to earning our pay."

A slight smile curled Jon's lips as he watched Guy over the edge of his coffee cup. What now, Mr. Smooth Talker?

Guy's smile became a bit tighter, but he was not going to admit defeat, that was obvious. "Why don't we cover this accounting business this weekend?"

"Certainly, Mr. Ramsey, just tell me what time and I'll schedule my team and my managing partner."

Guy flashed Jon a quick look of unmistakable meaning, and Jon regretfully rose to his feet. He had enjoyed this cup of coffee more than he had expected. "If you two will excuse me . . ." he said politely as he edged away. He wondered if he was asking for too much if he hoped that his date tonight had at least half the spirit of Guy's Miss James.

Guy's smile left with the other man. "All right, what's this accounting business you want to talk to me about?"

Maybe they'd get someplace now that he didn't have his friend to impress, Toni thought. "We've been trying to complete our audit and we need the invoices from some of your largest vendors. Rosie says she hasn't got your permission to give them to us, so all we got were the files from some very minor vendors. We really need those other documents to perform a quality audit."

Guy waved his hand in disgust. "Dumb broads, they make a big deal out of everything."

Toni did not doubt that she was included in that general classification.

"I'll take care of it."

"Will we have the documents when we're back next week?"

"I said I'd take care of it," Guy barked.

Toni smiled politely. "Thank you," she said as if it had

been a normal conversation, not a battle of wills. She turned to leave.

"Hey," Guy called in a low voice. "What you got planned for the weekend?"

Toni turned. "Why, Mr. Ramsey? Did you want me to schedule that meeting after all?"

A leering smile curled Guy's lips. "I was thinking of a more personal meeting."

"You mean with your family?"

"I keep my family out of my personal life," he snickered.

"Well, I keep my clients out of my personal life, Mr. Ramsey. Good afternoon. Have a good weekend." Her polite smile stayed firmly in place until she was out of his sight.

# CHAPTER THREE

With an exasperated sigh, Jon tossed back the dark brown sheet and sat up on the edge of his bed. The movement had been sudden and was instantly regretted as his head began to pound. The bright morning sunshine streaming into the room didn't help much either. He should have known better than to drink all that wine last night. And if he remembered correctly, it hadn't made his date seem any more interesting. What was her name anyway? Sally? Sadie? Sassy?

Who cares? he asked himself as he got to his feet and walked carefully across the deep white rug to the bathroom. After taking a couple of aspirin, he glared at himself in the mirror. His dark brown hair was mussed from the hours of tossing about trying to sleep, and his eyes looked puffy and bloodshot.

"You are an ass," he informed his reflection with disgust. "After thirty-three years of Dad's bullshit, you should have known what this latest dame would be like. Blonde, early twenties, terrific figure, and dollar-bill-green her favorite color."

He picked up the electric razor that lay on the glass shelf below the mirror and flicked it on, running it over the dark stubble on his cheeks. That was the last time he was going to let his father talk him into entertaining the daughter of a customer. No more favors. His workweek would be from nine to five, Monday through Friday, like everybody else's.

The phone interrupted his thoughts, and he put down the razor with a frown. He had a good mind to let it ring, and carefully put toothpaste on his toothbrush as he tried hard to ignore the impatient ringing in the bedroom. Unfortunately, the noise made the throbbing of his head unbearable.

Damn! Whoever was on the line seemed to know that he was just being stubborn. He put down his toothbrush and stomped into the other room.

"Jon? I hope I'm not disturbing anything." His father's sly laugh made him wince.

"I was brushing my teeth."

His father snickered with disbelief. "I was just thinking that you should bring Sissy up to the house tonight. Your mother's planning a barbecue, and you could bring your swimsuits. Nothing like a moonlight swim to heat up the blood, eh, son? Or maybe don't bring your suits. I've seen Sissy and I'd bet she'd be ripe for skinny-dipping. Your mother and I could discreetly disappear for a while."

"No thanks," Jon snapped. "Last I saw of Sissy"—was that really her name?—"it was about three o'clock in the morning and she was going off in a cab."

"What do you mean, the last you saw of her? You let her go off alone?" His father was horrified. "What kind of gentleman are you? She's just a kid. How can I face her father again?"

Jon bit back an impatient curse. "Look, she was above the legal drinking age and knew her way around the Rush Street bars like they were home. I was probably in more danger there than she was."

"My God, Jon! Is that any way to talk about a lady?"

But Jon had had enough, and hung up the phone. "Lady, my ass," he snapped as he strode back to the bathroom. "I should have told him that she was going to Sixteenth and Christiana because she insisted that was the only place in the city where she could get real Lebanon Red. Of course, the important thing was that she was born in Winnetka, went to the right schools, and had had a year of finishing school in Europe. So who cares if she majored in controlled substances? We can overlook these little quirks in her personality and plan the wedding, right Dad? Just think of how impressed all the old pisanos from Taylor Street would be to hear that your son was marrying some rich, highbrow dame. That would be the real sign that you've made it, wouldn't it?"

The phone began to ring again, but Jon was not going to listen to any more of his father's crap. He put on a pair of cutoffs and a faded gray T-shirt. Then a pair of socks and his shoes. He was out of the house by the time the phone was on its tenth ring.

Toni stood at the window of her apartment and stared down at the street, trying not to think about the plans she had had for this weekend. But even at its busiest, Dickens Street was not a hive of fascinating activity, and at 8:20 on a Saturday morning, there was nothing that could distract her attention.

With a sigh, she turned away from the window. It just was not possible to keep Bob and their canceled plans from her mind, she realized bitterly. Especially not today, on what should have been her wedding day.

She plugged in her electric coffee pot and pulled open the door of the refrigerator. She didn't really feel like eating breakfast, but she supposed she ought to have something before she started to clean up the apartment. A slice of toast should do.

While waiting for the coffee to finish, Toni flipped on the radio, to hear most of "He's a Taker." Waylon Jennings's ballad must have been written about Bob, Toni thought angrily. He certainly took everything she had to offer, took advantage of her love, and took her for granted. That realization suddenly galvanized her into action.

Bob was a bastard, a first-class creep, so why was she mourning him as if something fine and beautiful had gone out of her life? She had painted an unrealistic picture of him in her mind, and she should be glad that she had found out the truth before they had gotten married. She should be out cheering in the park, telling everyone of her lucky escape, instead of moping about inside.

With newfound determination, Toni unplugged the coffee pot and put the butter back in the refrigerator. Then she hurried into her bedroom. Her nightgown was quickly tossed on the bed as she pulled on a pair of shorts and a University of Michigan T-shirt. She slipped her Adidases over some short white socks, and after quickly brushing her hair, she pulled it back into a ponytail. Once a terry cloth sweatband was in place across her forehead to hold back the loose hairs, she was ready to go out running.

And run was exactly what she planned to do: run and

run and run until all the depression had been drained from her body. Until she was too tired even to remember what Bob looked like, let alone all the things he had said to her.

Toni tucked a key into a zippered pocket in her shorts and then let herself out of her apartment. She went down the creaking elevator and across Lincoln Park West to the park itself.

It was a beautiful June morning, Toni realized with some surprise as she began to run along one of the paths. The sun's warmth was like a caress, and a gentle breeze blew off Lake Michigan to dry the beads of sweat that formed along the edge of her hair.

She ran in front of the boathouse and along the edge of the lagoon. A small flock of ducks were swimming placidly along next to her until they sighted two young children throwing bread crusts into the water. All at once, there was a mad scramble for the food, and dignity was forgotten.

Toni laughed out loud at the ducks and realized how strange the sound was. How long had it been since she had felt like laughing? Or even enjoyed something?

Suddenly, Toni was glad that she had come out. She was alive again for the first time since that horrible night four weeks ago. Oh, she wasn't about to start singing or dancing or, heaven forbid, fall in love, but it was good to know that she could still smile and laugh.

As she ran, Toni began to notice the other people out enjoying the morning; some were running, but others were riding bikes or roller-skating. As she followed the edge of the lagoon south past the Farm-In-The-Zoo, where pets were forbidden, she noted the increase in the number of people walking dogs. Not that she minded them, but she could no longer enjoy the scenery as she ran. She had to start watching the pathway.

Not even that could dampen her enthusiasm for the day. Concentrating on the proper placement of her feet became a game. It was a challenge to keep to her rhythm and keep her shoes clean. She became oblivious to the people around her.

Vaguely aware that two teenagers were approaching on bikes, Toni still kept her eyes down, for runners stayed on the paths and bikers usually rode around them on the grass. What she did not see was that a man was running just behind her. As she suddenly slowed and veered to her right to avoid some dirt, he moved to his left to avoid the bikers.

They collided abruptly and Toni went down. Right into a mud puddle on the edge of the path.

Slightly stunned, Toni just stared at her mud-covered hands. She was not aware that someone was speaking to her until a hand reached down to help her to her feet.

"Are you all right?"

Toni looked up with an angry glare at the idiot who had knocked her down. She barely noticed that he was in his early thirties with dark curly hair and brown eyes, or that he looked strong and muscular with no excess weight on him. All that she saw was that his cutoffs and T-shirt were clean while she was sitting in the mud.

"Are you all right?" he repeated a little more anxiously.

Disdaining his hand, Toni climbed to her feet; her eyes flashed angrily. "Look what you did, you idiot! Can't you watch where you're going or do you just like to knock smaller people around?"

"Why didn't I watch?" he repeated in surprise. "You ran right in front of me."

"That's right. I was running in front of you, and since I don't have eyes in the back of my head, you pushed me down."

His jaw tightened, but she went on.

"What did you think I was going to do? I wanted to avoid that puddle."

The man looked down at her legs, liberally streaked with mud. "I would say that you didn't quite make it." A grin split his face.

The idea that he was laughing at her made Toni's blood boil. Her hands doubled into fists as she fought a surprisingly strong urge to reach out and hit him for spoiling her happy mood. Instead, she contented herself with a hateful glance as she looked around for something on which to wipe her hands.

"Want to use my shirt?" He held out the front of it with a mocking smile, obviously expecting her to refuse.

"Why not?" He deserved more than a muddy shirt, but

at least he would get that, she thought as she wiped her hands on the soft gray material.

Close to him as she was, she got a better look at his face, and an unpleasant thought nagged at her. There was something familiar about him. She frowned for a moment and then realized that she had seen him yesterday at Mid-America Supply. He was a friend of the obnoxious Mr. Ramsey! Damn! Just what she needed to spoil her day completely! She quickly dropped his shirtfront. Maybe she could get away before he recognized her.

"Hey, you're not done yet. Want the back of my shirt?"

"No, thank you. I'm all right now." She started to edge away but he followed her.

"How about my pants?" He gestured toward the front of his shorts.

"I said I was all right, and I am," she snapped. "Now, if you'll excuse me . . . ." This time she turned around and began to walk away.

"Look, I really am sorry."

Lord, he was coming with her!

"I know I shouldn't have laughed, but I couldn't help it." He paused, but she said nothing. "It was kind of funny, you know."

Toni shrugged slightly as she continued to walk. Maybe she was making too big a fuss over it. After all, the only thing hurt was her pride, and it was hardly his fault that that was so vulnerable these days. Before she had a chance to say anything, though, he began to speak again.

"Okay, so it wasn't funny." He shrugged. "If you want to clean up, my place is only a few blocks away."

"Very clever," she said sarcastically. "I may be muddy, but I'm not stupid."

Since he was not going to take any of her courteous hints that he leave, she would. Without even a glance at him, she started running again. Unfortunately, a wad of mud on her left shoe made her departure more awkward than dignified.

"Hey, you aren't hurt, are you?" He hurried after her, his laughter gone, and genuine concern on his face.

Toni continued to run. "No, just muddy."

"I wouldn't have laughed if you were hurt, you know."

Toni stopped to look at him. "Look, I said I was fine. Irritated, but fine."

His eyes narrowed slightly. "Say, haven't we met somewhere?"

"That's not a very original line." She began to run again.

"But we have, haven't we?" he insisted. When she said nothing, he continued to run along next to her, silently pondering the mystery. "I know," he cried, as they went through the Farm-In-The-Zoo. "You were in our office yesterday. You're our accountant." He looked remarkably pleased with his discovery.

Toni glanced at him, then slowed to a walk. Her eyes were on a young couple feeding the horses in a nearby enclosure. "Look, I agree that it's quite a coincidence that we met accidentally like this, but . . ." She paused, suddenly at a loss for words. How could she get rid of him without sounding rude and abrupt? "I really am fine, and I would not want to keep you from whatever plans you had made."

"In other words, get lost. Is that what you're trying to say?" He looked more puzzled than offended. "Tell me something before I go off and feed myself to the lions. Are you this friendly to everyone, or did I do something special to deserve it?"

Toni felt like screaming with exasperation. Why couldn't he just leave? "Look, didn't it ever occur to you that I might not want to be picked up by some lunatic in the park?"

Before he answered her, he took a long and thorough look at her. "I don't think I'd want to pick you up. You're too muddy."

His answer was so unexpected that Toni just stared at him for a moment, then burst into laughter. "Don't you even know when you've been insulted?" She laughed so hard that tears began to form in the corners of her eyes.

"Does this mean you aren't mad anymore?" he asked cautiously, still with a straight face.

Toni just shook her head. He wiped his forehead with his hand in an exaggerated sigh of relief.

"I'm sorry I was so nasty about it. I know it was just an accident," she said with a smile.

"Ah, but was it?" he asked mysteriously as they walked north through the park.

She looked at him with a frown.

"Perhaps it was a carefully planned plot to meet you."

A smile spread across her generous mouth. "That would make it a real dirty trick then."

He smiled back, an interested gleam in his eyes. "Let me make amends. Have dinner with me tonight."

Startled by his sudden invitation, Toni stopped walking. Things were getting a little out of hand and she was glad that they had reached the place for her to leave. "That's hardly necessary."

He smiled and stuck his hand out. "The name's Jon, Jon Morici. I know we haven't been formally introduced, but our Mr. Ramsey sometimes lacks in the social graces."

Unthinking, Toni put her muddy hand into his. Then, remembering the dirt, she tried to pull it back.

He just laughed. "So why can't you go out with me tonight? Do you have other plans for the evening?"

"Well, no," she admitted.

"Good. Is that where you live?" He gestured to the large apartment building across the street from them.

"Yes, but I really don't—"

"I'll pick you up around eight," he said, and then with a quick wave of his hand, he went back to his running.

Where was her mind these days? Toni asked herself as she stared after Jon's retreating figure. A laugh in the park was one thing, but dinner? She couldn't date a client. Why hadn't she made it clear that she was not going out with him?

She was not having dinner with Jon Morici, Toni decided while she showered off the mud. It was true that his take-charge manner had caught her off guard, but she was not going to be stampeded into a date she should not have. And she definitely should not have dinner with Jon Morici.

It was nothing personal, either, she assured herself. But, if Mid-America were a publicly owned firm and under the control of the Securities and Exchange Commission, she would be breaking the law by going on the date. As it was, her career as a CPA would not actually be in jeopardy, for

Mid-America's stock was privately held, but it still would be unwise to take the chance.

After her shower, she took her dirty clothes down to the basement laundry room. By that time, she was thinking less like a CPA and more like a woman. Just who did he think he was, assuming that she would be delighted to dine with him? Toni stuffed her clothes into a washing machine. Some women might jump at the chance for any date on a Saturday night, but she was not one of them. She would rather stay at home and read or watch television than endure the company of a conceited male chauvinist.

Unfortunately, Toni could not find Jon's telephone number listed, so her plans to cancel the date had to be postponed. Well, she'd just tell him when he got there, she told herself as she vacuumed her small living room.

By the time her clothes finished drying, the apartment was clean. There wasn't much to it: a small living room with a dining area off to one side, a tiny corridor kitchen, one bedroom, and a bathroom. Toni usually appreciated its compactness and that it only took a few hours to clean, but today she didn't. It was only a little after noon, and the rest of the day stretched endlessly ahead of her.

After a peanut butter sandwich for lunch, she wasted an hour rearranging her living room, only to put the rust-colored velvet sofa, the two chairs covered with a rust and cream plaid fabric, the two end tables, and the glass shelves back where they had been when she had started.

Relaxing with a glass of orange juice, Toni stared at the needlework picture of a lion that hung above the sofa. She wondered if it might not be nice to go out for dinner. Jon was fun and one date was hardly getting involved with a client. It was just a way to get out of the apartment and relax. Besides, it was better than thinking every ten minutes that this should have been her wedding day, and that tonight she and Bob would have been leaving for their honeymoon.

By the time she took a leisurely bath and washed her hair, Toni realized that she was looking forward to the evening out. It would provide a welcome break in her routine.

It was only when she went to her closet to choose a dress that a new set of doubts appeared. That black crepe was

Bob's favorite dress, and she had been wearing the deep purple voile when he had asked her to marry him. Next was a green satin backless sheath with a daring side slit. Bob had loved her in clothes that were rather risqué and had claimed that he had awakened the wicked woman in her.

That did not leave much besides the suits she wore to work each day, a pale blue dress that she had bought to wear on her honeymoon, and a cream-colored cotton. Toni took the cotton dress off its hanger and looked at it. She had bought the dress last year when she was in Mexico on vacation, having liked the bright flowers that were embroidered on the full skirt and wide sleeves. But Bob had not shared her appreciation of the fine handwork that had gone into it, preferring her other, more sophisticated dresses to the obvious ethnicity of this one.

With a shrug, Toni put her Mexican dress on. She had rarely worn it once she had begun to date Bob, so it brought back no painful memories. After slipping on a pair of low-heeled sandals, she brushed her hair and pinned it up in its usual style, but with more fullness.

The buzzer from the lobby rang as she was putting on a pair of simple gold earrings. Toni jumped as if she had not been expecting it. Why was she going out with this man? she thought frantically as she slipped on a bracelet and hurried to answer the bell.

Jon was wearing a dark blue suit with a white shirt and seemed far removed from the laughing man she had met in the park. She had to admit, though, that he was very attractive.

"I thought we would walk up to Ambria, if that's all right with you," he said as they left her apartment building and headed north.

She put her shawl over her arm, but a frown crossed her face. "That sounds great, but how did you ever get reservations at the last minute?"

He took her arm lightly in his, a teasing smile hovering on his lips. "Who said it was at the last minute? Maybe this is the way I spend all my Saturdays."

"Pushing girls in the mud and taking them to dinner afterwards?" Toni asked.

"Well, every exercise program should have a goal—"

Toni gave him a swift elbow in the ribs. "Be serious, now. How did you get a reservation on such short notice?"

He shook his head at her persistence, leaning over to murmur into her ear. "I sell restaurant supplies, remember? They're one of my customers."

Toni groaned, feeling really dense. The gleam in Jon's eyes told her that he was restraining his laughter with difficulty. "Don't you dare laugh!" she warned him. "Everybody forgets things sometimes."

But it was too late; his laughter had broken through, and before she knew it she had joined him. How silly to have stewed so over this date, she thought. He was marvelous company, relaxed and enjoyable. This evening was probably just what she needed after the past month of work and more work.

"Ever been here before?" Jon asked as they entered the lobby of the Belden-Stratford Hotel.

She smiled at him. "Sure, every Saturday that I can trick some guy into pushing me into the mud."

Jon gave her a stern look. "You know why donkeys don't go to college?"

She did not follow his train of thought, and shook her head. "No. Why?"

"Because no one likes a smart ass."

As the waiter poured their wine, Toni looked around the restaurant. Everything about its muted tones bespoke elegance, from the darkly paneled walls to the large mirrors that reflected the white linen tablecloths and gleaming crystal. From where she was seated at the dark leather bench that ran along one side of the room, Toni could see everything. A busboy was unobtrusively clearing a table near them, while a waiter was serving some delicious-looking fish to another couple.

Toni realized that the waiter had left their table, and she turned her attention back to Jon. He was watching her as he held up his glass of wine with a smile.

"Here's to muddy park paths."

Toni smiled wryly and tasted her wine. It was smooth and light and went down easily. She took another sip before she put her glass down.

"You can have the mud. I'll take the wine," she informed him.

After a few more sips, Toni was definitely glad that she had come. Jon was an amusing dinner companion, and she could relax in his company. It was nice to know that someone found her attractive.

As the waiter placed their salads on the table, Toni smiled up at him, then froze in horror. Right behind their waiter, the maitre d' was showing a couple to the table that had just been cleared. The woman was a tall blonde in a clinging red knit dress that left a great deal of skin exposed. Following closely behind her, and quite appreciative of the woman's show, was Bob Morgan.

Toni could not believe it! This was probably the only time in his life that Bob Morgan had gone to a restaurant that wasn't a steak joint, and she had to be there! Her shoulders drooped. There must be a black cloud hanging over her head, she decided, and watched morosely as they took their places. Of course, Bob was facing her. How long would it be before his attention strayed from his companion and he noticed her?

"Something wrong?" Jon asked Toni.

She blinked suddenly, and turned to face him with a bright smile. "No, of course not," she lied cheerfully, and took a steadying drink of wine. "I'm glad our salads got here. I'm starving."

She tried to dig into her salad with enthusiasm, but found her appetite had deserted her. Somehow in the past month she had managed to avoid Bob, so why did she have to run into him now?

As much as she would have liked to ignore his presence, Toni found her eyes drawn to his face. She tried to make a conscious effort to watch Jon as he spoke, but it was impossible. Her mind could make no sense of what he was saying. Putting a vague smile on her face, she let her eyes drift over to Bob.

He had spotted her by this time and was watching with a mocking smile. His eyes seemed hard and cruel.

When she saw the look on his face, Toni suddenly sat up straighter and turned to Jon with a wide smile. What was wrong with her? Jon was a very presentable companion and Bob had no way of knowing that she had just met him that day. Nor would she ever let Bob guess how deeply he had hurt her or how many lonely nights she had spent wishing things had turned out differently. This was her chance to salvage the pride that he had wounded so badly. She would prove to him that his cruel jibes had been meaningless for she had quickly replaced him with someone else.

Toni looked at Jon with an intimate smile while playing absently with her wineglass. "I just realized that I know almost nothing about you," she said with a slightly breathless laugh. "Have you always worked with your father?" Her eyes reflected an all-absorbing interest, for she sensed Bob watching her.

If Jon noticed any change in her behavior, he gave no sign. "Actually, I only joined the firm late last year. I was with a large construction company that was into everything: design, building, and remodeling. But then Dad had a heart attack, and I went to work with him."

"So you'll be running the company eventually," Toni noted as she sipped her wine.

Jon nodded and finished the last of his salad. While his head was bent, Toni bestowed a long, loving look on him that was not wasted on Bob. She saw his face when a busboy came to take her half-eaten salad away. It was obvious that he was quite surprised, and somewhat annoyed, at the turn of events.

"I certainly am impressed," Toni admitted once the busboy left the table. "I thought you were a product of nepotism."

"I see," Jon laughed. "The executive type turns you on."

Toni paused to take a drink of her wine and was surprised to discover that the glass was almost empty again. She drank what was left, and watched as the waiter hurried over to refill it.

"Actually, I like a man who knows where he's going." The look she gave him had an unmistakable meaning. Out of the corner of her eye she saw Bob frown deeply.

Jon leaned closer to her over the table. "And do you know what I like? I like a woman who knows just what she wants." His eyes held hers for a long moment and Toni felt a quiver of sensual excitement go through her.

Bob was suddenly the farthest thing from Toni's mind as Jon reached over to take her hand. His eyes seemed to caress her soul, and Toni realized with a shock just how potent his charm was. Although her mind might have been slowed from too much wine and too little food, her body wasn't. She felt an overpowering surge of desire race through her veins in response to his touch.

They ate their dinner in relative silence, although the air about them seemed charged with excitement. Toni's cheeks were flushed and her eyes glittered brightly as she picked at her broiled fish. Her appetite seemed to have deserted her under Jon's openly desirous gaze. Finally, their plates were taken away and coffee was declined.

"Ready to go?" Jon asked simply.

She nodded and slipped out of her seat. Jon took her arm possessively, leading her through the crowded tables.

As she passed Bob, Toni gave him a bright smile. "Well, hello, Bob," she said, feigning surprise. Bob nodded curtly as his companion chattered on. Toni bit back a laugh at his surly expression. His meal was going to cost him plenty, and he looked like he was going to choke on it.

"My home is just a few blocks from here." Jon slipped his arm around her waist once they were outside.

Toni nodded absently, savoring her revenge as they began to walk. Instead of behaving like the love-sick schoolgirl Bob had expected, she had been cool and controlled. She hadn't reacted angrily to his presence but had been completely uncaring, too wrapped up in her new interests to spare him a thought. The sulking pout on his face as they had left had been beautiful, she thought with a smile. She'd remember it forever.

Jon's arm pulled her closer as they waited to cross a street. "Do you know how beautiful you are?" He kissed her quickly on her neck.

She smiled back at him; the wine and his ardent attention made her feel beautiful, and it was heightened by the deliciously comfortable sensation of being desired.

After turning down another street and walking across a parking lot, they climbed a short flight of stairs to a brick townhouse. Jon unlocked the door and went in ahead of Toni, turning on a light and leading the way down a few steps into a spacious living room.

"This is really gorgeous," she said as she looked around her. One wall, to her right, was dark brick with framed art posters on it. Next to the fireplace in the corner was a wall of glass doors. They were covered now with bamboo blinds, but obviously, by the size of the plants in the other corner, they let in a great deal of sunshine during the day. A Navajo rug covered the floor, while several chairs in various shades of brown were around the room.

"What is this, looking for decorating ideas?" Jon murmured as he walked over to her and then kissed her slowly on the lips. "I promise to give you the full tour of the house if you like."

"Sounds fascinating."

"Not really, but we could arrange to get distracted along the way. Can I get you a drink?" He walked over to a bar cabinet across from the fireplace.

Toni shook her head and left her purse and shawl on one chair. In spite of her refusal, Jon handed her a wineglass with an amber-colored liquid in it.

"It's a dessert wine," Jon explained, and led her over to some large pillows scattered on the floor. Taking the glass from her hand, he placed it on the bricks in front of the fireplace. Then he gently pulled her down to the pillows beside him.

"Mmm, you smell so good." His lips nibbled at her ear and his hands moved with sure possession over her body as he aroused a desperate need in her. It was so good to feel this way again, she thought with a deep sigh. His fingers loosened her hair and it fell like a halo around her on the pillow.

When his lips left hers, she reached up to pull him back and kissed him longingly. She needed him so! While her lips were so pleasurably occupied, her hands opened his shirt and slid over the coarse hairs on his chest. Physical sensations seemed to consume her until she was barely conscious of who was arousing her.

The ringing of the telephone jarred her back to reality. With a muttered curse, Jon rose to his feet and hurried into the kitchen.

Toni sat up slowly and looked around her as if awakening from a dream. What in the world was she doing here? She took a deep breath and rose shakily to her feet. Good Lord, how could she have agreed to come to his home after knowing him for just a few hours? Had Bob's taunts made her so desperate that she would jump into bed with anyone?

She turned slightly as she heard Jon's voice rise in irritation.

"Look, I'm busy," she heard him say. "I'll call you back tomorrow." The receiver was slammed down.

"Sorry about that," Jon apologized with a laugh as he came back into the room. He frowned when he saw her standing up.

"I've changed my mind."

"You've what?"

And why shouldn't he sound surprised? Toni thought. She had hardly been reluctant for his caress. Taking a deep breath, she moved over to her purse. "Look, I'm sorry about all this . . ." She fumbled, seeking the right words. "I guess I had too much wine or something." She threw her shawl over her arm and clutched her purse tightly.

"Hey, that call wasn't from some girlfriend," he quickly assured her.

"It wasn't that. It's just that . . . well, I didn't really want to come."

"No?" Jon's voice suddenly became sarcastic. "I don't remember having to drag you here, and you seemed somewhat responsive, if not eager, a few minutes ago."

Toni blushed brightly, but she kept her head up high. "I said I was sorry. I didn't want to go out with you in the first place, but you didn't give me a chance to refuse."

"Look, lady, let's be honest with ourselves," he snapped, an icy look in his eyes. "You came on to me like you couldn't wait to jump into bed, so don't play the injured virgin now." He walked over to where his suitcoat lay on a chair and went through its pockets quickly. "I'll get my car keys and take you home." He spoke in clipped, measured tones.

"You don't have to."

He ignored her and went up the stairs to the second floor.

Toni waited only a moment before letting herself out the front door. The night seemed awfully black, and she pulled her shawl closely around her, hurrying down the steps and across the parking lot. As she walked, she kept glancing back behind her, almost expecting he might pursue her, but his front door stayed closed.

There were more people on Clark Street and she should have been able to relax slightly, but she kept up her brisk pace until she had reached the safety of her own apartment and had locked her door securely behind her.

She was still shaking, though, and sank down onto her sofa. What was she doing to herself? she wondered. Was she so desperate to prove Bob wrong that she would trade her self-respect for a few moments of pleasure with a man she barely knew?

# CHAPTER FOUR

Sam Morici hitched his shoulder up to hold the telephone to his ear. His sweaty palms could not hold the receiver and it kept slipping. "But it's only Wednesday. I just found out about her a few days—"

"We have a nice thing going at your place, Sam. I don't want even the smallest problem." There was a touch of impatience in the other man's voice.

"No, I don't either," Sam agreed. "I'll make sure Guy's handling it."

"We're old friends, Sam. We share things. I have problems, you have problems. I'm happy, you're happy."

Sam frowned down at his desk. "Lou, I understand. We'll stay on top of it, I promise. It won't get out of control."

"I still remember the old days, Sam, when a man's promise meant something. You remember those days?"

Sam's head bobbed affirmatively as he tried to keep the receiver in place. "Yeah, Lou, I remember. A promise still means somethin' ta me, too."

"I'm glad to hear it, Sam. Real glad."

The connection was abruptly broken and Sam hung up in the jerky movements of a puppet under the control of an amateur puppet master. He took a plain cotton handkerchief from a desk drawer and mopped his brow.

"Damn that Ramsey!" he muttered, and stood up to pace behind his desk.

After a moment he sat down again, leaning forward and drumming his fingers on the desk. The clammy sweat dripped down the back of his neck and he reached for the handkerchief again. This time, the mopping operation ended with a swipe under his shirt collar all around his neck.

"Damn him! When Lou put him in here he said Ramsey would take care of everything."

Sam's nervousness propelled him out the door. Guy's office was still empty so Sam took a few steps into the bullpen and looked around. He discovered Guy holding court with three of the office beauty queens just across the large room. The bile rose up, giving Sam a sour taste in his mouth.

"Tell Ramsey to get in here now. I have to cover something with him immediately," he barked at Mrs. Flores, and stomped back into his office.

She came quietly to his door a few minutes later. "Excuse me, sir. Mr. Ramsey is tied up with some personnel issues right now. He said he would get to you as soon as he could."

Sam exploded. "When I call a meeting for now, I mean right now. I don't have time to wait around for his majesty."

"I'm sorry, sir. I'm sure that Mr. Ramsey will do his best," she assured him.

Fifteen minutes later Guy strolled in. He was smoking an expensive cigar and looking at the *Wall Street Journal.* "Gotta check up on my investments." He smiled as he sat down, continuing his perusal of the newspaper. Sam just waited, drumming his fingers on his desk as his stomach churned.

Finally Guy put the *Journal* aside. He removed his cigar contentedly and blew a cloud of smoke at the ceiling. "I'm not doing too bad in this recessionary economy. How about you, old buddy?"

Sam's face was red with repressed anger. "Look, Ramsey, I didn't call you in here to talk about investments. I'm the boss around here and it's time everybody here realized that."

Guy's smirk could be seen around his cigar. "I'll put out a memo on it first thing after lunch." Before Sam could reply, he took the cigar from his mouth and went on. "Oh, by the way, the corporation just took over Jarulisis's operation, so we're adding fifteen new special salesmen."

"More of your bookmakers and leg breakers?" Sam's worry was evident in his voice. "How many men you think you can add to the payroll before somebody notices? We already got twice as many employees on the books than are showing up for work."

"We'll add as many as Lou wants," Guy informed him coldly. "How else are these guys going to get covered by Social Security and Workmen's Comp? And it ain't costin' you nothin', so cool it, grandpa."

Sam's hands clenched into tight fists of anger at Guy's contemptuous attitude. "I'm not your grandfather."

"From what I hear, you ain't nobody's grandpa." Guy's contempt grew. "What's the matter with your kid? Four years of college and graduate school and he ain't even learned to screw yet."

Sam felt the momentary lightness in his head that always accompanied his anger. Relations with Ramsey had never been good, but they'd gotten worse since Jon had joined the firm. Every business meeting degenerated into a family name-calling session.

With great restraint, Sam ignored Guy's remark and continued. "Lou called this morning and he's worried about that audit dolly nosing around."

Guy's smile disappeared and Sam realized that she had Mr. Smartass scared, too. The knowledge gave him confidence.

"What are you talking to Lou for? That's my area." Guy tried to hide his fear with anger.

"Sure. The next time he calls I'll tell him to call you and hang up. Right?"

Guy's glare wavered momentarily, but he quickly regained control of himself. "Just stay out of my sandbox." His voice was low and menacing.

Sam felt both pleasure and fear at Guy's discomfort. "I can't help it if Lou calls me. He's worried about that accountant."

Guy did not reply. He just clenched his jaws around the cigar and stared at the wall.

"The new one. The broad," Sam prompted.

"I ain't stupid. I know who they're talking about. And I got the dolly right where I want her."

"You layin' her?"

Guy turned to glare at Sam. "I got the whole thing under control."

"Maybe you ought to tell Lou."

"Maybe somebody ought to mind his own business or else his health will be a lot worse."

"This is my business," Sam replied hotly. "I started it, remember."

Guy got up from his seat, the smirk returning to his face. "Sure, Sam. It's your business. Now you just be a good boy and go out and do the things you're good at. Play a little golf or maybe you got a luncheon to go to, huh? Or maybe you got some big award to hand out."

Guy turned away, pausing at the door. "I ain't telling you again, Morici. Stay out of my sandbox. I talk to Lou."

The sweat started to trickle down his back again, but Sam forced a note of bravado into his voice. "Sure, next time I'll tell Lou straight out. You talk to Guy. I'm a big-picture man. I don't deal with the little details."

Hatred shot from Guy's eyes, radiating about the room until Sam saw tiny spots dancing in front of him and knew that his blood pressure was shooting up. With a deep breath, he looked away. His right hand, safely hidden in his pocket, was curled into a universally understood gesture, but he dared not let Guy see it. He heard Guy's footsteps recede into the distance and relaxed. Then he turned slowly and walked over to close his door.

Mrs. Flores looked up from her typing and saw Sam. "Would you like some fresh coffee?" she asked. Sam did not reply, and without a change in her expression, she returned to her typing.

All Wednesday morning as Toni supervised the work at Federal Drugs, she had managed to keep last Saturday's disaster out of her mind. As she neared Mid-America early in the afternoon, though, her feet automatically slowed. With a deep breath and a mental reminder of the job to be done, she pushed open the door. The receptionist let her into the office, and Toni walked briskly through it, glancing around as she did.

Mr. Ramsey's door was closed and Jon was nowhere to be seen. Come to think of it, she didn't even know where he did his work. The only place she had seen him was in the lunchroom.

With a shrug, she went down the hall to the room assigned her. Although George was not there, his briefcase was, so she assumed he was getting the files and computer printouts that they wanted. She decided to get herself a cup of coffee while she waited for him to return. It would be her lunch.

She took some change from her wallet and walked down to the lunchroom. It was empty, surprisingly enough, even though it was early afternoon. Lunches must be over and breaks not yet begun, she thought as she poured herself a cup and dropped her money into the change box.

Toni picked up her coffee and turned around, only to stop short. Standing in the doorway of the lunchroom was Jon Morici. A smile of welcome was not on his face.

Toni could not stop herself from blushing, but she did look directly at him. "Hello," she said.

He nodded coldly and walked around her to get his own cup of coffee.

Toni realized that she had her chance to leave without further conversation but couldn't. Part of her job was to keep relations smooth between her firm and their clients. Antagonizing the owner's son did not seem like the best way to do that.

After a quick glance at the door to make certain they were still alone, she turned back to him. "Mr. Morici. Jon," she corrected herself quickly. "I would like to apologize for the other night."

Only after his coffee was poured did he look at her, but his eyes were still cold and angry.

"I know I behaved very badly. Last Saturday was . . ." No, she would not tell him it should have been her wedding day. Instead she cleared her throat to strengthen her softening voice. "I'm afraid I had too much to drink and acted like a fool. I don't usually do that sort of thing."

"Look, Miss James." He was all impatience. "I don't care what your problem is. You can work out your sexual hang-ups with anybody you like. Just stay far away from me."

She was too stunned at first for anger. "That's a terrible thing to say. It wasn't like that at all."

"No?"

Toni just stared at him. She was suddenly through with explanations. He wouldn't believe her anyway. But what difference did it make? Men were all alike anyway: stupid, egotistical creeps.

Her anger helped restore her composure and Toni gave

him a sweet smile. "Has it ever occurred to you that I might not have liked your technique?"

Jon's face flushed and his eyes blazed angrily, but before he could respond a woman appeared in the doorway. The tension in the room was almost visible and she looked from Toni to Jon with open curiosity.

Toni smiled at the woman and turned briefly to Jon. "If you will excuse me, Mr. Morici," she said with perfect courtesy, and walked toward the door.

Her feeling of satisfaction only lasted a minute, though. Stupid! Stupid! Stupid! How could she have let herself talk to a client that way? She was supposed to aim for a win-win situation, or at the very least settle for a lose-win, where she came off as loser. She had handled far worse problems with much more diplomacy in the past. Why hadn't she bitten her tongue and let him think she was neurotic and repressed?

George was back in the room when Toni got there, but she did not see any files.

"Where are they now?" she snapped.

"Rosie said she'd check it out with Ramsey and get back to us."

Toni was furious with the further delay. Damn this place! "But we have permission to see those files."

George shrugged, holding his hands up to protest his innocence. "I'm just telling you what I was told."

"Look, this audit is your job, and I'm getting tired of wasting my time coming out here to find it hasn't progressed at all. I want to see some action on it. This is the only afternoon I can spare for the next two weeks. I've got to fly up to Madison tomorrow for two days and then I'm driving to Rockford next week. So go tell Rosie we want those files."

"All right, all right," he sighed, and walked to the door.

"And tell her Mr. Ramsey gave me permission for them last week," Toni called after him.

George nodded as he trudged out into the hall.

Jon frowned down at his cup of coffee. He had forgotten to put any cream into it because of that damn woman. Maybe his father was right. Women didn't belong in business. Just look at that one! She was more screwed up than old Sissy was. At least Sissy had known what she wanted.

It might have been Lebanon Red and not him, but she knew.

While he was in the hallway trying to decide if he should go back for his cream, a young man with curly reddish brown hair walked past him. The man glanced at him quickly, and then stopped and turned around.

"Say, aren't you Jonathan Morici?"

Jon nodded.

The man held out his hand. "You don't know me, but I'm George Manning. I went to New Trier too."

Shaking his hand, Jon tried to search his memories of high school for a George Manning but came up blank. "Were we in the same class?"

"No," George laughed. "You were a few years ahead of me, but we knew all about your exploits on the football field."

"Oh." The hell with the cream, he thought, and began to walk down the hall. He noticed that George was walking along with him, and felt that he ought to make some sort of conversation. "So what are you doing now? You don't work for my father, do you?"

"No." George shook his head. "Although there are days when I wonder if I want the job I do have." At Jon's confused look, he went on to explain. "I work for your accounting firm, and right now I'm the victim of my new manager's zeal."

Suddenly, Jon was more interested. "You mean Miss James?"

George grimaced. "Yeah, she's the first woman audit manager in our firm, so she's determined to be the best manager that there ever was."

"That's not so bad." Jon felt strangely obligated to defend her.

"No, except she's taking it out of my hide. She expects everyone on her team to work the same ghastly pace and hours that she does. But I guess since she couldn't make it as a woman, this is all she's got left."

"What do you mean by that?"

They had reached the end of the hall, and George started looking around for Rosie. "Oh, when she got her promotion her boyfriend dumped her."

Jon let out a low whistle. "Because of the promotion?"

George nodded. "The wedding was planned for last

weekend and everybody at the office had been invited, but I guess he couldn't take her being promoted first."

"She doesn't look like the type that would let a little thing like a wedding bother her."

George stopped searching for Rosie to shake his head. "That's because you didn't know her before. She was always good at her work, but she was more fun, too. You know, you could talk to her and kid around. Now, all she thinks about is her job." Suddenly he spotted the girl across the room, busy flirting with a young man cleaning her typewriter. "Oh, there's Rosie. I'd better catch her before my master comes after me, or is it my mistress?" He laughed and shook his head as he hurried off.

Jon thought about Toni as he watched George go. Maybe that explained some of her strange behavior. Suddenly he felt a little guilty for his harsh statements and found his feet retracing his steps down the hall.

He stopped at the doorway. She was sitting at a table with papers strewn out before her, but didn't appear to be looking at them. Her head was resting in her hands and she looked exhausted.

Jon took a step into the room. She started at the sound.

"Did you get—?" She stopped speaking when she saw Jon there. "Oh, Mr. Morici." She rose slowly to her feet. "Can I do something for you?"

Jon refused to be intimidated by her manner and smiled at her. "Yeah, you can."

She looked surprised and stared silently at him.

"You can take me out to dinner."

"I can what?"

Jon walked over and sat down on the edge of the table. "Well, the way I see it, you accepted my dinner invitation last Saturday, but you failed to fulfill your part."

"Now, wait a minute—"

He tried not to laugh. "You certainly are a testy little thing, aren't you? Anyway, you failed to give me the normal companionship that one expects in a dinner date, and instead treated me to an interesting theatrical display."

Toni's anger faded and she sat down slowly, a suspicious look still on her face.

"It's not that I begrudge the money I spent on the meal, but I do feel that I was rather cheated. After all, I could have seen a play at the Goodman for less money, and probably the acting would have been better."

The look on Toni's face changed to pure bewilderment as she stared at him. "Why in the world would you want to spend any more time with me? I was rude to you, completely bitchy. So why would you want to have dinner with me?"

Jon wasn't sure himself, and he wasn't about to try to explain that she seemed different to him. Vulnerable and very human. Instead he feigned a look of shame. "The truth?" he whispered.

She nodded suspiciously.

He took a deep breath and looked at her. "I've spent all my money and will starve to death unless you take pity on me."

He caught her by surprise and she suddenly found herself laughing. "Such a romantic plea! How can I refuse?"

Jon watched her with appreciation. She was beautiful when she relaxed. He remembered how gorgeous she had looked Saturday night, her hair loose and her face flushed with desire . . .

He rose to his feet abruptly to stop his thoughts. "I take it that's a yes?"

"Yes." Toni nodded with a smile. "Where did you want to go?"

"Oh, no. This is your date. You decide when and where and all that. You're a liberated woman now, so it's time you assumed some of the responsibility of your liberation. I am free on Friday."

Toni's face fell slightly. "I have to be in Madison Friday and my flight doesn't get back to O'Hare until five or six."

"That's no problem for me. Just tell me what airline and I'll pick you up. We can go from there. Unless you think you'll be too tired," he added, realizing that would be a long day for her.

"No, that should be fine," she agreed. "Can I call you and let you know my flight number and arrival time?"

Jon pulled a small case from his lapel pocket, taking out a business card. He wrote something on it and handed it to her. "My home phone's on the back, in case you can't reach me here."

She nodded and slipped it into the front of her notepad folder.

51

"See you Friday, then," Jon said. He walked to the door, but stopped to look back at her. "Better bring plenty of money; I expect to be starving by then."

She laughed lightly, and his breath caught at the beauty hidden there. He forced himself out the door even though he would have preferred to stay right there watching her.

Why had he done that? he wondered as he walked back down the hall. Some of his father's finds had been beautiful, yet he had never given any of them a second chance. What was there about Toni that stirred him so? She seemed so tough and strong, yet he sensed a vulnerability there and it had awoken a protective response within him. He wished Friday were closer.

# CHAPTER FIVE

Toni's flight touched down after seven o'clock Friday evening, and she was exhausted. The weather had been terrible, hot and humid. Her lightest summer suits were too heavy to be comfortable.

Then, everywhere she had gone she had found one problem after another. Even the flight home was a disaster, instead of a chance to relax and cool off. The usual business travelers had been replaced with vacationers taking advantage of the long Fourth of July weekend. Children screamed while several old ladies kept the plane in the air with their prayers. She was worn out by the time they reached O'Hare, but relief was not immediate. They had to circle endlessly and touched down more than an hour late.

Why did these things have to happen to her the one night she was going out with Jon? She wanted to prove to him that she could be a reasonable companion, and what does she do? She begins the evening by making him sit around the airport for more than an hour. She wouldn't be surprised if he had left, she thought as she waited her turn to deplane.

After getting her small suitcase from the luggage compartment near the door, Toni followed the other travelers off the plane. The terminal seemed to be swarming with people. The family pushing off the plane right behind her was met by an equally rambunctious group that blocked her way. She extricated herself with some difficulty and reached the main aisle, where she looked around only to find no sight of Jon. Everyone seemed to be moving about purposefully, and, with a sigh, she joined the throng that was trudging toward the exit.

"Toni, wait!"

She turned around and saw Jon hurrying to catch up with her.

"I was supposed to meet you here, remember?"

"I thought you must have left already since I was so late," she explained, unable to keep the weariness from her voice.

Jon reached down and took the suitcase from her. "Will the liberated lady in you object if I carry your suitcase?"

"If she does, ignore it," Toni said with a tired laugh. They walked toward the main terminal and parking lots. "I really am sorry about making you wait so long."

"I know, it was all your doing, too. You forced the pilot at gunpoint to keep flying. What happened? Didn't they give you enough time to finish your peanuts?"

"Right. They're so good, I like to savor them."

They walked through the terminal and went down the escalator to the pedestrian tunnel to the parking lot. As they rode down, Jon looked closely at Toni.

"Are you sure you want to go out tonight? We could do it tomorrow."

"Don't tell me I look that bad." She pushed some loose hair back from her face.

"You don't look bad, just tired."

"Well, tired I may be, but I'm also starving."

They reached the bottom of the escalator and began to walk forward. "I didn't have a chance to change after work," Jon said, "so why don't I drop you off at your apartment before we go out. It'll give us both a chance to freshen up."

Toni looked knowingly at his freshly laundered shirt. "You're a terrible liar, but I accept. I would love a shower."

An elevator took them up to the right floor of the parking lot. Jon's car, a silver Porsche with rich brown leather upholstery, was parked nearby. After putting Toni's case in the back, they settled themselves in the front.

"Very nice," Toni sighed, leaning back and relaxing as Jon backed the car out of the space.

"Don't be too impressed. It was a bribe." He shifted gears, and headed toward the exit. "When I went to work with my father, he insisted I get a company car."

"And this is it?" Toni asked in astonishment.

"Well, not all the salesmen have Porsches." Jon's voice

was cynical. "As director of marketing I rate higher." He stopped to pay the parking fee and then headed toward the Kennedy Expressway.

"Your father must be very happy to have you working with him."

Jon just shrugged and pulled around a slow-moving taxi. "So he says." He was silent for a minute. "However, I make it a policy, for the sake of my sanity, never to speak or even think about my job on weekends," he added with a grin.

"And do you succeed?"

"It depends. It takes real dedication to keep me distracted," he noted seriously. "So I hope you've got something really spectacular planned."

"I think so. I wasn't too sure what kind of food you liked, so I decided to play it safe and pick all kinds."

"You what?" he asked, clearly puzzled for a moment. "Oh, you mean Taste of Chicago."

To Toni's great relief, he sounded enthusiastic. Although the idea had appealed to her, she did not think Bob would have enjoyed a meal made up of samples of food from sixty of Chicago's best restaurants. Unless, of course, they were the sixty best steak houses.

About an hour later, Jon parked his car in the underground garage near Grant Park. Then he and Toni walked toward the brightly colored booths of A Taste of Chicago on Jackson Boulevard and Columbus Drive, two streets in the middle of Grant Park that were closed during the city's Fourth of July festivities.

Toni looked fresh and crisp in her dark green haltertopped cotton dress, and seemed to have shed her weariness along with her business suit. The cooler evening air along Lake Michigan had forced her to put on the shortsleeved jacket that matched her dress, but it had also put a soft glow of color into her cheeks. Her hair seductively brushed her shoulders in gentle curls and reminded Jon of that evening in his townhouse. With effort, he forced his thoughts to other matters, realizing that he was becoming more and more intrigued by Toni each time he saw her.

"Something sure smells good," he said appreciatively as they got closer.

"I would hope that there's more than one good thing here," Toni laughed. "Did you come to it last year?"

Jon shook his head as they got in line to buy tickets. "No, I was up at my family's house in Lake Geneva over the Fourth last year."

"Well, it was great. I think I ate everything in sight." She bought six books of tickets, putting four books in her small shoulder bag and keeping two in her hand. "Where should we begin?" She peered down at the map she had gotten with her tickets.

Jon eyed the cheesecake at a nearby booth. "How about over there?"

Toni looked up. "With cheesecake? We have the best dishes from Chicago's best restaurants to choose from, and you want to start with cheesecake? You'll be too full to eat much else."

Jon just laughed. "It's obvious that you don't know me very well if you think that little piece would fill me up." He took the map from her hand. "Why don't we start this way?" he said, pointing down a different row of booths away from the cheesecake.

As Jon and Toni walked along the booths on Jackson Boulevard, they listened to the Chicago Symphony Orchestra tuning up for their concert in the nearby Pertillo Music Shell. Between the music and the noise of the crowd, it was hard to make much conversation, but they did manage to eat. Jon made his way through some Bavarian-style bratwurst, a small dish of beef in pineapple sauce, and cold chicken wings. Toni had some Hungarian goulash, some crabmeat wontons, and an icy shrimp cocktail.

It was a bit quieter as they walked south along the booths on Columbus Drive. They stopped to sample some fried chicken and drink some beer.

Toni started to laugh as she saw a name on a booth. "I though I was done eating steak at Morton's every Friday, but it looks like I'm going to do it again."

Jon looked surprised. "You ate there every Friday?" he asked with a mouth full of chicken. "Is that some sort of religious custom?"

"Yeah," Toni laughed. "The Church of Traditional Dining." She took a drink of her beer before she went on. "No, actually, this guy I was dating liked to eat there."

"I have favorite restaurants, but I don't think I'd want to eat at the same ones every week. Sounds too boring."

"We always had a good time."

Jon watched her closely, wondering if the guy they were discussing was her former fiancé. He didn't say anything more, though, until they had gotten pieces of stuffed pizza, some more beer and had moved over to sit on the grass.

"So what happened to this guy?"

"Oh, we broke up," she admitted a little too casually. "I liked Morton's, but Bob turned out to be a jerk." She went back to eating her pizza, taking care not to look at him.

Jon was silent for a few moments, then asked, "This wouldn't be the same Bob that you spoke to at Ambria, would it?"

Even in the pale light, all the color seemed to leave Toni's face, and Jon cursed his thoughtlessness. "No, forget I asked. It's none of my business." He took the map out of the front pocket of her purse and began looking it over. "If I don't get my cheesecake soon, I won't have room for it."

Toni's laugh sounded rather forced, but Jon kept up a steady stream of chatter as they went back to the booths. He quickly got in line for some barbecued ribs, and by the time Toni had gotten herself an egg roll, he thought she was more relaxed again.

"Do you travel a lot, or was your trip this week a special one?"

"Oh, I do love egg rolls," Toni sighed as she bit into hers. "And, yes, I do travel a fair amount. To exciting places like Rockford, Peoria, and Madison." She took another bite and then went on. "But this trip wasn't a regular visit. I was getting complaints about one of my team members. The client in Madison just couldn't get along with him. They said he was an ass and wanted him off their account."

They began to walk north on Columbus Drive. "So did you manage to smooth everything out and keep everyone happy?"

Tony shrugged as she finished her egg roll. "Well, the client is, because I had to agree with him. Jerry is an ass."

"And what happens to good old Jerry?"

"I'm transferring him to the ranks of the unemployed." Toni grimaced and then said, "The joys of management. But then, some guys are born asses."

"Hey, that's a sexist remark."

"You're right," Toni laughed. "Women can be as bad. It's just that I've had more experience with men lately. Jerry, and before him, Bob."

"Oh."

"Don't you want your cheesecake? We're passing up the booth."

"Oh, yeah," Jon said quickly, wishing they had walked a little slower. He doubted that she would explain her comments about Bob now.

After he had eaten his slice, they passed a booth from an avant-garde French restaurant. "Their stuff is supposed to be good," Jon said, slowing his feet.

"Oh, no." Toni took his arm and pulled him on. "I refuse to eat there ever again."

Jon looked astonished but walked on with her. "Why?"

She shrugged and looked slightly embarrassed. "I got locked in their bathroom once." She acknowledged Jon's smile with a nod. "Yeah, I know it sounds funny, but it was actually kind of scary. The lock broke and I was in there for ten minutes before a busboy went to get a screwdriver and took off the doorknob so I could get out. I had gone to the restaurant with a client, and he heard a number of waiters snickering about my predicament. I was furious!"

"I can imagine." The smile was gone from his face and his eyes were sympathetic. "Did you give them all a good dressing down?"

Toni shook her head. "Not right away. I was too glad to get out of there, but I did write them a rather angry letter the next day."

Jon laughed. "And how many free dinners did they offer you?"

"Not a one. I never heard a word from them." Jon looked surprised. "I did learn from the situation though."

"You stay away from French restaurants?"

"No, I carry a tiny tool kit in my purse."

He laughed out loud and put his arm around her shoulders again, pulling her close to him. She was marvelous.

As they walked along, the crowd seemed thinner and quieter and the sounds of the orchestra drifted over. Toni got herself some strawberries coated with chocolate, and Jon got another slice of cheesecake. Then they found a clear spot in the grass to listen to the concert. Before very long the fireworks display began, accompanied by the *1812* Overture. The brilliant show lasted through quite a number of patriotic songs, ending with "The Stars and Stripes Forever."

"That was great," Toni said as Jon helped her to her feet. "Everybody should celebrate the Fourth this way."

"I think just about everybody has." Jon eyed the crowds of people moving toward the parking lots. "Want to wait a little before we leave?" He was reluctant to let the evening end anyway.

"Sure. I've still got some tickets left. We could see if they have any more food."

About forty-five minutes later, after a supertaco, an éclair, and a sourdough brownie for each of them, Jon and Toni walked toward his car. There were still a lot of people about, but the food stands closed at eleven, so there was no point in staying any longer. Soon they were driving north on Michigan Avenue.

"That was fun." Toni leaned back and relaxed.

"Yeah," Jon agreed, glancing over at her. Her eyes were closed and some of her weariness seemed to have returned. "Tired?"

"Just all of a sudden," she acknowledged sleepily. "I wasn't before."

"Must be the scintillating company. Maybe I need to hire an orchestra for the back seat."

"Either that or fireworks."

Jon smiled at her. "Fireworks I can manage myself."

Toni just laughed and fell silent. They were only a few blocks from her apartment when she spoke again.

"You were right, you know," she told him. "That was Bob at Ambria, and that's why I acted so strangely. Well, that and all the wine."

"Were you hoping to make him jealous?"

"Jealous?" Toni started to laugh, much to his surprise. "Good Lord, no. I wanted to show him I didn't care about him anymore."

"Oh."

"He was so certain I couldn't live without him that I had to prove that I could, and was."

"Well, that explains it." Jon was suddenly in a lighthearted mood. So she wasn't trying to make the jerk jealous. That was good to hear. "I noticed that you were different tonight. You ignored all my invitations to throw yourself at me."

Toni laughed as he pulled his car into a parking space. They walked the half block to her apartment building and into the lobby.

"Do you want to come up for some coffee?"

He shook his head, even though he would have liked nothing better. "You're going to fall asleep standing up. Just get to bed." He leaned forward and kissed her gently on the lips. "Good night."

"Good night," she said as he turned to walk toward the door. "Hey, I had a good time."

Jon turned at the doorway and grinned. "Yeah, so did I. Maybe I should let you take me out again sometime," he teased and, reluctantly, went out the door. As much as he'd like to rush this lady, he had the feeling she still needed some gentle handling after that bastard Bob, and he intended to give it to her.

# CHAPTER SIX

Toni settled back into the routine of work rather gratefully once the holiday weekend was over. Although she had enjoyed her evening with Jon, the rest of the weekend had seemed empty and flat. She had half expected him to call her on Saturday, but the phone had remained silent. Of course, he had not promised to call, she realized, and put him out of her thoughts as she went jogging in the park and worked on a financial report for the Anti-Cruelty Society. She even had time to read the latest issues of *Business Week* and *Working Woman,* and start on a novel that she had bought weeks ago.

By Monday evening she was pleased with all that she had accomplished, but the silence in her apartment had become oppressive. She decided to have dinner at John Barleycorn's, a small pub down the street where she knew a group of regular customers. It was crowded, but no one looked even vaguely familiar. The baseball game on the television behind the bar was her companion as she ate her hamburger. It was at times like this that Bob appeared in her thoughts.

She was relieved to drive down to Rockford on Tuesday and on to Peoria on Wednesday. Throwing herself into her work, she forced the loneliness of the weekend behind her. It was late by the time she got home Wednesday night, and she was too tired to do more than take a quick shower before falling into bed.

Her mind wandered back to Jon as she drifted off to sleep. Even if she never saw him again, she had reason to be grateful to him. The enjoyment of their evening together was proof that it wasn't Bob that she missed anymore, but the companionship that he had provided. She was actually getting over him.

Friday found Toni back at Mid-America again. She arrived just as George was leaving for lunch.

"I was hoping you'd come in today," he told her. "I found some places where the A/P printout didn't match the source documents early this week, and I wanted you to take a look at them." He handed her a stack of papers as he walked toward the door. "I marked them for you."

He was gone before Toni could ask him to explain, so she looked through the stack of papers he had given her. The computer printout of the firm's accounts payable had occasional figures marked in red. The rest of the papers were actual bills Mid-America had received. She spread all of it out on the work table and began to compare figures.

By the time George finally returned, Toni was waiting for him. The fact that he had taken a very long lunch hour was the least of her complaints.

"Why wasn't I notified of these discrepancies as soon as you found them?" she demanded as the door closed behind him.

George shrugged uneasily. "You said you were coming in today, so I figured it could wait a few days. After all, you were out of town earlier this week, so what could you have done anyway?"

She knew he had a valid point, but it didn't excuse his behavior. He had a responsibility to report any problems as soon as he discovered them. "You still should have let me know. And let me decide how serious this was." She stood up, gathering the papers together.

He watched her nervously. "Did you find the same mistakes?"

"Actually, I found seven more instances." She looked coldly over at him.

"Seven more? That's a lot of mistakes for someone to make."

"And that's just in the four months that you pulled. There could easily be more." She walked around the table to the door.

"You going to see Ramsey?"

"If someone's tampering with their accounts, he has to know," she said. "What's going to be hard to explain is why Martin didn't catch this. These are the files that you must have been auditing."

George looked uncomfortable. "Allbright wasn't what you would call pushy. We did compare invoices with their records once in a while, but it's so time-consuming . . ."

"That he usually just trusted their records," she finished for him, a disgusted look on her face. "I'll tell that to Mr. Ramsey, shall I?" Without another word, she left the room.

Toni's brisk walk hid a nervously beating heart. This would be the first time that she had had to confront a client with major discrepancies. She had found mistakes before, but it had always been someone else who had done the actual confronting. She hoped that she could handle it well.

Mr. Ramsey was standing near Mrs. Flores's desk, spreading his charm to several appreciative young ladies. He dismissed them all quickly when he saw her approaching and greeted her with a smile. "Well, hello, Toni. You certainly look lovely today."

She had not bought this dark green suit because it brought out the copper highlights in her hair, but because its straight, severe lines gave her an appearance of authority and height. She ignored his compliment, and asked, "May we talk privately, Mr. Ramsey?"

He looked slightly surprised at her formal tone, but indicated his office with a wave of his hand. "Surely this can't be as serious as you look." His voice was teasing as he followed her into the little room, closing the door behind him.

"I'm afraid it is."

Once they were both seated, he leaned forward, resting his elbows on his desk. "Now, tell me how I can help you."

His choice of words irritated her as she spread out her papers, but she refused to let it show. "We were doing a spot audit of your accounts payable and found several errors."

"I don't suppose a mistake or two is unusual."

Toni raised her eyebrows and went on. "In comparing the actual invoices to your accounts in the computer, we found twenty-seven occurrences where the amounts had differed." She was about to point out the errors on the printout, but he picked up the paper.

"The ones you've marked? That shouldn't be too hard to take care of. Some clerk must be daydreaming again. You

63

know how hard it is to get good help these days." He laughed, and rose to his feet. "I do thank you for bringing this to my attention."

She stared at him, astonished by his apparent dismissal. "But I don't think this can be a simple clerical error," she protested. "There seems to be a consistent pattern. If you get me some more files, I'll try to track it down for you."

Guy seemed amused by her persistence. "Now, Toni, you don't really think you've stumbled onto an embezzlement, do you?" His smile was condescending, and it made her angry. Why did he refuse to take her seriously?

"I don't know what it is, but you can't just type a few corrections into the computer and let it go at that." She had risen to her feet also, fighting to remain calm as she reached across his desk to point to the printout on top. "Look at this. It says that you paid Tempco Industries $538.16 for twenty cartons of paper products, yet their bill only charges you $269.08 for ten cartons."

"Yes, I understood what you said the problem was." He sounded slightly impatient and looked more than a little annoyed.

"Well, which amount did you pay?" she persisted. Her voice was brisk and businesslike. "If it wasn't just an entry mistake, why didn't the firm question the overpayment? Doesn't your accounting department spot-check the A/P checks as they're cut and compare the check amounts to the original invoice?"

The controller's anger was clearly growing, but he sat down slowly, leaned back, and put his feet up on the desk in an elaborate show of authority. "Look, sweetheart, since this is the first I've heard of it, no one must have complained. So it must be just an entry mistake and easily corrected."

Toni feared that his angry reaction meant she was handling this wrong. Regardless, she had to press on. "But these errors may have been propagated throughout your system. Your inventory is a good example. If these mistakes have gone into your inventory records, you've been paying too much property tax. We'll have to submit a petition for a refund."

"Believe it or not, I do know my job," he informed her tersely. "I've been doing it far longer than you've been doing yours, so when I want your advice, I'll ask for it."

She stared at him. He had gone from amusement to annoyance to rage in the blink of an eye. "I never insinuated that you did not know your job. But warning you of these things is part of my job."

"Oh, no, baby. Informing me of what you've found is your job. Correcting problems is my job and I'll take care of it." He spoke in clipped, careful tones, as if he could barely control his anger. "When I clean the shit out of the files, you'll get to see them. Got it?" He took his feet off the desk and bent forward to gather up the papers she had brought him.

There was no point in staying any longer, so Toni nodded slightly. The hands clenched at her sides were trembling, but she would not trade insults with him. She had done her job the best she could and had nothing to be ashamed of.

She left the room, barely noticing Mrs. Flores's smile as she passed. The walls of Ramsey's office were only seven-foot-high partitions, and it seemed to Toni that all eyes were on her as she walked through the bullpen office. It might just have been her imagination, but she was glad when she reached the safety of the workroom. She sank into a chair with a loud sigh of relief.

"How'd it go?"

She gave George a cynical smile. "Let's just say I've carried other business meetings off to a more successful conclusion."

"He got mad?" Surprise was in his voice.

She nodded. "Didn't want to hear any of the possible ramifications."

"That's strange." When Toni remained silent, he leaned forward slightly. "Say, if Ramsey's in a lousy mood, why don't we just take off early? We won't get any more out of him."

Toni nodded in an absent manner. "Sure, go ahead. See you in the office Monday morning for the staff meeting."

"Thanks for the reminder." He grimaced. After packing his briefcase, he gave her a little wave and left.

Toni gathered her papers together more slowly, deep in thought. George was right; it was strange. Some controllers might get defensive, but such anger was very odd. An audit is supposed to find problems and an audit manager is supposed to recommend the fix.

She closed her briefcase and squared her shoulders. She'd better get to the office and catch Simon before he left for the weekend. There could be more to this than sloppy keypunching.

"Send Rosie in," Guy ordered his secretary curtly, so angry that he could barely speak. That goddamn bitch! How did she get hold of those files?

He was seated at his desk, his right hand clutching the arm of his chair as he stared down at the papers Toni had left. A rage coursed through him that was stronger than any he had felt in a long time. Who'd she think she was, coming in here and telling him what to do? She probably slid into her job on her back, yet she acted as if she knew everything.

That was the whole trouble. The place was filled with idiots like her. Didn't get where they were by hard work, but because somebody gave it to them. Like Morici's son with his Harvard class ring. Neither him nor that broad ever had to earn anything, yet they acted as if they knew it all. So what if Guy had only gone two years to a city college? Miss Toni James was going to find out fast just who had the brains around here. He'd see how her fancy degree helped her when she came up against a real man. His smile turned unpleasant.

Guy Ramsey was nothing if not a real man. Strong and tough, he always won. He had proved that when he was eight and his parents had moved to Cicero, a suburb west of Chicago. His father had wanted to escape the coal mines of southern Illinois, but to Guy, the Hawthorn Works of Western Electric was no different. He had decided then that his future was going to be better.

Cicero, with its warring factions of Italians, Czechs, and Poles, had provided his schooling and he had been a very willing pupil. Money and power were everything, he had learned, and human nature could be depended on for greed and selfishness. Clean and dirty applied to clothes, not fights. They were won by the strongest, but strength could be measured in many ways. Sometimes it was just being smart enough to find your enemy's weakness.

Guy stared at the papers Toni had left without really seeing them. God, that broad seemed tough. Not like good old Martin. He was controllable and wouldn't push anything. Martin had been satisfied with the "discount" merchandise that he had received through Guy's acquaintances, and by lunches paid for by Mid-America and then expensed by Martin to the accounting firm.

Guy sneered again. Everyone had a price. All he had to do was find the right offer. Just because this dame put on a good show didn't mean anything. So she was on the job early in the morning, worked overtime, and precisely accounted for all of her expenses. She might not be the straight arrow she seemed, he tried to convince himself, but his palms were damp.

Things had been going too easy, and he knew he had gotten careless. Lou would hold *him* responsible, not that lazy bastard, Sam Morici. All he knew how to do was run to Lou and whine. Well, Guy'd fix this mess and bounce old Sam out on his big, fat tush. Then he'd be the big man with flunkies to do the work. Guy had paid his dues; let someone else take the heat for a while.

He leaned back and, in his nervousness, took a drag on his cigar. The burning in his lungs turned the quaking in his stomach into a spasm. If this blew, Sam would still be sitting in the catbird seat and it'd be old Guy that went down the pipes. The problem had to be fixed and now.

As Guy abruptly turned his chair away from the desk, he glanced at a double photograph frame standing on a small bookshelf. A smiling dark-haired woman was in one side, and two dark-haired little girls were in the other.

He stared at the pictures. That bitch Toni didn't belong in a business office any more than Angie did, except that his wife was smart enough to know that she was stupid. She could barely take care of the house and kids, and he had to tell her how to do that!

Looking at the picture of his wife brought some of Guy's confidence back. Hell, Toni was no different from Angie, so why was he so upset? Her price would be different than Martin's, but she wouldn't cause any more trouble.

He drew again on his cigar and leaned back in his chair, putting both feet on his desk. He could handle any woman alive. No different than a horse or a dog. Just need the right techniques. Pet 'em a little, praise 'em a little, and punish 'em when necessary. Once you show 'em who's boss, they'll do anything for you.

He tapped some ashes from the end of his cigar into the

amber glass ashtray and leaned back again, relaxed and in control.

Just look at Angie, he thought. He had married her before she had finished high school. She was pretty, and had adored him. When he had proposed, he had made no mention of love, but had promised that they'd live in a split-level house with a dishwasher, have several kids, and that he'd kill her if he ever found her looking at another man. She had been thrilled, and had married him in spite of her parents' objections.

After they were married, he had taught her to be the proper wife. Praised her a little for her cooking and cleaning. And punished her each time she got out of line. Split lips and black eyes were part of her education. God, the tears he had had to endure, and the pleading and promises not to do it again. She was always so eager to make amends that he usually stayed out late several nights in a row, just to make sure she really got the message. By that time she'd be a basket case and certain that he would send her back to her mother. But he would always generously relent, slap her around, and then screw her to show that she was forgiven.

Another pull on the cigar as he contemplated the situation. Hell's fire. Why didn't he think of it before? That was exactly little Miss Toni's problem. She didn't have anybody to show her the ropes. No wonder she puts in all that overtime. She was frustrated and not getting enough. Guy laughed out loud. He'd bet she wasn't gettin' any.

He contentedly puffed on his cigar as a warm glow spread throughout his body. First he'd play with her a little. All any woman really wanted was a good man. Poor little Miss Toni, playing around with college boys; she probably never had one.

He laughed coarsely again. He'd even let her pretend to be the perfect little accountant. Pet her, praise her, and then punish her for interfering in his business. In the end, he'd do her good. Might even be fun. She had a good-looking body under all that ice.

Guy was totally relaxed and in control by the time Rosie came to the door. He was delighted to see how worried she looked. Her clothes were as tasteless as ever and he suspected that she was trying to look sexy. Unfortunately, she came across like a street whore. The thought pleased him as he used his cigar like a pointer to beckon Rosie into his office, careful to keep his furious look in place. She silently closed the door behind her and sat down on the straight-backed chair that he indicated.

"What the hell did you think you were doing?" he demanded. "Who gave you permission to give out those files?"

Rosie bit her bottom lip as her eyes watched him warily. "But they said you gave them permission."

Her fear gave him a rush of erotic pleasure. He was in control as always. "They said?" he repeated with exaggerated astonishment. "Is that how you are supposed to do your job? Give them any files *they* say they have permission for?"

"No. But they said—"

"God damn it," he shouted suddenly, causing Rosie to jump. "There's that word again. Do you believe everything *they* tell you? If some punks broke in and told you *they* had permission to clean out the warehouse, what would you do? Help them carry the stock out to their truck?"

Rosie shook her head, tears forming in her eyes. "No, of course not. But you weren't here—"

"I see." His voice became haughty and frigid. "So it's my fault for not being here."

The tears began to flow in earnest. "No, no. It's all my fault. I shouldn't have done it." She covered her face with her hands.

He let her sob brokenly for a long moment, the tension in the room building with each minute that passed. Finally, she raised her tear-streaked face to look at him. "I'm sorry. I won't ever do it again."

Guy leaned forward and drew on his cigar and looked out over the office as if in deep thought. Jeez! This game was turning him on. He suppressed a snicker, almost laughing out loud, but it was close to quitting time. He'd better end his fun since he had a meeting with his board of directors tonight and they didn't tolerate tardiness. He'd have to cover this little situation with them—if Sam hadn't already spilled the beans.

Rosie's whining interrupted his thoughts. "Please. You can't fire me." Guy stared at her, refocusing his attention on the sodden-faced woman before him. "I need this job."

As she leaned toward him, the front of her dress fell forward. Guy's eyes lit up as he focused in on her ample breasts. Jeez, look at those boobs. Boy, he'd sure like to stomp around that melon patch with both feet.

He sat up suddenly and pushed the idea away. No, Lou always said, a smart bird doesn't shit in his own nest.

"I know that you didn't do it deliberately," he told her, becoming the understanding father. He sat back in his chair. "And I'm willing to give you another chance." He leaned forward again, resting his elbows on his desk. His face was concerned, but no longer angry. "But only one more, mind you. You have to learn to follow the rules."

Rosie's face was bathed in gratitude. "Oh, it won't happen again."

Guy nodded and waved her out of the room, watching her shapely little body disappear behind Mrs. Flores's desk. It was a shame to pass that up, but he'd make sure that accountant was worth it.

Guy watched the bartender carry two beers down to the other end of the bar, then drained his own stein. It was almost eleven o'clock at night, but the pickings were still slim at the Come Back Inn. The place was usually packed with lovely young bodies by this time.

He took a handful of peanuts and nervously cracked them. At least that meeting with the directors of Dunkirk Industries was finally over. Lou acted like Mid-America was the only company they held part ownership in, the way he zeroed in on the problems with Toni James. The memory made Guy's palms wet with sweat.

Old Morici must have been on the phone with them before she was out of his office that afternoon. It was a wonder his finger didn't wear out with all that dialing he did.

"Hey, gimme a burger. Dark bread. And another beer," he snapped to the bartender, then looked around the dark main barroom.

He had driven to the bar after the meeting for a drink and some fun, but it didn't look like he was going to get much. Jesus Christ must have come down and freed all the prisoners in the dog pound. He picked up his replenished beer. The three next to him at the bar had more hair on their chests than he did.

He finished the mug and ordered another beer, cracking

more peanuts as he waited. What a meeting! Fix it, Ramsey. That's all Lou had said. Just fix it, Ramsey, and the meeting had ended. No chance to tell him that he'd already had it all solved. Just fix it, Ramsey. The words seemed to echo in his head.

His hamburger came and Guy attacked it. Hell, he had everything under control. He'd take care of this little matter and then go to Lou with a bigger one. Sam was going. He wasn't puttin' up with him anymore. What'd they need Sam for anyway? All he did was sneak behind his back and call Lou. Mr. Guy Ramsey was the one who ran the place!

Too bad he had Lou hanging over his head, watching his every move. In the old days, he would handle a problem like Morici himself. Neat, clean, and very satisfying. Why'd everything get so damn civilized?

After eating the last of his french fries, Guy finished off his beer. He felt better, more relaxed. He could handle that accountant or any problem that came his way, and Lou would see that. There was nothing to worry about.

As he counted out his money for the bartender, he eyed the three girls next to him again. Hell, he could take them to a motel and twist their little tails. Which one would howl the loudest? With the lights off, they wouldn't look half bad.

As he moved in on them, though, the words continued to throb in his mind. Fix it, Ramsey.

# CHAPTER SEVEN

"No, it's all right, Mom. I understand," Toni sighed into the telephone. "Yes, I know. It's a chance that Melanie couldn't pass up. No, you mustn't worry about it. I hadn't started dinner yet." She wondered what she would do with the pan of lasagne in the refrigerator. "Yes, Mom, I'll see you soon. You two can come some other Sunday. Give my best to Melanie and tell her to have fun."

Toni hung up the phone with an exasperated sigh and glanced at the clock. It was past three. Why had her mother waited to tell her that she and Melanie weren't coming to Chicago? She must have known hours ago.

Opening the refrigerator and frowning at the foil-covered pan, Toni wondered why she had bothered to fix something so elaborate. She ought to know by now that her sister was bound to get a last-minute date and decide not to come. So there sat more lasagne than she could eat in a week, a beautiful tossed salad, and a light pineapple cream dessert.

"Damn!" she said, slamming the door closed. She had spent all morning making the stupid sauce, and the afternoon putting the fool thing together, and for what? Well, at least she'd gotten the homemaking instincts out of her system for another month.

She opened the refrigerator again and pulled out the bottle of Burgundy that she had planned to serve. After pouring herself a glass, she held it up in a bitter toast.

"Here's to Sundays."

She took a sip and then glanced down with a frown at her simple navy skirt and white blouse. She seemed a little overdressed for a solitary afternoon at home, and changed back into a dark green racquetball shirt and shorts. She pulled her hair into a ponytail, and left her shoes on the bedroom floor.

After getting her wine from the kitchen, she padded back into the living room and turned on the television. A Cubs game was on.

"Great, just what I need. A lost cause for a lousy day." She watched the game for a few minutes as she drank her wine, then turned it off to stare straight ahead of her.

If she socialized with anyone in her office, she could invite them over for dinner. But Bob had been so possessive of her time; they had never done anything with their co-workers. Once they had broken up, she had plunged into work with such vigor that she hadn't had time to rebuild her circle of friends.

She finished her wine with a sigh and put the glass in the kitchen sink. She might as well go running and save the day from being a complete waste. Who knows? Maybe she'd be lucky enough to get knocked in the mud again by some knight in shining armor. She stopped as she reached for her shoes. Why not?

She quickly searched through her wallet for the card Jon had given her, and went to the phone by the side of her bed. She felt a moment's misgivings as she stared at his name before her in bold black ink. Although this was the age of liberated women, she had never actually asked a man out. But, of course, this wasn't really a date. It was a plea to help her. If she had to eat all that lasagne herself, she'd gain about eight hundred pounds.

On that reasonable note, she picked up the phone and began to dial the number. By the fourth digit, her calm had disappeared. What in the world was she doing? The receiver was returned to its place quickly.

If he had wanted to see her again, he would have called her. She had taken him out last time. It was his turn. She frowned. Did liberated daters take turns? She tossed the card onto the table next to her bed and jumped to her feet. She'd never wanted to be a Harvey's Bristol Cream lady anyway!

"Look, Dad, we've been through this before. I don't see any reason to go over it all again." Jon's voice reflected his weariness and frustration.

A large white cat with a black ring around his left eye

jumped up on the kitchen counter next to the telephone and rubbed his head against Jon's hand. "I thought the reason I was joining the firm was to ease your work load, but obviously I was wrong."

"Hey, but you are," Sam protested. "You really are helping a lot."

Even over the phone Jon could sense his father's tension, but for once he was not going to be intimidated. He was going to say what was on his mind. "How? I'm not doing a damn thing! And I haven't the faintest idea how the company works!" Spike's demands became more insistent and Jon absently began to scratch his head.

"You have to be patient," Sam pleaded. "This ain't the same as working with your buildings. This is business."

"Dad, I have an MBA, remember?" There was no point in arguing his other statements. They would just divert him from the real issue. "I know as much about running a business as I know about architecture."

"Sure, sure," his father agreed.

Jon wondered why he sounded so worried. What was there to panic about?

"But whatever happened to that idea to combine the two?" Sam went on. "I thought you were going to study the plans for the old warehouse and see if we could renovate it."

"Yeah, I've been looking into it. But renovating the building is not getting you the rest your doctor said you need."

Sam seemed to relax suddenly. "Hey, what does that old quack know? I just want you to be happy. Doin' what you want to do. There's plenty of time for you to get tied down to the business. Enjoy yourself while you can."

Jon knew he had lost another round and made no attempt to hide his sarcasm. "Yeah, Dad, sure."

"Maybe your problem is that you've been working too hard." His father sounded as if he was back in control. "Boy, my vacation worked wonders for me. I'll bet that's just what you need: some time off. Why not take a month or so and travel around? Didn't you always say you wanted to go to Rio?"

"Dad, I've been on vacation ever since I started working for you. I want some real work, not more time off."

"Yeah, I know. It's just that—" The panic was back in

his father's voice, and Jon was tired of their whole circular argument.

"Look, let's forget I ever called, all right? I'll see you at the office tomorrow."

"But, Jon—"

"Good-bye, Dad." He hung up the phone, and tried counting to ten to ease his anger. It did not help.

Why was his father being so stubborn? He knew how much Jon hated what he was doing; why wouldn't he bring him into the business more? Jon's scratching got a little excessive and Spike reached over to bite his hand.

"Hey, what was that for?" he asked his cat in surprise. Spike turned away disdainfully and began to bathe himself. "I thought pets were supposed to be comforting."

What happened to all the plans he used to have? Jon asked himself as he wandered into his living room. He had loved his construction work, but he hadn't been unhappy when his father had needed him at Mid-America. Needed him! What a laugh! He was needed there about as much as they needed an extra wastebasket.

He sat down on the sofa, putting his feet up on the low table in front of it. He felt so useless and unnecessary. Not one person in the world really needed him. There was nothing he did that someone else could not do as well. He almost wished that he had married Mary Beth Fletcher after high school. He might not have a bunch of fancy degrees to hang on the wall, but at least he'd have a family that depended on him, something to give his life some purpose and direction.

He jumped to his feet suddenly. A direction is what he'd better choose and move in it before his father called back. The phone came to life just as he did, though. Its ringing seemed to echo loudly in the silence of the house.

"I'm not starting that whole argument again," he informed the phone as he took a few steps toward the kitchen. "You mention once what a great job I'm doing and I'm going to hang up on you."

The phone continued to ring, not frightened by his threats. He grabbed it. "Yes?"

"Jon?" It was not his father's voice that cracked nervously. "This is Toni."

He tried to shake off his anger and push his frustration from his mind in a long moment of silence. "Oh, hi, Toni."

"Look, I'm sorry. I called at a bad time. I didn't mean to interrupt you," she apologized quickly.

Her embarrassment got through to him, and he realized that she was about to hang up. "Hey, wait! You didn't interrupt anything. Honest."

"I was wondering if you were free for dinner," she said in a rush. "My mom and sister canceled out at the last minute and I've got this big dinner sitting here and I'll explode if I have to eat it all by myself." She ended abruptly and Jon felt his earlier anger melt away.

"I'd love to."

"You would?" She sounded surprised and he laughed.

"Hey, I thought that was why you called."

"Well, yeah, it was. But I didn't think you would. I've never invited a man out before," she admitted.

"You're kidding. And your invitation was so smooth and polished," he teased, seeing her face before him. The thought of her gentle beauty eased his bitterness. "When shall I come?"

"Oh, anytime. I thought we'd eat around five-thirty."

A peaceful, relaxing evening in her company sounded like heaven. "How about if I get there around five? Should I bring anything?"

"No, I have everything, except a body to eat the food."

He chuckled, thinking that he had just been bemoaning the fact that no one needed him. "You really know how to build a fellow up. Should I dress formally?"

"Oh, no, just dress regular."

"Regular?"

"Yeah, you know, shirt, pants, and stuff . . ." she finished off lamely, then added, "I'm wearing a blue skirt and a white blouse."

A teasing smile curved the corners of his mouth. "Do you want me to wear the same thing?"

"Do you know why donkeys don't go to college?" Toni shot out.

Jon roared with laughter as Toni took control of the conversation. "You may dress informally. There is no need to bring anything, and be here promptly at five o'clock, Mr. Morici."

"Yes, ma'am," he said meekly, and hung up the phone. Suddenly things did not look so bleak anymore.

\* \* \*

Toni had set her round dining table with care. Her dishes, a creamy white ironstone with tiny blue flowers, looked beautiful against her dark blue tablecloth. She was excited about having someone over for dinner; it had been a while since she had cooked for anyone but herself. The basket of flowers that Jon brought added just the right touch to the setting.

The lasagne smelled delicious and looked like an illustration in a cookbook, but Toni felt some misgivings as she placed it on the table.

"I probably have real nerve, serving lasagne to an Italian." She laughed nervously as she carried over a gravy boat of extra sauce.

Jon stopped pouring the wine and looked up. "Why? Don't you think Italians like it?"

"No, it's not that, but you probably get magnificent lasagne at home. Much better than mine." She looked down at the table to see if she had put everything out. There was the lasagne, some warm, crispy bread, butter, a tossed salad, and the wine. "I guess that's everything."

Jon held her chair for her, then sat down himself. "You have a slightly inaccurate picture of my family," he noted.

She put a large slice of the lasagne on his plate. "First of all, my home is that townhouse on Grant Place, and I've never had lasagne there since I've never tried to make it. I have made spaghetti sauce, but that's about as adventurous as I get." He took a bite of the rich cheesy pasta and sighed with pleasure.

"Secondly, although my mother is Italian, I can't remember the last time she actually cooked a meal. Since they moved up to Winnetka, there has been a succession of Evas, Maries, and Charmaines through their kitchen. Italian food was not their specialty." He took another bite. "This is really good. Your family will be sorry they missed it."

"Thanks." Toni smiled and began to eat her own. "But I'm sure Melanie would rather have a date than lasagne any day."

"Melanie? Is that your sister?"

She nodded, her mouth full of food. "My half sister, really," she said after a moment. "My father was husband number one; Melanie's was husband number three."

"Must have been a strange childhood for you." He reached over for a slice of bread.

"Oh, after each one left, Mom would rant and rave and get a job. Then there'd be a brief period of calm before another jerk would come along and convince her that he was different. That he wasn't looking for a free ride." She took a sip of her wine. "She finally wised up, though, after Melanie's father left town with a neighbor's teenage daughter and all Mom's savings. That was fifteen years ago, and she has kept her vow to rely on no one but herself."

"Do I detect a note of bitterness?"

"Nope, just realism," she corrected him lightly. She had not intended that her feelings be so obvious. "What about you? Do you have any brothers or sisters?"

"No, I'm the only one." He refilled her glass, then topped off his own. "All the hopes of generation after generation of Moricis are resting on my head."

She smiled at his bantering tone. "What a responsibility!"

"What a headache! Actually, I'm sure both my parents would have liked a large family to pamper and spoil. And seeing what a marvelous success I am, it's a shame, for the world's sake, that there's only one of me."

"Do I detect a note of conceit?"

"Nope, just realism."

They both laughed and their talk drifted into other areas. Toni told him about her experiences as a day-hop attending Notre Dame University, and he related stories about Yale and Harvard. By the time they finished eating, Toni had discovered how widely diverse Jon's interests were: horror films, anything with Woody Allen, country music and Crystal Gayle in particular, James Herriot's books, and westerns. He was not concerned with keeping up an image, but was content to be himself. It was such a refreshing change that Toni admitted she liked to square dance, a fact she had never mentioned to Bob.

When the food had been eaten, Jon helped Toni clear the table. He loaded the dishwasher and filled the sink with hot soapy water while she put away the leftovers.

"You will never know how much I appreciated your invitation today." He sighed, and began to wash the lasagne pan.

"Oh?" She took a clean towel from the drawer. "I wasn't

too sure when you answered the phone. In fact, I was imagining all sorts of things that I had interrupted."

Jon laughed when he saw her blush.

"I'm not doing that every time the phone rings."

"I didn't know. You sounded so grumpy, I was going to hang up."

"I know, and I'm sorry. It's been a terrible week. Where have you been anyway? I tried to call you early in the week, but you were never home."

"Tuesday was Rockford and Wednesday was Peoria."

"And Monday?"

She frowned. "I was home on Monday. Oh, except for an hour or so in the evening when I went over to John Barleycorn's for dinner. I've been home the rest of the week."

Jon smiled sheepishly as he handed her the pan to dry. "I went up to Lake Geneva over the weekend and didn't get back until late Monday. And then the rest of the week has been so bad that I wasn't fit company for anyone."

"Why?"

He let the water out of the sink. "It's my father. He just refuses to give an inch. He knows how I feel about my job, but he won't budge. All I do is visit hotel restaurants and try to convince them to buy more napkins, or saltshakers, or trays. I hate it, but he refuses to let me do anything else with the company." Jon shrugged. "I shouldn't bother you with all this."

"Don't be silly. It helps to talk about things." She put the pan away. "Should I make some coffee?"

"I have a better idea," he said, drying his hands on the towel. "Why don't we take a walk along the beach and then go over to my place and I'll make you some espresso."

"Sounds great. Just let me change my shoes and I'll be ready to go."

They left her apartment, walking through Lincoln Park to North Avenue Beach. It was only eight o'clock, but the beach was practically deserted.

Toni slipped off her sandals, and Jon followed suit. Then, holding hands, they walked along the edge of the water. The waves gently lapped at their feet.

After a few minutes of silence, Jon went back to their earlier conversation. "I don't know why, but suddenly I was fed up with my job. I decided that I was going to have it out with my father. That was the main reason I went to Lake Geneva. I thought we could talk undisturbed, but he had a houseful of people, so I might as well have stayed home. It wasn't until Wednesday that I finally cornered him and told him how I feel."

"And how is that?" Toni asked.

"I want more responsibility or he should let me go back to my old job."

"What did he say?"

"Nothing really." Jon shrugged, staring down at his feet as they walked. "Oh, there was a lot of talk that he was trying to work me into the business and how I shouldn't be so impatient, but it boiled down to nothing." He looked at her. "I'll be a sales manager all my life if it's up to him."

Toni frowned thoughtfully. "I thought you were the director of marketing."

"Fancy title, same job," he said bitterly.

"But when your father retires—"

"When? That's the real question. The doctor told him to, but he refuses to give up the reins of business."

Toni was silent for a while. The gentle rhythm of the waves was heard above the sounds of laughter down the beach. "What really bothers you?" she asked him finally. "Do you want more responsibility? Do you want to go back to your old job? Or are you worried about your father?"

"I don't know." He stopped walking and stared out across the lake at the sailboats silently gliding past. "I did like my old job, but I'm willing to help my father out. It's just that I have this terrible fear that he's going to have another heart attack and be forced to retire and I won't know a thing about the business. That was supposed to be the whole point of my joining the firm. I was supposed to learn to run it."

"Well, if that's the only problem, it's simple to solve," she laughed. "You just have to be sneaky."

Jon turned to look at her. She could see confusion in his eyes and laughed again. "A lot of women in business have the same trouble."

"They do?"

"Sure. They have a manager who refuses to train them for some reason. So they get the subordinates to do it." They began to walk again. "Look, if you want to learn how the inventory is controlled, you talk to the person who does the controlling. You can bet they understand it better than the manager anyway. If you want to learn billing, ask the billing clerk. For accounting, ask Guy."

"No, not him," Jon said quickly with a shake of his head as two joggers ran past them. "He's tighter with the information than my father."

"I thought you two were friends."

"No way. I've asked him questions about the company's finances and got nowhere fast. Between him and my father, I'm quite effectively shut out of the inside operation. I sometimes get the feeling that it's Guy that thinks I'm incapable of running the place."

They reached Fullerton Avenue and sat down on the rocks to brush the sand from their feet. After they put their shoes back on, they turned away from the beach and walked west along Fullerton, passing the north edge of the zoo and the Lincoln Park Conservatory.

"I admit that all that financial work that Ramsey does is not quite my thing, but that doesn't mean that I couldn't be an effective manager," Jon said with a touch of anger as they waited at a stoplight.

"No, but you may have to work extra hard to prove it," Toni pointed out. "Learn all you can about the other areas of the business, and then be patient. Sooner or later, you'll get your chance to prove yourself to both your father and Guy." The light changed and they crossed the street.

"I'm proving very well that I can take big customers to lunch, I can attend civic banquets effectively, and I make a good, respectable bagman when I attend political fund-raising shindigs."

"Now, come on," Toni cajoled, and squeezed his arm.

"Yes, I know." Jon nodded thoughtfully. "It makes sense, although I'm not a particularly patient person. But it is a lot better than my father's suggestions."

"What were they?"

"One was to use my architectural skills to renovate the warehouse."

"That old wreck!" she laughed. "I would think demolition might be a kinder fate for it."

"Hey, that 'old wreck' is filled with history," he protested mildly. "Rumrunners stored bootleg liquor there during Prohibition. The stuff was brought in on boats hauling newsprint from Canada, unloaded at night into rowboats, and then hidden beneath the false floors."

"Gee, think of what you might turn up. Bodies, a forgotten cache of money, very aged scotch . . ."

"Rats," he added, and laughed when Toni shuddered.

"And what else did your father suggest?" she asked.

"Today's idea was a month-long vacation in Rio."

"Rio as in Rio de Janeiro?" Toni stared at him in astonishment.

Jon made a face at her. "That was why I was so ticked off when you called. I had just hung up on him and thought he was calling back."

"Boy, when I ask for more responsibility, my boss just gives it to me."

"You're lucky."

"Yeah, I suppose. But there are times when I could use some of that paternalism," Toni admitted ruefully.

Jon looked at her and laughed. "It sounds good, but you wouldn't stand for it too long either." His humor faded. "That's his answer to everything. Whenever I get restless, he buys me a new toy. This time it was Rio, last winter it was the Caribbean, and before that the Porsche."

"He probably just wants you to be happy. Yet at the same time, he's reluctant to give up something that's been his for a long time."

Jon nodded reluctantly. "Yes, you're probably right."

They walked the few blocks to his home in comfortable silence. Toni thought how much better this Sunday evening was than the one last week. Her previous loneliness made her appreciate all the more having someone to share simple things, like dinner and a walk.

Jon's townhouse looked different this time because it was still light outside. He opened the screen doors at the end of the living room and a gentle lake breeze wafted through. The sounds of traffic were muted and seemed far away.

"Just sit down and relax," he told Toni, and disappeared into the kitchen.

"Can't I help?" She followed him through the dining area, which was off the living room. A low counter separated it from the kitchen.

"No, make yourself at home."

For a moment, she watched him get things out of his cabinets, then walked over to the tall, glass-enclosed shelves that lined the far wall of the dining room. They held a fascinating variety of things.

"Where did you get all this?"

Jon stopped what he was doing and peered over the counter to see which cabinet she was looking at. "Most of the pottery is from Tunisia. Those two tall urns are from Morocco, and the small round ones are American Indian. Hopi, mostly."

Toni turned to stare at him. "What were you doing in Morocco and Tunisia?"

Jon laughed at her expression and turned aside to rummage through a cabinet. "That's when I was working for Baylors, that construction outfit. We were doing work for some oil companies."

"Oh," Toni said simply, and moved to look at the pottery more carefully. "Somehow I had pictured you building houses out in suburbia."

"Well, I prefer something larger than houses, but after a while I got tired of moving around all the time. I like to have more of a home than you can when you turn nomad every couple of months."

Toni walked over to the next case. "Where are the baskets from? Not K-Mart, I know."

"The top shelf is from the Philippines, and most of the others are from Peru and Colombia. That large one in the back is Papago."

"More oil rigs?"

"Philippines was a bridge."

Toni moved down to the last case. "I'm almost afraid to ask about the mugs, but where did they come from?"

Jon came over to her side and opened the case. "The white pair trimmed with gold were my great grandmother's, on my mother's side. She brought them over from Italy. These with the covers are from Germany. That one is from Greece." He pointed to two delicate-looking ones. "These are from Korea, and those tiny ones are from Hong Kong and that crystal is from Ireland."

Toni shook her head. "No wonder your father suggested Rio. There's nowhere left."

Jon laughed. "I got most of these after I got my MBA from Harvard. My father decided I needed a break—and some polishing—before I settled down to work. Unfortu-

83

nately, it was on that trip that I met some people from Baylors and accepted a job offer."

Toni bent down to look at a dark blue mug with streaks of gold through it. "And where's this one from?"

"Sears Roebuck." He went back to the kitchen. "The coffee will be done soon. Why don't you just relax? Take off your shoes if you want. Or your clothes," he added with a distinct leer as Toni wandered back into the living room.

There was a stereo system in one corner, and after searching through his tapes, she put Willie Nelson on. His raspy voice filled the room as she went to sit down.

The meal, wine, and long walk had all been pleasant and now she felt deliciously relaxed. She kicked her shoes off and settled herself into the corner of the sofa. As she did so, she noticed a white furry ball uncurl itself from an opposite chair and stretch luxuriously.

"You have a cat!"

"Don't tell me that lazy bum has actually appeared?"

After stretching, the cat sat and stared unblinkingly at Toni. Then the cat gracefully jumped down and sauntered over to the sofa. With exquisite care, he sniffed her, his nose staying just a breath away from her skin.

"What's his name?" Toni called.

"That's Spike." She heard the clink of dishes as Jon spoke.

"What kind of a name is that for a cat?" Toni scoffed. Spike had finished his inspection of her and allowed her to scratch his chin. "You deserve a more dignified name than that," she told him.

"Well, he's not much of a cat," Jon informed her. "I don't think he could catch a mouse if his life depended on it."

Apparently to show his disdain for Jon's opinion, Spike carefully climbed into her lap. She stretched her legs out straight to accommodate him. By the time Jon, carrying the two cups of coffee, entered the room, Spike was fast asleep on her.

"Boy, the little twerp moves fast," Jon said in disgust when he saw where Spike was. He handed Toni her cup and sat down on the edge of the sofa next to her.

"I think he's sweet." Toni gently scratched the top of Spike's head.

"Sweet? He's a dirty old man." Jon drank some of his coffee and glared at the cat.

Toni smiled as she tasted hers. "You're just jealous because you aren't cute and furry."

A look of hope leaped into Jon's brown eyes. "Is that what it takes? How about if I just don't shave for a couple of days?"

Toni eyed him silently for a moment, then shook her head. "I think Spike'll still be cuter."

"I do have some talents that he lacks."

"Oh?"

Jon took her half-empty cup from her hand and put it on the coffee table along with his. Then he pushed Spike off her lap. With a muttered protest, the cat stalked over to the other chair and stretched out in it.

"Poor Spike."

"Yeah," Jon muttered unsympathetically as he moved closer to her. Placing one hand on either side of her on the back of the sofa, he leaned forward slowly and kissed her.

His touch was firm but had a gentle quality to it that was seductive as he teased the corners of her mouth with his tongue until Toni grew impatient for the feel of his lips against hers. When his mouth finally claimed hers, she needed little persuasion to open her lips beneath his, and the kiss deepened.

He shifted his weight against her suddenly, and Toni delighted in the feel of his body against hers. She slipped her arms around his neck, the fingers of one hand running through the soft curls along the edge of his collar while her other hand slid across his firmly muscled back. Jon's light cotton shirt was only a slight barrier to the explorations of her fingertips.

"See?" Jon pulled away slightly. "I told you I was better than that stupid cat."

Toni leaned her head against the back of the sofa and looked up at him languidly, while her hands rested on his shoulders. "Oh, I don't know," she teased with deliberate provocation. "I would need more data before I could confirm that."

Jon's eyes glittered with amusement. "Well, I'll certainly do my best." He slid his hands behind her back and pulled her close to him.

As Jon's mouth took hers again, Toni tightened her

arms around him, not content with the gentle brushing of her breasts against his chest. He tightened his hold also, so that her breasts were crushed against him and she was imprisoned in his arms.

She let her eyes close and reveled in the intoxication of his touch. It felt so right and so good as his mouth left hers to kiss the sensitive hollow below her ear, that a shiver of indescribable pleasure ran through her.

She grew bolder as the fever in her blood increased. The thin fabric of his shirt was suddenly in her way, and she slid her hands under it. They roamed across his hair-roughened skin, delighting in the feel of it and the spicy scent of his aftershave.

"God, you're beautiful," Jon murmured as his mouth came back to hers.

His lips were less gentle and more insistent this time. His hands, seeking the softness of her skin, slipped under her blouse to slide possessively across her back before unhooking her bra. Pulling away from her slightly, his right hand moved between them to free her breasts. The roughness of his skin caressed and tantalized the smooth fullness of them, leaving the tips hard and tingling with longing. His touch was gentle, but shock waves of desire raced through her.

Amid sensations of taste and smell, Toni was only aware of the pleasure of his body tightly pressed against hers. He seemed to have the power to ignite her with the slightest touch, and could arouse a depth of longing in her that Bob had never managed. Yet a flicker of fear awoke deep within her. This man was practically a stranger. How could she want him so desperately when she had never felt that strongly about Bob, whom she had loved?

When Jon finally pulled away from her, a curious sense of relief mingled with the burning desire that remained. She knew she needed time to think. She could still remember the pain and emptiness left by Bob.

"Isn't this when the phone is supposed to ring?" she joked lightly, trying to return to rationality.

"Why don't we move upstairs and I'll take the receiver off the hook?"

"And miss an important call? No, I don't think we'd better." She swung her feet around him to the floor and reached for her cold cup of coffee.

"Did you ever think that having someone else might be the best way to get over Bob?"

Toni stared up at him blankly. At first she was surprised at his assumption since Bob had not been at the center of her thoughts, but then she felt irritated. Who was he to know what was right or wrong for her?

"And you're unselfishly offering to be that someone else." She put down her coffee cup and reached behind her to fasten her bra. "Being the remedy for broken hearts must keep you busy."

"At least I don't deny my feelings and try to live in the past."

Toni rose to her feet, carefully tucking her blouse back into her skirt. "I'm not denying anything. I probably would enjoy the next couple of hours if I stayed, but I'm just not into one-night stands."

"Is that some sort of cue?" Jon's voice was cynical as he stood up also.

Toni glared at him. "Yes, it's a cue that I'm going home."

With an irritated sigh, he picked up the coffee cups. "I'll rinse these out, and then I'll walk you back."

"That's not necessary. It's only a few blocks, and I have to stop at the drugstore anyway."

He paused in the doorway of the dining room and gave her an impatient look. "What are you going to do, run away again?"

Toni just shrugged and sat back down on the edge of the sofa. After a glance at her, Jon turned around and went back into the kitchen where she heard water running.

As her anger faded, she felt slightly guilty. He probably was right in the assumption that he could wipe all thoughts of Bob from her mind, but that wasn't the problem. She was just learning to handle the loneliness that had been Bob's legacy and could not risk becoming dependent on anyone. She was not about to tell him that his hands held too much power over her. It was much safer letting him think she was still in love with Bob.

Her refusal had strictly been a matter of self-preservation. This man could arouse feelings in her that Bob never even approached, and instinctively she knew that if she let herself get close to Jon, the loneliness when he was gone would be unbearable.

Jon came back into the room and wordlessly turned off the stereo and closed the screen doors. "Ready?" he asked. No hint of his feelings was apparent.

Toni rose to her feet and nodded. She was sorry that their pleasant evening had to end like this, but what choice did she have? She was not going to let herself be hurt again, she vowed as she followed Jon up the steps to his front door.

He stopped as he reached the door, his hand on the knob. He turned to look at her. "Do you know you are as maddening as hell?"

Toni was taken aback. "I am?"

His hand left the knob. "First of all, you're so damn gorgeous that I can't think straight when I look at you, not to mention what happens when I touch you. And then, you're so easy to talk to that it seems like I've known you forever. How am I supposed to keep remembering you're still in love with that jerk?"

Toni bit back a smile. "Want me to write it on my forehead?"

Jon just glared at her and pulled the door open. "Are you going to have dinner with me tomorrow evening, or not?" he asked as she walked past him.

Stopping for a moment to look at him in surprise, Toni nodded slowly. "Sure."

"Good." He slammed the door behind him and they started down the steps.

# CHAPTER EIGHT

The traffic shouldn't have been bad at midday, but every summer the city went into a program of wrecking selected streets. By the end of July, the destruction was in full swing and Toni had to inch through the single-lane passages toward Mid-America. She arrived for her regular Friday visit hot, tired, and late. It helped slightly to see Jon in the reception area. They exchanged cool impersonal nods while their eyes smiled a greeting, and she went on into the office area feeling somewhat better. Still she was in no mood to play politics, and only hoped she could get through the afternoon without any problems. Her hopes dimmed when she saw Guy standing at Mrs. Flores's desk looking through some papers. They vanished completely when he put them down and came forward to meet her.

"I was hoping you'd come in today, Toni." He had stopped a few feet from her and stood blocking her way.

Toni looked at him, hoping that her animosity wasn't reflected in her eyes. Not that there was anything threatening about his manner, unless one counted his immaculate appearance. The red silk handkerchief in the breast pocket of his muted gray plaid suit looked as if it had been professionally inserted by a valet, and that bothered her, as did his perfect good looks. He reminded her of a model posing as an executive. Banishing such unprofessional thoughts from her mind, she gave him a cool, businesslike smile.

"Good afternoon, Mr. Ramsey."

"It's Guy, remember?" He kept his voice low. "Can we talk in my office?"

Toni nodded and followed him down the aisle between some desks and into his office. He carefully closed the door before turning to her with a crooked, boyish smile.

"I want to apologize for my behavior the other day." He seemed sincere and humble. "I am thoroughly ashamed of myself, and I only wish I had a good excuse to offer—besides the fact that I am a hot-tempered SOB," he added with a slight laugh.

She was somewhat surprised at his admission, but her skepticism remained, hidden under her professional veneer. "Don't give it another thought. We all have bad days."

"You're being kind and we both know it. And I certainly don't deserve your consideration." He glanced suddenly at his watch. "Let me take you out to lunch. It's the least I can do."

Toni was instinctively wary. "No, that's not necessary. I appreciate your offer, but there is no need for that." She took a step toward the door.

"Did you eat already?"

"No," Toni admitted. "But I usually just grab a sandwich after I'm finished here. I don't really have time."

"Then you have no excuse. Come on, we're supposed to be buddies. Besides, you can't refuse a client. I saw that in the *Official CPA Manual.*" He laughed heartily at his own humor.

Guy went on when he saw that Toni still hesitated. "Look, we should get together. I've been busy and I haven't spent as much time with you as a controller should with his auditing firm. Okay? Strictly business."

Toni hated to admit it, but he was right. Guy was a client and they hadn't had as many business meetings as they should've had.

"Look. Your predecessor and I went to lunch, so why can't you and I? If we don't, you could sue me for discrimination," he added with a charming smile.

Toni could not help herself and smiled back. Although a part of her still mistrusted him, she did admire the way he had removed the tension from the air. He was a pretty smooth customer.

"Does that smile mean I'm forgiven?"

"There is nothing to forgive, Mr. Ramsey. I'll be happy to have lunch with you."

"Guy," he reminded her patiently.

Guy drove them to the Chicago Claim Company, a trendy hamburger restaurant that was about fifteen minutes away from Mid-America and, coincidentally, just a few blocks from her apartment.

"I thought we'd better get out of that neighborhood to eat," he laughed as he held open the door for her and they entered the Claim Company's bar. "We'd either get ptomaine, mugged, or both."

Toni smiled slightly, deciding not to tell him of the good Spanish restaurants she had discovered around Mid-America.

An attractive young woman carrying a stack of menus came over to them. From the familiar look that she gave Guy, Toni guessed that he was a frequent customer. Her words confirmed it.

"Hi, Mr. Ramsey," she said, giving Toni a quick glance as she paused over his name. "Want to wait down here for a table?"

"Yeah, sure." He glanced around the room and then followed her shapely, jeans-clad body over to a table in the corner. Once they were seated, he turned back to the young hostess. "I'll have a Jack Daniels on the rocks, doll." He looked over at Toni expectantly. "Miss James?"

"Just a Coke," she replied.

"Hey, this is a celebration, remember? What kind of a party drink is that?"

"That is all I can handle when I have to stay awake and work the rest of the afternoon."

Although he continued smiling, Guy's eyes tightened as he nodded the hostess away. "How come I get the feeling that you still don't trust me?"

"Just because I ordered a Coke?" Toni avoided a direct answer to his question. "Who do you usually have lunch with?"

"People my mother wouldn't like," he admitted with a laugh. "You're really different from old Martin. Mid-America's lucky to have you."

The arrival of their drinks saved Toni the necessity of replying. She probably was being paranoid, but there was something too slick and smooth about Guy Ramsey. His compliments only made her wary.

"Have you worked for Mid-America long?"

"Long enough to know what a good job you're doing for us, and I'm gonna make sure your boss knows." He raised his glass slightly in a toast. "Here's to our getting to know each other better." He winked as he added, "From a professional point of view, of course."

"Of course." Toni found his tone of voice and the gleam in his eye a little too personal.

The hostess wasn't too thrilled either. "Your table's ready," she announced coldly.

Guy's solicitous manner as they climbed the flight of stairs to the dining room did not help matters, and Toni's irritation grew with each step. He did nothing concrete that she could object to. It was the general air of interest and concern that gave out an aura of possessiveness. Toni felt helpless to fight it, and that angered her even more.

The hostess led them to a tiny table across from the head of the stairs and just down the hall from the salad bar and the kitchen. Hardly a choice location, Toni realized, and so did Guy. His eyes grew dark with anger and he said in a loud voice, "Hey, sweetheart, if I want to watch parades, I'll go to the circus."

The woman clenched her jaw in suppressed anger. "Why don't you follow me please, sir? There might be something back here you'd prefer." She led them back to a table in a secluded corner.

Perfect for the tête-à-tête they weren't having, Toni thought as she sat down. Guy's anger had faded and he returned to magnanimity. "Thanks, doll." He smiled at the hostess as she handed them their menus.

That lady sure changed her tune fast when Guy hollered, Toni thought. The great master cracked his whip and the peons jumped. Toni tried to repress a feeling of disgust.

"Have you eaten here before?" Guy asked her, looking over the top of the large menu.

She nodded and put her menu down after a quick glance. "I'll have the Motherlode."

Guy smiled at her choice. "Just what I was going to recommend."

Maturity warred briefly with obstinacy, but she went ahead and ordered the hamburger anyway when the waitress came over.

"How do you know about this place? You live close by?"

"In the neighborhood." Toni's reply was vague.

There were several moments of silence between them and then Guy spoke. "You know, I did manage to track down the problem with the accounts payable. It was just some dumb broad. She was daydreaming instead of doing her job."

"How did you find out?"

"I just checked around. The supervisor of data entry told me that they had found a number of other mistakes. She'd corrected them, but apparently she missed a few."

Toni nodded as she sipped her Coke. It was a perfectly plausible explanation. Most of the mistakes auditors found were caused by somebody's carelessness, but Guy's almost blind anger when told of the errors still bothered her. "So, have the procedures been modified to trap these kinds of errors before they propagate through the system?"

Guy shrugged. "We have it under reasonable control."

"Would you like me and my staff to review them for you to make sure they'll meet your requirements?"

"You must have read my mind, Miss Audit Manager. I've decided to let you revamp our entire accounting system, with controls my mother couldn't sneak through," Guy replied with a wide smile. "Just to make sure we don't have a repeat of those problems."

Toni was surprised. Was he actually offering her firm a contract for more work? Before she could ask, he went on. "I'm going to tell your boss that it's a good thing for him that he finally wised up and put you on the account. That wasn't the first bit of crap that Martin let through. I was getting ready to change accounting firms."

"Thank you," Toni murmured quietly as their lunch came.

"Don't mention it." Guy raised his drink to his lips and then hesitated. "I got fifty thou' budgeted. You and your boy, George, just take your time and do a good job."

Why did she have the uneasy feeling that she'd just been handed a bribe?

Toni was glad when they finally returned to Mid-America and she was able to slip off to her workroom. Guy's behavior had further aroused all the suspicions that his explanation was supposed to have relieved. She couldn't wait to take another look at those files.

Luckily, she had kept a copy of them, and she spread them all out on the large work table. After two hours of study, she was still frowning. The usual attributes of clerical error just weren't there. No transposition of figures, no dropping of a digit. The figures in error were all exactly two or three times the correct amount, and that violated another pattern of clerical error, randomness.

By chance, she happened to be looking over the list of suppliers and noticed a vendor code after each name. This was a way of rating a particular vendor, but Mid-America did not seem to use these codes, for that field was usually zero. Except, Toni saw suddenly, in the accounts that had errors. These accounts had either a *B* or a *C* in the vendor code field. The *B* suppliers were billed twice the proper amount and the *C* suppliers were billed three times the correct amount. Something was very wrong.

Toni stared at the papers for a long time. Her first thought had been to tell Simon of her discovery, but then the new contract that Guy had given her came to mind. Would investigating this matter jeopardize it? She needed to bring in new contracts. It was part of her responsibilities as a manager, and this was her first one. Could she afford to risk it just because she didn't like Guy?

So he was rather pushy and his compliments didn't ring true. That didn't mean that his explanation of what had happened wasn't correct. She was letting her personal dislike of him color her professional judgment.

She stopped for a moment, remembering the feeling she had experienced when Guy had given her the contract. It had felt like a bribe then, and it still did. Her judgment was not being colored by her dislike of Guy, but by her desire for that contract. She was actually letting him bribe her into dropping her investigation, and that was wrong.

She picked up the papers slowly and glanced at her watch. It was late and she knew she'd never get back to the office before Simon left for the weekend, but her conscience would not let it wait until Monday. She packed her briefcase and walked down the street to a small bar where she could use the telephone without the danger of being overheard.

The few patrons in the tavern were watching a soccer game on a Spanish television station. No one paid any attention to her as she hurried to the phone booth in the back.

As precisely as she could, she explained the situation to

Simon. Even though her new contract might be jeopardized, she hoped that if she had discovered real wrongdoing, it could help her career. Such diligence ought to prove that she could be trusted with the more important accounts.

Simon was cautious. "Take it slow," he advised her. "And be careful. This can be a very touchy situation for the client."

"Isn't it to their advantage to find out if someone's messing around with their books?" she demanded. She was rather irritated with his attitude. After her moral dilemma about even telling him, she had hoped for more encouraging support. A cheer went up from the bar as one team scored a goal, and Toni turned her back to them, placing her hand over her other ear.

"Sure, they'll want to know, but what happens if it's the boss's brother or son that's kiting the funds? They aren't going to want that broadcast to the world."

Toni frowned. Jon wasn't involved in this. Guy was the one who was acting strange. "So what am I supposed to do? Forget about the mistakes?"

"Of course not," Simon sighed impatiently. "We just have to be absolutely sure. Check it all out, but do it discreetly. Everyone you meet there is not an embezzler, so make sure you don't alienate the wrong person. You don't want to be proven right and lose a client."

"I'll be careful," Toni promised wearily. She wished Simon a good weekend and hung up.

In spite of the fears Simon seemed to be harboring, she was not going to play detective and openly hunt down the culprit. She knew it was her job to advise and the client's responsibility to take action. He ought to have had more faith in her. She had proven herself in touchy situations before and this one would be no different. She'd be careful and discreet, but she'd find out what was happening.

Guy Ramsey put the phone down on his desk with a disgusted shake of his head. "All Lou keeps saying is 'Fix it, Ramsey, fix it.' Yet when I do, he won't believe it. You'd think it was the first problem I've ever handled."

He rose to his feet and reached over for the cigar resting in his ashtray. " 'Be careful. Be careful,' " he mocked. "Lou's showing his age. Worrying about little details."

He walked across his office and pulled a bottle of scotch out of the credenza. "Well, he may be too dumb to know I've won, but I'm not. I've got the little bitch just where I want her."

He poured himself a drink and gulped it down. The warmth that rushed through him paralleled the glow of satisfaction that was already there.

He had taken care of things real well. Toni James had swallowed his song and dance. She had been ripe for his lies, panting for just a bit of his sweet talk. And tossing in that $50,000 contract was a touch of genius. All accounting firms had to scramble for a buck, and that new contract would earn her the hero award for the month. No way she'd come back at him and give him some more trouble.

He smiled, savoring his victory, and poured himself another drink. While old Morici had whined, he had gotten the job done. And he'd make sure all the directors knew that. He was running the place, watching out for their interests. Using his brains to save their skins. Morici was worse than useless, he was in the way. It was time they tossed him out.

He finished his drink and then laughed aloud. Be careful. That's what Lou had said, be careful. And where would that have gotten him? A job in the mines in southern Illinois or a spot on some damn assembly line. Careful was for kids crossing the street. He got where he was by having guts, not piddling around bein' careful. Old age had leached the brass out of Lou's balls, but it was never doing the same to him.

# CHAPTER NINE

"What size is this army we're going to feed?" Toni asked Jon the next morning. She carried two grocery bags from his car across a park that was a few miles north of Mid-America.

"Just the normal size kids' soccer team." He was carrying a cooler filled with ice and cans of juice.

"I thought soccer was the sport that had small teams. Ten or something."

"Actually eleven are on the field at once," Jon told her. "But there are fifteen boys on the Dragons."

"If there's only fifteen, why are we bringing food for fifty?"

"Ever feed ten- and eleven-year-old boys before?" he laughed as two boys in orange-and-white uniforms came running toward them. Memo and Reyes took the cooler from Jon and he took the bags from Toni. Then she could see that Mid-America Supply was printed on the back of their shirts.

"Do all sponsors take such an interest in their teams?" she asked. The soccer field at one end of the park was in sight now, and a few more orange-and-white uniforms came rushing toward them.

"Well, my executive duties don't keep me too busy." He gave the bags to Juan and Carlos. "So I come out to the practices and games when I can."

Which probably was as often as they were scheduled, Toni thought, from the enthusiastic way the boys greeted him. They were curious about her also, for she noticed a number of them eyeing her and saying something to Jon, which he answered in Spanish.

After a particularly hearty burst of laughter, she could stand it no longer. "What are you talking about?"

97

"They just wanted to know who you were," he said innocently, shooing the boys onto the field to warm up for the game.

"And what did you tell them?"

"That you were my mother." He grinned and leaned over to kiss her mouth quickly. A chorus of cheers and whistles arose from the boys, causing Toni's cheeks to blush, but Jon was not in the least embarrassed. He just grinned even wider.

An older man named Ramon came over to the field and greeted Jon warmly. He turned out to be the head coach of the team and Jon was his assistant. Together they got the kids ready, and when a green team arrived, the game began.

Jon did not have much time for her, since he was too busy shouting instructions to the kids, but he did glance her way often and smile. Not that she was left alone, for it seemed like all the boys on Jon's team had brought their families to watch and they all thought it was their duty to take care of her.

One old gentleman, Reyes's grandfather, stood next to her throughout the whole game, providing her with a running commentary like an announcer. She couldn't understand much of what he said because her Spanish was sketchy and his was in a dialect, but she knew how the Dragons were faring by the excitement in his voice or the disgusted shake of his head.

At halftime she helped pass out cans of juice and the pieces of oranges that she and Jon had cut up earlier in her kitchen. Just as Jon had predicted, the boys devoured everything in sight. Then, when there was a victory to celebrate, Jon brought out the bag of doughnuts and more juice.

The boys and their families seemed to monopolize Jon's time, but Toni did not mind. She was seeing a new side of him, and quite enjoying herself. Jon was so relaxed and at ease that she could not help but compare him to Bob, who only cultivated influential friendships. He would never have bothered with these people unless he thought they could further his plans. That led Toni to wonder why he had bothered with her. What had he thought she could do for him?

"Tired?" Jon broke into her thoughts as they walked

back to his car. "It must have been a rather tedious afternoon for you."

"No, it was a lot of fun." She frowned as she lightly touched the tip of her nose. "Tell me the truth. Is my nose as sunburned as it feels?"

Jon planted a gentle kiss on it. "Worse. You look just like Bozo. But don't worry. I was going to cook dinner tonight, so no one but me'll see it."

She made a face at him. "If you're going to be nasty, maybe I'd rather eat by myself at home." Jon just laughed and kept his arm tightly around her shoulders.

A few of the boys had helped carry over Jon's cooler, and once he packed it into the car, he and Toni left. "I thought we'd stop and get a few steaks to grill and some salad fixings. That sound okay?"

Toni had closed her eyes and leaned her head back against the car seat. "Sounds great," she murmured contentedly. Although she had not spent much time alone with Jon that day, she felt very close to him. She liked him, respected him, and desired him. Maybe it was time to ignore that voice of doom in her mind and risk being close again. A thrill of anticipation raced through her when she thought about the evening ahead.

She opened her eyes when she felt the car turn into a parking lot. They had stopped at the grocery store a few blocks from Jon's home. Everyone else in Chicago seemed to be there too, picking up things for dinner. They chose a head of lettuce and a cucumber, but the tomatoes had to be weighed and the line at the scale was long.

"Why don't you get the steaks and I'll meet you at the express checkout?" Jon suggested.

Toni nodded and walked along the dairy case, past the bread and the eggs to the meat counter. She found some steaks nestled between the ground beef and pot roast and sorted through the packages until she found one that looked about the right size.

"Hi, Toni."

She spun around at the sound of the low voice and found Bob standing before her. "Hi," she said. Her own voice sounded breathless, but it was from surprise, not the joy of seeing him. Just to make sure he understood that, she frowned as she spoke again. "What are you doing in this neck of the woods?"

"Shopping for dinner." He held up a package of hot dogs, then reached over to take her hand. "Toni, I've missed you."

She just stared at him, totally amazed by this turn of events. Throughout all the pain he had caused months ago, she had never imagined him coming back to her. Now, the sight of him pleading his case while clutching her hand and a package of hot dogs was ridiculous, and she had to fight back the urge to giggle.

"Toni?" Bob took a step closer and tightened his hold on her hand. "Have dinner with me tonight. Show me that you're not still angry." His voice had become soft and pleading, almost a caress in its intensity, as he turned on his charm.

Was he stupid or just unbelievably egotistical? Toni wondered. Her inclination to laugh in his face had lessened as she thought what nerve he had, expecting her to forget his insults. Why, he hadn't even bothered to apologize! Well, she was not desperate for his companionship, and an uncharitable urge for revenge suddenly took over.

Toni's face softened into a look of adoration. "Oh, Bob, darling," she cooed as she slipped her hand from his to lay it gently against his cheek. She saw his eyes gleam with the satisfaction of victory. "You're such an asshole!"

He looked too stunned to feel the sharp little pat that she gave his cheek before she turned and walked away. He really was an idiot, she thought with a silent laugh, and she would have been one too if she had preferred him to Jon. Her step quickened. She hoped he was at the checkout counter so they could get back to his apartment. It wasn't dinner that she was anxious for!

Jon stared at the plastic bag of tomatoes in his hand. The line ahead of him hadn't moved in five minutes. The computerized scale had run out of labels and apparently the clerk had never loaded a new roll. At this speed, it'd be next weekend before he could make a salad.

A prepriced basket of cherry tomatoes was on a rack near him, so he made a quick exchange and hurried toward the checkout counter. The usual crowd of Saturday shoppers was waiting patiently in lines that stretched back into the aisles of food. He scanned each line, but Toni wasn't there. Wondering what could have happened to her, he retraced his steps back through the produce to the meat section.

Just past the bread, he stopped short. There was Toni all right, but some blonde guy was holding her hand like it was solid gold while she was gazing adoringly up into his eyes. Jon's stomach plummeted to his toes. It was Bob, the creep he had seen at Ambria on their first date. What was he doing here?

The answer seemed all too apparent from the pleased look on Bob's face and the loving one on Toni's. He had realized what a treasure Toni was and wanted her back. It looked as if he was succeeding, too, so Jon turned around and went back to the checkout counters. He took his place at the end of a depressingly long express line.

Dammit! Why hadn't he picked up the groceries last night when he came in for the oranges and juice? Or run in while Toni waited in the car? If he had been smart, none of this would have happened!

His reasoning seemed perfectly logical as he watched Toni approach. He wanted to believe that the smile of anticipation was for him, but he knew better and braced himself mentally, his anger turning against her. What feeble excuse would she use to cancel their plans for the evening?

To his surprise, Toni made no attempt at excuses, but slid her arm around his so that her body brushed against him. "New York strip okay?" she asked, holding up the package of steaks.

Jon nodded, distracted as their line inched forward. What was the sweet-and-loving act for? Did she feel obligated to stay and see the evening through? Well, he didn't want any favors! If she preferred that idiot to him, fine, good riddance to her. He loosened her hold on his arm by reaching into his pocket for his wallet.

"Are you sure you want to have dinner tonight?" He looked into his wallet. "If you're too tired, I'll understand."

Toni caught the basket of cherry tomatoes as it fell from his arms. "What's the matter? Can't you pay for all this? Or did you meet up with some hot tomato in the produce department and want to dump me?"

Jon looked up at her then, infuriated by her dishonesty. "Hey, I'm not the one making dates in the meat section. You don't have to play cute and coy about it. Just go."

"Go? Go where?" Her voice and eyes pretended to be stunned, but he was not fooled.

"What do I care where!" The elderly gentleman ahead of them in line turned around curiously. "Go anywhere you damn well please, but why not be honest and admit that the bastard's back and you're through with me!"

"What are you talking about?"

Two women in the next line stopped paging through their *National Enquirer* to watch with eager smiles.

"Don't play dumb with me." Fury added volume to Jon's voice. "I saw the two of you cuddling by the meat case. What's the matter? His budget doesn't run to steaks, so you thought you'd let me feed you before you went to him?"

Toni glared at Jon for a long moment, her green eyes blazing with such rage that he was sure his accusations had struck home.

"No wonder you work for your father. You're so damn stupid no one else would give you a job." She shoved the basket of tomatoes and the package of steaks into his hands and stomped toward the door.

Bob was waiting two lines away and put out his hand to stop her, but she swerved, avoiding his touch. "You can go to hell too!" she snapped, her voice echoing in the silence that had settled on the checkout counters.

Jon looked around to find a million pairs of eyes staring at him. "Holy shit!" he muttered.

He dumped all his groceries into the arms of a clerk who was supposed to be refilling the candy racks. Had he jumped to the wrong conclusion? She was the best thing that had ever happened to him. The most important thing in his life. Had he thrown it all away with his stupidity?

Jon hurried out the door, but Toni was nowhere in sight and a delivery truck was blocking his car. It was only about a half mile to her apartment and he headed toward it on foot.

# CHAPTER TEN

Later that Saturday, Melanie Langford frowned as she studied her reflection in the tarnished mirror. Why was it bars never had decent mirrors in their washrooms? Or decent lights, for that matter. She flashed an irritated glance at the small fluorescent light set in the tiled ceiling. She had been in a lot of bars in the Niles–South Bend area, and they were all equally deficient. You'd think Indiana had outlawed good lighting and Michigan had forbidden decent mirrors.

Biting back her impatience with a sigh, Melanie knew she had to forgive this bar its small faults. It was here, at the Scenic Cruiser, that Alan had finally noticed her.

Alan. Gorgeous, sexy Alan. Her hand reached up to adjust the gold chain that hung around her neck. She had been wearing it the other night, and it obviously had brought her luck, as it would tonight.

Who would have thought it? she thought as she laughed quietly. That something stodgy old Toni had given her two years ago when she had graduated from high school would have brought her such phenomenal luck? Who would have even thought that her sister's tastes could run to such sensuous elegance? Melanie had been expecting something like a pen-and-pencil set. Complete with little hints about going off to college and using it. Definitely not in her line at all.

She took her gold-encased lipstick brush from her purse and the tube of Passionate Persimmon and touched up her lips. Her large green eyes still looked perfect, for the Copper Haze and the Spun Sand that highlighted them didn't rub off easily, but her cheeks did need another sprinkling of Hushed Rose.

How could her mother not see the advantages of being a makeup consultant? That fabulous discount on the products made the small salary bearable. It was an investment in her future, for she was not going to spend the rest of her life working for nickels and dimes like her mother or pretending to find a business career fulfilling like Toni. No, she was going to find a man to take care of her, one who had money enough to buy her everything she wanted: a big house, expensive clothes, and a Mercedes-Benz 300SD.

She had been popular enough in high school and could have been married by this time, like some of her classmates, if she had wanted. Lord knows, Steve Turner had been eager enough, but his career plans had revolved around telephone repair and that would not put her into the tax bracket she aspired to. Of course, neither would her job at the drugstore, but it had given her the chance to transform herself from an attractive young lady to a gorgeous woman. Alan was proof that she had succeeded.

The thought of Alan Norris and his six-foot-two-inch body made her eyes sparkle and she quickly dropped the Hushed Rose and blusher brush back into her purse. Alan was a gem even without the family real estate agencies throughout southwest Michigan that Alan would one day run. His deep voice had always had the power to send shivers down her spine—not that he had ever noticed. Prissy old Priscilla Byers never let him stray far enough from her side to see that there were other girls around. But, if the other night was any indication, that had died the death that all high school romances deserved.

With a flick of her hairbrush, Melanie put a few strands of her pale blonde hair back into place. She had always worn her hair long and loose, but lately the color had varied. This icy platinum was it, though. Much better than her old reddish brown, because it really caught a man's attention. Once it was caught, she knew that her skintight black pants and red halter top would be able to hold it.

Melanie took one last glance in the mirror then went back into the smoky din of the bar. Her tall, lean body drew admiring glances from the men she passed, but she ignored them as her eyes searched the crowd for one certain sandy blonde head.

He had to come, she told herself as she moved toward the bar. Someone was vacating a stool, so she grabbed it quickly. By turning on it slightly, she had a good view of the small dance floor. There were familiar faces, but Alan's was not one of them. Neither was he at one of the tiny round tables that filled the corners of the room. Hell! It was past ten! Where was he?

Trying to hide her agitation, she pulled a pack of Virginia Slims from her purse and took one out, holding it between two long Persimmon Gloss-tipped fingers. The man next to her jumped to attention with his lighter, and she let him light the cigarette with a cool nod. He was just another Notre Dame stud who thought the local girls were nothing more than a quick lay. She was not going waste her time with him.

She ordered a rum and Coke and stared at the thick ropes and netting that hung on the wall behind the bar. It was the management's only attempt at nautical decor, but no one cared. The live band, cheap drinks, and the belief in all but the crudest IDs were what drew the young people of Niles and South Bend. Elegance and ambiance could be found elsewhere.

Was that where Alan was? she wondered suddenly. At a more elegant bar?

The bartender appeared with her drink and she paid him, trying to remember everything Alan had said to her last Thursday night. There had been the usual nonsense about where had she been all his life, and was she really the same girl that had sat behind him in algebra during their junior year. She had smiled coolly and pretended that she didn't care whether he sat down at her small table or not. When he did, she had practically fainted. Alan Norris had noticed her!

He had bought her a couple of drinks as they chatted about some of their former classmates at Niles Public High School. Then he had told her about his two years at Michigan State. She had been the perfect audience, attentive and impressed, yet by the time it was her turn to talk about her job, she had made sure his thoughts were elsewhere.

The deep valley between her breasts had been exposed by the V neck of her thin jersey print dress, and she sat so that her long legs could be seen next to the table. Crossed above the knee, the top one swung in a gentle seductive rhythm.

They had left the bar soon afterwards, retreating to the back seat of his Malibu where he had proceeded to show her the full extent of his admiration for her. She had been tempted to play cool and pull back at the last minute, but his hands had felt too good on her smooth skin. He had seemed to know just what to do to drive her wild with desire. Soon she could no more have stopped him from making love to her than she could have stopped breathing.

It had been perfect, Melanie thought, swirling the ice cubes around in the remains of her drink with a faint smile. He may have known what to do to please her, but she had been no slouch in satisfying him. Her hands had fanned his desire into an almost insatiable hunger with the techniques she had been perfecting since she was fourteen. When he had finally been spent, he had lain back from her, his face bathed in sweat, but tenderness had been in his eyes.

Melanie had almost laughed aloud in triumph. Had Prissy ever done that for you? she had wanted to ask him. Had she ever made you feel so great? Just in case he thought she had, Melanie had leaned over and taken him in her mouth, teasing and tormenting him until he had come again.

When Alan had fallen back against the side of the car, his eyes closed and his breathing ragged, Melanie had known she had won. He would be back for more. It had only been the first of August. By the time he was due to go back to school, he would know that he couldn't go without her.

Melanie glanced at the clock behind the bar again. Shit! It was almost eleven! Where the hell was he?

As if by magic, she felt someone come up behind her. "Hi, Mel." Her heart dropped as she recognized Steve Turner's voice. He ordered a scotch and water for himself before turning back to her. "Where've you been keeping yourself?" His eyes strayed down to her barely covered breasts.

Melanie fought the urge to turn away. She hadn't worn this outfit to impress him, but still, it was eleven o'clock on a Saturday night. Better to be seen with Steve Turner than nobody. "Oh, I've been around." Over his shoulder she saw several more of their former classmates come in. "Looks like this is reunion night."

Steve followed her line of vision and laughed. "Actually it's a continuation of one. We were all at Shakey's eating pizza until it closed. Then we came here to finish celebrating."

"Celebrating what?" Alan came through the door with Priscilla clinging to his arm and Melanie's heart stopped.

"Alan and Pris's engagement," Steve said casually. He took hold of her arm and pulled her to her feet, unaware of the anger that had suddenly raced through her. "Come and join us."

That bastard! she thought as Steve led her across the floor. She'd be damned if she was going to drink to their happiness, but she seemed unable to stop her feet.

Alan had found an empty table and, after seating Priscilla, turned to look around the bar. He waved when he spotted Steve and had the grace to look uneasy when he saw Melanie with him. She felt very determined suddenly.

Why should she feel ashamed? She had done nothing wrong. With a disdainful smile on her lips and an icy calm in her veins, she and Steve stopped at the table.

"Well, I hear congratulations are in order," she said, her eyes on Alan. "Although I must admit I was rather surprised." Alan paled noticeably.

"I don't see why." Priscilla sounded affronted. "We've been going together for four years. I would say it was about time we got married."

Melanie only laughed, and sat down across from the other girl so that she would be next to both Alan and Steve. With a pointed look at Priscilla's white cotton blouse and prairie-style skirt, Melanie leaned back in her chair and shook her hair provocatively so that it fell down her bare back. Then she took out a cigarette, knowing that both Steve and Alan were watching her while Priscilla radiated her disapproval.

"Alan, I wanted a glass of wine," Priscilla reminded him, her voice pouty and spoiled.

Alan rose obediently to his feet. "Sorry. Melanie? Can I get you anything?"

She favored him with a slow, intimate glance. "The usual. You know, a rum and Coke."

With a reddened face, Alan nodded and turned away. With a mysterious smile that she knew would annoy Priscilla, Melanie watched him go.

"I'm surprised you and Steve haven't decided to tie the knot," Priscilla noted cattily.

Melanie turned to her slowly; then her eyes went past her to favor Steve with a fond look. "As wonderful as he is, I know that high school sweethearts make the worst husbands. Just because we were attracted to each other as children doesn't mean that we have much in common now that we're adults."

Priscilla bristled. "I imagine Steve's surprised to hear that he was just a child."

Steve laughed uneasily. "She's only teasing you, Priss," he said with an uncertain glance at Melanie. She looked back at him innocently until he turned to Priscilla again. "Would Alan mind if we dance?"

With a nauseating giggle, Priscilla shook her head. "No, of course not." She rose to her feet.

Would you mind if Alan and I fucked in the parking lot? Melanie asked her silently.

"You will excuse us, won't you?" Priscilla asked Melanie condescendingly.

She nodded with a sweet smile, not bothering to watch as they wove through the other tables to the crowded dance floor.

Alan arrived with the drinks in time to see them leave. "I'm glad we have this chance to talk."

She picked up her drink and sipped it, her eyes mocking him over the rim of her glass.

"I hope you don't think I deliberately kept this from you last Thursday. But the truth is, I didn't know then."

Melanie looked skeptical. "You didn't know two days ago that you were getting engaged? Doesn't that make it awfully sudden?"

Alan shrugged, then looked over at Priscilla and Steve dancing. He turned back to Melanie after a moment. "I didn't exactly have a choice," he admitted uncomfortably.

She stared at him, and, as his meaning became clear, a malicious smile spread across her face. "You mean old Prissy's pregnant? God! Her parents must be pissed!"

Alan was startled by her reaction and glanced around them quickly, hoping she hadn't been overheard. "We're not exactly spreading it around yet. I just wanted you to know the truth. So you'd see that it doesn't change anything with us."

Her smile disappeared. "Oh?"

Alan leaned forward and covered her hand with his. "I won't be going back to school, unless it's a few classes at night, so we can meet someplace. Here, or if you get your own apartment, I could come there."

Melanie pretended to be shocked in order to hide her anger. "You mean you'd cheat on your wife?" Actually, she'd be the one cheated: out of the big house and rich life that she deserved. And all for what? The dubious pleasure of taking his tiny prick inside her.

"Well, it's not as if I was in love with her," Alan argued with another worried glance at the dance floor. "Hey, gorgeous, we made beautiful music together. You can't ignore that." He made his voice soft and coaxing.

Beautiful music! Christ, what a stupid phrase! How had she not noticed what an ass he was? She looked across the table at him, seeing the worry in his eyes and the weakness of his mouth. He was no man to waste her talents on. She rose to her feet.

"I don't know where you got the idea that there was an 'us,' " she said with a shrug. "We had a few laughs a couple of nights ago, that's all." She leaned over and picked up her glass to finish the rest. "Tell Priss to make sure I'm on the guest list. I would simply die if I missed something as exciting as your wedding." She smiled sweetly at his chagrined look and turned away.

"Mel." His voice sounded more than worried, it sounded terrified. "Mel, wouldn't it be better if you didn't come to the wedding? You know, if someone had seen us the other night and then saw you at the wedding . . ."

Melanie turned slowly; her eyes were cold and angry. "And how am I supposed to explain my absence? Our whole crowd will be there and it might seem a little odd if I wasn't."

"Yeah, but if you had a good excuse. Like if you were out of town. Couldn't you go visit your sister in Chicago?"

Melanie could think of few things less exciting than visiting Toni. "I'm not wasting my hard-earned money just to save you some embarrassment." She moved closer to the door.

"I could help you with that." Alan followed along behind her.

She felt him slip something into her purse, and turned

toward him. "Aren't you afraid that Priscilla will get back to the table before you?" He glanced behind him and Melanie took the chance to leave. God! He was a real wimp! She had no desire to go to his wedding, because she never wanted to see him again.

There was nothing quite as depressing as getting home before midnight on a Saturday night except to have reached eleven-thirty and still have no escort, Melanie thought. She backed mother's old Ford Fairlane out of its parking space and turned onto Eleventh Street. She headed north, passing a number of bars and restaurants. Their parking lots were filled and she could picture happy couples inside.

This town was the pits, she thought angrily as she turned onto a quiet side street. There was nobody and nothing worth a damn here, just a bunch of two-bit losers, like Alan. How had she ever thought she wanted him? She turned down another street, lined with small bungalows, and noticed that one further down the street was ablaze with lights.

"Swell!" Melanie muttered as she automatically slowed the car. "What is she still up for?" The last thing she needed right now was a friendly chat with her mother. She pulled her car into the driveway and noticed a trim little Scirocco parked right in front of the tiny one-car garage. So that was why her mother was still up—Toni was here.

Melanie was thoughtful as she got out of the car. Maybe there was an alternative to living in this dump after all.

"Goddamn stupid idiot! Hell! A girl could pitch better than that!"

Toni tried to ignore the man in front of the television set, but it was an impossible task. Mickey Thomas was as rude and obnoxious as he was fat and disgusting. She could hardly believe that her mother intended to marry him.

This was turning out to be some weekend, Toni thought as she picked up the remains of their Sunday dinner and carried the dirty dishes into the kitchen. First there was that disastrous argument with Jon and her late-afternoon drive to Michigan. Then her mother announced that she was getting married again.

Toni felt exhausted rather than refreshed by her visit home. Getting away had only provided her with more wor-

110

ries and tension. There had been no time to try to sort out her muddled feelings about Jon. It would be a relief to get back to the problems at Mid-America.

"You don't like him, do you?" Flo asked as the kitchen door swung closed. She was standing at the sink, her arms buried in suds up to her elbows and a worried frown in her eyes as she looked at her elder daughter.

Toni carried the dirty plates over to the garbage bag and began to scrape them. "I was surprised, that's all. I never expected you to get married again."

Flo turned back to the sink and began to stack the clean glasses in the dish drainer on the counter next to her. "I know what you're thinking. He's not exactly handsome, but I'm no Miss America either. Not with this extra forty pounds I'm carrying around or my gray hair."

Toni scraped the stub of Mickey's cigar and the surrounding mashed potatoes into the garbage. "I'm not so young that I judge a person by his looks. It's just that Mickey seems as dictatorial and opinionated as you said my father was, and Melanie's dad. They were disasters, so why won't this be?"

"Melanie's father and I were divorced more than fifteen years ago," Flo reminded her as she rinsed the soap from some knives. "And giving up my job at that diner isn't the same as quitting nursing school. Right now, I'm quite willing to trade my so-called liberation for some rest."

Toni looked around her mother's kitchen as she carried plates over to her. It was a small room, decorated in the avocado and turquoise that had been popular about twenty years ago, but it felt comfortable and safe. The small house had become her refuge, Toni realized, a place where she could hide from the world to rest or lick her wounds. That was why she had come running up last night, to try to escape from the pain Jon's distrust had caused. And instead of feeling soothed and comforted, she felt exhausted.

Was that why she disliked Mickey so, because his presence would destroy her little haven? Or was she truly worried about her mother's happiness? "He just doesn't seem to fit in here," Toni said with a shrug.

Flo took the pile of plates and pushed them under the water with such force that suds flew up onto the counters and the window over the sink. "I think he's gonna fit in fine, and his paycheck is gonna fit in even better," Flo said defiantly. "I'm tired of working my fingers to the bone at that damn slop house for measly quarter tips. It's my turn to take it easy for a change." She pushed a few strands of her short gray hair off her forehead with the back of one hand. "He wants to take care of me, and that's fine and dandy."

"Hey, Flo! How's about a beer?"

"Sure thing, Mickey!" Flo called back, her eyes daring Toni to make a comment. Looking away, Toni knew that her mother understood exactly what she was getting into. She had read it in her eyes. And just because Toni would never trade her independence for security, who was she to assume that that was the right course for others? After all, Toni had a career, work that she enjoyed, and her mother had given hers up twenty-eight years ago, when she was pregnant.

"I'll get it, Mom," Toni said quickly as her mother reached for a towel to dry her hands. "I think there's a few more things to clear off the table anyway."

Her mother went back to the dishes while Toni pulled a can of beer from the refrigerator. She was about to pull the pop-top open when her mother stopped her. "Oh, no, he likes to open them himself. Just bring out the can and one of those tall beer glasses on the top shelf."

Toni got the glass down, and could not help thinking that her mother wasn't going to stop being a waitress when she quit her job. Only she doubted that Mickey was likely to tip. Reminding herself that it was her mother's decision, she hid her feelings behind a bland look and carried in Mickey's beer.

"Damn, that's more like it!" Mickey shouted at the television set. A commercial flicked on the screen and he noticed Toni's presence just as she put the can and glass down on the table next to him. "Hey, don't run off, little girl." He nodded to a nearby chair as he flipped open the can. "We ain't hardly met." Giving all his attention to his drink, he carefully poured the beer down one side of the glass and watched as the foam rose on the top.

Toni stopped but did not sit down, hoping that the game would resume quickly. She might have decided not to question her mother's decision, but that didn't mean she and Mickey were going to be great pals.

"You know, you ain't a bad-looking gal," he told her easily. His beer poured, he took a long sip and set the glass down next to him. "I was real surprised when I first saw you, knowing that you were twenty-seven already. You don't look more than twenty-five or so."

"Gee, thanks."

Her humor was lost on him. "Not that twenty-five is much better. You should have settled down at least five years ago, maybe more." He took a long drink of beer, resting the hand holding the glass on his protruding belly.

"Settled down?"

He nodded solemnly. "Yeah. Now you're gonna have to settle for what you can get. You can't be too choosy when you're practically on the shelf." He took another drink of beer.

She didn't know whether to laugh or scream at his archaic ideas. For her mother's sake, she forced herself to remain polite. "I promise to keep that in mind."

"Course, with your training, it'll help 'cause you could always get a job. I know we got an opening for a timekeeper in our warehouse. You'd probably have a good chance for that."

"Golly, do you really think so?"

"Sure. I can help you too. I got a good rep in the warehouse. Thirty-one years and only three sick days. It didn't matter how bad the hangover, I went in. Hell, I can sleep better in that warehouse than I can at home." He belched and silently contemplated his man-of-the-world wisdom. Toni stood in stunned silence.

After another drink of beer, he looked back at her. "I can help you out in the pants department too."

"Pants? You mean slacks?" Toni asked. She thought he worked at Kawneer and made aluminum windows, not for any clothing manufacturer.

Mickey roared with laughter. "Nah, pants. You know, what's in 'em." He shook his head in disbelief. "Slacks! Oh, shit, college girls."

Recovering, Mickey went on. "Now seriously, little girl, I can find you a good man. I know a lotta people. Steady jobs. Real good." He thought for a moment. "There's Jeff Hester. He just got divorced and wouldn't mind you workin' 'cause his alimony and child support payments is eatin' him up. Or Bob Blumer. His Jessie ran out on him month before last and he sure could use help with them three brats of his. Two of 'em still in diapers."

And she thought she had problems now! With a little help from Mickey, they could triple! It was getting difficult to keep from laughing, but she managed to keep a straight face. "They sound very nice, but my job's in Chicago, and—"

Mickey just shook his head, seeing no problem. "Hey, I just told you, there's that timekeeping job. If that there don't pan out, there's all kinds of jobs for countin' and writin' numbers. We got banks, grocery stores, and all kinda things here in Niles. You could get a job easy." The baseball game resumed and the conversation was over.

Just in time, Toni thought as she walked away. Courtesy could only be stretched so far, and she had definitely reached the end of hers. The man was ridiculous, with his "all you need is a man" solution to everything. She ought to be laughing about it, except that she felt too tired to do anything.

She stopped at the dining room table and stared at the few remaining dishes to be cleared. It was time she got back to her own apartment. This wasn't where she belonged anymore, and it was stupid of her to keep trying to hold on to a little piece of childhood security. She lived alone because she liked being independent, both physically and emotionally. She didn't need her mother or Jon to take care of her.

She picked up the few cups and saucers that remained and carried them into the kitchen. Melanie was drying the dishes for their mother.

"I think I'd better be going," Toni told them both. "I've got a busy week ahead of me, and I don't want to get home too late tonight."

"Well, I'm glad that you came," Flo said. "You know, you're always welcome here. Mickey won't mind."

"Sure, Mom," Toni replied as she leaned over to kiss her. "I'll get my car loaded and then say good-bye."

Flo nodded and went back to the dishes, but Melanie followed Toni out of the kitchen and down the short hall to her bedroom.

"Toni, I've got to talk to you before you go," she said quietly.

Toni stopped, surprised by the urgent note in her sister's

voice, and turned to look at her. She looked quite young and innocent, maybe because her makeup was much lighter than usual and her cotton blouse was buttoned up modestly. What surprised Toni most was the look of worry on her face.

"Something wrong, Melanie?"

Melanie did not answer, but glanced down the hall toward the living room, and then pulled Toni into her small bedroom. "Toni, please, let me come to Chicago with you," she whispered.

Toni had not expected such a request and hardly knew what to respond. "Come with me?"

Melanie darted a nervous look into the hallway again, and then closed the bedroom door with care. Only when it was shut did she speak again. "I can't stay here." Her voice cracked with fear. "Please let me come with you. It'll only be for a few days, until I can get a job and find a place to stay."

"But why now? Wouldn't it be better to plan this out a little?"

Melanie blinked back the tears that had formed in her frightened eyes, and sat down slowly on the edge of her bed. A pink rabbit with soft, floppy ears lay on her pillow and she picked it up, stroking the soft fur. "I can't stay here anymore," she said. "Not after Mom marries him."

Toni sat down on the bed next to her sister. "You mean Mickey? I agree he's pretty strange, but if you keep your sense of humor, he's not so bad. And Mom wouldn't want you to feel this was no longer your home."

"If he's in it, it won't be."

The violence in Melanie's voice surprised Toni, and she frowned. "Mel, I know we haven't been close, but I am your sister. I'll help you any way I can. Has he done something?"

Melanie sighed and looked up at Toni, wiping a few tears from her cheeks. "Mom didn't believe me, and you won't either."

"Of course I will. You have no reason to lie to me about anything. Now what happened?"

Melanie rose to her feet slowly and walked over to her window. It looked out over the backyard, but she just played with the ruffled edge of the curtain and stared down at the floor. "He hasn't exactly done anything," she admitted. "It's just the way he watches me all the time and he pretends to be so friendly. Mom thinks he'll be a great stepfather, but I can tell that's not what he's thinking."

"Mel, are you sure? I admit I don't like him, but if he's marrying Mom—"

"If he's marrying Mom, why does he come around when he knows she's not home?" Melanie cried. "I may be only nineteen, but I've met up with men like him before. Just because I have to wear a lot of makeup for my job, they think I'm available. I've seen the way they watch me, and, believe me, they're not thinking they'd like to be my stepfather."

"What about Mom? She ought to know what he's like. Maybe we should both talk to her."

Melanie hurried over and took Toni's hand. "No, we can't. I already tried and she doesn't want to know. She's determined to marry him and won't listen to me. The best thing is for me to leave. Maybe then she'll never know."

Toni looked into Melanie's pleading eyes and nodded slowly. "All right, maybe that would be for the best. You can come with me tonight."

"Oh, thanks, Toni," she cried, throwing her arms around her sister. "I knew you'd help me."

# CHAPTER ELEVEN

"This is going to be fabulous!" Melanie purred. She got out of Toni's car and looked around her, excitement building inside her with everything she saw. "There are so many stores, I can hardly wait to go shopping tomorrow." She reached into the back of the car and took out one of the cases holding her makeup.

"Don't you think you ought to have a job before you start spending money?" Toni inquired dryly. "It's going to cost you more to live here than in Niles."

Her sister merely shrugged as she put her case on the sidewalk next to the car and reached into the back for another one. "I've got some money saved up and Mom gave me a little before we left."

Didn't that sound so terribly frugal of her? Actually her checking account had been overdrawn, but she sure wasn't going to waste that hundred that Alan had slipped her by covering some stupid checks. She didn't know whether he had intended to give her that much or if he had pulled out the wrong bill, but it hardly mattered. She had that, plus twenty from her mother and thirty from that her soon-to-be stepdad. Probably made him feel all paternal to slip her something. The big man taking care of the little girl. She wished she had had more time; she probably could have conned more out of him.

"Don't forget that you're going to have to pay for little things like food and insurance," Toni warned as she walked around the back of the car to open the trunk.

"I know all that," Melanie scoffed. "I've got plenty, so you don't have to be a wet blanket. I can hardly believe I'm here. Let me enjoy myself for a few days."

Toni put two suitcases on the sidewalk and closed the

trunk. "Mom seemed to take your leaving pretty well," she noted. They started walking toward her apartment.

Melanie was watching two young men cruising down the street in a red Triumph. Now there was some flesh worth an extra glance. "Yes," she agreed absently. "She knew how much I hated Niles and wanted to get out."

"I thought you wanted to move because of Mickey," Toni reminded her.

The sports car disappeared around the corner and Melanie turned back to her sister with an innocent smile. "Oh, yes, that too. But then I had to make up some other reason to satisfy her, didn't I?"

A handsome young man was walking toward them and Melanie could barely keep her eyes from devouring him. This was the mecca she had hoped it would be. Terrific men all over the place. And from the looks of their cars and clothes, she was sure their wallets would be just as attractive as their bodies.

Alan had actually done her a favor by showing himself as the fool he was before she wasted any more time on him. It had not taken her long to realize that she had been looking at things all wrong. Somewhere she had picked up some archaic ideas, and her desire for marriage was one of them. God! She had been almost as stupid as Alan. Why in the world would she want to get tied down to some jerk? If she played her cards right, she could have the house, clothes, and car that she wanted without the jerk tagging along.

Just look at last week. One evening with Alan and she had gotten a hundred dollars. Plus he was good for more. Just give her a few weeks to miss her period, and she could make a sobbing, desperate call to him. Jeez! It would be too easy! She'd bet she could make five hundred without any trouble while she looked around for some easy marks here.

Once all of Melanie's things were carried up to the apartment, Toni let her sister hang up dresses in one end of the closet and use a few bottom drawers of her dresser while she took a leisurely shower. It felt good to rinse the dirt from the trip off her body, and Toni felt some of her irritations fade away also.

She suspected strongly that Melanie had used her to get to Chicago for reasons of her own, but she was not going to let it bother her. So she had made up the story about Mickey in order to win Toni's sympathy. It had been unfair to Mickey, making him seem like a lecherous old man when he wasn't, but she could hardly send her back and make her apologize. No, she would just make sure that nothing in her life changed because her sister had moved in with her. Besides, Melanie would get her own place soon, and they'd probably see very little of each other.

Toni brushed her hair briskly and caught up the long curls with a barrette to keep them off the back of her neck. Then she put on a soft, white cotton batiste nightshirt that ended a few inches above her knees. The long full sleeves were trimmed with a lavish ecru lace at the cuffs, as was the deep V neckline. She tied the drawstrings to close the front at a more modest level and slipped on a pair of white satin scuffs. After a light snack and an hour or two of television, she was going to bed.

When Toni came out of her bathroom, she was surprised to find that Melanie had changed into a halter-topped sundress and a pair of wooden heels.

"I can't wait to see the neighborhood." She touched up her lipstick using the wall mirror near Toni's door.

Toni glanced down at her nightgown then back up at her sister. "I had no idea you would want to do something tonight. Other than have a light supper and watch some TV, that is."

Melanie's hand stilled, her lipstick brush held out from her lips as she turned toward Toni. "Hey, I don't need a babysitter or a tour guide. Go to bed early. It's okay with me; I can manage to find my way around."

"But it's your first night here—"

Melanie just laughed and went back to fixing her lips. "If I get lost, I'm sure I can find someone to help me."

Someone young, male, and good-looking, I'll bet, Toni thought. "Okay. I'll get you my extra key." She found it in a drawer of her dresser and put it down next to Melanie's purse.

"Don't bother to wait up." Melanie tossed her things into her purse. "I may be late."

Toni tried to stifle her emotions as she watched her sister go out the door. She was not certain if she was irritated or worried, but she knew that she would just have to get used to Melanie's presence and not let it bother her. Tomorrow morning would come soon enough, and her alarm would be ringing, not Melanie's.

She turned to go into the kitchen, but stopped suddenly, spotting the key still lying on the table where she had put it. Melanie had forgotten it.

Grabbing the key, Toni pulled the door open. The elevators were in sight down the hall, but her sister wasn't. She should have known that the elevators would come quickly the one time they shouldn't.

Toni closed the door with a sigh and put the key back down on the table. It looked like it was going to be a late night after all, she thought, going into the kitchen.

In a few minutes, Toni had managed to push Melanie to the back of her mind as the smell of sizzling bacon filled the room. She was hungry, that's all, Toni thought as she beat a couple of eggs. Once she had eaten, everything would fall back into perspective and Melanie's real reasons for coming would not bother her any more than Melanie's presence would.

When the bacon was almost done, she poured the eggs into the waiting pan and pushed the bread down in the toaster. It was just that the weekend had been so awful, one emotional surprise after another. After a good night's sleep and immersion in the routine of work, she wouldn't be thrown into a tizzy by unimportant little things. She pulled a sheet of paper towels from the roll and was about to remove her bacon from the pan when the doorbell rang.

"Oh, hell!" she muttered with a despairing glance from bacon to eggs to toaster. The bell rang again. What a time for Melanie to return for her key!

She darted to the intercom and slapped the button. "Come on up," she yelled, and ran back to the stove. Her bacon looked a tad crisp, but not too bad. She put it on the paper towels and stirred her eggs as the toast popped up.

The knock sounded at the door when she had the first piece buttered. She pushed the eggs back off the heat, hoping they would finish cooking slowly, and ran through the living room.

"Here's the key." She pulled open the door, turning at the same time to pick up the key from the table. She turned back to find Jon, not Melanie, staring at her.

"Does this mean you've forgiven me?" he asked with a hopeful grin.

She pulled her hand back, the key still safely inside. "I thought you were someone else. My sister," she added quickly, even before his frown registered in her mind.

"Then you *are* still mad at me."

Toni reached up and pushed some strands of her hair back from her face. She was glad to see him, but didn't want to be. Where was this independence she had been lecturing herself about? Why was she giving him the chance to make her miserable again?

"I haven't had time to think about it." She shrugged as if she had forgotten all about him and their fight. The air in the hallway seemed stifling compared to the air-conditioned comfort of her apartment. She stepped aside to let him enter so she could close the door.

"Does it count that I've been trying to apologize for the last thirty hours?" he asked her wearily.

Her heart twisted when she saw that the tiny lines around his eyes were more pronounced. She shook her head, trying to dispel the desire to smooth them away with her fingertips. "I was out of town."

"So I found out when I was about ready to call the police." In response to her startled look, he went on, running his fingers through his hair. "I kept calling and there was no answer and I was getting frantic. I didn't know what had happened to you. God!" he cried with impatient anger. "Don't ever scare me like that again!"

Toni had begun to feel guilty for running off as she had, but his anger wiped any such feeling away. "Then don't make all sorts of asinine assumptions about me," she snapped, and headed for the kitchen where her snack was congealing.

"I did it again, didn't I?" Jon sighed, trailing along behind her. There was a long moment of silence as they crossed her living room into the kitchen. "Can I tell you I like your outfit?" he inquired.

Toni looked down at her thin cotton nightgown and the long expanse of bare leg that was visible underneath it. She felt almost naked, and from the darkening of Jon's eyes, the transparency of her gown had not gone unnoticed by him. She turned away abruptly, not wanting to admit to herself the rush of desire that coursed through her in response to him. She didn't want him to have that kind of power over her. It made her too vulnerable and she wasn't sure she trusted him not to hurt her.

"It's been some weekend all the way around," she said as she stirred the solid mass of eggs in the pan. They looked awful, but her appetite was gone anyway. "My mother's marrying another idiot and my sister's moved in with me." She looked up to find him leaning against the cabinets, an unreadable expression on his face.

"I think it would have been more peaceful to stay here and continue our shouting match across the grocery store." She laughed uneasily and turned away. The bacon was cold as she picked up the paper towels. "Like some bacon?"

Jon took a piece, looked at a thoughtfully, and then, making a slight face, put it back down. "I had a hell of a weekend too. I figured that I had acted like such a fool that you'd never speak to me again." He paused as if it was her turn to speak.

What could she say? she asked herself, keeping her face free of emotion. Should she tell him that she hated fighting with him and had felt frightened and confused all weekend? Or that when she saw him at the door a few minutes ago, she realized how much she needed him? He probably would laugh and think she sounded like some love-sick fool.

She turned away, clutching the wooden spoon that lay on the stove. My God, did she do it again? Had she been so incredibly stupid as to let herself fall in love again?

Jon shifted his position. "Anyway, I think I surprised myself as much as you with my outburst. I didn't really figure the whole thing out until around lunchtime today."

Toni was barely listening as she fought back the panic. She had to think this all through, and she couldn't do that with him standing there talking to her. How could she get him to leave?

He was staring down at the bacon, and she grabbed the frying pan lined with cold eggs. "Want these?"

He shook his head impatiently. "Are you even listening to me?"

"Sure. You had a lousy weekend too." She turned away and dumped the eggs into the garbage bag. The toast followed. Why didn't he take the hint and go?

"I admit I acted like a damn fool. But there were

extenuating circumstances. For one thing, I can't stand the sight of that bastard you were talking to."

Her hands began to tremble uncontrollably, and she had to find something to do with them, so she carried the two dirty pans to the sink. After turning the water on, she stood staring at the growing soapsuds as the sink filled. She had been devoting all her energies to her career to avoid this very problem. Where had she gone wrong?

"Dammit! Will you listen to me?" Jon cried angrily. He had crossed the small kitchen and grabbed hold of her arm, spinning her around to face him. "Here I am, trying to tell you that I love you, and you're washing dishes."

His hands were on her upper arms and he must have felt her trembling, for his expression softened. "Toni, I love you."

She just stared at him. This wasn't what she had planned at all! "I thought we were just having fun," she protested, shaking her head. Her green eyes were open wide as she gazed at him.

A hint of a smile teased the corners of his mouth. "Being in love isn't fun?"

"Not usually, no."

His touch had become a caress as his hands slid lightly over her arms. "Maybe you just had the wrong partner."

"And I suppose you're the right one?" Her sarcasm was her only armor as she looked for a way to escape his hands and their seductive powers. He was blocking her way, though, and short of knocking him to the floor, there was no escape. His eyes seemed to pierce hers, cutting through her hastily erected fortifications. She was afraid of what he might read in them, things she had just learned about herself and wasn't ready to share.

To avoid his scrutiny, she spun around. With her eyes closed and her breathing rapid, she grasped the edge of the counter tightly only to touch something strange. Her eyes flew open and she stared down at the huge mountain of suds towering above the ready-to-overflow sink.

"Now, look at what you've done!" she cried as she leaned over and turned off the faucet. The delicate lace trim on her sleeves fell into the water and the soapsuds left damp spots where they brushed against her breasts. Both she and Jon reached for the kitchen towel at the same time and their hands collided.

"Tell me, do you flood your kitchen every time someone tells you that they love you?" He took the towel from her and mopped up the puddles that had formed on the counter.

"It's not funny." She pulled back her sleeve, and reached into the sink to let some of the water out.

"No, I don't suppose the people living below you think so either. Their ceiling will start to leak and they'll just look up and sigh, 'That Toni's got some poor fool all twisted up again.'"

She glared at him. "You make it sound like it's my fault. I didn't do anything." Her sleeve slipped down into the water and she had to squeeze the water out of it. "Rats!" she muttered.

Jon tossed the towel onto the counter and leaned back, crossing his arms over his chest as he watched her. "You know, that's pretty much how I feel right now. Somehow I had hoped for a slightly more enthusiastic response to my announcement."

She looked at him uneasily and reached for the towel. "It's just that I don't particularly want to be in love," she admitted. Keeping her eyes away from his, she squatted down and began to wipe the water from the front of the cabinet.

His feet came closer. "I don't remember hearing that you were. I thought I was the only fool under discussion."

Toni just shrugged and searched diligently for any damp spots that she might have missed. "I hate feeling dependent on someone else to be happy," she explained. "Anytime they choose, they can turn on you and twist everything around. They kill you with pain, but say it's your fault, all you have to do is change. Just conform to their unique image of a woman and you can have it all back again."

He came down to her level. "You've known some real gems," he commented, and took the towel from her hand. They both knew that the little water that had been there was long gone, and it was just another battlement she had thrown in his way. He tossed the towel up onto the counter with one hand as he raised her chin with his other. "I promise I won't make any demands. Well, no unreasonable ones," he qualified with a gentle smile. "And I'll never turn on you."

Toni watched him, wishing she could trust him. He did seem different from the others, yet admitting that you loved someone made you so vulnerable...

He leaned forward and touched her lips with his. "I have no desire to make you into something else, because I think you're almost perfect the way you are."

"Almost?" She couldn't help herself.

He smiled and her heart seemed to melt. "A touch of reciprocal passion would be all that is needed."

She smiled back, and when his lips returned to hers, she responded to his kiss. Was it so wrong to trust him? Wasn't it a bit too late to decide?

Jon's hands pulled her toward him so that they were both kneeling on the floor. "Tell me that you love me," he whispered as his arms encircled her body.

"I love you," she whispered back. "I didn't plan to, but I do." Wet sleeves forgotten, she put her arms around his neck and looked into his eyes. One hand came back to wipe away the lines of weariness that she had wanted to soothe before. "I missed you so much this weekend."

His embrace tightened and his lips sought hers again as his hands roamed over her back. She was crushed against his chest and delicious sensations were racing through her.

"You're the only thing that makes sense in my life and I was so afraid when you were gone. I was sure I had lost you." Jon moved from her lips to her neck. "You know, your nightgown is not helping my sanity at this moment."

"It's wet, too," she murmured, her eyes closed as he tugged open the V neck so that the valley between her breasts was exposed. "I might catch a cold if I leave it on much longer."

"And we wouldn't want that," he agreed, then stopped suddenly. "Did you say your sister has moved in with you?"

Toni laughed at the worried look on his face. "She's out for the evening. For a long evening."

He rose to his feet and pulled her up with him. "Here's hoping she stays out even longer."

She smiled at him. "We've got as long as we want. She forgot her key, remember?" She took his hand and led him down the hall to her bedroom.

# CHAPTER TWELVE

Melanie hurried across Toni's living room to answer the door. She couldn't have timed it better had she known when he was coming over. She had washed her hair about an hour ago and had just finished doing her nails, both fingers and toes. A pair of yellow knit shorts with a matching halter top showed off her golden tan, the product of five arduous days in the early August sun at North Avenue Beach.

"Well, you must be Melanie," the man at the door said. "I'm Jon Morici."

Melanie's smile was warm as she stepped aside to let him enter. "Of course. Toni told me about you." But she left out a few important details, Melanie thought, letting her eyes roam appreciatively over his broad shoulders and chest. How had her cold, strictly business sister ever found such a gorgeous hunk of man?

Jon looked past her into the living room. "Toni back yet?"

Melanie closed the door. "No, she called a while ago and said she was catching a later flight home." The disappointed look that crossed his face registered only faintly. There was something about this man that really attracted her, and she was going to get to know him better. Much better. Her glance took on a sensuous quality. "I promised to take care of you until she returns."

His smile seemed more obligatory than delighted. "Did she say what flight she was taking? Maybe I have time to meet it."

Melanie took his arm and led him into the living room. "Don't be silly. She should be home any time now, and I'm sure she'd much rather have you relaxing here than chasing out to the airport in Friday evening traffic."

Jon did not look convinced, but walked over to the chair near the window.

"So what can I get you to drink?" she asked him. "I'll bet you need something strong to unwind after a hard week at your office."

He shook his head. "I think I'll just wait for Toni. Thanks anyway."

Melanie forced her frown into a fetching pout. "What kind of a gentleman would make me drink alone? You may not need something, but after the day I've had, I do."

He turned toward her, his eyes softening a bit as if he had just really begun to see her. "Okay, I'll have a scotch on the rocks then."

Melanie nodded and sauntered over to the kitchen, conscious that his eyes were following her. "With Toni traveling all this week, we've hardly talked, so I don't know much about you," she called back to him. "Do you work with her at the accounting firm?"

Jon walked over to stand in the kitchen door while she got two glasses out of a cabinet. "No, actually I work for my father, and his firm is one of Toni's clients."

She flashed him an intimate smile. "Somehow, I didn't think you were an accountant, but my guess would have been athlete. Football, maybe."

Jon just laughed. "Not anymore. I'm a bit too old for that kind of nonsense."

"Oh, I doubt that," she scoffed, and pulled an ice tray from the freezer. "You look like you're in terrific shape."

"Not bad for an old man, I guess," he said. "But I owe it all to running. That's actually how Toni and I met. We were both running in the park."

Melanie poured some liquor over the ice cubes in each glass, hiding the impatient look on her face. "How interesting!" she murmured. Trips down memory lane were not her style and her sister was not her favorite topic of conversation. She handed him his drink. "Now tell me what kind of business you and your father are in. Is it just the two of you?"

"No, we're a bit bigger than that. We have a couple hundred employees."

"Really?" She shoved the ice tray back into the freezer

as she eyed the cut of his blue sport shirt and gray pants. Her instincts had not been wrong; she had known she smelled money.

She picked up her drink and followed Jon back into the living room. How could she have thought that this evening was going to be a dead bore? Not with such a juicy morsel to keep her company.

"So how do you like Chicago?" he asked as he sat down in the armchair by the window. Melanie curled up in one end of the sofa.

"Oh, I love the city, but it hasn't loved me back." He looked puzzled, so she went on. "I hate imposing on Toni like this, but I haven't been able to find a job. Nobody in this city seems to want me." She made her voice soft and seductive, but he seemed to miss the most obvious meaning.

"What kind of work are you looking for?"

"I'm afraid I'm not really qualified for much. I did some modeling back home," she said, stretching two high school fashion shows into a profession. "But I didn't want to get into that here. I'm not really searching for a career. I'd just like to make people happy." She glanced down at her drink, pretending to be embarrassed. "I guess I'm just an old-fashioned girl, at heart."

"Nothing wrong with that," he assured her, but before he could say anything else, footsteps were heard out in the hall. He turned toward the door, but they passed on.

It was to be expected, Melanie told herself, but she couldn't help feeling irritated that he'd found the promise of Toni's arrival more interesting than her actual presence. By the time he turned back, though, her angry look was gone and she was watching him innocently.

"What were we talking about?" he asked.

"Who cares?" she laughed, and shifted her position to stretch her long legs out in front of her. "It's just nice to have someone to talk to for a change."

He seemed embarrassed that his attention had strayed. "It must be rather lonely for you. Away from home and then here by yourself all week."

She smiled at his suggestion of her solitary week. It hadn't been quite that reclusive. "Oh, I've managed to keep busy." Her eyes fastened on his mouth, full and delicious-looking, and traveled slowly down his chest to the tantalizing bulge at his crotch. She licked her lips slowly as her hunger for him grew.

"Uh, when did you say Toni should be coming?" he asked, shifting his position uneasily.

Melanie just shrugged and rose to her feet. "Could be hours," she admitted, her appetite increasing steadily at the sight of his long tapered fingers. What a pleasure it would be to have a real man's hands on her for a change!

She picked up her empty glass. "Can I freshen up yours?" she asked. "Or are you ready for something a little more stimulating than alcohol?" She let her fingertips brush against his arm as she reached down for his glass.

"Look, Melanie, I think I'd better go. Maybe Toni could call when—" The sound of a key in the lock interrupted him. Their brief tryst was over. Jon rose to his feet, ignoring her and the offer in her eyes.

Toni pushed the door open and carried in her suitcase. Seeing Jon, she stopped short, a tender smile covering her face. "Hi," she said.

What sparkling dialogue! Melanie thought with a sneer. Jon apparently had no complaints, though, as he went forward to take her in his arms.

"I missed you," he murmured into her hair. "I hate it when you're away."

As she leaned back watching their performance, Melanie vowed to teach him to love Toni's trips. She finished the rest of her drink quickly, then let one of the ice cubes slide into her mouth. Her tongue played with it absently as she wondered about the extent of their relationship.

It looked like they must be lovers. She had wondered if Toni was too much of a prude to have reached that stage yet, but from the intensity of their embrace, it was clear that they weren't just pals. Of course, Jon just oozed sex appeal, Melanie thought. Just looking at his beautiful tight body had her panting. Toni would have to be dead not to have felt it too.

The sight of Toni's hands moving across Jon's back reminded Melanie of his rejection of her. Why should they have all the fun? "Would you two like me to disappear for a while?" she teased.

They broke apart slowly, their eyes continuing to communicate after their bodies no longer were touching. Toni's face glowed and her washed-out, haggard look was gone. With obvious reluctance, she tore her eyes from Jon to look across the room at her sister.

"Hi, Mel," she said. "How was your week? Looks like you got yourself a nice tan."

Melanie rose gracefully to her feet. "That's about all I got," she announced with a resentful glance at Jon.

"No job yet, eh?" Toni sympathized. "Say, maybe Jon could help you there." She turned toward him, apparently not noticing the stunned look on his face. "Couldn't you see if there'd be some opening at Mid-America for her?"

"Yeah, I guess so," he stammered.

Melanie smiled at him. "Oh, would you?" she purred. "I'd be ever so grateful." Her eyes told him the direction her gratitude would take, but he turned toward Toni.

Run away now, Melanie told him silently as she walked out to the kitchen. But she knew he'd change his mind pretty fast when she was working with him each day. She wouldn't be going there as Toni's sister, either. They had different last names thanks to the revolving door on their mother's bed, so no one would have to know. She'd be Jon's friend, that was all.

She made herself another drink, and when she brought it back into the living room, Jon was carrying Toni's case toward the bedroom. His other arm was around her shoulder. "What do you want to do tonight?" he was asking her softly.

Melanie could not hear Toni's reply, but Jon laughed and pulled her closer. "I think that can be arranged."

Melanie watched the two of them with a cynical smile. Just wait, she thought as she threw herself into a chair and took a long drink. Wait until Toni had to choose between him and her job. He'd find out where he ranked when he was left behind. Maybe then she'd give him another chance to sample her charms.

Jon came out of the bedroom a moment later. "We're going back to my place for dinner. Toni thought you'd probably have your own plans for the evening."

Melanie tossed her head so that her hair fell seductively over her shoulders. "Sure. You two have fun while you can. She'll be racing all over the country again next week." Jon frowned and Melanie softened her words with an understanding smile. "You ought to make her get a less demanding job."

Toni came into the room before he could respond. She had changed from her navy blue business suit to a snug-fitting pair of jeans and a lacy knitted top that Melanie would have been wearing if she had known it existed.

"Very nice." Jon smiled in approval. "Ready to go?"

Toni nodded and picked up her purse from the end table. "You don't mind, do you, Mel?"

Melanie's smile was gracious. "Not at all. Have a good time." She cheerfully watched them go out the door. Sooner or later, he'd tire of Toni's chill and come to find Melanie's fire.

By the time Friday's session at Mid-America rolled around, Toni was tired. The heat seemed worse than usual, even for Chicago in August, plus her car had broken down, forcing her to depend on cabs that were never there.

Her one bright spot was that it looked like she was close to getting a major new contract at Federal Drugs to redesign their chart of accounts, an enterprise that would keep three people busy full time for four months. With some of her other projects winding down, she needed that contract, especially if the one Guy offered her fell through.

Trying not to think such thoughts, she paid the cab driver and hurried into Mid-America. She had only routine tasks ahead of her, but soon she hoped she would be able to get back to those discrepancies. It was more than a week now since she had talked to the accounting firm that handled Tempco's books and they had promised to try to find out just what Mid-America had actually paid toward invoice #2641. It was a rather roundabout way to learn the amount of a check, but it had proven impossible to get such information from Guy. If she was going to learn what was happening in their books, it would be from using outside sources. She only wished she weren't so certain that Guy was involved. It hurt to watch that new contract slip away from her.

As if he had sensed her suspicious thoughts, Guy suddenly appeared next to her. "Well, well, well. My favorite lady executive has returned at last. Can I stop feeling like the poor little virgin left at the altar, or am I still out of favor?"

Toni stopped walking and forced herself to smile at him. "Don't be silly. It's just my job to point out problems. Anyway, I thought we settled all this when you took me out to lunch." Why did he throw sex into everything? Probably because he sensed it annoyed her.

"I guess I'm just not used to being scolded by a beautiful woman," he laughed. His eyes seemed to be looking through her deep blue suit and matching blouse to the silk camisole and French pants that lay next to her smooth skin.

Toni started walking again to escape those coal-black eyes, but he came right along, staying so close that her pleated skirt brushed against his leg. "Actually, I've been waiting for you to come back. I have those corrected files, and I wanted you to see what a good job we did with them."

"I'd be happy to look at them again." Toni kept her voice cool and businesslike, not allowing any of the irritation she felt to show. Certainly the aisles between the desks were narrow, but did he have to walk that close to her? She was relieved once they passed the last of the desks in the large office and were in the hallway that led to her workroom and the lunchroom. She moved away from him slightly. "Does George have them?"

"No, I'm keeping them just for you." They reached the door of her room, but he stopped her from going in by putting his right hand gently on the small of her back. "Shall I get them, and show you what I've done?"

"Fine." She nodded, pulling away from his touch. "Whenever you like." She went into the room.

George looked up. "More problems?"

She smoothed the annoyance from her face and shook her head. "None that I know of. Just a minor brush with Mr. Ramsey."

George looked surprised. "He's been real helpful lately."

"That's good." She put her briefcase down on the table and picked up some of the papers George was working on.

"So how is the audit going?" she asked. "Any further problems?"

"No, nothing unusual." He went on to elaborate what he had accomplished in the past week, while she glanced at his work. The small amount of work that he actually had accomplished barely registered in her mind, though, as it drifted back to the encounter with Guy.

What was he up to? she wondered. What was the reason for his sudden eagerness to please? Some of his actions could be labeled as sexual harassment, but why would it start now? Was he still angry that she had discovered those errors and was this his way of getting back at her?

No, she was willing to bet that it was more than that. Guy was a shrewd businessman, and no matter how angry he might have been when she found those errors, it was his business acumen that would govern his actions. And it would be her business sense that would dictate her response. She had to remain cool and professional, no matter what he said or what she felt. He was paying for her services, after all, and she could not afford to offend him; but then, neither was she going to let him make her look emotional and flighty. She wouldn't give him any reason to take offense and hurt her professionally.

Guy behaved very predictably when they went over the files in his office later. His every remark had a variety of interpretations; he was a master at turning even her most innocent comment into a sexual reference. There were a few times that his hand brushed against hers or that his eyes seemed to linger on her body, but he gave her nothing definite to complain about. She would have looked like a fool making an issue out of any of it. By the time they were finished, she was quite thoroughly frustrated and wished that a swift kick in the balls were an acceptable business practice.

"Let's get some coffee, shall we?" Guy suggested as he pushed back the stack of computer printouts. "I think we both deserve a break."

She reminded herself that he was her client and the success of her performance there depended on his continued goodwill, and she nodded her head. "Sure, why not?" She had endured his comments for the last half hour; she could certainly take them for another ten minutes. Maybe she could get that contract after all.

He opened the door and ushered her out. "You'll never know how much we appreciate all your hard work," he told her quietly. "With the turnover of help around here, God knows what kinds of mistakes were being made before we had you watching over us." His smile looked too practiced in its charming nonchalance, but she forced herself to smile back.

A satisfied look flitted across his face, and Toni felt puzzled. He apparently thought he had gotten her to respond to his sensuality.

Why should that please him? she wondered as they walked past her workroom. Had he pegged her as a quick lay and was this all nothing more than his way of getting into her bed? It was an interesting idea and she rolled it around in her mind, finding it quite possible. The fact that he hadn't made any play for her until she found those errors bothered her, though, and she could not get rid of the notion that the two were connected. Could this be a way to distract her? Lay on the charm, and she'd forget about everything but him?

She was angry that he might think that she could be so easily hoodwinked. She was not stupid, she thought, and almost collided with him when he stopped in the lunchroom doorway. Now he was probably convinced that she couldn't keep her hands off of him.

"Damn, I didn't think everyone else had a break now," he snapped, surveying the crowded room.

Toni was tempted to suggest they forget the coffee, but she still hoped to salvage that contract. It might be possible to keep her investigation quiet long enough to get him to agree to a contract and sign it quickly. "There's a table in the corner," she noted. "Why don't I grab it while you get the coffee?"

He nodded, and she wove through the tables to the one in the corner. Melanie and Rosie were with another girl at a table Toni passed, but her sister showed no sign of recognition. Apparently, she was still trying to make her own way, Toni thought with a cynical smile. She had noticed that Melanie's independence had not quite extended to exclude Jon. No, she was only too happy to make sure everyone knew that she had connections. She hadn't exactly bothered to explain them, though. Apparently, she was too busy chasing him to want to admit to the existence of a rival.

"I hope cream and sugar is okay." Guy came from behind her, and Toni looked up.

"Fine."

He sat down, moving his chair close to hers. "I had hoped that it would be a bit quieter in here. With all these people, you can barely hear yourself speak." His eyes grew bolder. "I guess I'll just have to take you out to dinner if I want to have a chance to get to know you."

Toni just sipped at her coffee. "Well, at least the coffee tastes good."

"I know a little place where the food's good and the atmosphere's even better," he said softly. "It's dark and very private. The perfect place for a man and a woman to be alone."

She raised her eyebrows in surprise at his invitation.

"So we could discuss business, of course," he added. "You must remember that other contract I mentioned. There never seems to be enough time during the workday to talk about it."

She was on touchy ground, she realized. "My team and I would be happy to stay late to help you out anytime you like," she offered. "It's part of our job."

"And what if they're not as dedicated as you are?"

"Oh, but they are. In fact, George would probably be happy to stay even if I couldn't."

"Oh, Mr. Ramsey, there you are," Mrs. Flores's voice interrupted them. "There's a long-distance call from New York on the line. They were very insistent that I find you."

"Damn!" he muttered under his breath, and smiled apologetically at Toni. "It shouldn't take long. Maybe you'll still be here when I'm through."

"I really have a lot to get done today," she pointed out. "I imagine I'll see you next time I'm in."

"I'll be looking forward to that," he promised softly. His smile showed that he knew he had had the last word. He went off looking very pleased with himself, while she fumed. She was a good accountant, she knew, but lousy at fending off seduction scenes.

Lost in thought, she was surprised when her body seemed suddenly charged with awareness. She turned, knowing that Jon had come up next to her table.

"Hi, Toni," he said.

She looked up, covering her surprise with a cool, friendly smile. What was he doing? They had always ignored each other at work. "Hi." She nodded as she rose to her feet.

He glanced at her half-filled cup of coffee. "Aren't you going to finish that? I'd sure like the company."

She looked beyond him. The room was emptying as people drifted back to their jobs, but George had just come in.

"Sorry." She smiled and slid past him. "I was just waiting for George so that we could go over some stuff." She flashed him a stiff smile and joined George at the coffee pot.

"Well, did Ramsey and his crew get the A/P discrepancies all straightened out?" George asked, pouring sugar into his cup.

"It appears so," Toni said with a shrug. She was conscious of Jon's eyes on her and wished he'd leave the room. They rarely ever saw each other here since they had begun dating two months ago. Why was he suddenly here and seeking her company? Didn't he know what kind of gossip that would start?

George was staring at her, and she smiled lamely, wondering what she had missed. "What's the problem, then?" he asked.

"Problem?"

"With Ramsey. I thought everything was going fine."

"I guess I don't trust his suddenly friendly attitude," she said, unwilling to explain her problems with the controller to him. Like most men, he would think she was making a mountain out of a molehill.

She let her eyes drift away from George and frowned when she saw Jon sit down with Melanie and her friends. A knot of jealousy twisted her stomach. She didn't like the way Melanie moved her chair closer to him and laughed so obviously at his jokes. God! Was she always so blatantly forward?

"What's wrong with being friendly?"

Toni turned to stare at George, realizing slowly that he was referring to Guy, not Melanie. "I think he's up to something, and I'd like to know what."

"You're just too suspicious." He shrugged.

George went on talking, but Toni heard little of what he said. Her eyes went back to where Jon was sitting. Melanie was listening to him in apparent fascination, seemingly oblivious to everyone else in the room. What was Jon thinking? Toni wondered. Was he as captivated by Melanie's youth and sensuality as Melanie hoped?

Damn! What was the matter with her? Wasn't this the very reason that she had decided to avoid love and its entanglements? She didn't have the time to indulge in jealousy. She put her half-empty cup on the table near her and left the room, not caring whether George had stopped speaking. If Jon thought Melanie was so terrific, he could have her. She didn't have time to flirt and play games to keep him. She had a job to do.

Toni felt no happier when she was finished for the day. In all honesty, she had admitted to herself that Jon had done little to encourage Melanie and that he could not help it if her sister was pursuing him so openly. It didn't help the nagging ache in her heart, though. She was still afraid to trust him. He seemed different from the other men she had dated, but then so had Bob. How could she be sure she wasn't laying herself open to hurt again by loving him?

George had already left by the time she was ready to go, and she packed up her briefcase slowly, not bothering to hide her weariness.

"Hard day?"

She turned and saw Jon leaning against the doorpost. He was wearing a charcoal gray suit, but the collar of his white shirt was open and no tie was in sight. "It wasn't too bad. What about you? All through for the day?"

He nodded and straightened up. "Yep, after long hard hours of praising our new saltshakers, I'm finally free to leave. Can I give you a lift?"

"I don't think that would be wise." She put the last of her papers into her case and closed it. When she looked up again, he was standing in front of her. His eyes seemed to be angry.

"Afraid someone's going to see us together?"

"Yes." She gave him a severe frown. "You know I don't want people here to know we're involved."

"And you know how I hate that word." He sat on the edge of the table and picked up her hand. His head was bent, so she could not see his face as he rubbed his thumb over her palm. She tried to pull her hand away but he would not let her as he raised his eyes to stare defiantly into hers. "I happen to love you and I'm not afraid to admit it."

Toni glanced toward the door, afraid that they might be overheard, but no one was in sight. The building sounded deserted, and she ought to be able to relax, so why couldn't she? She was startled when Jon dropped her hand and went over to close the door.

"That only makes it look worse."

He frowned. "I'll open it when you tell me you love me."

Toni sat down abruptly, too tired for his games. "What's the matter with you today? I've admitted I love you."

"Rather reluctantly, if I remember correctly." He walked around the table to stand in front of her.

"Is that so? Well, you must be getting senile then, because I remember telling you that I love you in quite a number of ways last night. And I don't think 'reluctant' would describe any of them."

He leaned against the table and shrugged in agreement. "All right, so sometimes you aren't. But only in private. In public, you pretend that you don't even know me."

"It's not public and private." She tried to explain her feelings to him. "It's my personal life and my business life. I want to keep our relationship separate from what happens here at work."

"Relationship! Involved! Boy, you've got all the right words, don't you?" He sounded very tired as he shook his head. "Why are you so afraid of the word *love?*"

Toni's patience was wearing thin. "We've been all through this before. I can't see that anything's changed just because we've said we love each other. Why can't you see my position in this?"

"Why can't you see mine?" he countered, shoving his hands into his pants pockets. "Can you imagine how I feel? You have coffee with George and coffee with Guy, but you'll barely speak to me."

"But I work with them!"

"I work here too."

Toni rose to her feet and walked slowly over to the window. Narrow venetian blinds obscured the view of the back alley, but she wasn't interested in looking out anyway. Why was it she could handle the problems that arose in her job, but felt so inadequate in her personal life?

"Toni, you scare me," Jon whispered. He had come up right behind her and she could feel the warmth of his breath on the back of her neck. "I can't pretend I don't know you, that we haven't loved each other. Your job may blind you to the things around you, but mine sure as hell can't. Actually, I can't think of any job that would be so engrossing that I wouldn't want to take the time to see you and talk to you. I'm not expecting you to throw yourself into my arms if we pass in the hallway, but you say I can't even smile at you or buy you a cup of coffee."

He put his hands on her upper arms and gently turned her around to face him. "You're so damned detached the whole time and it scares the hell out of me. Why do I need you so much more than you need me?"

She looked up into his eyes and the pain she saw there made her uncomfortable. "Oh, Jon," she sighed, letting her breath out slowly. She leaned forward to slip her arms around his waist and rest her head on his chest. "I'm so terrified myself that I hardly know what I'm doing."

His arms came around her and some of her tension melted away. "I'm so damned confused," she went on. "On the one hand, I don't want to admit to myself that I love you. Yet on the other hand, I'm so happy when I'm with you that I want to shout it to the world. The only thing I am sure of is that I can't let our love into my work. When I'm with my clients, I have to be one hundred percent the accountant."

He sighed and rested his head on top of hers. "Do you really think George and Guy keep their minds totally on their work?"

"They don't have to. They're men," she said bitterly. "Men are allowed to show emotion, but women aren't. Everything a woman does gets categorized: 'It's that time of the month,' or 'I wonder who she laid to get that.' We can't afford to be less than perfect."

"But that doesn't happen here," he protested.

The absurdity of his remark erased the bitterness and she just laughed. "Of course it does; it happens everywhere. The first time I met you, Guy made some remark about my being frozen because I wasn't willing to flirt with him. He wouldn't have said it about a man."

"Oh."

She pulled away from him enough to look up into his face. "It's become part of my job to field those remarks, but I couldn't take them about us. My love isn't covered with a thick skin that will protect it. I can only keep it safe if no one knows it's there."

"Don't you think I'd put a stop to any talk like that?" he asked, sounding hurt.

"How?" she teased. "Challenge them to a duel? I can see

it now: Lincoln Park at dawn. Dodging bullets or swords would certainly keep the joggers on their toes."

He smiled reluctantly. "All right, so it might be hard to keep the gossip down completely. But couldn't we compromise and at least speak to each other now and then? Have coffee once in a while?"

She leaned against his chest, reveling in the safety of his embrace. "It just wouldn't work. Can't you trust my love?"

She felt his lips brush the top of her head. "I guess I'll have to try. But not tonight. I *am* going to drive you home tonight."

She started to protest, and he put his fingers across her mouth. "This is a lousy neighborhood and it'll take you forever to get a cab. If you want, we can meet accidentally in the lobby and I shall offer you a ride quite loudly and innocently."

She shook her head with a smile. "All right. But your invitation had better be convincing."

He leaned down to kiss her lips and she reached up to meet him, meaning to break away quickly in case someone should come in, but it wasn't that simple. His touch was gentle and seductive and seemed to draw her pain and weariness away. It felt so right to be in his arms, here at the office or anywhere. His tongue knew how to soothe her lips and make her body feel alive again, while his hands moved rhythmically over her back, massaging away her tensions.

She became a woman again in his arms, caressed, desired, and intoxicated with the feel of his body next to hers. Memories of the past weeks danced in her head and she felt the strength that together they were. Tensions of the day would always be bearable when he was waiting for her at its end.

Slowly he drew his lips from hers and held her in his arms for a moment. "Five minutes enough time to get ready to leave?" he asked. His voice was ragged with passion.

"Sounds fine," she whispered. Her voice was equally unsteady.

She felt Jon nod, and then was released from the heaven of his arms. "You know," he laughed as he walked toward the door, "you may be right about all this. I don't think we'd convince anybody we're just friends."

# CHAPTER THIRTEEN

Jon raised himself up on one elbow so that he could watch Toni as she slept, curled up on her side with her left arm tucked under her head. She was so beautiful to him in a million ways that just the sight of her could make his breath catch. Her hair flowing over the pillow like molten copper. Her lips, so soft and moist and slightly apart as she slept. Even the faint freckles that were splashed over her shoulders were precious to him and had the power to turn his body to fire.

Toni stirred in her sleep and rolled onto her back. Her hair fell away from her neck and he saw the mosquito bite that she had gotten when they walked along the beach last night. There were red streaks where she had scratched it in her sleep, and he was tempted to kiss it. Would the red skin be hotter than the creamy white smoothness of her neck? He didn't try, though, because he didn't want to awaken her.

He treasured moments such as these, when she was all his, at least in his mind. He didn't have to fight all the ghosts in her past that threatened to tear them apart. He could lay here and watch her, loving the way she made him feel whole. She was everything that he needed in his life, and everything that he'd ever want.

He was constantly amazed at how completely she understood him. Not just his desire to succeed or his frustration with his job, either. But the deeper fears of being really alone with no one to turn to, and spending his life trapped in someone else's dream.

Maybe it was because they were alike in so many ways: their ideals, their goals, even their senses of humor. They ran in the park together, enjoyed the same restaurants, and cherished their quiet moments together. How could she not see how vital they were to each other's existence?

He wasn't just being paranoid. She visibly shied away from any form of commitment. Even light teasing remarks made her tense and frightened, like a wild animal afraid of being captured. But she had been engaged to Bob before they met. Why had she been willing to take a chance with Bob, yet now was terrified of even the vaguest sort of commitment to him? The rare times she talked about Bob, she readily admitted that he had been a mistake and that she had not really known him. Surely one error in judgment would not make her that wary of trusting again.

No matter how he tried to reason things out, though, he still was afraid of putting anything to the test. He told her that he loved her, and tried to show her in little ways, but he knew that she had no idea of the depth of his feelings. She was the person that he wanted to spend the rest of his life with. He wanted her at his side always, to love, to hold, to be safe within her arms. As if all that weren't enough to make her run and hide, he wanted more: he wanted a family. Not to provide an anchor for his life as he had once thought, but because children, their children, would be a natural part of their love. When, though, would she be ready to hear it?

She had been so loving last night as she tried to erase any hurt that remained from their misunderstanding at Mid-America, but he could see that deep down she was afraid. Afraid of hurting him, but also afraid of letting people know about their love. The fears had warred within her, but had not come to any resolution. She needed him to be understanding.

Maybe it was this vulnerability he sensed occasionally that made her so special. She could be a tough businesswoman and still be afraid. What she needed to learn was that she didn't have to fear him. He'd be there, no matter what.

But how long was it going to take to convince her of that? He knew that two months was not a great length of time for anyone to base a relationship on, especially someone as cautious as Toni. But the longer he knew her, the more irrevocably he felt himself bound to her and the more frightened he became that she would take flight.

Patience, he told himself. He just had to be patient. Wouldn't time prove to her that they belonged together?

Toni stirred again and opened her eyes. When he smiled down at her, she groaned and turned over on her side. "It can't be morning already."

He just laughed, reaching down to kiss her shoulder. " 'Fraid so. And getting hotter all the time. We'd better get moving if we're going to go running."

Toni burrowed under his sheet. "Wake me up when you get back," she murmured. Spike jumped up on the bed and leisurely began to curl himself up behind Toni's knees to go to sleep. "See, I can't let Spike down."

Jon picked up his cat and dropped him on the floor next to the bed. "Get up, lazybones, or I won't feed you breakfast."

Toni groaned loudly but did push herself up to sit on the edge of the bed. Her nightgown had been tossed on the floor and she reached down to get it, slipping it over her head. "Someday I'll get even with you for this," she vowed, punctuating it with a yawn. "I'll make you pay."

"Promises, promises."

Toni made a face and trudged past him to the bathroom. "I wish Melanie would find her own place soon."

"Why? I like having you here in the morning."

"Well, I like waking up in my own home," she pointed out, and disappeared through the door.

Jon bit back the urge to suggest that she move in with him so that this would be her home, and climbed out of bed himself. He pulled on his navy blue robe and followed her. She was brushing her teeth at the sink, so he picked up his razor and began to shave at the mirror next to her.

"So when's your mother getting married?" he asked. "You going up for the wedding?"

Apparently the question surprised Toni, for she stopped brushing her teeth to stare at him with a frown. "I don't know," she muttered with a mouth full of toothpaste. "Does it matter?"

"I wondered if you'd want me to go with you," he explained. "I'd like to meet your family."

Toni went back to brushing her teeth, then rinsed the paste from around her mouth. "You've met most of it already. I have no idea where my father is, and my mother's just a typical middle-aged housewife."

"Oh, I don't know about that. I thought I'd get to see what you'll look like twenty years from now," Jon teased.

"Gray hair and housedresses." Toni shrugged. "And about forty pounds overweight."

"Come on, there must be something else."

"Nope, nothing that I can describe. She's a nice average woman in her late forties. Not very spectacular or exciting."

"Yet, she's getting married for the fourth time."

"So she goes for quantity, not quality," Toni told him. "She's too dumb to see that they're all out for a free ride. Maid service and a cook and something to warm their beds. About four or five years from now, she'll wake up and notice that she's not getting anything from the deal, and get a divorce."

Toni's derisive tone made Jon sorry that he had brought up the subject. "Maybe this guy will make her happy," he pointed out.

Toni just stared at him for a minute, then walked back into the bedroom where she pulled her nightgown from over her head. "I thought we were going out."

Jon unplugged his razor and watched from the bathroom door as her soft body was revealed to him. Suddenly he needed reassurance that her cynical views on her mother's marriage would not also apply to him. He went over to her side and pulled the nightgown from her hands, dropping it on the floor. "Go out where?" he asked, pulling her up against him.

His robe was quickly disposed of and his hands were able to slide over her smooth back and firm buttocks as he pressed her closer and closer to him. His need for her was quite apparent and she laughed lightly.

"And I thought you were such a devoted runner," she teased. "What excuse do you use when I'm not here in the morning?"

Her lips tasted minty from the toothpaste, and her hair smelled faintly of smoke from the hamburgers they had barbecued last night. "It's only when you're here that I get distracted from my running," he said. "Other mornings, I'm a model of self-discipline."

He could not tell her that it was the lingering scent of her perfume in his bed that drove him into the park each morning to run out his longing for her. Nor could he explain the senselessness that forbade him to change his sheets after she'd gone. For those few blissful seconds each morning before he opened his eyes, her scent allowed him to dream that she was still there. That was worth the later agony of finding himself alone.

One day, he vowed, she'd be there to stay. Until then, he'd just keep showing her how much he needed and loved her, hoping she'd open her eyes and see the truth soon.

# CHAPTER FOURTEEN

At last, Toni thought as she hung up the phone. The accountant who handled Tempco's finances had just gotten back to her. After searching through the microfiche, he had found a copy of the check Mid-America had sent in payment for invoice #2641. It was for $269.08, the amount that had been on the bill she had seen. That other amount existed only in the records at Mid-America. Someone there was screwing around with the books and she had a good idea who.

Picking up her notes, she hurried down the hall to Simon's office. He was talking on the phone, but waved her in and finished his conversation.

"Now, what can I do for you?" he asked.

She put her notes on his desk. "It's that problem I spoke to you about at Mid-America Supply." She looked up expectantly, and he nodded his head. "I did some further checking and it appears that someone's tampering with their books."

Simon frowned and rubbed his chin with his hand. "That's a heavy charge. What proof do you have?"

"Nothing that would implicate anyone specifically." She opened up the folder and gave him a copy of the accounts payable computer printout. "The ones marked don't match up with their respective bills. And checking with Tempco Industries showed that they paid the amount on the bill, not the amount entered in the computer."

Simon looked at the printout sheet for a long time, then put it down before him on the desk. "Who did you talk to at Mid-America?"

"The controller. Mr. Ramsey."

"And what was his reply?"

She frowned in disgust. "It was a clerical error, he said. Some clerk was daydreaming, but she was fired a few months ago and unavailable to talk to."

"Obviously from your tone, you don't buy his excuse," Simon noted.

"No, I don't," she replied heatedly. Leaning forward, she pointed to the Tempco Industries entry on the printout sheet. "This was no clerical error. There were no transposed figures, or skipped digits. It was exactly twice the correct amount. And there were others two or three times what they should have been." She pointed to one column. "The amount of error seemed to depend on the vendor code."

Simon leaned back in his chair. "It certainly looks suspicious," he admitted. "Have you found anything in any other file?"

"Our access to files is very limited," she told him. "We have a great deal of trouble getting what we want."

"It looks like I'd better clue Mr. Morici in on your suspicions," Simon sighed, and gathered her papers together. "I'll hang on to these, but I'll keep you posted on what happens."

Toni nodded and left him to his work. She had a few odds and ends to finish up and then she'd be free for the evening. She was glad that she'd have time to stop at the grocery store before going home because she was celebrating tonight, and dinner was going to be special. Melanie was moving in with Rosie after work today, and her apartment was hers again.

Actually, the two and a half weeks since Melanie had moved to Chicago had not been that bad. Toni had spent most of her free time with Jon, and Melanie had her own social life, so they had not seen that much of each other. It would be nice, though, to have Jon spend the night at her place instead of her always staying at his.

Toni had felt as if she were on some crazy seesaw ride ever since she had admitted that she loved Jon. One day she would be deliriously happy, and the next, certain that he would decide that Melanie or some other woman was right for him. She was afraid, she realized. Since she had been hurt by love before, she was afraid it would happen again. The stupid part was, she could make it happen with her worries. She could drive him away by clinging to all her dumb hang-ups.

If she could just relax and learn to take things as they came, she'd be so much better off. Let the future take care of the future and just enjoy the present. It was a philosophy that was much easier to say than do, but she meant to try. She truly did love Jon, and she wanted to give their love a real chance.

Guy was feeling terrific as he sauntered back into Mid-America. He had found a new bar on Lincoln Avenue where the drinks were cheap and the women came on strong. One dizzy blonde with wild hair and huge tits had been panting for him by the time his hamburger and third drink had come. He had taken her up to that hotel on Belmont that rented rooms by the hour and was across the street from the Catholic grade school. She hadn't been too bad, although she did screech a bit during some of his better tricks. It had also been obvious she was a lady of the evening. Once he got her out in the daylight, she didn't take no beauty prizes. Still and all, it hadn't been a bad way to spend a lunch hour.

He glanced up at the clock on the far wall as he made his way across the large office, and shrugged when he saw it was past three-thirty. So what if it was more like a lunch-two-hours? He deserved the break. After all, who was it who did most of the work around here? Not that slob that called himself president. He didn't do anything but draw a fat paycheck and sit around his office looking important. Hell, Morici hadn't known what to do with that idiot Allbright who used to be their accountant. What kind of a mess would he have made with the one they had now?

The thought of Toni made Guy's stomach tighten with anticipation. It was only Wednesday and she usually didn't come in until Friday, but when she did, he'd be ready for her. He had had enough of her coyness. It was time she learned about the real world.

He had the whole thing planned, too. He'd watch until that redheaded wimp partner of hers left; then he'd bring in a file with an urgent problem. She'd have to stay to help him; it was her job. He'd make sure the problem wasn't solved until late, and it would be natural for him to take her out to dinner. An apology for keeping her so long after her regular hours. Then with a little wine and some smooth talk, she'd be ready to bed.

"Oh, Mr. Ramsey, I'm so glad you're back." Mrs. Flores met him at the door to his office. "Mr. Morici wants to see you. He's quite upset."

Guy bit back an impatient sigh and glanced longingly toward his office. He had wanted to relax with a cigar, not listen to Morici whine about parking privileges or the company picnic. He made a sudden decision. "Tell him I'm in my office if he wants to see me." He went into his office and closed the door.

He had barely gotten his cigar trimmed and lit before the door flew open and Sam Morici marched in. His short, round body was covered with a conservatively tailored gray suit, but his face was bright red. He looked ready to burst.

"What the hell is going on, Ramsey?" he demanded, slamming the door behind him.

Guy bristled and leaned back in his chair, putting his feet up on the desk in a little demonstration of authority. If all this was just because he took a long lunch hour, Mr. Sam Morici was going to be told some hard facts. He drew in deeply on the cigar, then let the smoke out of his mouth slowly. "Just what exactly are you talking about?"

Sam walked over to the front of Guy's desk and leaned his hands on it. "I'm talking about our books. Our accounts payable. That were so stupidly kept that some damn broad could spot something wrong."

Guy's feet came back to the floor with a thud and his teeth clamped down on his cigar. "How did you find out about that?"

"Oh, so this isn't all a surprise? You knew about the nosy little bitch and just sat there playing with yourself while she ruins us?" Sam was trying to keep his voice from being overheard outside the office, but anger was making him louder and louder.

"Calm down," Guy snapped. His voice was quiet and deadly as he nodded to a chair. "Tell me how you found out. Did she come to you?"

Sam sank into the chair and mopped his sweaty forehead with a wrinkled handkerchief. "No, her boss did. Seems that she found some errors a few weeks ago and reported them to you."

Guy nodded impatiently. "I told her they were clerical mistakes."

"Well, she didn't believe you. Went snooping on her own to see what amount was really being paid and then turned everything over to this Bradley."

Guy frowned and looked down at his cigar thoughtfully. "That bitch!" he muttered under his breath.

"She's more than just some bitch," Sam argued, edging forward on his chair. "She could ruin us. You've got to do something. If that dame blows the lid, we're all in trouble."

Guy glanced up. "Yeah, then it'd be bye-bye home in Winnetka, and bye-bye country club. How I'd cry for you!"

"Don't play the smart ass with me," Sam told him. "When I sold half of this business to your bosses, we made a deal. They promised you'd take care of things like this."

"Yeah, and I will," Guy snapped. "It's not the end of the world that you seem to think it is. There's absolutely no reason to panic. All we have to do is get rid of that accountant."

Sam paled suddenly and jumped to his feet. "I don't want to hear about it," he cried with a shake of his head. "I don't want to have anything to do with that."

"I mean I'll get her removed from our account," he pointed out sarcastically. "What'd you think? I was measuring her for cement boots?"

"Well, I didn't know." Sam was defensive. "I don't know how you guys work." He moved over to the door, but turned back with his hand on the knob. "I just don't want any trouble. Either control her or get her out of here." He left, closing the door solidly behind him.

Guy ground out his cigar impatiently. He should have known that that broad would be up to something. She thought she was so damn smart, playing macho and acting like she had balls. He'd like to get her flat on her back for a few hours. He'd show her just where she belonged.

His earlier idea was still tempting, but he knew he had to be more careful now. Bedding her would be a pleasant diversion, but getting her nose out of their books was more important.

It wouldn't be too hard, either. A private meeting with Mr. Bradley, and maybe even Mr. Henderson and Mr.

Smythe. He would be so sincere and so apologetic that they'd never doubt him. Of course, he'd be fair, too. Praise her efforts and dedication, even if they were somewhat misguided. And it was such a shame that they could not work comfortably together, but after she had made such a fuss over a simple clerical error . . .

He laughed aloud suddenly and pulled his bottle of scotch from the cabinet next to his desk. He poured a hefty measure into a glass and drank it with pleasure.

It was almost too simple. That accounting firm would bend over backward to keep their business. Anyway, if push came to shove, they could always apply pressure of their own. Henderson, the oldest of the partners, probably wouldn't want it to become general knowledge that he liked to play cowboy with twelve-year-old boys. Guy snickered to himself. Nah, no sweat, there'd be no problem in removing little Miss James from their account since that was all he was asking. It wasn't like he was demanding that they fire her. No, he was not vindictive, just an ordinary man trying to run his business without her harassment.

Having solved the problem of Toni's interference—in his mind, at least—Guy was free to handle his routine chores. When he was through, it was past dinnertime. He leaned back in his chair and stretched. He was undecided whether to go home and make Angie whine and dance a little or whether he should go out and hunt some big game. As he sat there mulling over two pleasant choices, his direct line rang.

Guy came up with a start. What now? His hand trembled slightly as he picked up the receiver. "Yeah?"

There was silence for a moment, then a cold voice spoke. "I would advise you to show a little more respect for your elders."

Guy swallowed nervously. "I'm sorry. I—"

" 'Yeah' is not a greeting of respect."

"I'm sorry, Lou. I didn't know it was you."

"You have others calling you on this line?"

Fear stabbed Guy's stomach. "Oh no, Lou. Absolutely not. No one else has this number. It's just that I was thinking of something else and I forgot."

Lou's impatience came clearly over the line. "That sounds like a lack of mental discipline, Ramsey. Lose that discipline and you get careless. You get careless and you get problems. That's why I'm calling you. You got a big problem now."

Guy paled and licked his lips nervously. "Sir, I promise you. It's all taken care of. She'll be removed from our account and there won't be any more fuss."

"Removed? What do you mean removed? You sound like a street punk still running numbers in the wards."

Against his will, Guy found himself laughing in a high-pitched squeak. "No, no, Lou. You got me all wrong. There won't be any rough stuff. Just strictly business. A conflict of personalities. They deal with that kind of stuff all the time."

"Managers solve problems, Ramsey. They don't make them."

"Yes, sir, I understand that. I'm sorry about this situation, Lou. It just sort of happened."

"Managers who let things 'just sort of happen' find their careers not progressing as they would like."

"I . . . I understand, Lou."

"Some even find their careers coming to a rather abrupt end."

Guy was stunned and found himself unable to speak.

"A very abrupt end, Ramsey."

Guy had a sudden and powerful urge to urinate. "Lou, honest to God, I promise. This will all be taken care off. I promise."

"Do you understand what a promise means, Ramsey?"

"Yes, sir, I do, I—" The line went dead and Guy slowly replaced the receiver. The clamminess in his armpits felt very unpleasant.

"That dirty son of a bitch. He did it again. Every goddamned time something comes up, old Morici runs over to them." Tears of fear mixed with rage came to Guy's eyes.

He turned quickly and pulled the bottle of scotch from the cabinet. There was an empty coffee cup on his desk and Guy filled it three-quarters full with scotch, then drank it down like water. He welcomed the burning sensation that ran from the back of his mouth down to his stomach. After a deep breath, he could will his hands to stop shaking. The liquor and the discipline brought quiet to his nerves as he stood up and walked to his door, then stared for a long moment at the dark empty office of Sam Morici. "You're a dead man. You got one or two aces in your hand right now, but let them fall out for one second and you're gone." He turned off his office lights and went out to his car.

There was no way in hell he was going home now. All he had to do lately was look cross-eyed at Angie and she'd start screaming like a banshee. His nerves were just not up to that tonight. Since lunch had been rather satisfying, Guy drove the few miles over to the same bar on Lincoln Avenue. It was more crowded than it had been at lunchtime, and most of the patrons were young and female. He got himself a whiskey and leaned against the bar, surveying the pickings.

A number of the women had come with friends, so he excluded them. He wasn't in the mood for a crowd tonight, no matter how tempting some of their bodies looked.

Suddenly a blonde across the room caught his eye, for she was openly watching him. Her skimpy little knit dress had to be the only thing she had on, and it sure wasn't keeping much a secret. Her hair was long, her mouth wide. She sure looked like she knew what her body was for as she walked across the room toward him. Her long legs moved slowly, rhythmically, in a sensuous gait, and her full breasts pushed out against the soft fabric of her dress, the hard nipples clearly visible.

He felt a tightening in his crotch. He was going to score again.

"Well, hi, Mr. Ramsey," she said softly. "Fancy meeting you here."

Shit! How'd she know who he was? Was this some of the jailbait that babysat his kids?

"I'm Melanie Langford," she reminded him as she slid up next to the bar. Her bare arm brushed his jacket, and her breasts were so close that he would hardly have to reach out to touch them. "I started working for you last week."

"Oh, yeah." Hell! The one hot number in the place and she had to be from that damn office! He gulped down his drink. "Well, it was nice seeing you here."

"Hey, don't go," she cried. Her arm slipped through his. "I thought we were going to get to know each other better."

"Look, Melanie," he said. "I only came in here for a

drink before I went home. I'm a married man." Angie was a convenient excuse.

"Who cares?" Her eyes roamed over his chest and arms.

She was awfully tempting and he decided to level with her. "Actually, Melanie, it's bad business to see an employee socially."

Melanie just laughed, a sensuous throaty sound that somehow moved his body closer to hers. Her eyes gleamed when she felt his hardness against her leg and she lifted her thigh up into his crotch, giving him a gentle ride. "So fire me, why don't you? But buy me a drink first."

Guy smiled. Why not? He always could fire her. "Are you old enough to drink?"

Her thigh continued swaying gently. "Back home they always told us farm girls that when you're old enough to bleed, you're old enough to butcher. Get me a rum and Coke."

Guy dragged his eyes from her to summon the bartender. Soon her drink was in her hand and she sipped it greedily. He watched her put it down after a moment, her tongue sliding over her lips wiping traces of the brown liquid away.

"Do you have your own place near here?" His voice was suddenly thick and hoarse.

She shook her head slowly. "Nope, you don't pay me enough to have my own place." Her hands went down to take the place of her thigh. "Yet."

He smiled and tried to control his pleasure while he let his eyes wander over her ripe body. He remembered her now. Morici's son brought her in and got her the job, so he must be screwing her. All those years of college and here was his woman out cruising the bars. What she needed was someone like him who could do it right. Leaving her wanting more, not wanting someone else.

So what if she was an employee; he could always fix that like she said. Poor little thing. Her hot little body just burning for a real man. He thought of the hotel again, the one across the street from the Catholic school. Why not? He smiled to himself. It would be an act of Christian charity. He finished his drink in a quick gulp. "Let's go."

# CHAPTER FIFTEEN

"I don't know why I let you talk me into this," Toni declared. It was Labor Day weekend and she was looking in the mirror, braiding her hair. "I have the feeling it's going to be a gigantic mistake."

Jon glanced up from the Sunday newspaper, which was spread all over her bed. "Hey, we're going to a picnic, not the guillotine."

"Might as well be." She slipped an elastic band around the bottom of the finished braid. "I just hope you appreciate what I'm doing for you."

He turned a page of the sports section. "Oh, I do, I do," he said absently.

Toni made a face at his back and began to braid the hair that hung down on the left side. It wasn't that she hated picnics as a rule, but this one was Mid-America's company picnic. All the employees and their families would be there, and for her to come with Jon . . . well, it seemed to make their relationship so official, so public. The whole idea made her uneasy.

Jon was suddenly behind her and kissed the back of her neck with great tenderness. "You haven't got a thing to worry about," he assured her as his hands slid around her waist and under the white knit shirt she wore. "In this outfit, no one there will ever recognize you as the same stern-faced lady accountant that haunts the halls."

"I don't haunt the halls," she protested, trying to ignore his caresses and finish her hair.

He kissed her neck again. "You haunt mine. I see you everywhere."

She slipped a band on the braid and turned around in his arms so that he could kiss her properly. His hands slid around to her bare back, soothing and delighting as they pulled her nearer. His lips, meanwhile, were sampling the sweetness of her skin: the thickness of her earlobe, the smooth cool surface of her neck, and the moist recesses of her mouth.

Toni slowly wrapped her arms around his neck and shifted her position so that she could be the giver. She planted light little kisses all around his mouth, teasing his lips with the tip of her tongue, while her body pressed ever closer to his. She moved in a gentle, seductive rhythm until he could stand her temptations no longer. With passion heightened by impatience, he took her lips with his own. Toni sighed deep within her.

"Want to stay home?" she asked.

He just laughed and reluctantly left the circle of her arms. "And miss a terrific picnic? Not a chance."

Toni wrinkled her nose and went off in search of her shoes. It was always the same, she thought. In his embrace, she was safe and her worries disappeared. Unfortunately, she knew she couldn't hide there forever.

"I guess we might as well get this over with," she sighed.

"Such enthusiasm."

After walking over to Jon's townhouse to feed Spike, they drove to the far northern end of Lincoln Park. It was a little before noon, but some people were already there. Tables of food were being set up under some trees, while a softball game was in progress in the large open area.

Jon parked his car in the narrow strip between the lake and the park. She stared out the window glumly. Why had she agreed to come when she knew she shouldn't?

Jon reached over and planted a light kiss on her lips. "Buck up," he laughed. "Maybe it'll rain."

Since there wasn't a cloud in the sky, it was only a mockery of her worries. Why didn't he understand? Part of it was that she knew she should not be dating a client because of all the problems it could bring to her work life. Could she remain objective when dealing with his company? And even if she could, would others believe that she was, or would they accuse her of overlooking irregularities or sloppy record keeping? Worse, though, would be the sly insinuations about the relationship. She would no longer be the accountant that happened to be a woman, but a woman that happened to be the accountant. It was a big difference that a man might not even notice. But there would be more sexual remarks and speculative glances. The respect that she had worked so hard to achieve might slip away as others saw her as a sexual creature first, and a businesswoman second.

There were personal fears also, and they were as strong as her professional ones. She was appearing in public with him. As a couple, they were going to see people they knew and this would link their names together. Rather than make her feel confident and strong about their relationship, that made her feel more vulnerable. Everyone would know, and if they split up, she could not hide behind a wall of cool indifference. She would not be able to pretend that her heart had not been involved or that it had been a physical attraction that had worn out. They would all know.

There was one other reason for her worries, and she was almost too embarrassed to admit it to herself, but she was worried about meeting Jon's parents. It seemed so silly, so adolescent, but the worry was there nonetheless. Jon's father had been cold and unwelcoming at Mid-America and she had been relieved that she had had little to do with him. He didn't like women in business, but that had not bothered her, because as a professional woman, she had come up against such people before. She could handle them, although it made her job simpler when she didn't have to deal with them too often. But to meet him as the father of the man she was involved with, the father of her lover, well, that was a different story. How would he react? Worse still, how would she react to coldness or indifference on his part? Without her professional veneer to guide her actions, she was liable to make a mess of things.

Jon had gotten out of his door and slowly walked around to her side. All this worry was stupid, she told herself. She was here for one reason, and that far outweighed all the problems she was building in her mind. She was here because she loved Jon and he wanted her to be. Keeping their love a secret was hurting him. He felt that she didn't really care about him if she wouldn't admit it to anyone, so this was her way of showing that she did indeed love him. Surely that love would keep her safe.

She got out of the car and waited while Jon locked the

door. "I love you," she whispered as he turned to take her hand.

He gave it a comforting squeeze. "I love you too," he said. "You'll see, everything will go great." He gave her a quick peck on the cheek and, tucking her hand under his arm, led her toward the picnic area.

She hoped so. She certainly hoped so.

Sam smiled down at the two little girls who stood before him. Their cheeks were rosy-pink clean and their black hair was pulled into ponytails, with green plastic barrettes holding down any stray strands. "Such lovely young ladies," he exclaimed. "Why, you two have grown up overnight. I'll bet you have loads of boyfriends now, don't you?"

The littlest girl just giggled, and clung to her sister's hand. "I'm only seven, Mr. Morici," the older girl pointed out seriously. "Seven-year-olds don't have boyfriends."

Sam pretended to be relieved. "Then you're not too old for one of one of my suckers?"

She shook her head while her sister giggled again.

Sam reached into the box on the table behind him and pulled out two huge lollypops. Six inches across, they were spirals of red and green candy.

"Oooh!" the little girl breathed in awe as Sam put one in her hand.

"Thank you," her older sister said properly, giving the younger girl a sharp nudge with her elbow.

"Oh, thank you," she echoed.

"You're very welcome," Sam laughed, and patted them on the head before they scurried off with their treasure. How he enjoyed these picnics! Made him feel like a grandfather and Santa Claus all rolled into one.

"I don't know why you keep giving that candy away," a tired voice next to him sighed. "You know we find half of them in pieces around the park before we leave."

"Yeah, but the kids love them so." When he was a kid, he had seen suckers like that in old Mr. Caverelli's candy store and would have sold his soul for one. But that wasn't something his wife would understand. Frances was too practical in her generosity. She hadn't grown up scraping and stealing for every little thing.

He glanced up at her, for she was several inches taller than he was. She looked so cool in her white Izod shirt and knitted skirt. Her gray hair was neat, as was her light covering of makeup. Not one drop of sweat was on her face, in spite of the oppressively hot sun. How could a person forbid their body to sweat? he wondered as he wiped his own forehead for the hundredth time.

Frances had always been one classy lady, he thought, remembering how she had impressed him when they had first met. She had such grace and style, it was a wonder that she'd noticed him at all. Of course, he had seen himself as a grubby little pisano trying to fight his way out of that Taylor Street ghetto, while she had seen him as a serious young businessman starting out with his own company.

Oh, he had done well for his family, all right. From a series of apartments on the west side, they had moved to a house in Winnetka. Jon had been able to go to the best schools and mingle with the sons and daughters of the best people. Frances had been accepted with ease, also. She had adapted quickly to designer clothes and tennis lessons. Charity luncheons became a way of life, while the socially elite passed through their lives.

It was only in his case that he felt some doubts. There were times that he sensed his wealthy neighbors were just tolerating him, that he might have had the money to buy a house in their midst, but he could never buy their acceptance. That was what was so great about these picnics. He was the elite here. People were honored when he spoke to them, and felt hurt when he didn't. But best of all, he could look at the poor bastards that loaded his trucks or sorted the mail and see just how far he had come. He had escaped the ghetto they were stuck in because he had brains and guts, and that would keep him from slipping back. He refused to move in any direction but up, and this picnic was a celebration of that fact.

"Oh, here comes Jon." Frances sounded more excited than she had all morning.

"Is he the only reason you agreed to come?" Sam teased.

"Who's that with him?" A frown crossed her face. "I didn't know he had a girlfriend."

Sam laughed as a little boy came over to say hello and get his lollypop. He was still laughing when the lad left. "Frances, a man Jon's age always has a girlfriend. If he didn't, we ought to worry."

"She's very pretty, whoever she is," Frances went on. "I wonder if we know her family."

"Hell, he probably just brought her here to impress her. You know, son-of-the-boss type of thing. I bet that's one monkey that'll perform some fancy tricks tonight."

Frances turned to him. "You amaze me, Sam. Each year you sink to new levels of grossness."

Sam just laughed, more interested in watching the young lady than in his son. Boy, he had to hand it to Jon, he could really pick 'em. This one sure had a terrific set of legs. His gaze traveled slowly upward from them, appreciating her trim hips and tiny waist. Nice tits, he thought, and not a bad face either. He frowned thoughtfully. She looked vaguely familiar. Had Jon brought her up to the lake this summer? It would be embarrassing if they had met and he didn't remember.

"Hi, Mom. Dad." Jon leaned over to kiss his mother's cheek, then pulled the young lady closer to him. "Mom, this is Toni James. She works for Mid-America's accounting firm, and is our very own audit manager."

Audit manager? Mother of God! Sam felt his stomach tie into a knot. It couldn't be her, could it? His palms were suddenly wet. It had to be. They only had one audit manager, and he remembered that Bradley fellow mentioning somebody named James. He had been too worried to catch the name, but it had to be her. The one who had pushed her nose into his affairs and was trying to ruin them.

He got out his handkerchief and mopped the sweat from his forehead. Everyone was watching him suddenly, and he was aware that Frances's voice had stopped.

"Uh, good to see you again, Toni," he said, and looked down at the damp handkerchief in his hand. "Wish it wasn't so hot, though."

"Yes, you'd think it would be cooler in September," she agreed.

There was a moment of awkward silence while Sam mopped his brow again. God! What did she really know? What had she told Jon?

"You any good at softball?" Jon asked Toni.

"Hey, I'm a CPA and we're terrific at anything our client wants to do." She laughed as Sam swallowed nervously.

"Maybe I'll let you be on my team then," Jon told her.

"Go and have some fun," Frances said. "Let's sit together when we eat."

"I'd like that," Toni agreed.

Sam watched them walk away with a meaningless sigh of relief. He knew that she wouldn't have said anything here at a picnic, but he was relieved nevertheless. And maybe he was worrying over nothing. "It was nice of Jon to invite her," he noted. "We ought to invite the people that handle our various chores. I just never thought of it before. Good business sense, though. Shows Jon's really on his toes."

Frances just stared at him for a minute, then laughed. "You're kidding, right? You can't really believe that he invited her to improve your public relations. Anyone with eyes in his head could see he's in love with her."

The panic returned and seemed to close off Sam's throat so breathing was impossible. "No he's not. Just because he shows up with some good-looking broad doesn't mean that he's in love."

Frances ignored him and turned to watch Jon and Toni as they joined the softball game. "Wouldn't it be wonderful if he finally found someone special? It's time that he was settling down, and she really looks nice."

Sam could not believe what she was saying! After all his years of work, of taking care of his family and sheltering them, she was fussing over the one person who could take it all away from him. Not just his business, but his son, the reason that he'd done all that he had. Where the hell was Ramsey?

"It's not my fault Mary Lou spilt that milk on her dress," Angie protested.

"You shouldn't have even given it to her when we were getting ready to leave." Guy pulled into the parking strip and looked about him. Hell! The place was packed. He drove slowly down the narrow lane, and finally found a spot that must have been a half mile from the picnic area. Just what he had wanted—an hour-long hike! Trust Angie to screw things up.

By the time they got to the picnic, the girls were cranky and Angie's pout was in full force. "Try and look pleasant," he told her as they approached Sam and Frances.

"Act like you've got some manners, or we'll have to have a few private lessons again."

Angie shot a glance at him, her dark brown eyes reflecting the painful fear/hate mixture of a chained, beaten dog, but Guy just smirked and looked away. She needed him too much to fight back, even if she had the guts, and when she turned to the others, her smile was friendly. "Hello, Mrs. Morici. Mr. Morici."

They exchanged a few meaningless pleasantries, and the girls were given their lollypops. Then Sam pulled Guy off to one side. "Just a little business talk, ladies," he laughed, but Guy was not fooled. What the hell was bothering him now?

"I thought you said you were going to get rid of that accountant bitch," Sam hissed.

"I am." Guy frowned. "You can't do it overnight. We've got an appointment with Bradley Tuesday morning."

"Well, Tuesday morning may be too late. She's here with Jon."

A slight smile lifted the corners of Guy's mouth. "Afraid she'll spill the beans to the straight arrow, eh?"

"There are no beans to spill," Sam snapped, while glancing worriedly about.

"Sure," Guy snickered. "You just made a business deal with some run-of-the-mill businessmen. He'll understand." Who'd he think he was fooling with his sanctimonious attitude?

"Dammit, Ramsey. You're supposed to handle this. That was the agreement."

The smile left Guy's face and his eyes grew cold and hard. "No, it wasn't. I handle the business. What lies you tell your family are none of my affair. If you don't want them to know who paid the Harvard tuition or footed the bill for those expensive vacations, then make sure no one tells them. I think you should never have brought the son and heir into the business."

Sam's belligerence had flown and he looked pathetically frightened. "But he'll be taking over the company one day and—"

"Is that right?" Guy glanced around him, tired of Morici's whining. "I think you have some people waiting to talk to you." He nodded toward three little children standing a few feet away. "And I'm ready for something to drink."

He turned and walked away, irritated with Sam's demands that he do something. That fool couldn't handle anything on his own. How'd he manage to get dressed in the morning?

Guy walked around the small groups of people, nodding occasionally but never stopping until he reached the table where the keg of beer was resting. He got himself a glass and drank it thirstily. First Angie, then Morici. Why was he surrounded by jerks?

Over the top of his glass, he saw Toni and Jon sitting at a green picnic bench with Frances Morici. Toni was all smiles, and watching Jon as he spoke. So that was why she kept refusing him; she was after a bigger fish, or so she thought. Shows how stupid she was, passing up the one with real power for a limp weenie with a Harvard ring. Come Tuesday morning, though, she'd realize her mistake. He finished the rest of his beer, and turned back to get another one.

Even when he was no longer watching her, he could still see Toni before him in her clinging knit top and long bare legs. And each of her rejections seemed to ring in his ears. Damn bitch! Where'd she get the idea she was such hot stuff?

Suddenly it wasn't enough to get her removed from the Mid-America account; he wanted her to pay for his humiliations. She needed to be taught a lesson, and he was going to be the one to do it.

He lifted his beer to his lips, but stopped suddenly as an idea began to grow in his mind. The perfect idea. Career women like her were such easy prey. Alone and vulnerable, yet sure they could handle anything. She was no different, thinking she was so tough, a macho lady that could beat him. This would be the way to show her.

By the late afternoon, Jon was tired of sharing Toni with everyone. He wanted her to himself again, and when the volleyball game they were playing was finished, he suggested that they leave.

"What happened to your great love of picnics?" she laughed.

"It's being sorely tested each time one of these young studs tries to pick you up."

She laughed again and slipped her hand in his as they

walked slowly toward the car. It had been a good afternoon, he thought. Toni had shed her nervousness quickly and had charmed everyone, just as he had known she would. His mother had loved her, too, and he could tell she was dying to get him alone and plague him with questions.

"Hey, Jon!" He saw his father approaching them. "I've hardly seen you all day. Let's go get us a beer."

Jon glanced briefly at Toni, reluctance evident in his eyes.

She squeezed his hand. "We have hardly seen him," she pointed out quietly. "And another few minutes here isn't going to matter."

"It will to me," he grumbled, but turned around with her to face his father.

Sam seemed somewhat uneasy, and glanced nervously from Toni to Jon. "Uh, I thought just the two of us could go. You know, man talk."

Jon frowned; his father's avoidance of them all afternoon took on new meaning. Just what was the old man up to? His grasp of Toni's hand tightened protectively. "Look, Dad—" he began, his voice harsh with warning.

"I don't mind," Toni interrupted him quickly. "I've been wanting to talk to Melanie anyway and see how she's doing. This will give me a chance." She smiled at Sam. "Just don't keep him too long," she added. After a quick kiss on Jon's cheek, she hurried away from them.

Jon watched her go, admiring her diplomacy but not liking it. He turned back to his father, his eyes flashing suspiciously.

"How about that beer?" Sam started toward the beer table.

Jon walked along with him. "I'm not thirsty right now, Dad. What was so important that you had to tell me in private? There some problem?"

His father wiped his forehead with a wet gray rag that used to be clean white linen, and his hands trembled noticeably. Jon felt a pang of the guilt that always appeared with any indication of his father's ill health.

"Problem? Oh, problem. No! Hell no!" Sam's laugh sounded forced. "Nothing that giving up twenty years wouldn't cure."

They had come to the beer keg, which was tended by a

Spanish man. He filled a glass and handed it to Sam, then looked expectantly at Jon. He smiled and shook his head. His father had already turned away without acknowledging the man and was gulping his beer. Irritation was seeping back, and Jon felt it concentrate in his shoulder muscles, tightening them.

"Dad, what is it that you want? We want to go."

His father forced out another hearty laugh. "What do I want? Hmm. Well, what I'd really like is a little piece of that stuff you brought to the picnic."

Jon stopped walking and stood still. "What did you say?" he asked quietly. He misunderstood him, he told himself, forcibly willing back the black anger that had filled his veins.

Sam seemed unaware of Jon's rage. "That is sure some foxy lady you got there, son. Is it true what they say about lady executives? Ice on the outside, and fire on the inside?"

His father was old and sick, Jon reminded himself, his hands clenching tightly into fists. He thought he was being funny. "I don't know what they say. I make it a practice never to listen to assholes." His voice was quiet and his manner radiated a warning of danger.

Two boys playing with a Frisbee nearby sensed the violence in the air and moved away nervously, but Sam just laughed and finished his beer. "Well, she looks like a lively one, Jon. Do you think she could handle the two of us?"

The anger Jon had been fighting exploded in his head, and all thoughts of his father's health vanished. Jon's hand reached out and grabbed the front of Sam's shirt. "Listen, old man, that lady is very important to me. More important than your stupid job or that ridiculous company. I intend to marry her, and if you don't like that, then the hell with you! I'll walk out of this damn park and that's the last you'll ever see of me." He dropped his hand as if he had discovered he had been touching vermin.

Sam's face was a ghostly white. "Hey, I was joking, son. Just making a joke."

But Jon had turned away, his hands still clenched in angry fists as he sought to regain control. What the hell had gotten into his father? Had senility overtaken any sense he had once had?

"Jon, son. Hey, I didn't mean it." His father's whining

voice followed him as he strode from the picnic, but Jon did not turn back. A very primitive urge to strike out and cause pain was still present. He had better leave before he gave in to those desires.

Melanie thought the whole thing was a bore. Picnics were not really her thing at any time, but ones overrun with little kids were worse than the plague. To seek some relief, she wandered over to the lake.

There was no beach at Montrose Avenue, just a paved area that people ran or biked along, and a causeway that stretched into the lake. Since the day was so beautiful, numerous fishermen, complete with encouraging families, were trying their luck from it. She had no desire to join another crowd, so she just walked slowly along the edge of the lake. When she came to a relatively deserted stretch, she sat down in the sun to relax.

That job of hers was the pits. She had thought she'd meet someone like Alan, rich both in money and exploitive value, but the place was filled with women and blind old men. Jon and Guy were the only real men there, but Jon seemed to be avoiding her, and while Guy was fun, he didn't have the kind of money he'd need to keep her faithful to him. No, she needed to find some more lucrative friendships if she was going to be able to live as she wanted, and she sure wasn't going to do that stuck behind a desk at Mid-America.

She paused in her thoughts to smile invitingly at a young man strolling along the lake. He smiled back, but kept on walking. Damn jerk. She glared after him. He probably was as lousy a lover as Alan.

Her lips curved into a smile as she thought of Alan. It was time she gave the dear boy a call. She'd been gone almost a month. Plenty of time to learn she was pregnant and needed his help. His wedding ought to be any day now, too. Her smile grew wider. He'd have heart failure when she begged him not to abandon her and their child. Might even pay more than the five hundred she was hoping for.

"Hi, Mel. Picnic too much for you?"

Melanie looked up and found Toni smiling down at her. Just what she needed: Goody Two-Shoes. "Yeah, well, I guess I'm a little homesick," she improvised. "Everybody was there with their families and all."

"You should have joined Jon and me," Toni said, settling herself down on the pavement.

Melanie looked past her. "Where is he, anyway?"

"Talking to his father. He's going to meet me here when they're done. I saw you and thought it was a good chance to see how you're doing. How do you like your job?"

Melanie shrugged and stared at the sailboats gliding along on the surface of the lake. "It's all right. Not too exciting, but it'll do until something better comes along."

"It's hard to get started in a new city," Toni said.

Getting started was easy; getting enough was the hard part, Melanie thought.

"You know, Melanie, we don't know each other very well, and don't always seem to have the same values, but I have had a bit more experience being on my own," Toni said. "And I think I could help you over some of the rough spots."

Melanie turned to look at her. How could Rebecca of Sunnybrook Farm help?

"You have to learn to take care of yourself," her sister pointed out. "Stand on your own two feet, and decide what you want to do with your life."

Standing wasn't her best position. Not that she was bad at it; she just excelled at certain other approaches.

"Decide where your skills lie and develop them," Toni went on. "That's what I did while I was in college, so I was able to get a good-paying job. Now I have my own apartment and the kind of life-style I want."

Melanie turned back to the lake, hiding the smile Toni's words caused. Her sister was so pompous it was ridiculous. The whole Puritan ethic of hard work. Well, for once she agreed with her. Hard work and independence would get her what she wanted. She had very unusual talents and had definitely developed them to a high degree of excellence. She thought of Alan in the back seat of his car and of Guy the other night. It was a beginning, she guessed, and she supposed Guy had potential. Not as the lead act, of course, but he might do for an opener.

Toni's lecture continued. "You're a smart girl, Melanie. You can go far on your own. And you'll find that men will like the fact that you're independent. They don't want clinging vines anymore."

Depends on what the vine has wrapped itself around,

Melanie thought with a tiny smile. She had been foolish to disregard Guy just because he wasn't wealthy enough to take care of her by himself. He was available and willing, and would do until something better came along.

"Well, when I'm terribly successful, you'll know it was all due to your good advice," Melanie said, doubting that Toni even noticed the sarcasm in her voice. She rose to her feet and stretched. "I think I'll get back to the picnic and work on my skills."

Toni looked puzzled, but Melanie just smiled innocently and sauntered away. Mr. Guy Ramsey was in for a real treat, she thought.

Guy was trudging down toward his car when she met him. He was carrying a bag that had to be his wife's, with things to clean up the kids and a change of clothes for them. Two lollypops were sticking out.

"Well, hello there," she said with a smile. "I see someone's put you to work."

Guy glared down at the bag in his hand. "It was better than staying at the picnic."

She glided up to him, her hand gently brushing his arm. "I know what you mean. Family get-togethers can be the pits."

Guy's eyes darkened with remembered passion. "Friday was a long time ago. When are we going to repeat the performance? I've time for a quickie now."

Melanie sighed and drew back. "I don't know," she admitted. "Rosie might come back to the apartment."

"So who needs the apartment?"

Melanie turned away, loudly stifling a sob, but in reality she was hiding a smile of triumph. This was going to be so easy. "No, I can't go back to one of those hotels. I felt like a tramp checking in, and my ass still itches from the fleas and the bedbugs."

Out of the corner of her eyes she saw Guy frown. "I know it wasn't the Ritz, but it wasn't all that bad either."

She flashed him a brave smile. "It was just the way the place felt. The stale smell in the room, and the way the desk clerk seemed to smirk at us. I just couldn't bear to go through it all again." She sighed pathetically, and moved so that he could see the swell of her full breasts down the front of her blouse.

"I've got something in my pocket that might ease all that terrible humiliation," he suggested.

She frowned at him.

"My MasterCard," he explained, slipping his arm around her shoulders. "I'll bet we can find someplace that's open on the way to the hotel and get you a little trinket."

She smiled appreciatively, although the word "little" bothered her. It had better be something good, or his "quickie" was going to be a lot quicker than he expected.

# CHAPTER SIXTEEN

"Well, are you feeling better now?" Toni asked, slipping her arm through Jon's as they walked out of the restaurant.

"What do you mean, better? I feel fine." He frowned. "Why shouldn't I?"

His tone was not rude, but did not invite any arguments either, so Toni just snuggled up closer to him and rested her head on his shoulder. "This was a terrific idea of yours," she said. "I wish you had had it earlier, so we could have spent the whole weekend up here in Milwaukee instead of just this evening and tomorrow."

He put his arm around her waist. "Well, maybe if you're good, I'll bring you back some other weekend."

His teasing seemed rather forced, and Toni wondered, not for the first time, just what had happened between him and his father at that picnic. He had been waiting for her after she had left Melanie, and had hustled her into the car with little comment. She had been able to feel his tension and anger, but since he had denied that anything was wrong, she had not pressed him. Was there something wrong in their firm, or was it something to do with her? They were the only reasons she could think of that Sam would not have wanted her around.

She had tried to hide her nervousness as Jon had driven toward her apartment. It was ridiculous of her to feel threatened just because Jon was upset, she had tried to convince herself. It probably had nothing to do with her or them. Maybe someone was ill and he was concerned. Yet it hadn't been worry that she had sensed, but anger. Deep, raging anger.

She had glanced at him as another thought had come to

her. Was it those damn discrepancies? Had he found out about her further investigation and felt she should have been more loyal to them?

She had been somewhat comforted when Jon had suggested that they pick up a change of clothes and drive up to Milwaukee for the rest of the weekend. He hadn't seemed to be on the verge of discarding her, so whatever had happened between him and his father, his feelings toward her appeared to be unchanged. She had hoped that he would confide in her as they drove to Milwaukee.

He hadn't though. He had remained silent during the hour-and-a-half drive, responding vaguely to her attempts at conversation until she had given up and had stared out the window in silence. Once they had gotten to the city and checked into the Pfister Hotel, he had begun to relax. During their dinner at Mader's, an old German restaurant, he had even made some light conversation, although she knew that he had stayed far from what was really on his mind.

"What now?" he asked, breaking into her thoughts. "Want to see a movie?" They had reached his car, and he had her door open.

She got inside and waited until he was in also. "There something special you want to see?"

He shook his head and she sensed his distraction returning.

"Good, because I'd much rather go back to our hotel." She leaned across the gearshift and kissed him slowly with seductive gentleness. "I have something much more interesting than a movie in mind."

He smiled at her with such a look of tenderness in his eyes that Toni suddenly realized how deep the bond between them was. It was no longer just a matter of enjoying each other's company or a physical attraction; it went far beyond that.

She had thought she had been in love with him a month ago, but what she had felt then seemed weak and pale beside what she felt now. Her love was no longer a selfish wish for someone to satisfy her needs: a sexual partner, a companion, and a confidant.

No, now her love was focused more on him and his needs. The desire to cherish and protect was very strong. She longed to stand at his side and help him fight his battles, even if it was just invisibly in the form of her loving support. She hungered to be his refuge from pain, his strength in weariness, and his comfort in sorrow.

Her love had grown beyond anything she had experienced before. This selfless need to give was totally new to her, yet she did not feel afraid as she had earlier. In giving of herself completely, the risk seemed to disappear. She loved Jon because she had to; it was a part of her now and as natural and necessary as breathing.

They parked the car and walked through the lobby and up to their room. The halls were dimly lit and silent as a tomb. The downtown hotels that catered to business travelers weren't too crowded on holiday weekends. Their room was sumptuous and welcoming as Jon closed the door behind him. The sound of his bolting the door echoed loudly, then faded away as they stood staring at each other.

Toni moved softly across the plush rug and took him into her arms. He bent his head to bury it in her hair; his breathing was deep and ragged. His arms came up around her, holding her tightly as if she might disappear.

She held on to him for several minutes; her hands moved slowly across his back, soothing and easing away his tension. As she felt him relax, her eyes closed and she let her head rest on his chest. The rhythm of her love changed as her hands caressed and her fingertips told him of her need.

He seemed to gain strength from her hands, and lifted his head slowly. Her mouth moved to meet his. His kiss pleaded with her, begging for something she could not understand. Her lips promised him everything that she was and all that she had to give. Her love was his.

Slowly, under the persuasion of her lips and her hands, the tension and anger melted from his body. He began to return her caresses with rising passion until the power of their love erased everything else from their minds.

There was no need for words as she led him over to the bed. With whisper-light movements, she slid the suitcoat off his shoulders and let it fall back onto the foot of the bed. Then she loosened his tie, slowly pulling it off to join his coat. His shirt was next. The buttons seemed to unbutton themselves and she was able to slide her hands across his chest.

His skin was slightly damp from sweat and had a salty

taste to it when she leaned over to kiss his neck. She kissed him again and again and felt a sigh deep within him as his hands pulled her closer to him. Her hands slid around his waist as her lips continued their explorations, kissing and tasting as they went down lower and lower.

With a groan, he pulled her back up to his lips. His hands framed her face and his lips came down on hers, ravaging yet tender as they proclaimed his desperate need for her.

Her arms wound around his neck, pulling him closer, as his went around her waist. A sudden coolness on her back told her that one of his hands had pulled down the zipper on her light cotton dress, and then she was free of its irritating confinement.

Her breasts brushed lightly against his chest. The air in the room seemed cool to her heated skin, but his flesh was warm. She snuggled even closer to him, the hairs on his chest tickling and teasing her sensitive nipples, making her hungry for his touch.

With infinite gentleness he laid her back on the bed. One hand pushed her hair back from her face as he bent down to kiss her eyebrows, her cheeks, her lips. The other hand roamed over her breasts, pushing her dress farther out of the way, and then over her flat stomach.

His movements seemed so slow, so deliberate, that Toni wanted to cry out with impatience. Her desire was already at a fever peak and she wanted the feel of his hands on her, bringing her desire even higher. With an abrupt twist of her body, she pulled her dress out from under her and let it fall to the floor. Her shoes were kicked off so that she was left in a silken pair of dusty rose pants.

Jon's hands moved lower seeking out the warmth between her legs, and she curled up closer to him. Her hands went out to loosen his belt, but with him bent over her, it was difficult. He sat up and pulled it off himself. Then the rest of his clothes went on the floor as she disposed of her panties.

Their hands became gentle suddenly, almost reverent as they explored each other's body. Passion was flaring, but it was their love that they were expressing. Each movement became a declaration of love until they could hold back no longer. They became one.

\* \* \*

Toni was in a large room crowded with people. Jon was with her, she knew, but everywhere she looked there were strangers. A tremor of fear crept into her heart, but she kept moving about, searching for him. Suddenly, there he was, at her side.

"Promise me you'll never leave me, Toni," he whispered, his eyes full of love and need.

"I'll never go," she vowed as they melted into each other's embrace.

"I love you. Never leave me," he said over and over.

People began to push at them, and he released her. Still facing her, his eyes were sad. "Don't leave me," he repeated even as he walked backward with slow steady steps, each one taking him farther and farther from her side.

"Jon!" she cried, terrified and unable to move for some reason. "Jon, come back." But she was too late; he was gone and so was everyone else. She was alone with just the echo of his words.

"Jon!" she called again. But there was no answer. She was alone and terrified. Jon was gone, and she knew he would never come back.

Toni sat up, trembling violently. It had only been a dream, she realized. She turned in the darkened hotel room to see Jon fast asleep at her side. One arm was flung out toward her, as if he were reassuring himself that she was still there. Her worries had just given her a nightmare, that was all. Just a silly, scary dream.

She lay back down, curling up closely to Jon. The security of his touch drove away the cold loneliness that had crept around her heart. He moved in his sleep, turning slightly toward her, keeping her safe. She closed her eyes, sighing in relief. Don't leave me, Jon. Don't ever leave me, she silently pleaded as she fell back asleep.

# CHAPTER SEVENTEEN

Her bedroom was dark when the phone rang, pitch dark as Toni was thrown out of a sound sleep into uncertain wakefulness. She opened her eyes slowly, trying to get the fog out of her mind, when the shrill sound split the night again. The lighted digital clock on her nightstand said it was 2:30 in the morning. Who would be calling at that hour? she asked herself, reaching over for the phone.

"Hello," she mumbled. There was dead silence, but a twinge in the pit of her stomach told her there was still someone on the line. It brought her out of her pleasant euphoria into irritation.

"Hello? Is someone there?" she repeated, more impatiently. When the silence continued, she slammed down the phone and rolled over.

It was a prank, she told herself. She had been awakened out of a peaceful sleep by some stupid kid playing jokes, and she tried to relax by thinking about Jon and their weekend in Milwaukee.

The phone rang again just as she was drifting toward sleep. The noise seemed harsher and more threatening than before. She snatched up the receiver angrily. "Yes?"

The silence was the same, but suddenly turned into harsh, guttural laughter. Then a raspy voice came on the phone. "I got something for you, sweetheart. It's so round, so firm, so fully packed, so fine and easy on the draw."

Toni was stunned and still on the edge of sleep. "What?"

"I got a big cock you can suck, you stupid bitch." He laughed mirthlessly again.

Toni was fully awake now and slammed the receiver down. She was shivering with fear and the shock of being jolted awake. He had sounded so close, as if he had been right there next to her.

She jumped to her feet and turned on the light. Her hand was trembling visibly and she took several deep breaths, willing herself to calm down. She'd had calls like these occasionally. Any woman living alone got them, but that knowledge didn't really help.

The phone began to ring again. The noise echoed around the room, taunting her, mocking her. She stared at the instrument, refusing to answer in spite of its persistence, but even the ringing seemed tainted and dirty. Finally she could stand it no longer. She had to stop the noise and grabbed the receiver.

"Leave me alone!" she shouted into it. An awful phlegmy laughter filled the room as she forcibly hung up.

That was stupid, she told herself. That's what they want, to know that you're afraid.

She was still shivering and sat down on the edge of her bed. It wasn't so much being afraid, she thought, as being outraged. That man had violated her home. He had come into her bedroom and right into her bed. She closed her eyes and took a deep breath. She wasn't in danger, though, she was safe here, she repeated over and over to herself.

She was not surprised when the phone began to ring again, but this time she was not tempted to answer it. Her fear had eased somewhat, and she would not play into his hands again. She shivered momentarily at the thought of his hands on her, but pushed the idea away by standing up. Getting a quilt from the closet, she put the phone on the floor and took the receiver off. Then she covered both pieces with the quilt.

The silence in the room seemed almost as threatening as the phone because it suddenly was so noticeable. She looked around her neat bedroom, reminding herself that she was safe here. No one could get in. Their voice might come in on the phone but that was all. That was the only way they could threaten her.

Her shivering finally stopped, but Toni knew that sleep was far away. She was almost tempted to call Jon, knowing that his arms would really make her feel safe, but she shook her head. She was a big girl. With her own job, her own home, and her own life. She could handle little irritations like obscene phone calls. She didn't need a man to run to.

Her arguments did not convince her, but she walked slowly away from the phone. Being independent wasn't everything it was cracked up to be, but she had chosen it and had to take the good with the bad. And that meant you didn't run for help at the first sign of trouble.

Instead, Toni went into the bathroom and took a shower, trying to wash the filth from her mind. After changing from her short lacy nightgown to a sensible cotton one, she felt better, but still wide awake. She went into the living room and found her latest copy of *Working Woman*.

He was probably some goddamn little wimp who wouldn't say boo to her on the street, she thought. She knew some of the women in the office were into karate; she'd ask them about classes tomorrow. Tomorrow, hell. It was already Tuesday and in a few hours she had to drive down to Peoria. Toni sighed and settled down with her magazine. It was going to be another ripsnorting week.

"How would you like your coffee, Mr. Bradley?" Mrs. Flores asked.

"Black, with just a touch of sugar, please," Simon replied, settling himself down in the comfortable guest chair in Sam Morici's office. He assumed this urgent meeting had something to do with those discrepancies that Toni had found, but he wondered what course Mr. Morici had chosen to take. With these small firms, he never knew whether they'd be congratulated for the firm's persistence, or lose the account completely. He certainly hoped that the latter wasn't going to happen.

Guy Ramsey was seated across from him on the couch along the wall, while Sam was sitting nervously behind his desk. It was impossible to guess what was in Morici's mind, and Simon was not reassured. Sam was far from his idea of a strong company president, while Guy seemed to be too confident and powerful. It was an uneasy mixture that required delicate handling on his part.

"Well, Simon," Guy asked, as he lit a cigar and puffed at it to keep it going, "what do ya think the Bears' chances are this season?"

Simon smiled tightly. He did not care about Chicago's pro football team, but he had done his homework on the train that morning. He had perused the first three paragraphs of every sportswriter's column in the *Chicago Tribune*. "Well, they seem to have changed their coaching philosophy for the better, but the offensive line is still weak. I'd say it will be a long season for them."

"Yeah, Chicago oughtta adopt some other team in the league. Right, Sam?" Guy said. He glanced in Sam Morici's direction.

Sam glanced about, startled. "Huh? Oh, yeah, sure. The Bears haven't been anything since 1963."

Simon remembered that Sam had had a heart attack last year and wondered if he was having medical problems again. He certainly looked sick with his pasty white complexion and distracted air. Either sick or worried.

Who would take over the firm if something happened to the senior Morici? Would his son step in or would Guy Ramsey shoulder everyone else aside and assume control? He didn't care either way, and would become disturbed only if his firm was threatened.

Mrs. Flores came back in with the coffee and rolls. "Are you sure you won't have a sweet roll, Mr. Bradley? They're very good."

"I'm sure they are, Mrs. Flores, but I am not that partial to sweets. Thank you."

She passed out the cups of coffee and left a small plate of sweet rolls on the edge of Sam's desk. Then she looked around at the men. "Is there anything else I can do, gentlemen?"

"No, we're all set, Mrs. Flores," Guy said grandly. "Thank you."

Simon noticed that she glanced at Sam, who shook his head. "No, there's nothing else."

She made a slight bowing gesture and left the room, gently closing the door behind her.

Simon sipped his coffee and then set the cup down. He was anxious to find out the reason for his summons. "Well, what can I do for you this morning, gentlemen?" He addressed them both, but looked at Sam.

Sam fingered a paperweight on his desk and spoke quietly without looking up. "Guy has some items he would like to discuss with you."

Guy gave Sam an amused glance, then took his cigar

from his mouth as he leaned forward. Resting his elbows on his knees, he looked over at Simon.

"Simon, we would like you to make some changes in the personnel servicing our account."

Simon picked up his cup and took another sip of coffee. He was careful not to let his face reveal any emotion, although he had felt a wave of relief at Ramsey's words. Their small-business division was not growing at an acceptable rate, and losing this account would only set them back farther. "I see. Any changes in particular that you would like to suggest?"

Guy hitched himself around to face Simon more directly and crossed one leg over the other. "As a matter of fact, yes, there are some changes in particular." He puffed on his cigar while Simon looked at him. "We would like a change in audit managers."

"You would like Miss James removed?" Simon calmly asked. He had not really been surprised. The times Toni had briefed him on the problem here, she had seemed a little too eager to get somebody's head on her pike. Someone here must have thought so also.

Guy laughed. "Yes, Miss James, the bro—" He caught himself. "Yes, the lady accountant."

"Have you any specific complaints about her?" Simon directed his question at Sam.

"No," Guy replied. "We haven't any specific complaints. It's just that things aren't working out and we think it would be better for everybody if we made a change." He paused to pull at his cigar again. "Actually, Miss James is really a fine lady and we really appreciated how she found those mistakes."

Simon stared at him. Then why were they asking for her removal?

"I know she never believed that they were some clerical error, but we didn't mind 'cause she's been real friendly and she does try real hard."

Maybe too hard, Simon thought. "I see."

Guy continued. "This ain't exactly the best neighborhood for ladies and we worry about her."

"Do you make special provisions for your female clerical workers?" Simon asked.

Guy answered again. "Nah, they're just some broads from the neighborhood and they take care of themselves.

Toni's different, you know? She dresses fancy and walks around like she owns the place, you know? It could bother some people."

It obviously did bother at least one person. "So, for her own welfare, you would suggest that we change?" Simon asked. He did not bother to play the game of looking at Sam, but turned right to Guy.

Guy puffed on his cigar importantly. "Yeah, that's it. You know yourself that this is a tough industry. We really need a hard, aggressive audit manager. Somebody that would fit in, you know? That's hard for a lady to do."

Simon looked down into his cup of coffee. Toni had thirteen other accounts. Would this be the only one that complained or the first one? It appeared he'd have to make a few discreet inquiries when he got back to the office. He finished his cup of coffee and turned to Sam. "I was the one who placed her on this account. I hope that I haven't caused your firm any problems."

Sam shrugged while Guy answered. "Hey, don't worry about it. The personal chemistry just wasn't there." He leaned back with a leer. "For business, that is."

Simon smiled thinly, sure that Toni would not tolerate him on a personal basis and probably had trouble with him on a business basis. That was probably where the real trouble lay. Toni forgot that she should never let her real feelings toward a client show. It looked like she still had some things to learn about business politics.

Simon stood up to leave. "Well, gentlemen. We'll look into the problem. I hope that our firm hasn't inconvenienced you in any way."

Guy stood up also and slapped Simon on the back and winked at Sam. "Hey, man. Don't lose no sleep over it. It's just something that didn't work out. We like your work or we wouldn't be giving you that new contract."

Simon was surprised. Fifty thousand from this little outfit was not exactly chicken feed. This, plus the Federal Drugs contract, meant that Toni had brought in more new work in one quarter than her predecessor had in two years.

"That's right, Simon," Sam interrupted his thoughts. "It's not really a matter of competence or incompetence. It's just that firms have personalities just like people and our respective personalities just didn't mesh."

Simon nodded solemnly. "Yes, I can understand that.

This certainly wouldn't be the first time that sort of thing has happened." Simon turned to Sam and extended his hand. "Well, good to see you again, Sam. And thank you for your time."

"Not at all, Simon. Thank you for coming by on such short notice. Maybe we can get some tickets for a ball game some Sunday."

Simon smiled thinly. "I understand Bears tickets are difficult to get, but I do suppose we can try."

"Remember, if tickets are too easy to get," Sam said, "it means that the game's going to be a waste of time."

Simon turned to Guy. "Thank you for your time, Mr. Ramsey."

"Hey, sure, why not?" Guy waved his cigar in a careless gesture. "And remember what I said, Simon. Don't lose no sleep over this. After all, you can't teach a dog to talk."

"I beg your pardon?"

Sam frowned, but Guy ignored him. "You know, if it ain't right, don't force it. Women just don't have the logical minds required for accounting and management and things like that."

Simon's eyes tightened slightly, realizing some of what Toni had been up against. "I see."

"Sure, you know." Guy laughed heartily. "It's like the monkey said to the elephant."

"Yes, I do believe I've heard."

Guy seemed unaware of Sam's irritated frown and Simon's coolness. "If it don't fit, don't force it," he repeated with a laugh.

Simon's smile was strained as he nodded to both men. "Good day, gentlemen. Thank you for your time."

Simon had finally rid himself of Guy's escort and was signing out with the receptionist when a young man with reddish brown hair slouched in. There was a worried look on his face.

Simon rapidly searched the appropriate memory bank in his brain. The readout came quickly. George Manning: employed at Henderson, Bradley and Smythe for approximately three years, mediocre performer, no significant accomplishments, should be dropped soon. He nodded curtly to the man.

The young man nodded in return and then a puzzled look crossed his face. "Uhh, Mr. Bradley. Hi."

"How do you do, Mr. Manning?" Simon crisply replied, and headed toward the door.

"Mr. Bradley, wait."

Simon stopped, holding the door open. "Yes?"

"Can I see you for a minute? We could talk in the audit room."

Simon sighed and turned back to the receptionist. "Is there any reason for me to sign in again?"

She shook her head as George spoke up in a deep, suddenly authoritative voice. "He'll be with me. I'll take full responsibility."

The receptionist failed to look impressed and went back to putting new tabs on file folders as Simon followed George into the office area. Since he had no desire for any coffee, he waited rather impatiently in the drab room while George got himself a cup and returned. When George finally came back, he sat down and slurped at his coffee, saying nothing to Simon for a moment.

Impatient and getting more irritated by the second, Simon did not wait for another slurping session. "What is it you wanted to discuss with me?" he inquired.

George took another nervous gulp of coffee and then put the cup down. He looked up at Simon; his expression could only be called a pout. "Well, you see, sir, it's about my manager."

"Miss James?"

George nodded and twisted his hands in front of him nervously.

Simon's jaw tightened. "And what is it you'd like to discuss about Miss James?"

"She isn't fair. I had my performance appraisal with her last Friday and she gave me a C6."

Simon silently looked at the nervous young man in front of him. So Toni had put him on a three-month improvement plan, after which he was likely to be dumped. Somehow Simon was not surprised.

"In what way was Miss James unfair in her appraisal of your efforts?"

"Well, sir. My wife just had a baby last month."

Simon's eyebrows rose. "How does that affect your job performance? Have there been problems at home?"

George gulped his coffee more quickly now that it had cooled. "Oh, no. Everything's all right." He gulped at his coffee again. "Most everything is all right."

"Most everything?"

"I ain't getting any right now."

Simon stared silently at the young man. How had this ass slipped through the initial interview process?

George continued. "You got kids, Mr. Bradley. You remember how it was right after they were born." He laughed in a man-to-man fashion.

Simon ignored the remark. "Could we discuss the difference of opinion that you and Miss James have regarding your job performance, please?"

"I think she just doesn't like guys."

"What do Miss James's alleged sexual preferences have to do with your job performance?" Simon let impatience creep into his voice.

George raised his hands and stammered. "Oh, I didn't mean she's a butch or anything like that."

Simon let his statement hang in the air.

George laughed nervously and wiped his sweaty palms on his pants underneath the work table. "She probably isn't getting any anywhere. That's why she's so crabby."

"Crabby?"

"Yes, she's just really hard to get along with. It doesn't matter what you do. She's never satisfied. She picks on everybody. She can't even get along with the clients."

"All clients?"

George shrugged and looked down at the table. "I dunno." He looked up quickly. "But I do know that she and Guy Ramsey don't get along."

"That's curious. Through her efforts, Mr. Ramsey just recently gave us a fifty-thousand-dollar contract to help him implement some more stringent accounting controls."

George wiped his mouth with the back of his hand. "Yes, she knows her stuff. But she sure doesn't know how to get along. She's always pushing, you know?"

Simon nodded. "I see. A good accountant, but a poor people person?"

George swallowed nervously and stood up. "I'm gonna get another cup of coffee, Mr. Bradley. How about you?"

"No, thank you. I have to get back to the office." He turned to go out the door and George followed him.

They parted at the door, going in opposite ways, but George called back to Simon after going a few steps. "Hey, Mr. Bradley?"

"Yes?"

"Thanks for coming up to see me."

Simon suppressed a contemptuous smile. "Think nothing of it, Mr. Manning."

"Didn't I tell you I could handle it?" Guy bragged. He sauntered back into Sam's office after having escorted Simon out to the lobby. "Didn't I tell you there was nothin' ta worry about?"

Sam nodded distractedly. Just because Guy had gotten Toni James out of their books didn't mean there was nothing to worry about. Hell! Who knew what she had told Jon about the firm? It might already be too late. She might have told him all about the partners and the way more money seemed to be flowing out of the company than into it.

He closed his eyes briefly. There was no way that she could know any of that, not know for certain, he reminded himself. And even if she suspected something and told Jon, Jon wouldn't necessarily believe her. No, he'd come to his father and ask him for the truth, and Sam could convince him that it was all a vicious lie, that Toni was mad at them because they had gotten her off their account. Would he believe it?

Sam opened his eyes as he pulled out his handkerchief and wiped his forehead. He was glad to see that Guy had left the room. Ramsey might know his job, but Sam hated having to work with him. He thought he was so smart, but he was just a two-bit punk hood. He didn't even have the sense to see that people like Bradley could smell the street on him. They knew exactly what he was, and as much as they'd tolerate him for the sake of their business, he'd never be one of them.

Sam knew it was the same with him. He didn't have the polish and class to fit in with guys like Bradley or most of his neighbors. He used to think that once he had enough money all those differences would disappear, but they didn't. He still was an outsider, but a smarter one than Ramsey. He knew when to keep his mouth shut. He might look uneducated, but never like an ass.

The reason for his carefulness was Jon. He would fit in where Guy and Sam never could. Because of Sam's deal years ago, his son had gotten the education he would need, and one of these days he'd have Mid-America. It didn't matter how much Guy wanted to be the president, the job would go to Jon. Nobody, not Guy Ramsey or Toni James, was going to get in the way of Sam's plans for his son.

"Mr. Morici?" Mrs. Flores stood at the door to his office. "Did you say you wanted to see your son? He's down in his office now."

Sam nodded gratefully and rose to his feet. He had handled things badly at that picnic on Sunday, and he wasn't going to make that mistake again. Yesterday had been spent in hard thinking, and he had come up with a terrific plan. A plan that just might see Miss Toni James really out of their lives.

He walked over to Jon's office and knocked lightly on the door. "Got a minute, son?"

Jon's eyes were cold and unwelcoming, but Sam ignored them and came in. He closed the door behind him and walked over to Jon's desk. He was sorting through some papers, putting some in his briefcase and tossing some into the wastebasket. He did not glance again at his father.

Sam coughed uneasily. "Hey, I'm really sorry about Sunday. It was so damn hot, I kept gettin' another beer to drink." He shrugged with embarrassment. "I guess I just had a few too many."

Jon stopped going through the papers and turned to his father. "Don't try that line on me. We both know that it doesn't matter how much you have to drink; you still are in perfect control of everything you say and do. It's one trait I've always admired in you," he added bitterly, and turned back to his papers.

"You're not being fair," Sam protested. "How was I to know that she was something special? You never told me about her. Besides, all I did was make a few jokes. Nobody else heard them but us."

"You really don't understand, do you?"

The conversation wasn't going quite as Sam had planned. He hadn't expected Jon to be obstinate. Maybe it was time for his next move. "I understand that you're angry with me, and I want to show you how sorry I am," Sam said. He wiped his brow and sank into a chair with a sigh. "God, it's hot in here." He thought Jon's coldness melted a little. It usually did when Sam reminded him of his ill health. "I know how unhappy you've been with your job, and I think I may have found a solution."

Jon looked interested in spite of himself, and put the papers down on his desk. "Oh?"

Sam nodded. "There's a small paper-products firm up in Combined Locks, Wisconsin, that we've been dealing with for years. Good company, quality products."

Jon sat down as he listened to his father, and Sam hid a smile. It was working just as he had known it would. "Anyway, the owner of the firm died a few months ago and the place is up for sale. I've been thinking of buying it, but only if it could be renovated to handle all our paper needs. We're buying now from five different firms and I'd like to see all those products made in a firm of our own."

"So where do I fit in?" Jon asked cautiously, but Sam saw that the forbidding look was gone from his face.

"I was hoping that you'd go up and take a good look at the place. See if the building's in reasonable shape," he tossed in innocently. "See if it could supply all our needs."

"I don't know much about paper manufacturing," Jon pointed out.

Sam just shrugged. "There's a good manager up there to show you around. And Mrs. Flores made a list of some of the other paper-products firms in Wisconsin and Michigan. I thought you could travel to a few of them. Get an idea of what they're doing and how it compares to our plans."

"Then what?" Jon still sounded cautious.

"Then if we decide to buy the place, I'd like you to go up there for a few months and oversee the changes we want to make. It could be a permanent position if you like it, or just a temporary one." Sam left the option up to him.

"I thought I was supposed to be learning this business."

Sam nodded. "And you would be. It's all tied in together." He could see Jon was still hesitating, so he took his last shot. "Actually, I'm getting ready to retire. There's just a few deals I want to see through, so by the time you'd be back, I'd be willing to start turning things over to you."

"It sounds like it might be interesting," Jon admitted slowly. "When would I have to leave?"

"That's the catch." Sam sounded apologetic. "I've heard someone else is interested in the place, so I'd want you to get up there immediately."

"How immediately?"

"Leave today. Tomorrow at the latest."

Jon leaned back in his chair, absently running his hand through his hair. "That's pretty short notice."

"The place is a steal at the price they're asking," Sam said. "We have to move fast if we want it."

There was a long silence in the room and Sam tried to look relaxed and unaffected, as if he didn't care which way Jon decided.

"All right, I'll go," Jon announced. "I'll leave the first thing in the morning."

"That's great." Sam stood up and beamed. "I'll have Mrs. Flores get all the papers to you." He leaned over and shook Jon's hand. "Old Mid-America's gonna be a great place when you're at the helm." Jon just shrugged with a wry smile as Sam left the room.

Sam felt victorious. He had won! He knew that he had. Toni James would never leave Chicago to go to a tiny place in the middle of nowhere like Combined Locks, and he would soon get tired of weekend drives to be with her. Especially once winter set in and all that snow was blowing around the roads. No, a few months from now, Jon would barely remember her name.

Sam quickly put out of his mind the promise he had made Jon that he'd be ready to retire soon. Time enough to think about that when Jon came back.

Guy hung up the phone with a scowl of anger creasing his forehead. What the hell did Lou know anyway? He had done it! He had beaten that bitch twice now with barely the blink of an eye.

The phone call last night showed her she was nothing more than a stupid broad, and today he proved she didn't belong in the business either. All her fancy degrees and proud ways didn't help her at all. Old Bradley knew the score, and it was listed in dollars and cents. When it came to the bottom line, Toni James was expendable. How he'd love to see her face when she found that out!

But Lou was like an old lady. Guy had every right to call him and tell him the good news. With all his "Fix it, Ramsey" speeches, he'd think Lou would be relieved to know that he had. And had done it well, too. Instead, all he did was complain about the problems and warn him that there'd better not be any more.

How'd Lou expect the problems to end as long as Morici was still loose in the place? He had less brains than a cockroach, yet Lou was dragging his feet about getting rid of him. And he knew why. If Morici was gone, who'd keep them informed of each little thing that happened around here? Sam probably called them every time somebody peed crooked.

Guy rose to his feet, too restless and triumphant to sit still. He didn't care what the partners said, he had done one hell of a good job and deserved a reward. Wandering out of his office, he glanced across the large room. What he wanted was a little party. A celebration to mark the end of Sam Morici's reign and the beginning of his, and he knew just the person to party with.

Melanie was filing some papers at the bank of gray cabinets along the far wall, and she was quite obviously bored. Most of the men in the room were watching as her tempting little ass swayed each time she shifted her weight. Guy noticed with satisfaction that she was not covertly watching any of them. His women had to be faithful to him, not little cockteases that would flirt with anything in pants.

He took a stroll that happened past her filing cabinet. "Meet me in front of Mario's in half an hour," he said softly.

She flashed a pouty look at him, but then shrugged an agreement as she went back to her work.

Guy spent the half hour before lunchtime began by wandering around the building playing boss. Flirting with the girls, and talking macho with the men. They all liked him, he knew. Better than Morici with his big house. He ought to be the boss, and one of these days he would be.

A few minutes after he saw Melanie leave, he slipped from the building too, and picked her up in his white Cadillac Seville in front of the bar down the street.

"Hi, gorgeous, in a party mood?"

Melanie shrugged. "Maybe."

He laughed and pushed the gas pedal down further. "Well, get in one fast, 'cause we're going to have fun today."

She turned her new diamond-studded watch around on

her wrist. "You're sure in a good mood. What happened? You win the lottery?"

"Better than that," he laughed. His hand reached over to slide up the inside of her thigh. She never wore any underwear, and he grasped a handful of the soft tangled hair, giving it a sharp tug that made her cry out suddenly. "I'm gonna be boss of that place soon."

"Oh, yeah? And what does Mr. Morici have to say about that?" She tried to move away from him, but his hand had begun a caressing movement.

"He won't have a thing to say about it. He don't do nothing now, and his partners are gonna have him out soon."

"Partners? I haven't seen any partners around." Melanie's voice had turned hoarse and she slid over closer to him. Her hand went down between his legs.

"You won't, either. They don't exactly advertise their existence." He turned into a parking place near the hotel that they had used before. Melanie could see the little children playing on the school playground across the street and abruptly withdrew her hand.

"Here again? I hate this place."

Guy snickered at the repulsion in her voice and turned toward the seedy-looking building. So did he, he realized suddenly. What was he doing at a dump like this? He was no stupid truck driver picking up ass off the street. He deserved better and that was what he was going to have. It would be his bonus for dumping Miss Toni James.

"Well, I'm not renting a suite at the Ritz-Carlton for an hour, but if you're real sweet to me, I'll give you a present."

They got out of the car, and Melanie slid up alongside him, her hand creeping across his chest. "What kind of present, sugar?"

Guy smiled. Melanie always liked her pay up front, like any good whore. "How'd you like your own place?"

Her eyes widened with surprise. "Really? My very own apartment?"

"Mine, too," he pointed out.

"Well, of course," she purred. Her hand slid down his chest. "You could come by at lunch, or after work. We'd have such fun."

They walked along the sidewalk toward the entrance. "I'm going to need money for new clothes and stuff," Melanie pointed out thoughtfully. "An apartment costs a lot besides rent."

"You have a job."

"If you want me to be good, I can only concentrate on one thing at a time."

Guy frowned at her. She was a greedy little thing, but then, it wasn't his money so what difference did it make? As they turned into the shabby doorway, Guy waved gaily at the nun who was watching the children. He snickered at her scowl and turned back to Melanie. "How'd you like to be an outside salesman?"

She glared at him suspiciously. A new job had not been her goal, apparently. "What do I have to do?"

"Just sign a time card once a week and give it to me."

"What if someone finds out?" she said, frowning.

"We've got a bunch of guys doing it. It's no big deal."

"Okay," she agreed, and melted her body against his. "You're my bossman."

"Make sure you remember that," he warned, and went into the office to get a room.

# CHAPTER EIGHTEEN

The phone woke Toni from a sound sleep, and an immediate fear seized her. Sitting up slowly on the edge of the bed, she reached over and turned on the light. It was a few minutes before six o'clock. Time she was getting up anyway. Wednesday had already begun. She flicked off her alarm, then reached for the phone, picking it up on its fourth ring.

"I was beginning to think you were still in Peoria," Jon laughed.

Toni had not noticed that she had been holding her breath until she relaxed and let it go. "No, I'm here. Didn't get in until almost midnight because of that thunderstorm, but I'm here now. What are you doing up at the crack of dawn?" She propped her pillows up against the headboard and leaned back.

"I'm trying to share some terrific news with you," he said.

Toni heard the smile in his voice and could see him in her mind, lying on his bed just as she was. His dark hair would be slightly mussed, and his tanned skin would smell slightly of sweat and English Leather. She longed to be there with him. "You're coming over for breakfast?" she guessed hopefully.

"Wish I could, but I'm meeting Dad up at their house for breakfast. He's sending me up to Wisconsin and we're going to go over some last-minute details."

"He's sending you to Wisconsin?" A sudden emptiness appeared in the pit of her stomach. "Why?"

Jon was too excited to notice the worry in her voice. "That's the terrific news. I'm finally doing something more than sell saltshakers. He wants me to check over a paper plant he's thinking of buying, and once that's settled, he's going to retire."

"That's wonderful for you," Toni murmured, forcing some enthusiasm into her voice. She swallowed and asked the question foremost in her mind. "How long will you be gone?"

"A few days probably. No more than a week, I'm sure."

A week without him! That seemed like forever! "That doesn't seem very long," she lied, not wanting to spoil his happiness. "I'll have to think of a special way to welcome you home."

He laughed, then sighed. "I wish you hadn't gotten home so late last night. Monday seems like ages ago. I'm going to miss you."

"I'll miss you too," she admitted. They were both silent for a long moment.

"I guess I'd better get moving. Dad's expecting me before seven."

"My shower's waiting for me."

There was another long silence, as each was reluctant to break the connection.

"I love you," Jon whispered.

"I love you, too," she whispered back. "Come home soon." There was a quiet click as he hung up the phone.

Toni rose to her feet. The apartment seemed empty and she had the ridiculous urge to burst into tears. That was stupid, she scolded herself. She went on business trips all the time, and although she certainly missed Jon, she never felt frightened at the thought of being without him. Not being able to live without someone was a ploy used to sell valentines and had no relation to reality. She would miss his company for the next few days, but it was hardly the end of the world. Or the end of their relationship. No, not relationship, their love, she corrected herself quickly.

She turned on the radio as she made her bed, but the warning of an accident on the Northwest Tollway and construction delays on the Skyway did not dispel the loneliness in her heart.

It seemed as if every one of Toni's clients had called her while she was in Peoria, for a large stack of messages was waiting for her when she got to the office. She was able to pass off a few to members of her team, but most were vaguely stated and required a return call.

She sat down at her desk, feeling tired before she even began. So many of these calls were just a waste of her time. If the client needed a question answered, usually the best person to ask was the senior accountant assigned to his account, but few clients bothered with the underlings. They had to talk to the manager or the partner. The rest of the calls would be complaints, she knew, mostly about their bills. This was one part of managing that she would gladly give up.

Before Toni had made much of a dent in the stack, Sara Myers, Simon's secretary, knocked on her door. "Toni? Didn't you see the note that Simon wanted to see you first thing this morning?"

"Lord, no," Toni sighed, and rose to her feet. "Has he been waiting long?"

Sara smiled as she shook her head. "He's just finishing up a few calls and asked me to see if you were free."

"For him, sure," Toni said. She smoothed out her gray skirt and adjusted the floppy bow tie of burgundy silk. "Why the summons? Is he going to chop off my head?"

Sara was the perfect secretary and knew how to answer without offending. "He's in a good mood, I wouldn't worry."

Great, Toni thought as they went out her door and down the hall. That means he's looking forward to my execution.

Sara smiled encouragingly as she settled herself at her desk. Toni went past her to the door and tapped lightly on the wood.

Simon had been going over some papers on his desk, but he looked up with an easy smile. "Toni, come in." He waved his hand toward a plush wingback chair in front of his desk. "Would you like some coffee before we begin?"

Toni settled herself into the wide chair and shook her head. She hated these mysteriously requested meetings. They made her feel like a little girl called before the principal.

Simon's eyes seemed to be thin and piercing as he gazed at Toni. "I have a few minor items to cover before we get to the reason for our meeting."

Toni nodded slightly. Right, he'd point out the few

things that he liked about her, then he'd pitch her out onto the street.

"First of all, we have the problem of Mid-America."

She opened her mouth to speak, but Simon stopped her with a quietly raised hand. "As you may know, I met with Mr. Ramsey and Mr. Morici yesterday morning."

She had known and had wondered why. Her blood seemed to race a little faster.

"It was their request that you be removed as audit manager of their account," Simon went on.

"Who requested it?" Her voice was remarkably steady as her hands clenched convulsively once before she forced them to relax.

"As I understood it," he replied, "it was a management decision by the executives of the firm."

"I can believe that," she scoffed, unable to keep the bitterness from her voice. "Guy Ramsey is up to his neck in something strange and Sam Morici is either too dumb to see what's going on or in it himself."

Simon raised his hand again and Toni bit back a sigh of frustration. She leaned back in her seat, saying nothing further.

"I think, Miss James, that we had better review a few basic facts before we go much further," he said with quiet authority. No longer a friend and adviser, he put himself back in the role of her managing partner. His voice was scolding and his manner unbending. "First of all, Mid-America is not a large publicly held corporation, but a small privately held firm. Mr. Morici is the majority owner and can do what he wants with his company. He can give his product away or throw it into the river; it's none of our business. Secondly, Mid-America is not our firm. We may have some opinions on how it should be run, but they are opinions only. We discharged our responsibility when we notified executive management of our concerns. Unless we have proof of laws being broken we are covered by what we have done to date."

Toni sat quietly for a moment. She knew that Simon was correct, but at the same time, she hated to give up the pursuit. Guy Ramsey was up to no good and maybe Jon's father too, yet there wasn't a thing she could prove.

Simon seemed able to read her mind. "You identified

some problems. You notified those in authority. You have discharged your responsibility, Miss James."

Toni clenched her teeth. "Yes, sir," she said with obvious reluctance. Guy was going to walk free. He could get her fired, and there wasn't anything she could do. She tried to put her anger and frustration behind her and remember that she was a professional. If she couldn't take the knocks and fighting, she should have stayed in Niles.

She looked up after a long moment of painful silence. "I'm sorry if I have caused problems for the firm, sir. But I still believe I'm correct."

"That's okay, Toni," he said gently. "You did what you felt was right."

His apparent understanding surprised her. "You're not mad at me?"

He frowned slightly and a crease appeared in his forehead. "I'm somewhat disappointed. I think that you could have handled things in a more mature manner and you should have hidden your personal feelings toward the individuals concerned. But we are going to remain as their accounting firm and the new contract that you obtained is still ours." A slight smile played on his lips. "And in the final analysis, Miss James, that's what the game's all about."

Toni could not bring herself to smile back. Apparently the only thing that really mattered to him was that they kept the account. Guy's unfairness to her and his possible illegalities were unimportant as long as they didn't lose a client. And what would happen to her now?

"So! The bottom line, Toni, is that you will no longer be the audit manager for the Mid-America account."

She had known it was coming, but hearing the actual words knocked her breath from her. She could feel a slight quiver to her chin and she took a deep breath.

"Now, there's another matter I would like to cover with you."

She forced herself to look at him. "Yes, sir."

"I had a chat with George Manning before I left Mid-America. He felt that you were being unfair in putting him on a three-month improvement plan."

Toni's face grew hot and flushed. "I gave him any number of chances to improve. In fact, I probably gave him too much leeway."

"Are you aware that Mr. Manning's wife recently had a baby?"

She was confused for a moment as she tried to remember. It vaguely came back to her. George had remarked one day that he hadn't said anything because he didn't think she smoked cigars. "Yes, sir. I think it was just a few months ago."

"Are you aware whether there were any problems with his wife or child?"

Her heart sank as she replied in hushed tones. "No, sir, I wasn't."

Simon looked at her for a moment before answering her in a matter-of-fact tone. "Well, there weren't any."

Toni caught her breath in a confused mixture of anger and relief. What was this game he was playing?

"I reviewed Mr. Manning's file yesterday. Whenever you put an employee on an improvement plan you are to be sure that every *i* is dotted and every *t* is crossed. You didn't cover yourself on one or two points. Your CYA efforts left a little to be desired."

Toni was angry now. Damn! What a bunch of Mickey Mouse crap! CYA, cover your ass, indeed. Wasn't there more to management than that?

"Actually, I agree with you," Simon went on. "I feel that Mr. Manning is of little use to the firm and I will be quite happy to see him go after his improvement-plan period has expired. His performance has been less than stellar over the years."

"Thank you, sir." Toni felt tired. If she had made that many mistakes, they certainly didn't want her around. Why didn't he just get it over with?

"If Mr. Manning had any kind of political acumen and had been in with one of the other partners, he could have caused us problems." Simon's gaze was stern. "I expect in the future that your procedures will be a little more tidy."

"Yes, sir," Toni replied. She barely heard what Simon was saying.

"Okay, now to the main issue that I would like to cover. I've been giving a great deal of thought to our small-business unit, or what is referred to as 'pots and pans.' "

Yes, she was sure he had, Toni thought to herself. And

he probably decided to blame any problems he discovered on the audit manager.

Simon quickly glanced at a paper he had in front of him. "I have reviewed our revenue figures from that unit for the past five years and there has been absolutely no growth."

Toni clenched her teeth, waiting for the words she knew were coming. It was over. Her dream for the past ten years was over. Down the drain because of that bastard Ramsey.

Simon droned on, unaware of her tension and despair. "Without growth in small business any firm will die. It is a natural growth progression for any company to expand its small-business customers and then grow with them."

Her hands were clenched in her lap, and she tried hard not to scream out.

"That's how our business grew when we first started it, but we seemed to have lost sight of that basic business strategy in the last few years. So, I am going to make some changes in that area."

Toni steeled herself for the blow she was sure was coming.

"I've decided to split the small-business unit in half and have two audit managers instead of one. In addition to managing his half of the client set, each audit manager will also be charged with finding new customers. I will expect his revenue base and client base to grow by a reasonable percentage per year."

Simon stopped and looked into Toni's strained face, a mischievous smile playing on his lips. "Or rather, I should say 'managing his or her client set.'"

Toni's eyes took on a slightly bewildered look. Wasn't she being fired? What about the Mid-America mess? Everybody in the office knew about it. Old George had had diarrhea of the mouth and made sure everybody was aware she was having problems.

"I know that this isn't the same as making you a partner," Simon assured her, "but it is an interesting new challenge. And, I assure you, it is extremely important to the health of the firm." Simon looked at her anxious face. "For your own personal growth, you will have to get more marketing oriented. Revenue doesn't sit on trees waiting to be plucked. The accounting firms that survive in the future will be those that aggressively go out and market their services."

Toni nodded. "Yes sir, I understand that."

"Very good." Simon took the paper he had laid on the corner of his desk and handed it to Toni. "This will be your new client set. The rest will be given to Bob Morgan. I will announce his promotion this morning. Please review his new clients with him at your earliest convenience."

"Yes, sir."

Simon turned to a stack of reports on his desk. "Are there any questions?" he asked, not looking up.

"No, sir. Not right now."

He glanced back up at her. "Very good. I will get back to you and Morgan with my expectations for revenue and client growth."

"Fine, Mr. Bradley. Bob and I will get the transfers taken care of quickly."

Toni got up and moved to leave the office.

"Oh, Miss James."

Toni turned at the door. Simon had a slight smile on his face, but it looked more cold and calculating than friendly. "My expectations will be high. I'm sure you and Morgan will find them interesting and challenging."

Toni forced a smile to her face. "I'm sure we will, sir."

Somehow Toni made it through the rest of the day. She even managed to congratulate Bob on his promotion and promise to go over the accounts with him in the next day or two. He was as smug and condescending as she expected.

By late afternoon, she was a nervous wreck from trying to hold her battered emotions in check. When Doug Miller, a tax manager, suggested she join a bunch of them for a drink downstairs in the Chicago Bar and Grill, she was torn. Would it be better to keep up the brave front a little longer or should she go home and give in to her impulse to cry?

With Jon out of town, the evening stretched endlessly before her, and it seemed rather self-pitying to have nothing else planned but a good cry. Maybe if she pretended a little longer that she was fine and excited about her new challenge, she would come to believe it herself.

After finishing up the last of her phone calls, she met the others in the bar. It was a dark place, decorated in polished woods and brass trim. The people from her office were scattered around several tables and she found a place between Mike Derwinski, another audit manager, and Denise Taylor, a senior accountant in the tax department.

"I think it's terrible what Bradley did to you today," Denise said in a low voice as Toni sat down. "If it was me, I'd take him to court for discrimination."

The anger in Denise's voice made Toni slightly uneasy and she glanced around her. Mike was telling some loud, involved story that seemed to have the rest of the table engrossed. Toni turned back to Denise, wishing that she had remembered Denise's rather militant reputation before she had sat down.

"It wasn't anything like that," Toni corrected her. The waitress approached and she ordered a piña colada.

"Oh, he probably was pretty careful not to let himself get caught," Denise agreed as soon as the woman left with Toni's order. "But I'll bet the same thing wouldn't have happened to a man."

This was just what she needed, Toni groaned mentally. "It had nothing to do with my being a woman," she insisted. Guy might have made some suggestive remarks, but he'd had her removed because of her persistence, not her sex. "Simon wants to expand the small-business area, and this was how he chose to do it."

Denise looked unbelieving as she lit a cigarette and took a deep drag on it. "That's a bunch of crap, and we both know it."

Toni glanced away, pretending to listen to Mike's anecdote, even though she didn't have the slightest idea what he was talking about. Once her drink came, she'd just drink it quickly and get away from this fanatic.

"I've talked the whole thing over with Anita in auditing and Jane in management consulting and we think it's time to take a stand," Denise went on.

Toni's drink arrived just in time and she took a large gulp to soothe her indignation. "Take a stand?" she whispered harshly. Her eyes were open wide in horror. "What are you talking about?"

"We can't let them get away with this." Denise's voice was low and intense. "If they push you around, they'll try it with all of us. We've got to stop them now."

"You know nothing about this situation," Toni informed

her. "I'm perfectly happy with the way things turned out." She was no longer concerned about appearing rude and picked up her drink as she rose to her feet. "I am not a recruit for your army."

Toni walked across the room, uncertain where she was going. She was sorry that she had bothered to come, and wished she could just fade into the woodwork.

"Toni?"

She was surprised to find Don Smythe next to her. He was the youngest of the firm's partners, probably in his late forties, and had only spoken to Toni once or twice before in her four years with the company.

"I was sorry to hear what happened with your account," he said.

Toni didn't bother to argue with him. As a partner, he'd know what had really happened. "I guess I didn't play my cards right," she admitted.

Don nodded toward the empty table next to them. "That kind of situation is really tough," he pointed out as they sat down. "Especially when you know you're right."

Toni was flattered by his belief in her and smiled at him. "Yes, but keeping the customer happy is more important than being right."

"To some people maybe." He raised his hand to call the waitress over, giving her his now-empty glass and asking for another Manhattan. "What about you? Can I buy you a drink?"

"I've still got most of mine," she said, holding up her glass. "Thanks anyway."

Don turned in his chair as he nodded to the waitress, his leg resting lightly against Toni's. Suddenly her senses were alert and on guard, memories of Guy's "accidental" touches flooding her mind. Had she jumped from Denise's frying pan into Don's fire?

Toni picked up her drink and sipped it thoughtfully. When she put it down, she shifted her position nonchalantly away from his touch. "Actually, Simon's new arrangement may work out well. I'll enjoy the challenge of finding new clients—".

Don's skepticism was obvious as he leaned closer, resting his hand on the back on her chair. "Selling nickel-and-dime contracts will get old quick. Why don't you come over to my side of the house and play with the big boys? They have more money and a more rational way of doing business." He sipped his drink, then winked at her. "Besides, I'm a real nice guy and will treat you good."

Sure he would, Toni thought cynically, and what kind of bonuses would she be expected to provide? "I think I'll just stay where I am, thank you."

He moved away as the waitress approached their table and put his drink down on a white cocktail napkin. "Thanks, sugar," he said to the woman, and handed her a five-dollar bill. "Keep the change."

The waitress was obviously impressed with him, but to Toni it was all too similar to Guy's behavior when he had taken her out to lunch. As if her day hadn't been enough of a disaster already. Now, she had to fend off a groping boss. She quickly finished her drink so that when Don turned back to her, she was ready to leave.

"Now, how can I convince you to transfer to my division?" he asked her softly.

"You can't." Her voice was crisp and curt as she reached for her purse. "I'm quite satisfied where I am. My work is interesting and Simon is quite pleasant to work for. In fact, I'm beginning to think he's the only one of his kind. A manager who treats me like a person instead of a sex object." She rose to her feet and pulled her purse over her shoulder. "Good night, Mr. Smythe."

She turned and hurried between the tables to the door, but he caught up with her before she reached it. "Hey, that's a heavy charge," he protested. Grabbing hold of her arm, he turned her around to face him. Toni could see he was angry. "All I was trying to do was be nice to somebody who'd had a few tough breaks lately. I don't need to hear that kind of shit."

Toni took a deep steadying breath. She tried to find something specific to counter his argument, but suddenly nothing seemed very damning. So he brushed against her leg or leaned closer to her as he spoke; was that a crime? She thought she had matured beyond jumping at every slight innuendo, but apparently the events of the day had erased some of her growth.

"I'm very sorry if I've misjudged you," she said quietly. "I appear to be overreacting to everything today."

"Hey, no sweat," he said, shaking his head with a forgiving smile. "Come on back and let me buy you that drink."

Toni shook her head in return. "No, I think with the day I've had, I'd better go home before I bring total disaster down on my head. Thanks just the same."

He shrugged and walked back to his table as she left the bar. "Good Lord," she sighed once she was out of sight. What was she trying to do, ruin her whole career? She had better pull herself together and do it fast.

By the time Toni got home, she was ready to burst into tears. It was all the fault of that damn Ramsey, she thought, tossing her shoes into the back of her closet and sitting down on the edge of her bed. She was doing too good of a job there and he was getting scared. He was worried about what she was likely to turn up. Why didn't Simon see that?

She stood up restlessly and unbuttoned her white blouse. How did she know that Simon hadn't understood perfectly what the situation was? She ought to have learned by now that there were few white knights riding about corporate America, doing what is fair and just. No, everybody was out for themselves or out for the company. Since the firm didn't suffer, Simon had been willing to keep her punishment simple. Just a little humiliation and fear, that's all. Next time, she'd know not to do what is right, but to do what is safe.

This kind of thinking was only making her feel worse, and Toni decided to go out running. The storm last night had left the air cool and clean feeling. It would feel good to let it ease her tensions by soothing her troubled spirit.

She slipped out of her skirt and panty hose, and into a pair of pale blue knitted shorts and a matching sweatshirt. How much of the truth did Jon's father know? she wondered suddenly. If he knew nothing, why would he have agreed to her dismissal from the account?

She put on her running shoes and tied them up. He had to have known about Guy's manipulations. Whatever Guy was doing, Mr. Morici had to have known about it. They were too close for him not to.

That brought Toni up to an unpleasant hurdle. If Sam knew, did Jon?

She turned aside from her closet as if she could turn aside from her thoughts, but they followed her over to the dresser. Wasn't it a strange coincidence that Jon went out of town the day she was being taken off the Mid-America account? Was he really out of town, or was he avoiding her?

The thought so unnerved her that her hands began to tremble. She glanced toward the phone, but she knew she could not dial his number. What if he answered? Wouldn't that prove her suspicions? And where would it leave their love?

Ignorance might not be bliss, but in some cases suspicions were easier to live with than the truth. She grabbed a rubber band from her top drawer and pulled her hair into a ponytail, scolding herself for her doubts.

Jon would not pretend to leave town when he hadn't. He wouldn't lie to her, and he wouldn't be a party to his father's schemes. Unfortunately, the scene at the Mid-America picnic came to her mind. Jon had been very upset and had never given her any explanation. Could his father have told him of her investigation and the need to get rid of her? Hadn't she suspected that at the time?

Toni was getting frightened and didn't know what to think. Nothing and everything seemed to fall into place.

The ringing of the phone split the silence of the apartment. Toni knew it was Jon calling her, but she just stared at the phone from across the room. What could she say to him? That his father's plan had succeeded? That she needed his comfort, but could understand his guilty conscience forcing him to stay away?

No, there was nothing she could say to him. Not now, not tonight when the hurt was so fresh. Slowly, she backed out of the room and left the apartment. The phone was still ringing when she headed down the hall toward the elevator.

# CHAPTER NINETEEN

"So the great accountant wasn't as great as she thought," Bob snickered as Toni sat down at her desk.

"Let's just get to these files, shall we?" She tried to keep her voice cool and businesslike and not give in to the anger she felt.

"Sure thing, hotshot."

Toni pushed back a loose strand of hair that had fallen onto her forehead and reminded herself once again that she was a professional. She would not exchange insults with him, no matter what level he sank to. Flipping through the pile of folders on her desk, she pulled one out.

"I think we ought to cover Mid-America first," she said briskly. "There are some special problems there."

A knowing look settled on Bob's face. "They're the ones that tried to get you canned, aren't they?"

She held her breath for a moment, then let it out slowly, forcing the tension from her body at the same time. "They didn't try to get me canned. They merely asked that I be removed as their audit manager. I did, however, get a large contract from them."

"Oh, yeah? Well, we'll see how it compares to the ones I get."

He was so smug and sure of himself that Toni longed to hit him. Instead, she opened the folder and spread out a few papers. "The president of the firm is Sam Morici, but you'll probably have very little to do with him. The one you will deal with is Guy Ramsey, the controller."

"Which is the one you couldn't get along with?"

Toni glanced briefly at him. She knew other women might say he looked very attractive in his navy three-piece suit, but she could not see beyond his sneering eyes.

"George Manning is the senior accountant on this account and he was just recently put on an improvement plan. I found his work to be very sloppy, and this was partially responsible for some of the problems I encountered."

Bob leaned back in his chair, crossing his right leg over left. "Right. It was all George's fault."

"No, it was not all his fault," she corrected him curtly. "I didn't say it was, but there were mistakes in the bookkeeping that I discovered that should have been found months ago. You will have to keep close tabs on him."

"I can handle George."

Toni was skeptical but silent as she went back to her papers. She had been stewing all night about how much of her suspicions of Guy she should confide to Bob. Since they were both professionals and working for the same company, she had decided that she should tell him everything. It was not going to be easy, though. Not with his attitude.

"I did have some trouble getting along with Mr. Ramsey," Toni said, looking across her desk at Bob. "He found it difficult to accept me as the audit manager because I was a woman, and I found him personally distasteful."

"Gone back to being a prude, eh?"

She forced herself to ignore his jeering and went on. "Our difficulty in getting along was not the reason they asked to have me removed. I'm sure that, given time, we would have reached some sort of truce. The actual problem arose in the work I was doing."

Surprisingly Bob made no cutting remark, so she continued, playing nervously with the buttons on the sleeve of her tan suit while she spoke. "In going over their accounts payable, we found a large number of discrepancies. Places where the amount listed in their records was larger than the amount they were billed for or the amount actually paid."

"So somebody entered the data wrong." He shrugged. "It happens all the time. Nobody's perfect, not even you."

"The amount wouldn't be exactly doubled or tripled, though. No, this wasn't just an accident. The amounts were systematically inflated."

Bob looked highly skeptical. "And you're telling me that's why you were removed? For finding this problem?"

"Yes," she insisted. "Because Ramsey, and probably

Sam Morici, were the ones making the changes. No one had caught it before, and when I did, they wanted me out."

"Are you listening to yourself, Toni? You aren't making any sense. Just what did you think was going on? Embezzlement? Embezzlers don't inflate funds, they deflate them."

"I know it wasn't embezzlement," she protested hotly. "But they sure as hell were doing something they didn't want known."

"Come off it, Toni." He was obviously impatient with her explanation. "Stop trying to make excuses instead of admitting you did a lousy job. Just what did you decide they were doing—laundering money? Shades of Watergate, right? Hell, the president probably just wanted to make the place look bigger."

Toni leaned forward on her desk. "Why? He would just have to pay more taxes."

"Maybe he's very civic minded," Bob suggested sarcastically. "The guy's a greaseball, right? It was probably a macho thing. Wanted the company to look big to impress his mob buddies. No wonder they wanted you out of there if that was your attitude."

Toni swallowed the angry retort that came to her lips. There was no way that she was going to convince Bob that her suspicions had legitimate grounds. She hadn't been able to convince Simon, who was more on her side than Bob would ever be. She closed the folder on Mid-America and pushed it across the desk toward him. "I just thought you should be filled in on all that's happened, since Simon's taking you there this afternoon. Shall we go on to Star Communications?"

"You know, this place was once used as a hideout by Al Capone," Bob Morgan confided with a touch of pride in his voice.

Guy looked around at the trendy copper bar and curved walls of The Brewery restaurant and grunted. "Oh?"

"Really," Bob assured him. "They had telephone lines and escape tunnels in the basement."

Guy's eyes were impassive as he watched Bob sip his wine, but his thoughts were disgusted. Another college boy trying to convince everybody he was a man of the world, but only succeeding in looking like an ass. Guy drank half of his martini.

Bob put down his glass and leaned closer across the table. "Actually, I think it's the Cosa Nostra that gives Chicago its unique vibrancy."

"Cosa Nostra?" Guy's eyes went cold as they searched Bob's carefully, but he found no ulterior motives lurking there.

"You know, the mob. La Cosa Nostra means Our Thing."

"I see," Guy replied. Apparently, Morgan's enthusiasm was his idea of the dynamic executive.

"Those mob guys are really something else," Bob gushed. "Sort of reminds you of Robin Hood."

"Robin Hood?"

"Sure, you know what I mean. They operate above the law, doing what they want like real men yet never actually hurting anybody."

Guy snickered slightly at the man's stupidity, but Bob seemed to take it as an invitation to continue. "A lot of these old buildings were used by the mob during Prohibition. They had tunnels and hideouts all over the city and in some of the older suburbs. Your building is fairly old, isn't it?"

"Yes, it's a dump."

"Hey, don't knock it." Bob's tone became slightly patronizing. "It may have some tunnels too. Probably should be on the historical register."

"That's good to know. If we need a little extra money, we'll open it to the tourists."

Bob laughed heartily as Guy continued to snicker. A long, strained silence followed; then Bob spoke again. "I thought that Simon would be joining us, but he's always busy. He doesn't seem to spend much time with any individual client."

"That's okay. I got his phone number." After a meaningful pause, Guy finished his drink and signaled the waitress for a refill. "Besides, he don't look like a party guy to me."

Bob chuckled with forced gusto. "You're right there. You can say a lot of things about Simon Bradley, but you sure can't call him a party boy."

The waitress placed Guy's drink in front of him. "Thanks, doll," he said, caressing her roughly with his eyes. She had a polished but hard look about her and did not shrink from his attention. Probably a good lay, but cash in advance. Expensive, too. He gave her a wink before turning back to Bob. "How about you, Bob? Do you like to party?"

"Absolutely. In fact, I'd like to party with her right now." He nodded toward the waitress who had just left. "Unless you want her first. My clients always get first dibs with me."

Guy tried hard not to laugh aloud at his pompous generosity. "Nah, that's okay. I got my own stable and I'm already immune to their germs."

"That's a good idea." Bob nodded. "You'd think with all the money and brains around, they would have cured herpes long ago."

Guy took a sip of his drink. "You got a stable of broadies you keep happy, Bob?"

"As much as I can afford."

His eyebrows rising in surprise, Guy snickered. "You mean, you gotta pay?"

Bob stammered nervously. "Well, not directly. But, you know, you got to buy them enough to keep them alive. Otherwise they go picking up some other action and who knows what they'll bring back."

Guy pulled a cigar from his pocket and lit it, looking Bob over with narrowed eyes. Just like he thought, a real weenie. Guy's girls took care of themselves, and when he called, they came ready, willing, and clean.

The waitress came over to take their luncheon order and Guy watched with smug amusement as she ignored Bob's come-ons. This was a lady that could smell a man's gold from a country mile, and she could tell Morgan had nothing in his pocket or his pants. Too bad she was so hard or he'd give her a tumble himself. At his age, though, he liked them soft and young. Made for a more comfortable bounce.

After she left, Guy let the silence drag out, enjoying the sight of Bob squirming a little. Then he asked quietly, "Do you know Toni James very well?"

Bob snorted with vicious mirth. "Do I? She and I almost had a thing going once."

Guy was surprised, and looked up with interest. "What happened?"

"When I finally got inside, I turned blue from the cold."

Guy laughed with Bob at his feeble attempt at humor. Toni James was one tough lady and she needed a real man to keep her happy. Look how she enjoyed his little calls.

"Hell," Bob went on as the waitress brought over their food, "I had to pay two broadies to take turns holding it for forty-eight hours straight before I could use it again."

Guy ignored him and patted the waitress on her fanny. "Hey, sweet thing, the next time you're this way bring the catsup."

"We have a good hot sauce."

"The only thing I like hot is my woman, honey babe. Just bring the catsup." He turned back to Bob, suddenly all business. "So, did you and Ms. James finish passing the baton?"

Bob followed his lead and nodded seriously. "Yes, sir. There won't be any need to involve her with Mid-America again."

"And you know everything there is to know about us?"

He nodded again. "Yes, sir. I do know that the intricacies of your business require some very unique accounting procedures."

"But you don't visualize yourself running into some of the same problems as Ms. James?"

"Oh no, sir. Absolutely not." Bob shook his head. "Toni asked for all the trouble she got. I always figure life gives me enough trouble. I don't need to look for more."

Guy felt a warm glow of satisfaction spread through his being. So little Toni had a few problems. Guy smiled broadly at Bob without really seeing him. Pretty soon Ms. James would be finding out that she'd just got the down payment. The best was yet to come.

Bob's voice brought Guy out of his happy reverie. "There are a few questions that I may have, but I don't see that they should cause either of us problems."

Guy was glad to hear it. That meant he wasn't going to rock the boat. Bob Morgan was another Martin, just younger. Lou would be relieved.

When the check came, Guy reached for it first. "We've got a lot of money. It'll be my treat."

"But, I really should—" Bob protested.

Guy smiled and signed his credit card charge. "What's

the matter? You guys got a quota on how many times you're supposed to take a client to lunch?"

"They do like us to do our share."

Guy took the receipt that he had torn off the restaurant check and threw it across the table to him. "Here, I've got my credit card receipt. You can use this so you won't get into trouble."

Bob quickly grabbed the piece of paper. "I insist that the next time is my treat."

"Sure, no sweat." Guy rose to his feet and moved lazily toward the door.

Bob followed. "In fact, can we get together next week?"

They passed their waitress and she smiled at Guy. "Thank you, sir."

Guy reached out and rubbed her gently on the small of her back. "Take care of yourself, beautiful."

"No one else will," she replied.

Guy winked and went through the door, Bob following close behind him. "In fact, sir, I like to keep in close personal contact with the executives in my accounts. I think we should have lunch together once a week as a rule."

"Sure, no problem. Sounds like a good idea." The fool would probably be just as cheap as old Martin. Things were back on an even keel again. He fingered the piece of paper the waitress had slipped in his pocket and smiled. He thought he might give her a call later. After all, a man was never too old to learn new tricks.

Jon tapped his foot impatiently while he listened to the phone ring. The damn hotel had such a short cord on their phone that he couldn't even pace in the small space next to the bed.

Where was she? He had been unable to reach Toni last night, and it looked like she was out again tonight. Had she gone out of town herself, or was something wrong?

The phone had rung at least six times and he was about ready to give up, when someone picked up the receiver at the other end.

"Hello?"

"Toni?" It sounded like her, but then again, it didn't. "Is that you?"

He heard her sigh. "Yeah, of course it's me. Who else

would be answering my phone?" Before he had time to respond, she went on. "So, how's Wisconsin?"

"Fine," he said, frowning. She didn't sound like herself at all. "Is something wrong?"

She just laughed slightly. "It's been a hectic week. Is your paper plant as interesting as you had hoped?"

Her evasiveness worried him even more, but he decided to play her game for a while. "Yeah, it's been pretty interesting. The building's in good shape, but we'd need to make some changes." He sat down on the thick blue-and-white bedspread, running his fingers absently over the uneven weave. "There isn't much to Combined Locks, but Appleton, where most of the people live, is really nice. It's got a college and a great art museum. It's different from Chicago, but I bet you'd really like it."

She made a monosyllabic reply that he could not understand, and then there was an awkward moment of silence.

"Toni, what's the matter?" He pressed more gently this time.

He was not sure she was going to answer, but after another bit of silence, she sighed again and spoke. "Look, Jon, I don't think I can talk about it yet. I'm not angry with you about leaving when you did, but it just hurts too much to talk about it right now." Her voice sounded raw with anguish, and that alarmed him as much as the fact that he didn't know what she was talking about.

"Toni, for God's sake, what's wrong?"

"I said not now." Her voice broke and she sounded close to tears. "I'm dealing with it the best I can."

"Dealing with what? Why won't you tell me what you're talking about?" He was close to panic. "Should I come home tonight?"

"No, no," she said quickly. He was sure she was crying openly now, for her words seemed to come in bunches between sobs. "Don't be silly. I'm fine. I'm really fine."

She sounded terrible, but he was not about to argue that point. "It's only eight o'clock. If I leave now, I can be there before midnight."

"No," she said brokenly. She must have held the phone away from her, because he could only hear muted sounds for a moment. "Look, I really can't talk now. Why don't you call me tomorrow night? I promise I'll be better then."

"Toni—" But he was too late. She had hung up the phone.

Jon put down the receiver slowly, lines of worry crossing his forehead. He hadn't the slightest idea what she had been talking about, but she seemed to think he did. What could have happened?

He frowned at the phone. He'd be damned if he'd wait until tomorrow to find out what was going on. He'd give her five minutes and then he'd call her back. Well, maybe ten. She didn't cry very often, but when she got started, it took her a while to stop.

Jon rose to his feet and walked over to the window. He stared out at the parking lot, seeking distraction, but there was only his car and two others, both with Wisconsin license plates. Beyond the parking lot, in the space between the motel and the highway, was a swimming pool. Even though the temperature was in the sixties, two teenagers were splashing around in it as if they didn't have a care in the world.

He turned away in frustration and glanced at his watch. Only three minutes had passed.

What in the world could be the matter? he wondered. He felt so damn helpless up here, miles and hours away from her. Well, if she wouldn't talk to him this time, he'd drive back down there. The hell with his appointment for tomorrow morning.

After six minutes, he went back to the phone and dialed her number. Again he waited interminably while it rang and rang. She could have gone out, he knew, or just be sitting there, refusing to answer. He was not going to hang up.

"Yes?" Her voice sounded tired, but more in control.

"Toni, don't do that to me again," he pleaded. "I love you. Don't keep shutting me out."

"Oh, Jon," she sighed.

"No, you've got to listen," he said quickly before she could get into all those meaningless phrases again. "I know something's wrong, but I haven't got any idea what it is. You've got to tell me what happened."

"I was sure you knew," she said slowly, as if she was considering a new possibility. "I'm not much of a believer in coincidences."

"Toni." He tried to call her back to the explanations.

"It really was too much to believe that you should just happen to go out of town that day."

So it happened yesterday, he thought, not wanting to interrupt her again. She seemed to be getting to the point, however slowly, so he held his breath and waited for her to go on.

"Of course, I never thought you were part of the decision. I figured it was all Guy's doing."

The hand that held the phone felt wet with sweat as he waited for her next words. What had that bastard done?

"You know, after Simon took the account away from me, I just kept remembering how upset you had been after the picnic. I figured it all had to be tied up together."

"He took you off the Mid-America account?"

"At the request of Guy and your father." She could not keep the bitterness from her voice.

"And you were told on Wednesday. The day I was sent on my wonderful trip." The bitterness in his voice matched hers. "I guess I'm not much into coincidences either."

He became silent as he digested the news. An anger was growing inside him, but he was careful to keep it out of his voice. She was upset enough without adding his anger to everything. "Was it because of us?"

"Us?" She sounded puzzled for a moment. "You mean because we're seeing each other? Oh no, I'm sure it wasn't. It was more . . ." She was suddenly silent. "It was because Guy and I just couldn't get along. You know how he was."

Jon certainly did, and that knowledge didn't do much for his temper. "They'd take away the account just because Guy is an ass? I would have thought your boss was smart enough to see him for what he is." He chose not to think about his father's role in the whole matter.

"Oh, how I love you!" Her laugh was tired but relaxed. "However, Simon is more concerned about keeping the customer happy than fighting for my integrity. He had no qualms at all about giving Mid-America to Bob Morgan."

No wonder she had been upset! "He gave it to that jerk?"

She just laughed at his indignation. "At least I don't have to worry that you're going to fall for my replacement."

He was too angry to notice her attempt at humor. "I have a good mind to come home tonight and confront my father with this. Why the hell is he agreeing to this?"

"No, Jon, don't," she said quietly, her laughter all gone. "It won't change anything. Simon didn't just take Mid-America away, he took half my accounts away. Said he has some big plan for growth in the small-business area, so he wants to free me up for more marketing. Mid-America wasn't the only one Bob got."

That took the wind out of his sails. "Toni, I'm sorry," he sighed. Why was he up here when she needed him so? "That was rotten luck."

"Yes."

The silence this time was more companionable, but it only increased his desire to see her, to hold her, to know that she was really all right. "I think I should come home," he said suddenly.

"Jon, don't be silly," she scolded. "You have a job to do and so do I."

"Well, I'll come home tomorrow then," he persisted. "I was going to work through the weekend so I could get finished sooner, but I don't have to."

"No, work through the weekend. I already told Mom I was coming up for a visit, so I won't be here anyway."

"Dammit, Toni, stop being so reasonable!" he cried, only to have her burst into laughter. "I'm furious about all this. Why aren't you?"

"Because you love me," she said simply. "I was feeling miserable before, and I guess I still do, but not quite as bad because I know you're still on my side."

"I'll always be on your side," he told her, then paused. "If I can't come home, why don't you come up here?"

She laughed again. "Don't be silly. I've hardly eaten or slept since this happened, and once we get off the phone I'm going to fix myself a sinfully huge ice cream sundae and then I'm going to bed. See how you've helped me?"

"I could help you more if we were together," he said dryly.

"I love you," she whispered.

"I love you too," he said, and listened in resignation as she hung up the phone. He waited only a moment and then dialed another number. His father answered the phone at the other end.

"Jon, what a surprise. How's Wisconsin?"

"Why was I sent up here when Toni was going to be taken off the account?" he demanded.

His father was startled. "Oh, that," he muttered. "I guess I should have told you about that."

He could sense his father's uneasiness as Sam fumbled for an explanation. "It's sounds to me like I was set up," Jon pointed out.

"Oh, no," his father protested quickly. "It wasn't like that at all. It was Ramsey. You know how he is, and he was really making things tough for Toni."

"So why didn't you make him stop? You're supposed to be in charge there."

"Yeah, I know." Sam was breathing heavily. "But it's not that easy. Ramsey does a lot of work around here. I can't afford to lose him because of your girlfriend."

"Dad, that's not the point."

"Some women are tough and they can handle a bastard like Ramsey," Sam went on, his words coming a bit faster. "But Toni's such a nice kid. I worried about her having to work with him. And after the mess I made of things at the picnic, I decided to do something to make up for it."

"And firing her from the account was it?" Jon was astonished.

"Hey, you're making it sound like something terrible," Sam protested. "I was doing it for her own good. Lots of auditors get changed. It's no big deal, doesn't count against them or anything. Hellsfire, she's still an audit manager, and on top of it she's getting credit for that additional bit of business we bought."

Jon could not think of a reply, and his father jumped into the gap left by his silence.

"Jon, I was just trying to protect her. I thought you would want me to," he added, sounding confused.

Jon was speechless, not certain what to believe. It sounded so farfetched, it might actually be the truth. His father did have an old-fashioned, protective feeling about women.

"I don't want you to be mad about it," his father said. "And I sure didn't mean to hurt Toni's feelings. You want me to get her back on the account?"

"No, Dad," he sighed. "I guess you meant well."

"Is she upset?" Sam asked worriedly. "Want me to call her myself?"

"No, she's okay. Don't worry about it, Dad. I'll tell her what you said." He was tired and confused and needed some time to think. "See you in a week or so."

"I never meant to cause any trouble."

"Yeah, I know, Dad."

Jon hung up the phone with a sigh. Why couldn't his father leave well enough alone?

Toni sat on her sofa happily smashing the caramel sauce into the large mound of vanilla ice cream. She liked her sundaes gooey and soft. Smiling to herself, she remembered Jon had said that watching her eat a sundae would gross out even the least fastidious pig. Finally the ice cream was brought to the right consistency and Toni popped a glob into her mouth. Before she could really savor the deliciousness of it, the phone rang.

"Oh, if it's that man again, I will go up to Wisconsin tonight. And stuff this mess right into his ear." She hurried across the room and picked up the receiver. "Hello," she said brightly, though somewhat incoherently. Most of the ice cream in her mouth had been swallowed, but the cold sensation gave her the feeling of a full mouth.

There was a momentary silence on the line, and then a guttural voice rasped, "You sound real happy, sweetheart. Whose dick do you have in your mouth?"

Confusion and shock raced through Toni's mind. "What?" she asked, more an involuntary gasp than a question.

"I said, whose dick you got in your mouth now? Listen when I talk to you, bitch."

Rage flooded through her and she screamed into the phone, "You get out of my house."

He laughed harshly. "Thanks for the invitation. I'm gonna do that; then you can play with my pecker."

"You're garbage. You're pure filth. You're . . . you're not even human."

"I love you too, cunt."

"Go to hell, you ass—" Toni stopped, shocked at herself. What was she doing? Hang up, she thought. Just hang up on the moron.

The man seemed to read her mind and screamed into the

phone. "Don't hang up. I know where you live. I'm gonna visit you, sweet tits. I know where you li—"

After she crashed the receiver into the cradle, the jarred bell mechanism seemed to echo through the dead silence of her apartment. "I know where you live," he had said. "I'm gonna visit you." The two sentences raced across her mind as she sat down on the edge of her sofa. Fear instead of rage fueled her violently shaking limbs.

She got up and began to pace about her apartment. Her hands were crossed in front of her, clutching at her arms in a concerted effort to still her shaking. She should take Jon's invitation and run away to Wisconsin. He would see that nothing happened to her.

She stopped at the window, then jumped back. What if he could see her?

Toni shook her head angrily. That creep would have to be Superman to look in. She lived in a high-rise and was high up enough to look out into empty sky. Nevertheless, she turned off the light and moved over to the side of the window.

From her hiding place, she looked down into the street, seeing a number of people walking around, but none of them was her caller. She let the drapery fall back into place and sat down on the sofa again, a hysterical laugh bursting from her lips. How did you spot an obscene caller in a crowd of people? Did he wear a sign? Her ridiculousness made her laugh again, but it quickly turned to tears. There was no way she could know who he was. She was helpless.

Toni walked into her kitchen and washed the liquid remains of the sundae down the drain. As she wiped the dishes she glared at the phone, knowing that her hate and distrust were unreasonable. But she could not help herself. The phone now seemed an instrument of evil. It had brought that filthy slime into her house. She felt betrayed.

As Toni got ready for bed, she could not rid herself of that sense of betrayal. Finally it dawned on her that the telephone wasn't always a friend. There were times it intruded when she needed privacy. But, that was usually at work and a secretary would screen the calls.

She turned off her light, then tossed about on the bed as she tried to settle down to sleep. Wouldn't it be nice to bring one of the secretaries home? Borrow one like an Apple computer when she wanted to work at home after hours?

Of course, she thought, sitting up suddenly. She could hire a secretary to screen her calls. First thing in the morning she would hire an answering service. That would take care of the slimy nerd, she assured herself, and lay back down, ready for sleep.

# CHAPTER TWENTY

"Well, what do you think of it?" Melanie asked, leaning against the closed front door. A satisfied smile settled on her face as she watched Toni's glance take in her new apartment.

"Very nice," Toni said simply. "How long have you been in here?"

Melanie straightened up and walked casually over to the white velvet sofa that, along with a floor lamp, was the only furniture in the living room. "I found it on Tuesday and moved in on Wednesday. I hated that tiny place Rosie had, and it was good to get out." She sat down in one corner of the sofa, her right arm lying along the back as she faced her sister.

Toni said nothing as she continued to glance around the room. Melanie's eyes followed hers and knew when Toni noticed the solid wall of windows at the far end of the room. Through the loosely woven draperies, the north end of Lincoln Park was visible, and beyond that, Lake Michigan. A bit more interesting than Toni's view of the street, Melanie thought but refrained from pointing it out.

"I haven't gotten too much furniture yet," Melanie said instead. "I hate the carpeting and I'm waiting until the new one is put down before I get too much stuff in here."

"Your sofa is gorgeous," Toni admitted and sat down. She ran her hand over the plush fabric. "It must have been expensive."

Melanie just shrugged, playing absently with her new gold bracelet. Anything really good was expensive, but some things were worth the extra money. Guy would certainly agree with that after last night. "Hey, you can get all sorts of furniture from these rental places. They even had a grand piano, and a marble-topped bar."

"But they're not coming until after the new rug, right?"

"Sure," Melanie teased, and rose gracefully to her feet. "Why don't I get us each a Coke while you look around at the rest of the place?"

Toni nodded and went down the short hallway to the bedroom. Melanie loved that room the best, with its wall of mirrors opposite the same spectacular view as the living room. She had wanted to get a circular bed with a white fur bedspread, but she hadn't been able to find one to rent. While she mulled over the possibility of actually buying it, she had settled for a regular king-sized one.

Melanie poured the soda into glasses and brought them back into the living room just as Toni returned. A frown was on her sister's face.

"How can you possibly afford a place like this?" Toni asked, taking one glass from Melanie. "Your job at Mid-America could barely support you as Rosie's roommate."

"I got promoted," Melanie said lightly. She took a drink of the Coke and then sat down again. "They liked my work."

Toni's frown did not disappear. "So what's your new position? Chairman of the board?"

Melanie was looking forward to telling Toni the truth about her new job. Her sister would be so shocked to learn that she did nothing more than sign a time card to earn her paycheck. Would she insist that Melanie quit and go out and get a "proper" job? Melanie decided to prolong the fun with vague hints. "No, I'm in sales now."

"Oh, really?" Obviously impressed, Toni joined her sister on the sofa. "Then I guess congratulations are in order. I know you weren't too crazy about that other job, so I hope this one works out better."

"I'm sure it will," Melanie agreed with confidence. "It's something I'm perfectly suited for."

Toni looked puzzled, but settled more comfortably on the sofa. "So when do you start your new job? Do you have to take any special training?"

Melanie laughed and shook her head. "Good Lord, no. I know everything I need to." Guy was constantly amazed at her expertise.

Toni pondered that silently for a moment, staring down

into her glass. "Melanie, I'm really happy that things are starting to go well for you, but are you sure this new job is one you can handle? You've only got a high school diploma, and selling cosmetics isn't exactly the same as being in sales for a large company."

Melanie's deep laughter only increased the puzzled look on Toni's face. "Lord, Toni, what's wrong? Are you afraid that the duties will be more than I can handle?"

"Well, they might be," she pointed out.

Melanie finished her drink and put the glass down on the floor near the corner of the sofa. She could not keep the amused gleam from her eyes. "Toni, all I have to do is sign a time card and turn it in. I don't really think that's too difficult for even little old me."

"Just sign a time card?" Toni asked. "What kind of sales job is that?"

"The same kind that a lot of guys have around there." Melanie shrugged.

"It sounds pretty strange to me. How can it pay enough to rent an apartment like this?"

"Who said the rent comes from that measly salary?" Melanie shook her head so that her hair fell back from her shoulders. "This is a company apartment. Mid-America's paying the rent, not me. Lord, even with the better job, I'm barely getting enough to buy my clothes. If it wasn't for the expense account, I'd still be at Rosie's."

Toni looked stunned as she shook her head. "You get all that for just signing a time card? What kind of sales department is Jon running?"

"I never mentioned Jon, did I?" Melanie asked as she rose to her feet. She stretched her arms above her head, then picked up her empty glass. "I don't know about you, but I'd like something a little stronger."

Toni followed her into the kitchen. "If you're not working for Jon, who are you working for? He's the director of marketing."

Melanie poured herself another glass of Coke and then added a hefty shot of rum. She looked questioningly at Toni, who just shook her head. "I'm part of a special group of salesmen. We report right to Mr. Ramsey." She put the bottles away and went back into the living room.

"Guy? You had better be careful with him." The alarm in Toni's manner made Melanie smile. "I wouldn't trust him with my garbage." When Melanie said nothing, Toni became more insistent. "I mean it, Mel. If he's your new boss, your job sounds pretty precarious to me."

"And yours wasn't?" Melanie's voice was gently sarcastic as she sat down, folding her blue-jeans-clad legs beneath her.

Toni had stopped just inside the doorway and was frowning. "How did you know about that?"

Melanie just shrugged, taking a long drink of her rum and Coke. "Hey, our jobs were basically the same. As long as Guy stayed happy, we were fine. You made the mistake of forgetting that, and he removed you. I won't be that careless."

Toni took another glance around the apartment. She appeared to find new meaning in the expensive surroundings, and Melanie's smile grew. "Melanie, be careful," she warned. "What do you think will happen to this great new job when Mr. Morici finds out? How will Guy take care of you then?"

"You really know nothing about that place, do you?" Melanie scoffed. "Old Morici can't do a thing. Guy runs it. Him and some mysterious partners that give him his orders. Morici's just a figurehead, and he won't even be that much longer. Guy's getting him out."

"My Lord, did Guy tell you that?" Toni said in a voice quiet with worry. "Mel, you've got to be careful. He's nobody to fool around with."

Melanie's laughter filled the room. "Fool around?" she teased. "I haven't heard that since I was in seventh grade."

Toni took a step closer to the sofa. "Melanie, listen to me—" She was interrupted by the sound of Melanie's doorbell.

"Must be the bossman," Melanie said lightly, and rose to her feet. "He said he would come by if he could get around to it. Maybe you'd better slip out the back door. I haven't broken the news to him about my various relatives yet."

Toni picked up her glass and carried it with her, depositing it in the sink. "I don't think I ever would, if I were you."

Melanie just smiled as she walked over to the intercom. The buzzer rang again impatiently. "Say hello to Mom for me when you go down this weekend. I told her I couldn't make the wedding because of the pressures of work." As she pressed the button to let Guy in, she heard the back door close behind Toni.

Toni put her suitcase into the car and glanced around her. Nothing looked out of the ordinary. A few people were running in the park, and some others were walking along the sidewalks. No one looked at all suspicious, yet she could not rid herself of the vague feeling that she was being watched.

It was because of those damn phone calls earlier in the week, she told herself as she got into her car. The threats had unnerved her and hiring an answering service was not going to change that immediately. Right now, her imagination was working overtime: seeing strangers lurking in doorways and hearing footsteps that echoed hers. In a few days, she would relax.

Driving south on Lake Shore Drive to the Dan Ryan Expressway, Toni hummed along with the radio. She tried to force her thoughts to the upcoming weekend and her mother's wedding, but they kept wandering. If it wasn't the phone call, then it was Melanie's situation. The traffic was just too light to be distracting. By the time she reached the Indiana border, she was certain of two things: that she was right to leave town for the weekend and that she should have stayed to talk some sense into Melanie's head.

What could Melanie be thinking of? Toni wondered. Obviously she did not share Toni's personal distaste for Guy, but couldn't she sense his underlying violence? That type of relationship was precarious regardless of the man involved, but with him, it would be even worse. He was so egotistical and hated to be crossed. Toni had seen that for herself the few times they had had to work together and could not imagine what it would be like to be with him for longer stretches. Melanie would have to be very astute to read his moods quickly and accurately, but even if she did, what would she get out of such a relationship?

To Toni's way of thinking, there were no pluses to Melanie's arrangement, but her sister obviously did not agree with her. What could she be hoping to gain? Advancement in her career? Hardly, Toni thought with a wry smile. At least not according to her definition of career. But Melanie did not share her goals, she knew that. Working hard for a sense of achievement had never been one of Melanie's fondest dreams. Did she see Guy as her ticket to gaining wealth without the work?

Certainly Melanie was not the first person to think of such a scheme, but its lack of originality was not what bothered Toni. It was more the feeling that her sister was in way over her head. Although Melanie might be very experienced in certain areas, Guy was not the typical man that Melanie was used to in Niles and South Bend. He was not going to be manipulated as easily as others might have been.

Toni bit her lip thoughtfully as she passed a tollway oasis. She readily admitted that she could not prostitute herself as Melanie was, and that the idea of being Guy's mistress assaulted her senses in every way. Putting both those issues aside, though, there was still something nagging at her. Where was all this money coming from? How could a controller in a small firm have the money to live as Guy did? His clothes were expensive and so was his car. He had a house and a family out in the western suburbs somewhere, so how did he have money to throw away on Melanie?

The statements Melanie had made about Mid-America bothered Toni also. What was this special force of salesmen who did no work? And why did they report to the controller instead of the sales manager? Then there was that apartment. She didn't doubt that Mid-America was paying the rent, but she'd bet that Melanie and Guy were the only ones that ever used it. How did Guy have the power to dole out such favors?

He could do it if Melanie's assertion was right, Toni thought suddenly, and Guy and some partners ran the company, not Sam. She had no trouble believing that either. Not from the things she had seen or from what Jon had told her. Guy certainly acted like he was in control. Where did that leave Sam, though? And Jon?

Something very strange was going on there. First it was the inflated accounts payable that she had found and now it was an inflated sales staff. Why in the world would anyone want to make their company look substantially larger than it was? That sounded like an expensive ego trip. The whole affair left a bad taste in her mouth. Even though she had been taken off Mid-America's account, she sensed her involvement in it was not over.

She was relieved to see the South Bend exit appear. At least for this weekend, she could relax and forget about everything.

"I can't believe you're actually selling the house," Toni sighed. She looked around the bedroom that had been hers since she was four. Her mother had broken the news to her as they had been driving back to the house after the wedding.

"What's the point of keeping it?" her mother said with a shrug. She stopped behind Toni in the narrow hallway and glanced into the room. "Mickey's house is big enough for the two of us, bigger than this place, actually. And there's room for you when you come for a visit, too."

Toni nodded, unable to explain to her mother that she wasn't worried about having a place to sleep if and when she wanted to come to Niles. It was losing that last link with the security of childhood that made her sad. "What shall I do with all the stuff once I have it packed up?"

"Oh, just leave it in the room. Mickey'll bring everything over to his place." She laughed quickly and twisted the new gold band on her left hand. "I mean, our place. We'll just keep it in the attic there."

"Okay," Toni said, and walked over to the dresser. She opened the small cedar box filled with old ticket stubs and dance programs. "I imagine I'll need more garbage bags than packing boxes, though."

"Hey, what're you girls doing? Gonna gab all afternoon?" Mickey's heavy walk could be heard coming toward the room, and then he appeared in the doorway.

"Is it time to go already?" Flo glanced at her watch in surprise.

"Naw, it's not even five yet," Mickey laughed. "I'm not gonna let us be late for our own dinner party. I just thought I'd see if I could get a beer while we wait."

"I think there's still a couple left in the icebox," Flo said. She squeezed past his large form and disappeared down the hall.

Why anybody'd want a beer before they went out to dinner was beyond Toni. She closed the box on her dresser and walked over to the bookshelves under the window. The

Anne of Green Gables stories and a few Nancy Drew mysteries were mixed in among college texts and high school yearbooks.

"Your mom was glad ya came down for the wedding," Mickey said. He took a few steps into the room and sat down with a sigh on the edge of the bed. "Made it more special, you know."

Special was not the word Toni would have used to describe the ten-minute ceremony in the minister's office. Depressing was more like it. Weddings were supposed to be romantic, love-filled occasions. This one reminded her of a bowling banquet. There was no music, no bouquets of flowers, and no starry-eyed lovers. Was she the only one who had thought something was missing?

Mickey had been in a navy blue suit that looked too small for him. Her mother had worn the same tan knitted pants suit, floral print overblouse, and tan vest that she had worn when Toni had taken her out to dinner for her birthday last May. The only festive touches were the carnation boutonniere and the orchid corsage.

Besides herself, there had been three friends of Mickey and two of her mother. They had met in the church parking lot and gone into the parsonage together. In fifteen minutes, they were back in their cars. It took longer to apply for a charge account.

"What happened to Melanie?"

Toni looked up at Mickey. What could he have possibly heard about her?

"I thought she'd be comin' with you," he went on. "It ain't like she moved across the country or nothin'."

Toni shrugged uneasily and sat down in the ruffled chair in the corner. "I talked to her last night, but she told me she couldn't get away. Said she had to work."

"Musta had some guy nipping at the bait," he said in disgust, and then shrugged at Toni's surprise. "Hey, I ain't blind. I can see her for the little bitch she is. Wouldn't say nothin' like that to your mom, but you've gotta know what she's like."

"Well, yes," Toni agreed reluctantly. "Was Mom upset that she wasn't coming?"

Mickey shook his head and rose to his feet as they heard Flo coming down the hall. "She didn't say much about it," he said quietly.

Flo came into the room with a smile. "Better make this last. It's the only beer in the house."

Mickey took it from her, putting the glass on Toni's old dresser while he opened the can. "I'll nurse it through the end of the ball game; then we're gonna have to leave for the restaurant."

Flo watched him leave the room, then sat down on the bed where he had been. "Are you sure you want to stay here by yourself tonight? There's plenty of room for you at the other house."

"No, this'll be fine, Mom," Toni assured her. "I can get started cleaning out this room. Besides, you'll be on your honeymoon. What would you want me around for?" Toni meant her remark to be teasing, but her mother frowned.

"It's not like that," she said.

Toni was tempted to pretend to misunderstand, but didn't. "Then why did you marry him? If you don't love him, how can this marriage be any different from your others?"

Her mother sighed impatiently and rose to her feet. "Sometimes, I can't believe how young you are," she said, and smoothed out the wrinkles in the bedspread. "Are you still waiting for your knight in shining armor to rescue you?"

"I don't need to be rescued from anything," Toni told her with a frown.

"But you still believe in love?"

"Don't you?"

Flo laughed bitterly. "Sure. I love the idea of never going to that damn diner again. I love the idea of having someone else to bring in the garbage cans. And I love the idea of not waking up alone in the middle of the night."

"Mom," Toni said impatiently.

"You and your knights," Flo scoffed. "Who do you think would end up polishing all that armor and cleaning up after the horse? Grow up, Toni. You can be happy settling for somebody real ordinary."

"Mom, I really wasn't criticizing. I just want things to work out for you, that's all."

"Hey, gals. We got to get going," Mickey called from the other room. "I need another beer."

"He ain't as handsome as your dad," Flo said as Toni got to her feet. "But then, he don't get mad and hit me either, or run after girls like Melanie's father did. When you get to my age, you're willing to settle for a lot less."

Toni followed her mother out the door and down the hallway to where Mickey was waiting for them. Why was it no one seemed to believe in love anymore? she wondered sadly. Melanie was only out for money, and her mother wanted someone to take care of the garbage. And Mickey, what did he want from the marriage? Toni watched as he hitched up his trousers and then straightened his tie in the mirror over the television. Was he just looking for a housekeeper?

"I thought we'd all go in one car," he told Toni as she and her mother picked up their purses. "Then we'll drop you off here on our way back to the house."

Toni caught her mother's anxious glance and smiled easily at Mickey. "That sounds fine," she said.

As they walked out to his Oldsmobile, Toni tried to imagine Jon in twenty or thirty years and saw a vague picture of Sam in her mind. Jon's father must have been enthusiastic about his company when he started it, yet now he seemed resigned to having Guy run things. Were dreams something only the young believed in?

She got in the back seat of the car and stared out the window. Mickey had some baseball game on the radio, so no one spoke, but it hardly mattered to her. She was so depressed that even the wittiest conversation would probably leave her in tears. She must be getting horny, she decided as they pulled into a parking lot. Jon had better get back from Wisconsin soon or she was going to have to go up there.

The restaurant where her mother and Mickey were throwing the small dinner party turned out to be the local American Legion Hall. "They've got a great buffet on Saturday nights," Mickey told Toni. "All ya can eat for four ninety-eight plus a band."

Toni said nothing, but Mickey didn't seem to expect an answer as he called hello to another couple getting out of a car a few spaces down from them. Together the five of them went into the hall and found that several more of the guests had already arrived. They were gathered at the bar off to the right of the door, and shouted out greetings to the newcomers.

"Well, me and the missus are here. Let's get this party rolling," Mickey laughed back, taking Flo's arm and leading her into the bar. "Ain't nobody allowed to drink more beer than me tonight."

Toni tried to stay in the background, smiling vaguely at the guests, but Mickey was not going to allow it. Once he had a beer in his hand and Flo was settled with some of her waitress buddies, he took Toni away from the older couple she had been chatting with.

"Got a surprise for you," Mickey said with a grin. He led her over to a group of men sharing a table, and a plump blonde man with greasy-looking hair rose to his feet. "This here is Bob Blumer. You remember, I told you about him."

Toni didn't remember, but stuck her hand out politely. "Hi, Bob."

"Hey, in this here town we kiss pretty ladies," he said, and leaned forward to kiss her on the lips. The other men laughed heartily.

"Ain't he the fast one?" Mickey roared, and thumped him on the back proudly. "Sure don't waste time."

No one seemed to notice that Toni did not join in the laughter. She wasn't averse to kisses from strangers, but she liked to have a choice in the matter. Besides, this one stank of cigarette smoke, whiskey, and sour milk. Suddenly, she remembered Bob. He was one of the men Mickey had offered her in August. Maybe she should have brought Jon along to dispel Mickey's obsession with finding her a man.

"So grab a seat," Bob offered graciously after Mickey moved back to his other friends. He pulled a chair over from a neighboring table. She didn't see any easy way of getting rid of Bob, so she sat down. She'd been stuck with jerks for a few hours before and survived. She could do so again.

"Let me buy you a drink," he offered.

"Thanks, I've got one," she pointed out, holding up her highball. The other men drifted back to their own conversations, leaving her feeling like she was alone with Bob. Her smile was stiff as she took a sip of her drink.

"So Mickey tells me you do bookkeeping," Bob said, sliding his arm over the back of her chair.

"I'm a CPA."

"Hey, I knew a guy who was one of them. He did taxes for people and that kind of thing. Can you do taxes?"

"Oh, yes. Both the long and short form," she murmured.

He whistled in surprise. "Hey, that's real good."

Toni quickly took a swallow of her drink to force down the need to laugh. Jon would never believe this conversation when she told him.

Bob's arm moved slightly so that it was on her shoulders. "Must get awful lonesome there in the big city by yourself. Me, I tried living in Detroit once, but I couldn't take it. I need room around me. A house with a little garden, and my family."

Toni turned in her chair so that his arm fell away from her. "I have a lot of friends and a huge park right across the street from me."

"But it ain't the same," he said. "A woman especially needs to have her own place."

"Oh?"

"It's the same with this dog I bought," he went on, looking pleased that she was listening so avidly to his words. "I'm gonna let her have a litter of puppies before I get her fixed, 'cause otherwise, she wouldn't never be normal."

"She'd never be normal?"

"Sure," he said with a nod. "Any female's got to have kids or they ain't gonna be happy. You'd see it too, if you was to give your job back to the man you took it from and got yourself a family."

"No, thanks," Toni said, rising to her feet. "I'm not in the mood to trade in my career for an ironing board."

"Go ahead and be snippy," he said, shrugging. "But you ain't gonna get too many offers at your age."

Toni walked away from the table as Mickey finished talking to the maitre d'. "Our tables're ready," he called out to the group, then spotted Toni without Bob. "Say, whatcha doing alone? How are you and Bob hitting it off?"

"Not too well," she admitted. "I refused to quit my job to start having babies."

"Oh, no! Is he on that kick again?" Mickey sounded disgusted, much to her surprise. "I told him a hundred times that you could get a real good job here in Niles. Hell, he can't even support the brats he's got now, and he's talking about more. You were right not to hang around him if he's that stupid. Next time you visit, I'll do better, I promise. I'll get Jeff Hester to come around."

Toni smiled vaguely at him. Would he be as solicitous about her mother's wishes? Toni hoped so.

# CHAPTER TWENTY-ONE

Someone was following her. Toni had suspected it often during the past week since she had returned from Niles, but she was sure of it this time. She could sense his presence although no one looked suspicious when she glanced around her.

Why had she come out after dark? she scolded herself. As paranoid as she felt lately, she should have stayed safely locked up in her apartment, bolts bolted, and had a sandwich for her dinner. It was stupid to have gone grocery shopping at eight o'clock on a Friday evening even if the store was only four blocks from her apartment.

Clutching the grocery bag tightly to her chest, she began to walk faster. She was being silly, she thought. The sun might have already set, but it was hardly dark. Not with the streetlights, shop lights, and car headlights. And there were a lot of people around. The date crowd had already emerged to mingle with a number of neighborhood shoppers like herself. She was perfectly safe.

The more she assured herself she was safe, the faster her feet moved. Why hadn't she just stayed in her apartment and waited for Jon's call?

Toni turned the corner at Dickens Street and found herself virtually alone. It was darker, too, but she was almost home and felt some of the tensions ease. She was tired, that was all, and had an imagination that liked to work overtime. With the way things had been going at work for the past week and a half, it was only natural that she should feel slightly threatened.

Toni was halfway down the block when she glanced behind her and saw that a man had turned the corner also. Her hands started to sweat and there was an empty feeling in the pit of her stomach. Maybe it was just someone who lived in her building, she tried to reason with herself. She'd look like a fool if she ran away from a neighbor. Refusing to turn around again, she glanced instead up to her right. The light was on in her kitchen; the security of her apartment was close at hand. She held her breath as a movement caught her eye. Was it just her imagination or was the man getting closer?

Still a short way from the corner of Lincoln Park West, Toni took advantage of a break in the traffic and crossed the street. When the man behind her did the same, she thought her heart would stop. Lord! He really was following her!

It was impossible to run with a full bag of groceries in her arms and in the low heels that she always wore to work. Besides, what good would running do? Her pursuer had nothing in his arms to slow him down. He could keep up with her easily.

If she could just reach the corner, she thought, she'd be fine. Once out of his sight, she could make a mad dash down the half block to her apartment entrance. Her hopes rose as she got closer and closer to Lincoln Park West. Just another storefront to pass and she'd be safe. Just a few more yards.

She glanced behind her to find that the man had also increased his pace. The half block that had separated them was now no more than ten feet and getting less with each step. What could he want? she wondered, her mouth suddenly dry with fear. Was he a purse snatcher? The ugly words from those phone calls came back to her. Oh God! Was this her caller? Had he gotten angry that she had hired an answering service and come after her in person?

Stifling the scream that was rising in her throat, Toni raced for the corner. She did not care if the man was merely out for a stroll and thought she was an idiot. She was terrified and not about to wait around to get mugged, or worse.

In just a few steps Toni was at the corner. As she turned, though, she glanced over her shoulder to see where the man was and collided with someone coming toward her. The impact knocked the breath from her for a moment, and, as someone grabbed her arms to steady her, a tremor of fear flashed through her.

"Sorry!" a familiar voice laughed. "You okay?"

Toni glanced up quickly, certain that her imagination must be playing tricks on her. But even in the dim light she could recognize his features. "Jon! What are you doing here?"

He seemed as surprised as she was. "Wondering where you were, actually," he admitted. His hands were still on her arms, and he felt her slight trembling. "Are you okay?" he repeated, frowning down at her.

"Sure," she laughed, and glanced around her. The man who had been following her was nowhere in sight. She felt rather foolish and glanced down into her grocery bag. "I hope you didn't break the eggs. I know you enjoy knocking people down, but—"

Ignoring the bag of food in her arms, he pulled her closer to him and touched his lips to hers. His mouth was tender and loving, and awoke a flood of remembered passion. Her breath became unsteady as his tongue teased her lips, tormenting their softness as it slid along her mouth.

The grocery bag in her arms was forgotten until the smell of fresh bread and peaches came wafting up to mix with the scent of Jon's aftershave. Toni pulled away regretfully and stared down into the bag. "I love you dearly," she sighed. "But you aren't too good for my bread."

Jon just grinned and took the bag from her. He carried it with one arm and put the other one around her shoulders. They started toward her apartment building. "So tell me, why were you out grocery shopping when I was coming to see you?"

"How was I supposed to know that? You told me last night you wouldn't be able to make it down this weekend."

"Well, I changed my mind." He opened the door to her building and followed her in. "Do you know how frustrating it is to be missing you desperately, needing to hear the sound of your voice, and then get that damn answering service? Why didn't you just change your phone number?"

They got into the elevator and Toni pushed the button for her floor. He had his arm around her, and she leaned comfortably against him. She felt so safe suddenly. Even the terror she had just experienced on the street had receded into a bad dream. "It seemed easier this way. I didn't have to contact everyone who had reason to have my number and give them the new one. Besides, my friend might have had access to the new number, too."

The elevator stopped and they got out. "Well, you should let me start answering your phone then. I'd like a chance at that guy," Jon said.

Toni got her key out of her pocket. "You weren't here, remember?" She unlocked her door and pushed it open. "Besides, I'm a big girl. I'm supposed to handle my own problems."

Jon gave her a strange look and then went past her with the groceries. "I assume you want these in the kitchen?"

"No, the bedroom," she laughed, and took her key from the lock.

"Fine with me," he called over his shoulder, but went toward the kitchen anyway.

Toni had a smile on her face as she pushed the door closed. How good it was to have him back home!

The smile died as she noticed a piece of paper lying on the floor near the door. She glanced back over her shoulder. Seeing that Jon was not watching, she bent down quickly and grabbed the paper. Her hand was trembling as it crushed the paper into a ball, not even bothering to unfold it.

"I'll have you know that I even—" Jon stopped with a frown as Toni spun around to face him. "What's wrong?"

"Nothing," she lied. A smile was forced on her face as her hand slipped casually into her pocket, leaving the crumpled paper hidden there. She crossed the small space between them and put her arms around his neck as she stood on her tiptoes to kiss him. "Do you have any idea how much I missed you?"

"I can prove how much I missed you," he teased. His hands slid under the jacket of her blue twill suit and softly caressed her back.

"Oh?"

He leaned over to kiss the side of her neck. Gently. With whispery light touches. "I put your ice cream in the freezer and your milk and yogurt in the frig. Your groceries don't need you as much as I do."

Toni laughed. The note in her pocket was forgotten as her hands pulled at his shirt. It came out of his jeans and she quickly unbuttoned it, sliding her hands over the rough hair of his chest. "Are you suggesting I should delay putting my groceries away?"

"You're so clever," he whispered.

Suddenly the time for joking was gone. Their need for each other was too intense to be postponed any longer. Jon's hands slipped underneath her blouse and loosened her bra, fondling and caressing her breasts with the urgency of his passion. The sensitive tips seemed starved for his touch and her body moved in a sensuous rhythm with his caress.

Their mouths met in a blinding hunger. They drank the sweetness of each other's lips and tasted desire in the movement of their fingers.

Toni's jacket was on the floor and then was joined by the pins that held her hair up. Jon's shirt was next as she pushed it from his shoulders. She wanted to feel him close to her, closer than their clothes would allow.

"I've never made love in the foyer before," she teased gently. Her lips left a moist trail across his chest and her hands roamed over his flat stomach.

"Let's not try it then," he said.

Toni's hands stopped their explorations in surprise, but Jon just laughed as he swung her up in his arms. "I have missed you like I never would have believed," he told her. "I knew I loved you, but, God! I never thought love could hurt so much!"

Toni slid her arms around his neck and laid her head on his shoulder.

"For the last ten days, I have thought of this night," Jon went on, seemingly oblivious to the tiny kisses Toni was scattering across his neck and face. "And I don't plan to spend it on a cold, hard floor."

"As long as you spend it here with me," she sighed, reaching around him to flick on her bedroom light.

Jon laid her gently on the bed. The satin quilt felt cool against her love-fevered skin, and the smoothness of the fabric only deepened her need to feel his body against hers.

Slowly Jon began to unbutton her blouse. His lips were on hers, then on her neck, and then seeking the valley between her breasts. Lower and lower his kisses went as each button was released.

When the blouse was finally out of his way, he began a painstaking removal of her bra. His mouth sought the rosy tips of her breasts, his tongue teasing them until they were hard. As her longing for him grew, so did her impatience. She tried to help him pull off her skirt, but he stopped her.

"I've been dreaming of this night for days. I longed to touch every inch of you and now I'm going to do it."

Toni bit back her frustration and began her own exploration of his body. His back was tight and firm with ripples of muscles that seemed to dance under her fingertips. His chest was covered with coarse, dark hair. They tickled her lips, yet felt soft beneath her hands.

She loosened his belt and let her hands slide lower down his back. "I think we should give up business trips," she murmured.

"Sounds good to me." His voice was muffled for he was busy elsewhere. Her skirt and her stockings had finally come off, and his lips seemed determined to taste every inch of her. "I think we should ban business altogether," he added after a moment, "and just stay here forever."

Toni sighed with deepening pleasure. His hands, his mouth, his whole body was becoming part of hers. How did she ever think she could manage away from him? she wondered briefly before she gave in to the delight of their love.

"Are you sure you don't want to go out to eat?" Jon called to Toni as he pulled his jeans on.

She came out of the bathroom wearing her white batiste nightshirt and brushing her hair as she spoke. "Don't be silly. You're probably sick of restaurant food after being gone for ten days. Besides," she said, and glanced down at the revealing nightshirt with its deep V neckline, "I'm not exactly dressed for a night on the town."

"Oh, I don't know about that," Jon teased.

She made a face and put the brush down on her dresser. "I'll make the French toast. You can set the table," she informed him, leaving the room.

It was amazing how everything seemed terrific when Jon was around, Toni thought. She walked across the living room and into the kitchen, the tile floor cool to her bare feet. She took some eggs and milk from the refrigerator. The bread was still in the grocery bag on the counter along with a bag of peaches and a box of cornflakes. So she emptied that next, folding up the bag and slipping it into the space next to the dishwasher. Even the mess at work seemed manageable with Jon behind her.

She broke a couple of eggs into a mixing bowl and beat them. For the past week, she had moped about feeling defeated and persecuted, but no more. She would turn the sow's ear of her new job into a silk purse. Simon wanted new business, so she would get him new business. More new clients than her team could handle. He'd see that the mess at Mid-America was none of her doing.

She might even find that Guy had done her a favor. Working with all those pots-and-pans accounts was a little like being responsible for one of the eighteen wheels on a trailer truck: she could do a good, competent job for years and not get noticed. Now, suddenly, she had been switched to a unicycle. Others might shun the limelight for fear of falling, but she didn't. This was her chance to be the star. When she brought in new client after new client, the partners could not help but see how talented she was. She might even get that partnership earlier than she had hoped.

Her life was back on the right track again, she thought as she heard Jon coming across the living room. Looking toward the door with a smile, she wondered how he'd feel about some wine with his French toast. She was in a mood to celebrate.

"What's this?" Jon stopped in the doorway with a crumpled paper in one hand, his shirt and her jacket in the other.

Toni recognized the note she had found slipped under her door, but she didn't really want to talk about it. She was in a good mood, optimistic once again, and that would just spoil it. "It's just some prankster," she said with a shrug, and opened the milk carton.

"A prank!" he cried. "I read the filth in here and it doesn't sound like some prank to me."

She said nothing as she poured some milk into the eggs.

"This isn't the first one, is it?" he asked suspiciously.

Toni glanced up at him. His dark eyes were flashing with anger and the hand holding the note was trembling. It did not seem likely that she would be able to brush his concern aside. "No," she admitted. "That's the third."

"The third!" He was furious. "Why didn't you tell me?"

She sighed and put the milk carton back in the refrigerator. "What was the point? You weren't here, so what could you do about them? The police can't even do anything."

"At least you had the sense to call them," he muttered, and tossed their clothes onto the dining room chair behind him. "Have they questioned people in the building? That lobby attendant?"

"I don't know who they questioned, if anybody. Obscene notes get only slightly more attention than obscene phone calls," she pointed out impatiently. "It's only on television that they have the time and manpower to trace paper types and kinds of ink." She opened the package of bread and took out several slices. "I was advised to keep my door locked and stay inside after dark."

As soon as she said the last phrase, she regretted it. Jon jumped on it, just as she had known he would.

"Then what were you doing out tonight?"

Toni turned away from him, taking out the frying pan. "For God's sake! I needed groceries, so I went to get some. Is that such a crime?" She was irritable with him although she knew she shouldn't be. He loved her and was worried. That should make her relieved, but instead it angered her. She had put away her fears and he was bringing them all back. "I can't stay locked up here for the rest of my life, you know."

"Of course not. It's just that there's so damn many weirdos out there." She could sense his agitation as he walked toward her and put his hand on her arm, turning her to face him. "Toni, let's stop all this nonsense and get married."

"Married?" Toni was stunned. "Because I've been getting obscene phone calls?"

"Don't be dumb. We love each other, you know that." He frowned at her. "I've wanted to marry you for a while now. The reason I never mentioned it was your damn independence, but that seems a little silly under these circumstances."

"Oh, does it?"

"For God's sake, Toni, don't get mad," he said. His voice had lost its belligerence. "I've thought it all out. Maybe this isn't the perfect time or the most romantic way, but I really do want to marry you."

His manner had become so loving and gentle that Toni

sighed, the tensions and anger melting from her as she leaned forward into his arms.

He went on, looking down tenderly at her. "I got the idea earlier this week when I found out about the obscene calls. I was so worried about you, alone here in this damn neighborhood. The target for any nut who came along."

"Now, wait a minute," she argued, lifting her head from his chest.

He leaned down to silence her with a kiss. "Appleton is such a nice little town. Quiet, with pretty houses and yards. It seemed like the perfect place."

Some of Toni's tensions returned as she listened to him speak, but she said nothing.

"I know that Dad's not ready to retire, but I could take over that paper plant once he buys it. The renovations I'm suggesting would take a while to finish, and even once they're done, we could stay on. It'd be a great place to live."

"Appleton, Wisconsin?" she asked quietly as she moved away from him.

"Yes." He nodded.

"What I am supposed to do in Appleton, Wisconsin? We don't have a branch office there."

He frowned. "Hey, they've treated you like dirt there. What the hell are you worrying about them for? Just cut your losses and leave."

She could not believe her ears. "After all the years that I've put in, after all my hard work, you expect me just to quit?" He sighed, and she could see that he was losing patience with her. Not that she cared, for she had already lost patience with him.

"Did all those years of hard work mean anything when Guy complained about you?" Jon asked.

"That's not the issue," she argued. "I want to know what you expect me to do up there in Appleton while you run your paper plant. Iron your shirts and have babies?"

Her anger seemed to infect him also. "And what's wrong with that? Why not take advantage of the year or two we'd be up there to start a family?"

"And then what? After that time I can just come back and expect that they've held my job open for me?"

"Your job?" he cried. "Why the hell is that job so important to you? Guy's done us a favor getting you demoted.

He's given us the perfect chance to leave. To start a good life up there. We'd be safe from all the nuts that roam these streets. Why won't you see that?"

"See that I should be grateful to Guy?" She laughed bitterly. "Don't you mean grateful to you?" Suddenly a lot of things seemed clear. "You were in on this whole thing, weren't you? You knew that Guy wanted me out, and decided to use it to force me to marry you."

"Toni, you're not making any sense." His voice was weary. "I love you."

She was too angry to listen or even think. "This whole time I was blaming Guy and those damn discrepancies. I was so sure that he and your father were up to no good with those secret partners and that special sales force that did no work. And the accounts payable with all those inflated bills. They were all distractions, though. You were the one that wanted me out so that you could convince me to marry you."

"What are you talking about?"

"You must have known that I wouldn't just dump my career easily, and thought you'd give me the perfect reason—"

Jon grabbed hold of her shoulders and shook her. "What are you talking about? Secret partners? My father owns the whole company."

She pulled away from his hands and walked to the other side of the kitchen. "Sure he does. Just like he runs the place. Just like all those extra salesmen who do nothing but sign a time card to get paid. Hey, I know about that place. The only reason Ramsey got me out was because they're up to their necks in something crooked and I was getting too suspicious. I started tracking down some of those bills that didn't match."

"Just what are you saying?" he asked, his voice frozen and forbidding. "Are you saying my father is involved in something illegal?"

"They got rid of me before I got the proof, remember?" she said. "But I know the reason that extra money's added to the accounts isn't because he's Santa Claus."

"How can you say these things about my father?"

"How?" she repeated in surprise. "I was the accountant, my sister's shacked up in some company apartment, screwing the controller, and you want to know how I know things? I'd like to know how come you don't know them."

Jon just stared at her silently for a long moment; then he turned to pick up his shirt. "I can't believe that you would stoop that low," he said softly as he put his shirt on. "Just because you had a run of bad luck and got demoted, that's no reason to start throwing mud around on my family."

"The mud was there," she snapped. "I can't help it if you were too blind to see it."

Without buttoning the shirt, he stuffed it into his pants. "Good-bye, Toni." His voice was quiet as he turned aside. "I don't think there's anything left to say."

She watched as he walked through the living room and out the door. It was only after he was gone that she realized she was crying.

Jon poured himself a stiff measure of whiskey and drank it down quickly, not even bothering to move away from the small bar cabinet. He should have known better than to get involved with that dame, he told himself. She had been strange the first time they went out, and he should have seen what she was like.

He poured himself another glass and carried it over to his sofa. It was dark in the room; the only light was coming in from the kitchen, but he did not move to turn on the lamp next to him. If he lit it, he might see his reflection in the glass-covered paintings on the opposite wall, and that was one sight he would like to avoid. He had no desire to look at such a fool.

Damn! He put his glass down on the table next to him and leaned forward, burying his face in his hands. To think he had wanted to marry her! To think he had let himself fall in love with her! He was a first-class idiot. A-number-1. He ought to win some sort of prize for self-delusion.

He got to his feet, too restless to sit still, and wandered over to the sliding glass doors. They were open, letting in the cool night air and the sounds of traffic that never ceased along Clark Street.

In all honesty, he could not blame Toni. She never pretended that she was anything but a businesswoman. A professional. Dedicated to her career above all else. She might even have loved him, as much as she was able to love anyone. But it wasn't the same kind of love that he felt. Her avoidance of commitment should have warned him of that.

He turned around to face the room. The digital clock on the stereo said it was 10:32. He had been back in town less than two hours and was already thoroughly disillusioned. He wished he had stayed up in Appleton, safe with his dreams.

Jon walked back to the table and picked up his drink. It was Toni's attack on his father that bothered him the most, awakening protective feelings toward the older man. He might not have been the perfect father, but he tried. He worked damn hard to send him to the best schools and then to Europe. He was so proud of that company, and Jon could not remember how many times he had said that it would all be Jon's one day. Toni's statements were ridiculous.

Jon glanced at the clock again. It wasn't all that late, really. Maybe he'd give his father a call. Tell him he had driven down and make plans to spend the day up at his parents' house tomorrow. A whole day together was something they had not had for a long time.

Jon went to the kitchen and dialed the number. His father answered almost immediately, and seemed surprised that Jon was back home.

"Finished up already?" Sam asked.

"Just taking a break," Jon laughed. "Say, what have you got planned for tomorrow? I thought I could come up and fill you in on some of the details of the plant. Maybe we could even get in a round of golf."

"Sounds great to me. Your mother'll be glad to see you too. You'd think that cat of yours was her son, the way she's been spoiling it while you've been away. If you come up, it'll give the poor thing a chance to rest."

Jon laughed. "Spike probably loves it. He may not want to come home to me again." Jon was silent for a moment, Toni's words rankling in his mind. He had to know. He had to hear his father deny them. "You know, Dad, I really think that paper plant is going to be a terrific move. I think we should go ahead and buy it before someone else does. I've brought some papers home with me and I think you should sign them."

"Well, you made your mind up pretty quick," Sam teased. "I'll give you your chance tomorrow to convince me."

Something egged Jon on further. "What's the matter, Dad? Got some secret partners you have to check with before you can buy the place?"

There was a long pause and then Sam forced a laugh. "What's that supposed to mean?"

Jon had heard the fear in his father's voice. His mouth went dry. "It was just a joke, Dad," he claimed. "You're always thinking things over for so long that I wondered who actually makes the decisions."

There was another nervous moment before Sam answered. "Sometimes a man feels like he has to think things out before he makes a decision."

He could feel his father's tension over the phone and had to defuse it. "I'll bet Mom's the real boss there, right?"

Sam laughed. "Hey, you found me out. She's not only the beauty here, but the brains as well."

"Tell the beautiful brainy one that I'll be up to see you both tomorrow morning. And tell Spike not to worry. I'm not quite ready to take him home."

Once Jon had hung up, his smile faded. What the hell was going on? He didn't want to believe that Toni was right. He couldn't believe it. Yet something was clearly wrong.

Little things flashed into his mind. His father's reluctance to let him have any responsibility with the company. His tension whenever Jon tried to pin him down. Even the crude way he had responded to Toni's presence at the company picnic. He was afraid to guess what it all might add up to.

Tomorrow was suddenly too far away. He needed to talk to his father tonight. And not over the phone, but face-to-face. He would confront him directly with Toni's accusations and get the truth out of him.

He poured the rest of his drink down the kitchen sink and hurried out of the house.

Sam put the phone down slowly, sweat running down the side of his face. He could hear Frances laughing and talking to some friends in the parlor as they played bridge. They would be expecting him to come back in soon, but there was no way that he could. Not now.

He went down the hall, away from the parlor and the laughter, and into his den. Its rich paneled walls usually assured him that he had made it, but they seemed more like a stifling prison now. He went to the sideboard and poured himself a brandy, taking it back to the leather chair behind the desk.

She had told him. He was sure of that. That damn accountant had told Jon everything. She was probably pissed off that she was removed from the account and told him the truth to get even. Shit! He should never have trusted Ramsey to handle it.

Sam took a long drink of the brandy and began to choke. Damn rich man's drink, he thought, and put it down on his desk. There were just some things that couldn't be faked.

What was Jon thinking? Sam wondered. Would he understand?

Sam rose to his feet and nervously paced the room. He hadn't seemed angry, but he was going to have questions. He was going to want the truth when he came up the next day.

Sam stopped walking and leaned on the edge of the desk as he thought of Jon's visit. If Jon was upset and wanted to know everything, how could he keep Frances from learning the truth? Jon would never be able to play it cool and keep his mother from finding out.

Pulling a handkerchief from his pocket, he mopped up the sweat. Why hadn't he told Jon the truth years ago? Why hadn't he told him the truth just now on the phone?

Sam frowned and nodded slowly to himself. That was it. He'd go down to Jon's apartment and talk to him. Keep Frances out of it entirely. If Jon was too upset, he just wouldn't come up tomorrow. She didn't know he might, so there'd be no explanations to make.

Sam gulped down the rest of his brandy, coughing as he put the empty glass back on the desk. He should have done this years ago.

# CHAPTER TWENTY-TWO

Toni stopped crying and decided that she had to talk to Jon. She had handled things so terribly, he might not ever forgive her, but she had to try. It was no excuse that his proposal had taken her by surprise. Neither could she claim that his assumption that she would quit her job to join him in Wisconsin was reason enough to have acted the way she had. She loved him and he loved her. They should have been able to talk things out.

She tossed her nightshirt onto the bed, trying hard not to remember how tenderly they had made love there just an hour ago. Instead, she turned away, pulling on a worn pair of jeans and a thick sweatshirt. Her blue running shoes went on over her bare feet.

Jon would listen to her. He just had to. She would tell him how often she had heard her mother crying far into the night over her latest husband. And how Melanie used everyone in sight, and cared about no one. She would admit that she was afraid of being hurt, afraid of being used, and afraid of becoming too dependent on someone else. Her job had become her security, the one thing that she could trust when everything else failed. It was frightening to be told to give it up even if it was no longer everything she wanted it to be.

This past week had been hell. She had been confused and hurt and alone. It had been awful, and she just hadn't been able to handle another shock, even if it should have been a pleasant one. Jon would understand. She would not give up until he did.

Toni slipped a warm-up jacket on, although she feared Jon's coldness more than the chill of the September night. She dropped her key ring into the pocket of her jeans and let herself out the door. It was much darker outside now, for it was past eleven and most of the stores were closed. The restaurants and bars were still open, but only a few of them lay between her apartment and Jon's townhouse. The streets were practically deserted.

Her mind concentrating on what she would say to Jon, Toni was just vaguely aware of the relative silence. She hurried past a couple strolling leisurely toward a bar in the next block. Their arm-in-arm happiness made her heart ache, and the need to see Jon even greater. She dashed across Clark Street during a lull in traffic. Then she hurried around the corner and down Webster.

She didn't want to give up her job, but neither did she want to lose Jon. There had to be a solution, and she was determined that they find one. Marry him, she would, in spite of her fears. She loved him desperately, and needed him so much. If he was going to be in Wisconsin for the next several months, then they would commute back and forth. She was willing to give in if he would too.

The issue of children was harder. She had been so afraid of marriage and its chains that she had never really considered having a family. How important was that to Jon? she wondered. Would he be willing to wait a little while to let her get used to the idea? It was all so frightening to be actually considering—

Her thoughts stopped as her body suddenly became electrified with fear. No longer lost in her thoughts, she was aware of her surroundings. It was late at night, and the street was dark. The commercial strip on Clark Street seemed far away and she was alone. No, she wasn't quite alone. That was the problem. There was someone right behind her. She sensed his presence rather than actually seeing or hearing him.

Her stomach became a knot of fear, and she swallowed the lump in her throat as her ears strained for the sound of his footsteps. She heard them. Soft and muffled as if he was wearing running shoes also. Oh Lord, why had she come out? Maybe Jon was right. Maybe she should quit her job and move to Wisconsin with him. She'd really consider it if she just got to his home safely.

The sound of someone closing a window in one of the houses she was passing awoke her to action. She was not going to stand around to get mugged or worse. It was less than a block to Jon's house if she cut through the parking lot. With a speed born of fear, she began to run.

Time stood still and she felt as if she were moving backward with each step while her pursuer was coming closer and closer. His breath was loud and so were his steps now that he was making no effort to hide his presence. Every muscle in her body tightened, screaming with each step to go faster.

Although she seemed to have been running for hours, she was barely in the parking lot when someone grabbed her arm from behind and pulled her to a stop.

"Whatcha runnin' from, sweetheart?" he muttered in her ear as his right hand went over her mouth. His left hand was tight around her waist, pinning her arms to her sides.

Toni squirmed, trying to free herself. Her heart was in her mouth; she had never known such terror. She glanced ahead, feeling that if she could just see Jon's home, she would be safe, but she couldn't.

The man's hand covered her mouth and her nose. The dirty smell of it was making her sick to her stomach, while the lack of air made her feel dizzy. She struggled helplessly. Jon, where are you? she called silently to him.

Her assailant was a big man. Pulled roughly against his body, she could tell that he was considerably taller than she was and much heavier. Her feeble kicks and elbowing only made him laugh. His hold tightened on her mouth, bruising her lips, as his other hand slid under her sweatshirt.

"Now, ain't you the nice one," he murmured.

His hand roughly fondled her breast and her fear doubled, but so did her strength. She bit his hand, kicked him hard against the shins, and twisted her body at the same time. The movement took him by surprise and his hold loosened for a split second.

Toni took advantage of her chance and pulled away from him. "Jon!" she screamed out, her vision blurred by tears of terror. "Jon!"

She raced across the parking lot, conscious every second that the man was gaining on her again. She dodged between two cars, feeling that she was moving incredibly slow. The man made another grab for her. He caught the sleeve of her jacket, but the smooth fabric slid through his fingers.

She ran across the open lane, and in between two more cars. Her foot lost some traction as she slipped on some stones and suddenly she was in his grasp again.

"You little bitch," he snarled. His grasp was cruelly tight as he spun her around to face him and pushed her against the car. The door handle of the car dug into her back and she gasped with pain. "You wanna play games, that's fine. I like games."

She knew that she could expect no mercy from him and fought in terrified desperation, kicking at his shins and ankles.

He just laughed and taunted her, his hands never loosening their grip. "Them sissy running shoes ain't too good in a fight, are they, sweetheart?"

Her breath was coming in short gasps and fear was eating up her strength. She had to do something to get away, she knew.

The man shifted his weight as he moved closer, and she drove her knee upward toward his crotch. He was rather tall, though, and she caught him on the inside of his thigh.

"Fuckin' bitch. Tryin' to smash the family jewels, are ya?" His hands released her for a split second and a fist came from nowhere. It smashed into the side of her face so that she tasted her own blood and saw pinwheel sparklers before her eyes. A small click before her face seemed terrifying, and through her daze, she saw a knife gleaming before her.

Hypnotized by the blade and still stunned, Toni could not make a sound. She tried to inch away, sliding along the edge of the car, but he grabbed her arm with his free hand and spun her about as he twisted it behind her. Tears appeared in her eyes. Then laughing, he pressed his body against hers. The knife was still in front of her face, and taunted her fear as it gleamed.

"I'm gonna carve my name on your face. That way everyone'll know you belong to me, sweetie." His voice was hoarse and his laugh sent shivers of terror through her body. He laughed even more as he felt them.

The knife gleamed again and suddenly Toni awoke from the fear that had paralyzed her. The knife was gleaming in headlights. A car had pulled into the parking lot. Out of the corner of her eye she saw it approaching. She didn't know if her assailant had seen it or not. Perhaps he was so cocky that he didn't care who saw him, or maybe he hadn't seen it yet. If not, there might be a split second of distraction—

It came suddenly. His attention wandered for a fraction of a second and his grasp loosened slightly. She slid down in the loop formed by his arm and drove her elbow into his crotch. This time his height worked to her advantage. A groan escaped his lips in a gasp. Snarling some curse, he grabbed at her, but again the slippery fabric of her jacket saved her and she ran.

Sam's headlights caught two people in the parking lot. The woman could barely be seen, but the back of the man's jacket proclaimed proudly that he was a Demon, a member of a vicious bikers' gang.

"Lord!" Sam muttered softly, wishing he could just back the car out and disappear. He didn't want to get involved in any Demon quarrel.

As he watched, the woman broke away and ran toward his car. Pure terror was on her face as she reached his door and pounded on it, pleading with him for help. Lord, it was Toni. What the hell was she doing out here at this time of night? Surprise moved him out of his car and she fell against him, sobbing and trembling.

"Hey, it's okay," he said, awkwardly patting her back. He glanced over to where the man had been, but the parking lot seemed deserted. "You're safe now. Let's just get you inside."

Leaving his car where it stood, he led her to the door of Jon's apartment. Between sobs, she was trying to speak, but he couldn't make much sense of it and knocked impatiently on Jon's door. There was no answer, and, after a nervous glance around them, he knocked again. A little more sharply this time.

"I've got a key," Toni said. Her voice was hoarse and shaky as she pulled away from him. She dug into her pocket and produced a key ring.

"Maybe he's in the john and didn't hear us," Sam suggested. He opened the door and let her go in ahead of him. A few lights were on, but the house seemed quiet and deserted.

"Jon?" Sam called from the doorway. There was no answer, so he went in a little further. His hand was on Toni's back, urging her forward also. "Jon?" Only silence. "Seems kind of funny that he'd go out if you were coming over," Sam said slowly.

Toni was wiping the tears from her face with her hand and he silently handed her his handkerchief. "He didn't know I was coming over," she admitted. "We . . . we had a big fight earlier."

"Oh." Sam was uneasy watching her distress and looked away. The front door was standing open. "Uh, I'd better park my car. You be okay for a few minutes?"

She nodded, and wrapped her arms around the top of her body, trying hard to control the violent trembling that had just begun.

"Why don't you go sit down? I'll take your keys to let myself back in." Without waiting for her reply, Sam went out the door and closed it behind him.

The quiet purr of his car's motor was the only sound Sam heard as he went slowly down the steps, but he wasn't really worried about going back to his car. The man that had attacked Toni was probably long gone. No, it was the Demon business that bothered him. Was it just pure coincidence that the biker had chosen Toni as a victim, or was there more to it than that? The Demons were not exactly friendly people on their own, but Guy and his partners often hired them to do especially dirty jobs. Was roughing up Toni one of them?

Sam carefully checked the back seat of the car before he got in. Then he drove into a nearby space, got out, and locked the doors. Jon might be able to accept the fact that he had sold out part of the company, but if something happened to Toni because of it, Sam knew he'd never be forgiven. He clenched his hands nervously and reached for his handkerchief to wipe the sweat from his forehead, but remembered that he had given it to Toni. Lord, she had everything: his handkerchief, Jon, the truth about the company. He took a deep breath and unlocked Jon's front door.

Toni was sitting on the edge of the sofa when Sam went back in. She jumped at the sound of the door; her face was white and her eyes looked huge. He felt a twinge of guilt at her obvious relief at his return. "Was he still out there?" she asked.

"Nah, he's probably miles away by now," Sam assured her. He walked down the few steps into the living room and across to Jon's bar cabinet. Opening a bottle of Jim Beam, he poured a stiff measure into two glasses. "Here, this'll help you relax," he said, and handed her a glass.

Sam sat down in a chair opposite the sofa and took a long drink of the whiskey, watching her at the same time. Her lip looked slightly swollen, and she had a vicious-looking bruise on the side of her face. "He didn't hurt you, did he?" he asked. "I mean, except for . . ." He waved his hand awkwardly.

Toni shook her head and gulped some of the liquor down. "No, you came just in time." Her breath seemed to quiver, and she closed her eyes briefly. "He had a knife and—" The trembling returned and she put the back of her hand to her mouth.

"Hey, don't think about it," Sam said. He moved over to sit next to her on the sofa and took her right hand in his. In spite of all the trouble she had caused him, he felt sorry for her. She was probably a nice kid. Both Jon and Frances seemed to think so. "You just picked the wrong time to go out, that's all. You won't see him again."

His assurances must not have been too effective for Toni shook her head. "No, he's been following me for days." Her voice was a harsh whisper. "He's probably the one that made the calls and left the notes . . ." Her hand clung to his as she lifted the glass to her lips.

Sam did the same with his glass. It wasn't just some random mugging then. Somebody was out to get her. He looked down at her hand clutching his and then up at her tear-streaked face. "Jon is certainly fond of you," he said for no reason.

She tried to smile. "I'm not sure after tonight."

Sam nodded slowly. She had told Jon about Mid-America tonight, he knew, and suddenly he felt very old and tired. Patting her hand gently, he rose to his feet. "I'd better call the police and have them look for that guy. You want another drink?"

Toni shook her head, so Sam just poured more for himself. "Call me if you need me," he told her simply, and went up to the phone in Jon's bedroom. He didn't want to be overheard since it wasn't the police he was planning on calling.

Sam barely had time to sit on the edge of Jon's bed before a gruff voice answered the phone. Sam identified himself, but wasted no time on niceties. "I want to talk to Lou," he insisted. "Tell him it's an emergency." He gave the man Jon's phone number and hung up the phone. He took a long drink of the whiskey. The phone was ringing before he had time to put the glass down.

"What's the problem, Sam?"

Ignoring Lou's suppressed anger, Sam asked, "Are you guys after that accountant we used to have?"

"What for? She causing trouble again?" Lou sounded impatient.

"No, she's not doing anything," Sam assured him. "She's not on the account anymore. Some other jerk is, but he ain't gonna cause any problems. Somebody's after the lady, though, and roughed her up a bit."

The other man sighed. "So call the cops. Why bother us about it?"

"The guy after her tonight was a Demon. I know you use them sometimes."

"What's that prove? No action's been authorized against her. He was probably out for a little fun."

"It's more than that," Sam insisted hotly. "If you didn't plan it, then someone's free-lancing. She's had calls and notes before tonight."

There was a moment of silence at the other end. "I will look into it," Lou said slowly. "I promise there won't be any more incidents."

Sam felt a bit better as he hung up the phone. He may have made some mistakes in the past, but at least he had this one off his conscience. He finished up most of the whiskey in his glass and then went back downstairs. Toni was huddled at the end of the sofa.

"Everything'll be okay now," he said, and looked around. "No sign of Jon?"

She shook her head, a look of desolation in her eyes. "It's getting late. Where do you think he could have gone?"

"Hey, he's a big boy. He can take care of himself. Probably went out for a drink." Sam sat down in the chair and sighed. His optimistic outlook disappeared as he watched her. She looked so small and defenseless, hugging her knees to her chest and surrounded by the pillows of the sofa. How had everything gotten so screwed up that he was afraid to face his own son? "Look, who am I fooling? You two may have had a fight, but he sure wasn't too thrilled with me when we talked an hour ago."

Her eyes were dark pools in her pale face. "What was he upset about?"

Sam ignored her question and rose restlessly to his feet. "Hell, it's not like I deliberately set out to trick him."

"No." Toni turned away uneasily.

Sam looked down into his empty glass and walked over to refill it. "Sometimes things happen," he sighed. "They're not what you planned, they just happen. You're in a bind and suddenly there's a way out so you take it. Later you might wish you had done things different, but it's too late."

He turned back to her and found her watching him. Her eyes were sad, but not condemning. "He was such a good kid. I wish we could have had a dozen more, just like him. He deserved the best, and that's what I thought I was giving him."

He drank down part of the drink and came back to the chair. Feeling very weary, he sank down slowly. "That's what a father's supposed to do, you know. Take care of his kids. Give 'em a good start. Help them over the rough spots."

"My father sure didn't do that," Toni said quietly. "Jon was lucky that he had you."

Sam's smile was sad. "Tell him that. He thinks I'm just a stupid old man, and maybe he's right." He felt rather light-headed suddenly, and took another long drink. The burning sensation of the liquor helped clear the fogginess away. "Maybe I was stupid for trying to do so much. It was all for him and now he hates me for it."

"He loves you," Toni assured him. "Look how he came to work with you when you needed him. That love isn't going to stop."

How he wished he could believe her! "No, it's you he's not going to stop loving. You didn't do anything wrong. Just told him the truth." Some of the fogginess returned. He tried to blink it away, but it didn't help. His hand touched wetness on his face. Were those tears? "I guess I was always afraid to talk to him. Afraid he wouldn't understand. I just kept putting it off because I couldn't bear to see the disgust in his eyes."

He could feel his hands trembling and his breath was coming in gasps. There was a strange feeling of pressure in his chest and he heard the sound of glass breaking. "I just don't want him to hate me," he told Toni, but his voice sounded strange and she looked far away.

Toni was worried. Sam was getting more and more agitated as he spoke. His face had become alarmingly pale and his speech was slurred. Was it the liquor or something else?

As a client she had found him arrogant and difficult to work with, but now he was just a frightened old man. Jon's father. Someone who needed comfort.

"Mr. Morici, please don't get so upset," she said quietly, but he just continued babbling about Jon, tears streaming down his face. She moved forward on the sofa and reached over to take his hand. "Just give him a chance. Don't worry so." Suddenly his hands began to tremble violently, and the glass fell to the floor.

"Sam!" she called out, and jumped to her feet, alarmed. But he seemed not to see or hear her. Gasping for breath, he clutched futilely at his chest as he fell forward.

"Oh Lord," Toni muttered. Desperately, she rolled him over on his back, careful to keep him away from the broken glass. His face was pale with flushed blotches. His lips were blue as she loosened his collar. The pulse in his neck seemed erratic.

She jumped up and raced to the phone in the kitchen. Her hands shook slightly as she dialed 911. After three interminable rings, someone answered and she was able to ask for an ambulance.

By the time she got back to Sam's side, his eyes had fluttered open. She took his hand in hers, not certain if he could hear her.

"I've called for an ambulance. They'll be here soon. Just lie still. You'll be fine." How insane to expect him to believe her soothing words when she was crying!

For a moment he continued to stare up at the ceiling, but then he slowly turned his head so that he could see her. His mouth worked silently for a time before he managed to form any words. "Don't let . . . him . . . hate me," he gasped, his eyes pleading with her.

"No, he won't. I promise Jon won't hate you," she said. Her tears splashed down onto the front of his shirt leaving a growing number of wet circles. Where was that damn ambulance?

"I . . . just . . ."

Toni shook her head. "Don't talk now," she begged him. "Save your strength. You've got to keep going until the ambulance comes."

The sound of a siren approaching made her squeeze his hand gently. "I've got to let them in, but I'll be right back."

She wasn't certain he understood, but hurried to the door. She pulled it open as the ambulance turned into the parking lot, and she waved them to the right townhouse.

The attendants hurried past her and one settled on the floor next to Sam as the other one pushed the furniture out of the way. They worked quickly and efficiently, checking blood pressure and responses. An IV and some monitors were attached and a stretcher was wheeled in.

"Are you family?" one attendant asked her.

She just shook her head; her voice had deserted her momentarily. "No, I'm a friend of his son's." She watched as they lifted him onto the stretcher. "Can I come with him to the hospital?"

They had already started wheeling him out the door. "Might be a good idea if you can help us reach his family."

Toni grabbed her keys from the small table near the stairs, closed the door, and ran after them to the ambulance. There was a small seat out of the way, where she perched herself, watching fearfully as the monitors recorded each gasp for breath and labored heartbeat.

Jon led his mother into the emergency room at Grant Hospital and up to the nurse's desk. "We're Sam Morici's family," he said. "We got a call that he was brought in here."

The nurse looked up. "The doctor is still with him, but I'll tell him you've come. The young lady that brought him in is in there." She rose to her feet and nodded toward the waiting area before she disappeared down the hall.

"Young lady?" Frances clutched Jon's arm, pain in her voice.

Jon put his hand over his mother's and squeezed it.

What else had the old bastard been up to? "Don't jump to conclusions, Mother," he said gently in spite of his own thoughts. He turned her around and they went into the waiting area.

His eyes fastened suspiciously on a young blonde near the door. She was wearing a tight black dress and paging listlessly through a magazine. He felt a wave of disgust for his father's behavior, and wished there had been some way to spare his mother this knowledge.

Suddenly he felt his mother sigh as her hand left his arm. "It's Toni," she cried.

Startled, Jon turned toward his mother to find her crossing the room. Sure enough, there was Toni rising from a chair that had been hidden from his line of vision by a plastic plant. What was she doing here?

His mother embraced her, and then they both sat down, clinging to each other's hands, but Jon wasn't sure he was ready to face Toni yet. He still felt too confused and angry. Her words had caused him to question things about his father that he never would have otherwise, and now his father lay in the hospital. Jon felt as if his anger had put his father there. His steps were slow as he walked over to where they sat.

"Toni thinks it was a heart attack," his mother said glancing up at him.

He nodded, trying not to look at Toni, but found that his eyes kept straying toward her. Her head was bent and all he saw was the curtain of her hair.

"They were at your apartment waiting for you," his mother went on.

Jon frowned at her. "At my place? While I was waiting up at the house for him?" Just what he needed to hear. His phone call had so worried his father, that he had driven down to see him that night. Jon turned away, staring blindly at the wall.

"I had no idea where Sam had gone," Jon heard his mother tell Toni. "I didn't even know that Jon had called earlier until he was at the door. We were just sitting around talking, waiting for Sam to come home, and then the hospital called—" She gulped back the words as tears rushed to her eyes.

"Don't think about it," Toni said softly. "Just wait until the doctor comes out here. Maybe it's not that serious."

Jon turned back to them. "I wonder where the doctor is."

Toni looked up at him, the hair falling away from her face and exposing a bruise along her jawline. He frowned when he saw it.

"What happened to you?" he demanded.

Her hand went up to her face, and she self-consciously pulled the hair forward again. "It's nothing," she stammered, looking away.

Jon reached down and moved the hair aside. His movements had no gentleness to them, and neither did his voice. "That's nothing?"

"Jon!" his mother scolded him sharply, then turned back to Toni. Her voice was gentle and full of concern. "What happened?"

Toni shrugged her shoulders, both her hands clutching his mother's hands for support. "There was someone following me when I went to Jon's," she admitted.

Damn! Jon thought with an angry intake of breath that stopped her words for a moment. Another offense to nail on his door.

She went on, "He caught up with me in the parking lot, but Mr. Morici came before anything happened."

"Thank God he did," Frances said.

True, Jon thought bitterly. But *he* should have been there to help her since it had been his anger that had made her leave her safe apartment. He jammed his hands into his pants pockets, angry at himself and angry at her for making him feel that way. "What in the world were you doing out at that time? You were just asking for trouble."

His mother looked at him in astonishment, while Toni just kept her head bent, her face shielded by her hair. He knew he was behaving terribly, but couldn't seem to stop himself. There had been too much piled on him at once. He could only handle so much anger and guilt without striking back. Even if it meant striking back at someone he thought he loved.

"I'm going to find that doctor," he said, and walked back to the admitting desk. The nurse there just shook her head and went back to her work.

Jon turned away, not knowing where to go. He was angry. Unbelievably angry at himself, at Toni, at his father, at the world.

Rather than return to Toni and his mother, Jon went out

the exit and stood in the darkness next to the wall. What was the matter with him?

He pounded his fist against the bricks until it hurt. How could he have spoken that way to Toni? What was the matter with him? He loved her, and she loved him. She deserved his protection and his concern, not his anger. This attack was the very thing he had feared while he was up in Wisconsin, and he had caused it. If it hadn't been for him, she would have been safe at home. If it hadn't been for his father, who knows what might have happened?

Tears of rage and pain came to his eyes. What was he supposed to do?

He was torn with indecision as he heard the door open behind him and soft footsteps approach. All he knew was that he needed Toni's warmth and love. "Toni," he said, turning around as he spoke.

The nurse stood before him. "The doctor's waiting to speak to you, Mr. Morici."

# CHAPTER TWENTY-THREE

Toni walked down the long corridor to the intensive care unit in Grant Hospital. It was after one o'clock on Saturday afternoon, almost twelve hours since she had caused Sam's heart attack, fourteen hours since her disastrous argument with Jon. Lord, so much had happened since she had left work yesterday. It was no wonder she felt numb. But she actually hoped that the numbness would last, for it was preferable to the misery of last night. She thought she had grown out of crying herself to sleep years ago, but yesterday's trip back to adolescence proved she was wrong.

She reached the doors of the ICU, but they were closed, so she went into the small lounge off to one side. Frances Morici was standing at the window, leaning against the wall as she stared out.

"Hello, Mrs. Morici," Toni said softly.

The woman turned; a smile touched the corners of her mouth, but her eyes were sad. "Oh, Toni. It's good to see you." She came away from the window and embraced the younger woman. "I was hoping you would come back today. But I'm afraid you just missed Jon. I was finally able to convince him to go home and get some rest."

"I'm sure I'll see him later," Toni said lightly, not wanting to admit that relations were still strained between them. It was at his mother's insistence that he had driven her home from the hospital last night. In the strained silence of the car she had tried to apologize for their earlier fight and express her sympathy and guilt for his father's condition, but he had been silent and withdrawn. After her attempts to talk had failed, she had given up, glad that the hospital was only a few blocks from her apartment.

Putting Jon determinedly from her mind, Toni took

Frances's hand. "How is Mr. Morici this morning? Is there any change?"

Frances shook her head. Her face was pale and her shoulders drooped. She looked exhausted. "No, he still hasn't regained consciousness." She closed her eyes briefly as her grip on Toni's hand tightened. "They keep telling me that we have to be patient, that he can still pull through; but they've got him on so many machines, Toni. How can he possibly get better if he can't even breathe for himself?"

"You have to keep hoping and praying," Toni said. She glanced around the small room, and then led Frances over to the sofa near the door. "Now what have the doctors said? Have you talked to them since last night?"

Frances shrugged. "They say he's holding his own, that's all." Tears came to her eyes. "But, Toni, he looks so terrible. Machines and monitors all around him. What will I do if he dies?" She looked so much older than she had when Toni had met her at the Mid-America picnic. Older and frightened.

"You'll remember all the good times you had together and be grateful for them," Toni said. "But you don't know that he's going to die. You can't give up hope."

"I know," Frances sighed, nodding her head slowly. Toni noticed that her hands were trembling. "But I just can't imagine my life without Sam. We've been together for so long, you know . . ."

Her voice trailed off, full of pain, and Toni put her arms around her. For a time, Frances just leaned against her, crying quietly, and then she straightened up. "I'm so glad you're here, Toni. You have such strength that even being with you makes me feel stronger. More able to cope."

"I don't know how you can bear to have me here," Toni admitted. "If I hadn't been so stupid as to go out last night, he wouldn't have exerted himself, and wouldn't be here now."

Frances was surprised. "Toni, it's not your fault. Sam's had a bad heart for years. This could have happened at any time. Neither Jon nor I blame you. We're only thankful he was there to help you."

Toni wished she could believe her, and said nothing.

"Surely Jon didn't say anything last night that made you feel this way." Frances looked worried.

"No, no," Toni quickly assured her. "Jon didn't say anything last night." How true that was!

The other woman relaxed and patted Toni's hand. "Even if he had, he didn't mean it. He's suffering too, I know, but he was so remote it was impossible to talk to him. I don't think he heard much of what I said. That's what he does when he's upset. Just pulls all inside himself and won't let anyone near. You mustn't let him shut you out, though, Toni. Make him talk to you. Make him lean on you. Deep down he needs you as much as you need him. He just won't show it."

Toni nodded, pretending to agree with everything Frances said. But Frances did not know everything. Even if Jon didn't blame her for his father's heart attack, he had already turned away from her before Sam was stricken. The wall that was between them now was not a barrier to hide his grief, but a way to keep her out. And the worst thing was, she understood. The accusations she had hurled were about his father, who was possibly dying this very minute. How could she expect him to forgive her? He had a deep sense of loyalty toward his family, and it had multiplied now that his father could not defend himself. She felt miserable, for she could see no possible happy ending for them.

"Tell me," Toni said, forcing her dejection away from her, "have you eaten any lunch? Did you even have breakfast?"

Frances shook her head. "No, Jon took me to his apartment about four this morning and wanted me to rest. He came back around ten with some doughnuts and made some coffee, but I just couldn't get anything down." She looked rather sheepish. "Actually, I promised I would have some lunch while he took his turn resting. That was the only way I got him to agree to leave."

"Then that's what we must do," Toni announced, rising to her feet. She took Frances's hand and pulled her up also. "We'll tell the nurses that we're going down to the cafeteria so they'll know where we are." Frances looked ready to protest, but Toni just shook her head scoldingly. "It would be a fine thing if Sam wakes up to find that you're in the hospital too."

"Oh, Toni," Frances laughed. "You sound just like Jon. What a pair the two of you make."

\* \* \*

Jon had not gone to his apartment, for he knew sleep would never come. Not with Toni's accusations festering in his mind. Instead he had gone to Mid-America. He had been determined to find out the truth.

Unfortunately, as he slammed shut a drawer in his father's desk, he realized how difficult that was going to be. He didn't even know what to look for. Would there be secret papers to identify the secret partners? Exhausted, he leaned back in the padded leather executive chair and stared dully around the room. Toni was just paranoid and didn't know what she was talking about.

He felt like an intruder sneaking around his father's room. The man's values and life were laid out here. All the things that were important to him. The walls were covered with pictures of Jon and his mother. There was his mother holding him as a baby. And the two of them standing in front of a school on his first day. There were athletic award certificates and pictures from Yale and Harvard. With a catch in his throat, Jon saw that his father had the team photo for each of his soccer teams since he was six years old.

He put his arms on his father's desk and let his head fall onto them. His breath came in shudders as he wiped a tear from his eye. What did that stupid broad know?

His father started this business from nothing and built it into the best restaurant supplier in northeast Illinois. The man's sweat and blood were embedded in the walls of this building. Mid-America was Sam Morici and Sam Morici was Mid-America. Jon blinked back tears. Many was the time that his father would rush up from the city to see Jon in a soccer game on a Saturday morning and then rush right back to work, not returning until late at night.

He lifted his head, looking proudly at the letters on his father's desk. There was a letter requesting his participation in a fund-raising dinner for the athletic department of DePaul University. Others that thanked him for his efforts in a recent Boy Scout fund-raising drive and for speaking at the graduation ceremonies for chefs at Washburn Vocational High School. The letters went on and on. His father was an important man in the business. Anyone could see it.

Jon rose from the chair angrily and walked to the door. He looked out over the darkened bullpen and closed offices of the other executives. The power and control emanated from this corner office. Jon could feel it. But what did she know about power and control, about struggling and fighting, about winning and losing?

Jon's irritation grew. She had it made with all these equal opportunity laws. She just had to be in the right place at the right time. He pushed back the nagging thought that Toni had been the first woman audit manager in her firm and how the first Christians had met the hungriest lions. He also pushed from his mind the picture of women in his own business school. How the prettiest girls had to fight twice as hard as anybody for professional respect.

Jon hit his father's door with the bottom of his fist. "Shit," he said aloud. "What the hell does she know?"

Jon wandered into Guy's office. He briefly glanced at the various papers on the desk and saw that Guy's tastes seemed to run to computer reports. Among others, he found an aged accounts receivable report, and an accounts payable register. Jon snorted. The infamous accounts payable or, as Toni indicated, the charitable arm of Mid-America. That was so stupid. Why would they pay suppliers more than they were billed? But then, she didn't say they were actually paid more. Mid-America just pretended they were. Jon shook his head. None of it made any sense.

On another pile lay a requisition for a new truck and Guy's signature was the last one required. His father certainly delegated a lot, and that was going to change when he took over. Mr. Ramsey would find his wings trimmed a bit.

In Guy's out-basket he saw more reports, many with personal notes attached. An overtime list was being returned to a foreman in the warehouse with Guy's demand that the excessive overtime be explained. The dealer who maintained Mid-America's trucks was to explain last month's abnormally high maintenance costs.

Jon threw down the papers with disgust. That wasn't Guy's department. He really pushed himself into everything.

Leaving Guy's domain, Jon wandered through the rest of the offices. The inventory manager had his reports and files concerning orders, reorder points, and stock usage. The payroll manager had the usual weekly payroll lists and various deduction and government forms. Jon remembered seeing a number of reports concerning payroll in Guy's office and snorted. Those ghost salesmen, no doubt. That damn woman makes this sound like city hall. An accountant ought to be smart enough to realize that a small private business can't operate that way.

Jon realized the futility of his visit, and left the office area for the warehouse. It had been open for a few hours that morning, but was dark and quiet now as he glanced down the aisles between supply-laden shelves. He stopped at the main foreman's office, but it was a clutter of papers that held no interest for him. He passed the office by.

Once out in the warehouse, Jon took a deep breath. This place was part of his father, even down to the faint musty smell. When the business had been smaller, Sam had worked in the warehouse himself and brought that musty scent home.

Jon glanced around at the thick wooden supports that held the roof up and the floor blocks stained with years of grease and grime. Sometimes he thought he knew more about buildings than people, but maybe they weren't all that different. Take this old place. Nobody used all this wood for structural supports anymore. It was too expensive, a fire hazard, and steel was stronger. But that was what made this place special. The adherence to the old ways. And that was what made his father special. His belief in all sorts of old-fashioned values like hard work and honesty. Nobody, not Toni, not anybody, would ever convince him otherwise.

Lost in his thoughts, Jon found himself in a back corner of the warehouse. The wooden floor blocks had a different pattern in one place that was partially hidden by a dusty pile of used equipment. That must be the trapdoor, he thought, remembering the tale of an old warehouse worker. There was supposed to be a tunnel around here that had been used for bootlegging liquor during Prohibition. What secrets the old building had!

Jon had found the similarities between his father and the building reassuring earlier, but now they nagged at him. Did his father have secrets that he had kept hidden all these years also?

His thoughts brought back all his worries and doubt and anger. With a troubled mind, he walked back into the office area and to his own office. There he sat down, a sardonic smile on his lips.

"Now this is where the real power in the company lies," he mocked himself. "Just look at all the information and control reports that cross this desk." He disgustedly flipped through the letters requesting help in fund raising, attendance at political dinners, association reports . . .

Suddenly it came to him. The certainty was there. A rage welled up in his throat, making him shove everything from his desk onto the floor. But it did nothing to exhaust his anger as tears formed in his eyes.

He had been the stupid one. The argument with Toni. The attempt to talk to his father. His father's heart attack. The night without sleep. They had clouded his senses, but now he understood. Something had bothered him since he had gone through Mid-America's offices, but he hadn't seen it until that moment.

They were the same. His office and his father's. They were exactly the same: offices of useless figureheads. The business did not need either of them. Guy Ramsey really did run Mid-America.

Eventually Jon's anger died away, leaving him feeling weak and spent. He had to talk to his father, he thought, rising slowly to his feet. He had to make the old man tell him why he had done it.


"I don't care if it's not visiting hours yet," Jon snapped at the nurse blocking his way. "I need to talk to him."

"Mr. Morici, your father cannot talk to anyone. He's still unconscious," the nurse explained with extreme patience. "We will tell you when there is some change."

Jon glanced toward the cubicle where his father lay. Monitors on the wall above him whirred rhythmically as countless tubes and wires ran in and out of his body. What had he done? Why hadn't he told his own son the truth? He felt his anger growing again, and jammed his clenched fists into his pockets.

"Please, Mr. Morici." The nurse lightly touched his arm and he started, having forgotten she was there. "Please wait in the lounge down the hall. We will call you as soon as there's any change."

Jon nodded silently and went out the door. His head was bent and his eyes were staring at his feet, but they saw only his father lying in that bed. Would he ever learn the truth?

"Jon, what's wrong? Has there been some change?"

He looked up to find his mother hurrying down the hall toward him. A little way behind her was Toni. Although he tried to turn back toward his mother, his eyes would not budge from Toni. She looked tired, he thought, recognizing it from the droop in her shoulders and the way her hair was pulled back. She always fixed it that way when she was too tired to fuss with it.

His gaze went on to her face, his heart softening at the shadows around her eyes and the bruise on her chin that her makeup could not hide. Why couldn't he just go over to her and hold her? Lose himself in her embrace as her eyes begged him to do? Why did he feel so torn, as if going to her would be an act of disloyalty to his father?

He forced his eyes back to his mother. "No," he told her. "Nothing's changed."

# CHAPTER TWENTY-FOUR

Toni eased herself off the waiting room sofa slowly, careful not to disturb Mrs. Morici. It must be close to three o'clock in the morning, Toni thought. Monday already, and Toni suspected that this was the first sleep Frances had gotten since Sam's heart attack. Not that she had gotten much rest herself, she thought, and stretched some of the stiffness from her limbs. With each passing hour, Frances had seemed to cling to her more so that Toni hated to leave her. Even when she did go back to her apartment, sleep was elusive. All she needed was the slightest thing to remind her of Jon and she felt too miserable to close her eyes.

She glanced at her watch and found that her estimate of the time had been close. She was due at her office in five hours. She had better get herself some rest or she'd never make it through the day.

A half-empty cup of coffee sat on a table in the corner next to a box of Fig Newtons that Jon had brought last night. She had tried to eat one but could just manage half, and that only because she was trying to get Frances to eat also. When she was tired, everything tasted like cardboard and the thought of food was appalling.

She picked up the coffee cup and stared down into its cold contents, not able to remember how old it was. She had gotten it before Jon had left, she knew, and that had been around midnight. So it was at least three hours old. She put it back down on the table. Coffee was the last thing she needed anyway, especially if she still hoped to get some rest before it was time to report to work.

From where she stood, Toni glanced back at Frances. The older woman was slumped against the padded arm of the sofa, a sweater of Jon's tossed over her shoulders.

Should she wake her up and tell her that she was going home to get some rest? She hated to leave Frances alone, though, and Jon might not be back for hours. He had looked terrible, she remembered, and her heart twisted painfully. As if he hadn't slept for days.

Maybe a drink of water and a trip to the washroom would help, she decided, knowing that she could not leave yet. It wasn't that Jon had asked her to be there or even acknowledged her presence much, but she still had to stay. She loved him, no matter what his feelings for her were. And even if he never spoke to her again, this is where she belonged right now.

She was too tired to think about the future, anyway. The dull pain in her heart was competing with the empty feeling in her stomach from lack of food and the ache in her head from exhaustion. Her whole body seemed to be bruised and battered. She'd like nothing better than to hide away someplace and sleep for several years.

The water in the drinking fountain was cool and refreshing in spite of its slightly metallic taste. Then she went into the nearby washroom and splashed cold water on her face. She felt somewhat invigorated after she combed her hair, and she went back down toward the lounge.

If she had her choice, she knew just where she'd choose to hide away to sleep, she thought. She'd curl up next to Jon in his king-sized bed and let him hold her until she felt alive again. And when she woke up, all this unhappiness would have disappeared because he would still love her.

It made for a pleasant dream, but a yawn interrupted her thoughts and brought her back to reality. A nurse was standing just outside the doors to intensive care. Toni hurried down to where she was waiting.

"I'm afraid Mr. Morici is sinking," she told Toni quietly. "If there's anyone who ought to be here, you'd better call them now."

Toni stared dumbly at her for a moment, then nodded. "Yes, all right." She watched as the nurse went back into the unit, then walked back down the hall to the phones. Her hands trembled as she searched for some change. She had no dimes, but found a quarter at the bottom of her purse.

The phone rang twice before Jon picked it up. He had

been asleep and his voice was hoarse. Toni's hand tightened around the receiver.

"Jon? It's Toni." She sensed he was more awake and went on. "They want you to come down to the hospital."

"Is he awake?"

She winced at the hope in his voice. "I don't know. I haven't seen him and your mother is still asleep in the lounge. The nurse said his family should come now so I thought I'd call you first."

"Oh. I'll be there in a few minutes." He hung up the phone without saying anything else.

Toni hung the phone up slowly and then went back to the lounge. She shook Frances gently. "Mrs. Morici, they want you in intensive care."

The woman woke up quickly, a look of fear covering her features. "Sam?" she cried, clutching Toni's hand in a tight grip. "What's happened to Sam?"

"He's not doing too well," Toni told her gently. "I've called Jon and he'll be here in a few minutes."

Toni did not feel it was her place to go into the unit with Jon and his mother. She was not part of the family, and she did not want to intrude in something so private. Mrs. Morici, though, seemed incapable of moving on her own. Toni had to lift her to her feet and lead her to the ICU. Frances was trembling uncontrollably and clung to Toni's hand.

"He can't die," she said, as if her words would be enough to keep him alive. "How can I go on without him?"

Toni pushed open the ICU door and helped her inside. The nurse looked up and nodded to them. They went past the desk to the cubicle where Sam lay. A different nurse was taking his blood pressure and she carefully recorded the figures before glancing their way.

"The doctor should be here soon," she told them.

Frances said nothing for she was staring at Sam's body. Toni looked back at the nurse and nodded. "Thank you. I called his son and he should be here shortly."

The nurse slipped past them as Frances turned to Toni. "He can't die, Toni," she said. Her face crumpled with tears. "He just can't."

She leaned against Toni's chest and sobbed. Toni put her arms around her, trying to comfort her the best she could, but she didn't really know what to say. On the monitor on the wall, she could see that Sam's heartbeat was erratic and slowing down as she watched. How could she lie to Frances and tell her that he would be all right? They stood like that, silently for longer than Toni realized.

She felt someone near them and turned around to see that Jon had come. He seemed to be suffering his own agonies and was barely aware of her presence. Toni turned to Frances. "Jon's here," she told her gently.

Frances looked up and met his eyes. Toni loosened her hold, leading her over to him, then she slipped from the unit.

It was a relief to be back in the lounge, and she sat down on the sofa letting her eyes close. She tried not to think of the coming day. She just let herself relax.

She wasn't sure how long she sat there, but opened her eyes suddenly at the sound of footsteps approaching. Jon came in and she rose to her feet.

"Is he—?"

Jon nodded, then cleared his throat awkwardly. "I'm going to take Mother back to my apartment. She's pretty upset, and the doctor gave me some tranquilizers for her."

"She needs the rest."

He nodded again as his eyes seemed to focus on a place somewhere beyond her. "I, . . . I want to thank you for staying with her so much. She really needed a woman with her. I know it made it a lot easier for her."

Toni did not know what to say. It didn't seem to be the time to remind him that she loved him and had been willing to help him in any way she could. Besides, he ought to have known that, and if he didn't, what was left of their relationship? She said nothing.

He coughed again and glanced over his shoulder uneasily. "I'd better get Mother and go then. Can we drop you off at your apartment?"

Toni found her voice. The thought of sharing another silent ride with him was more than she could handle. "No, I'll get a cab. You just take care of your mother."

Jon accepted her decision easily and turned away. She watched him pass from her sight with a sigh of resignation. In a way, she envied Frances. Sam might be gone, but he hadn't turned his back on her love. She had her memories to cherish without the bitterness of betrayal to taint them.

Toni picked up her purse and her sweater and walked wearily out of the hospital.

Guy smiled at the young receptionist as she let him into the office. Ellie had just started working at Mid-America last week and was doing her best to brighten the place up. His gaze traveled down the loose front of her dress and lingered on the swell of her ripe breasts. He took a step closer to her, so that his leg brushed against hers. His smile deepened when she did not move away. "Hi, sexy. You keep on wearing that dress and no jury in the world will ever convict me of rape."

Ellie's laugh was harsh and deep in her throat. "Oh, Mistah Ramsey. You do carry on so."

Guy laughed and slapped her backside. "Lady, lady. That dress and your southern drawl just makes my blood churn."

"Well now, Mistah Ramsey. Ah got just the thing to cool you down." Her voice was soft as a morning breeze and did not match the burning hunger in her eyes.

"I gotta check you later, honey. I got a business to run." His eyes rode roughly over her body, stopping on her large breasts. Kentucky lost a few hills when she came up here.

"You do what you gotta do, Mistah Ramsey. I ain't goin' no place."

Guy moved rapidly toward his office, a crude smile on his face. He was through passing up goodies like that. This place was filled with hot young things just panting for him, and he had earned the right to have them. "Good morning, Mrs. Flores. How are you today?"

The older woman looked sad. "I'm fine, sir. But have you heard about poor Mr. Morici?"

Guy nodded solemnly, wiping the smile from his face. Had to put on a good show for the peons. "Yeah, it was too bad, but it happens to the best of us."

"That's true, Mr. Ramsey. Death is the destination of all our journeys."

"Right," he said, picking up the pile of mail on her desk. If he didn't stifle this conversation, she'd be telling him next about the better life they were all going to. "Any messages?"

Mrs. Flores checked a paper on her desk. "The younger

Mr. Morici said he'd be tied up today, but he'd like to meet with you tomorrow morning."

"Is that right?" Guy grunted as he read an advertising flyer from a manufacturer of stainless-steel tableware. So the hotshot was starting already. It was going to be fun to shoot him down.

"Shall I set up a time for both of you to meet?"

"No, I'll get around to him when I have a chance." He tossed the mail back onto the secretary's desk. "Hold my calls. I got a bunch of stuff to do this morning."

Guy walked into his office and shut the door behind him. As he sat down, a wide smile split his face. Everything was working out better than he could have planned.

He pulled a cigar out and lit it, staring at the wall contemplatively. Maybe he should put Ellie into the apartment with Melanie. After all, the place had two bedrooms.

He puffed a few times on his cigar and then decided. That was what he'd do. The convenience of having two hot women in the same place outweighed any problems that he could see. And old Melanie might even appreciate the help. She'd have to be tired sometime.

He unlocked his credenza and brought out his bottle of scotch. He started for the intercom to order Mrs. Flores to get some ice, but shook his head. He was just going to have a little sip. As the whiskey laid a warm path down his throat and through his stomach, Guy chuckled.

Soon he was laughing out loud and couldn't stop even though tears came to his eyes. It couldn't have gone better if he had planned the whole thing. Donny had called Saturday morning and told him how he had massaged Toni's face a bit but hadn't been as thorough as he would have liked because some old guy had pulled up into the parking lot. When Guy had heard over the radio how Sam Morici, a civic leader, had died after having a heart attack in his son's townhouse, he had put two and two together.

Guy shook his head and wiped his eyes. God, it was beautiful! Things were going great. Now he had the title as well as the responsibility.

Relaxed, he leaned back in this chair and put his feet on his desk. He would even play around with sweet little Toni for a while longer. Then he'd let her know that he could make life easier for her. After she begged a bit, he'd give her a touch of his power-hammer, but then he'd throw her

273

back. She wouldn't be that interesting in the long haul. Too damn frigid.

Guy leaned his head back and blew smoke rings toward the ceiling. Jon Morici was another one. He probably should fire the jerk. Throw him out there on his own and see if he could survive. The only thing he probably could do was bag groceries.

He took his feet off the desk and snapped his body forward. No, he'd keep him around for laughs. He could do the same junk he did now, but Guy'd jerk his chain every so often to remind him who was boss.

Guy finished off the scotch in his glass and pulled on the cigar. Everything tasted good today. He was in the catbird seat and life was getting better by the minute.

He turned to the telephone, dialing a number that was burned into his memory. He'd better give the partners a call and get the ball rolling. There wasn't any reason to wait. Lou could make him president and then he could start fixing things up. As he waited for someone to answer the phone, he stared at the wall in front of him. He thought he'd knock that wall out and make one big—

"Yeah?" a voice grunted into the phone.

"Hey, Gus. How's the boy?" Guy said exuberantly. "Is Lou there? I gotta talk to him."

"I'll see if he wants to." There was a sudden silence.

That dumb punk, Guy thought. He wasn't tough enough to hack it on the street, so they made him a combination secretary/shoeshine boy. Shoulda made him target practice.

"What do you want, Ramsey?" Lou barked.

Guy was taken aback at the tone of voice. "Uh, I thought that we should get together real soon. You know, Sam Morici died over the weekend."

"So?"

"Well, I just thought that we should get some things settled. You know, like who's running this place." Guy's voice cracked slightly and he could feel himself start to sweat. "I don't think Sam ever told his kid about you guys."

"So what?"

"Well, he thinks it's his place now and that he's gonna run it." A tiny whine had slipped into his voice.

"The board has a lot of talking to do. We got some items

to check out, and when that's done we'll make the necessary decisions on Mid-America."

Guy tried to sound more authoritative. "When you guys gonna do this talking? I can come over."

"You're not a member of the board."

"But I can help." The whine slipped in again.

"We'll let you know if we need your help."

"When are you gonna be done with your discussions?"

"When we tell you, Ramsey." Lou sounded impatient, and Guy hurried to explain things.

"Yeah, but Junior is gonna be here tomorrow. And he thinks it's his place. What am I supposed to do?"

"Just keep your mouth shut and take care of things, Ramsey. We'll be back to you. Real soon." The line went dead.

Guy hung up slowly, staring with hatred at the telephone. The scotch that had given his stomach such a warm glow was now giving him a sour, burning sensation. Stupid old fool. "Take care of things, Ramsey." "Keep your mouth shut." He spun back to his desk and slammed his fist down. Junior had better not give him any trouble or he'd bust his face.

He picked up the phone again, but Melanie did not answer until the sixteenth ring. Before she could mumble a greeting, Guy barked into the phone. "Where were you? You think I got nothing to do but listen to your phone ring off the wall?"

"Hey, I spent all night taking care of you. What do you want this early in the morning?"

Guy chewed his cigar a moment before answering. The broad was getting an awfully big mouth lately. She was gonna have to be taken down a peg or two.

"Take a walk for a couple hours around noon. I need the apartment for a business meeting."

"You want me to stay and help?"

He smiled at the idea of her staying to help him and Ellie, but did not let his voice show it. "No. The people I'm gonna meet with get nervous with company around."

"Well, what am I supposed to do for two hours? I'm not into hiking, you know. And I don't have enough money to go shopping."

"Use your charge card. I gotta tell you how to do everything?"

"I don't know what kind of a limit I have. For all I know I could blow it all with one lunch."

"You'd need one huge lunch. You got a five-grand limit."

He could feel the anger and irritation melt away. She giggled merrily. "That should take care of one lunch hour. I'll tell you what, take three or four hours if you need it, honey babe. Bye-bye."

"Money-grubbing little bitch," Guy muttered aloud as he hung up. A little competition would keep her in line. He'd give old Ellie the test this afternoon, but he thought he'd better wait before he moved her in with Melanie. Those hillbillies start young, but they burn out fast. For all he knew she might be twenty-two going on forty.

He got up from his desk to go find Ellie. He had to make sure the day didn't turn into a complete disaster.

"Guenther, you got a message to call the doctor at the nursing home. It's about your aunt."

Guenther Weiland, a building inspector for the city of Chicago, walked across the drab office of the Inspections Department and took the message. It was marked "urgent," but these messages always said that. He looked back up. "Thanks, Loretta. I'll take care of it."

The middle-aged black lady smiled at him sympathetically. "How's she doing? She's been sick a few years now, ain't she?"

Guenther nodded. "Oh, she has her ups and downs, Loretta. She's doing as well as can be expected."

"Does she have any children of her own?"

"No," he replied brusquely. "She never married."

Loretta leaned her bulk toward him. "I know that you're trying to keep it a secret, so I won't tell anybody. But you really are a nice man, Mr. Weiland."

No smile or emotion crossed his face. "Is that right?"

"That's right," she said. "I may not know electricity or plumbing like you guys do, but I do know people. In fact, you're probably the nicest person in this department."

"Is that right?" he repeated quietly.

Loretta was laughing heartily and shaking her head as he made his way back to his gray steel desk on one side of a large bullpen office. A single phone was shared by four desks, but none of his neighbors was in the office as he picked it up and dialed the number.

"Westview Nursing Home," a woman's voice answered.

"This is Guenther Weiland. I have a message to call Dr. Janus."

"Oh yes, Mr. Weiland. Dr. Janus isn't here right now. He did leave a number and said for you to call him at two this afternoon."

She gave him the number and Guenther repeated it, but did not write it down. Once off the phone, he glanced at his watch. It was ten minutes to two, so he'd better hurry. He'd gotten back to the office later than he had expected, but it had been worth it. Laura would really be surprised.

He picked up his light blue jacket and walked past Loretta's desk to the door. "I'm gonna be gone about an hour," he told her.

"Okay, Guenther. I'll hold down the fort."

Guenther left the building and made his way down the street to the Greyhound bus depot. As always, he moved quickly and lightly. With his cold blue eyes and unsmiling face, the pedestrian traffic seemed to part for him.

Under the cold exterior he was smiling, though, as he thought how surprised Laura was going to be. He knew that she had wanted a car, but she was such a good kid that she never actually said so. Figured that he and Edna couldn't afford another one. Edna would be excited too, because now Laura could come home more often.

Laura was their oldest. A bright girl, she was in her junior year at Northwestern University and planned to go to their graduate school of journalism. She was hoping to be an investigative reporter for one of the large dailies in Chicago, or possibly one of the television news stations.

Yes, sir. She was really going to be surprised when she saw what her old dad got her for her birthday. He had gone to the Toyota-Saab dealer on Wabash Avenue, planning to buy her a Toyota. He had changed his mind when he saw the Saabs, though, and had picked out a turbo-charged, two-door hatchback. It was a real beauty. A silvery brown with tan leather seats.

He'd have to go to the mattress and pick up another eight thou. More than twice what he had expected to pay, but that was all right. That was what a father worked for. Those odd jobs certainly came in handy.

He went into the depot and saw that it was almost two o'clock. He moved rapidly to a bank of public phones and dialed the number he had memorized.

"Guenther?"

"Yeah, Sammy. Whatcha got?"

"Old warehouse building just south of North Avenue close by the river. Mid-America Supply. It's got to go real quick."

"This week?"

"Wednesday at the latest."

"Okay. I'll check it out, but it can't go down tomorrow. We're having dinner at Edna's mother's for Laura's birthday. I don't see any problem with doing the job Wednesday night, though."

"Sounds real good. I'll give our clients the word."

"What's the setup at the place? Anybody in the place at night?"

"Nah, they said everybody's out by seven. And there's just a night service that comes by every couple of hours."

"Okay. Good."

"Hey, Guenther. Did Moochie give you a good deal on the Toyota?"

"No, I got my kid a Saab instead."

"Whew, big spender. How much more did it cost ya?"

"Eight thou."

"I'll call Moochie. You bring an extra six thou."

"Thanks, Sammy. I appreciate that."

"That's okay, Guenther. You do good work. My clients never got any complaints when you do the job."

# CHAPTER TWENTY-FIVE

Frances had insisted. The funeral mass had to be at Our Lady of Pompeii and the burial at Queen of Heaven Cemetery. Sam would have wanted to be buried from the old neighborhood, she had assured Jon. It had not mattered to him, so he had made all the arrangements for Wednesday morning just as she had wanted.

The post-burial brunch at Scalzetti's turned out to be more than he had bargained for, though. The hordes of distant relatives and old family friends that hugged him tearfully seemed to have little to do with his own sense of loss. But when two elderly cousins began to argue about which of them would die next, he escaped to the bar at the end of the room.

"A glass of rosé, please," he ordered.

The gray-haired bartender's smile was friendly. "If you're finished with dessert, how about a little anisette, Mr. Morici? I got first-class stuff."

"Hey, I ordered rosé and that's what I want," Jon snapped.

The man's face froze and his black eyes stared hard at Jon. With elaborate slowness, he poured the glass of wine. "Whatever you say, buddy."

Jon was ashamed of his outburst. He had no right to relieve the tensions of the past few days on this man. "I'm sorry," he said simply. "This hasn't been my best day."

"Forget it." The bartender shook his head. "Some people like suggestions, some don't."

"That didn't give me the right to be rude," Jon pointed out.

The man gave an expressive Latin shrug and reached for

the bottle of rosé. He poured himself a glass, then raised it toward Jon. "Salute," he said.

"Salute." Jon stumbled over the word.

"Been out of the neighborhood a long time?"

Jon glanced up quickly. "Do I look that out of place?"

There were no other patrons at the bar, so the man sipped his wine while leaning his elbows comfortably on the counter. His smile was easy. "You look like a guy who don't live in the neighborhood." A quick shrug. "There's a lotta people like that."

Jon turned to gaze at the crowd.

"Some people seem to leave, but not really. Like your mother," the bartender said with a wave of his hand. "It's like she never left."

Jon's eyes found his mother as she moved among the relatives, restauranteurs who had done business with his father, and politicians from city hall. Frances had Toni on her arm and was chatting with Vito Marzullo, the ageless alderman from the neighborhood.

"See how easy she moves around? She's a fine-looking woman." He turned quickly toward Jon. "No offense meant. Just a compliment for a fine lady."

"None taken," Jon replied.

"That redheaded kid with her ain't bad, either."

"Yeah." Jon turned away from the sight of Toni. Even though she had been at the wake last night and with his mother since the funeral early this morning, he had barely spoken to her and had managed to keep her from his thoughts.

It seemed like years since their argument, not just five days. But so much had happened since then that he couldn't even remember how he felt about her. Had he loved her? Did he still? He certainly needed her. The nights had been pure hell. He'd toss and turn for hours, dreading the moment he'd fall asleep, for she haunted his dreams. Could they ever regain what they had once had?

Jon drained his glass and placed it on the bar with a thump. "Well, guess I better do my duty and mingle."

The bartender chuckled sympathetically. "Don't push anything, son. Just float around and everything will be fine. We take care of our own, you know."

Trouble was, he didn't feel like he was one of their own, he thought as he was grabbed by a large, elderly woman dressed entirely in black. She kissed him and murmured, "May his soul rest in peace."

Jon nodded, feeling awkward. "Yeah."

"He was such a good man. He took care of his family as best he could and never turned his back on his friends."

Jon nodded again. "Yes, he did his best."

"And no one can do any better than that," she pointed out solemnly. After giving his arm a slight squeeze, she moved away.

Who was that? Jon wondered as he watched her move across the floor. He turned back to find a short, grandfatherly man standing before him.

"Hello, Jon." He extended his hand. "Please accept my sympathies on the death of your father."

Jon took the man's hand, wondering who he was. Probably some uncle or cousin that he didn't remember. "Thank you, sir," he said, then paused. "I'm sorry to be so blunt, but I'm not doing too well today. Where should I know you from?"

The elderly man's eyes twinkled, surprising Jon with their blueness. "My name's Lou Alexander, son. Your father and I were friends. We grew up together."

"Well, it was nice of you to come."

"That's what friends are for." He drew at his cigar and let a black cloud escape slowly into the atmosphere as his eyes moved over to where Jon's mother and Toni stood. "That lady accountant is a good-looker."

Jon was surprised. His mother must have introduced Toni to everyone here. She probably could do better with the names than he was doing. "Yes, she is very attractive."

"Seems real sharp, too."

Jon nodded, fighting a creeping suspicion. Had his mother sent this old coot over to try to patch things up between Toni and him? "Yeah," he noted. "She's an intelligent lady."

"A man could do a lot worse."

Jon chose not to reply.

Lou took the cigar from his mouth and stared at the tip thoughtfully. "She looks a little tired, but her run of bad luck should be over."

Jon tried not feel irritated. Mr. Alexander was an old man and deserved his courtesy, but how did he know so much about Toni? Was his mother telling everyone Toni's life story? Rather than be rude, he made no reply again.

Lou pulled a business card from his pocket and handed it to Jon. "We should talk sometime soon. Give me a call when you have a chance."

"Sure thing. Thanks again for coming, sir." Jon shook the man's hand and slipped the card into his pocket.

His mother and Toni were free, so he walked over to join them. There were lines of fatigue around his mother's eyes, but she looked quiet and composed. He leaned down and kissed her on the cheek.

"Hi, Mom. How you holding up?" He nodded toward Toni without really looking at her.

"Real good, Jon." Frances glanced quickly around the room. "It feels comfortable here."

"Comfortable?" Jon was astonished.

"Yes, like home."

He stared at his mother.

"How are you feeling?" Toni asked him. "You don't look like you've had much sleep."

Jon shrugged uneasily, noticing she didn't look too rested herself. "It's been a hectic few days." He turned back to his mother. "I'll take you home when you're ready, Mom."

Frances smiled at Toni and squeezed her hand. "No, Toni's going to take me up to the house and help me pack."

"Pack?"

"Yes," his mother said. "I can't wear these clothes forever."

Jon was lost. What was she talking about?

"The top floor in my cousin Helen's apartment is vacant and she said I could have it," Frances explained. "I'm going to sleep in her spare bedroom until I get my own stuff moved in, though."

"You're moving?"

"I'm coming home," she corrected him. "Back to the neighborhood I love."

"But you've got a home. In Winnetka."

"I have a house in Winnetka, Jon. That can be sold. I want to be comfortable, Jon. I want to walk to the grocery store and the bakery. I want to chat and laugh with friends. I want to talk to little children. I want to have someone to cry with when I need it."

Jon felt a twinge of guilt. Had he let his mother down? "Mom, I'll be around more. I promise."

His mother's eyes glistened and a tender smile came to her lips. "You're around enough. I don't want to be an old lady waiting for her son to give her the only human contact. I want to live my life."

"But what about your friends in Winnetka?"

"I've got acquaintances in Winnetka. I've got friends here that I haven't seen for years. We have a lot to catch up on."

Jon must have looked as confused as he felt, because his mother just laughed quietly and turned to Toni. "You talk to him," she said. "Convince him I haven't gone off the deep end." She left the two of them together.

Jon looked hesitantly at Toni. This was his chance to tell that he missed her and was sorry for all that had happened. He didn't know how to start, though, and while he was fumbling for the words, she began to speak.

"It's what she wants, Jon," she said, obviously not sharing his awkwardness. "She doesn't want to go back to that big old house by herself. It has too many memories."

Jon stiffened slightly, feeling embarrassed that his thoughts had been so personal when all she wanted was to discuss his mother. But then, he had thought all along that he was more deeply involved than she was.

"It seems like such a major step," he said. "My father worked so hard to leave that neighborhood, and she can't wait to get back."

"But he's not here anymore," Toni reminded him. "And she still is. Would you rather see her lonely in the big house or happy in a small apartment?"

"It's not that," he argued, all too conscious of her nearness. A strand of hair had come loose from her pins and his hands longed to smooth it back.

"And from a financial point of view, the move makes sense," Toni went on. "She can invest the money from selling the house and live off the interest."

"Boy, she sure did some sales job on you," Jon noted with a trace of bitterness in his voice. She was every inch the accountant, safe and secure in her world of assets and debits. Her eyes were like the green numbers on his calculator—bright and vivid, but no heart behind them.

Toni blinked in surprise at his tone, but Frances joined

them before she could say anything. "Well, is he convinced?" His mother carried two glasses of Coke.

Toni took one with a forced laugh. "I'm not sure."

"It's just that I'll worry about you," Jon pointed out. "That's not exactly a safe neighborhood."

Frances shook her head with a smile. "Jon, darling, you're so funny. I'll have a police sergeant living downstairs and a street boss for the outfit next door. I could sleep in the middle of the street and be safe."

He suspected his mother was making fun of him and his frown did not move. "Well, if you're sure it's what you want to do," he said grudgingly.

Frances reached up to pat his cheek. "It is, honey, it is."

Jon sighed, and hugged her. "I'm not really such a grump. I just want you to be happy."

"I know," his mother said. "It's been a bad time, and my monopolizing Toni hasn't helped. But she's been so wonderful. I honestly don't think I could have gotten through it without her."

Jon did not look at either of them, but across the room. "Yeah. I'm glad she was able to help. If you'll excuse me, I think I'd better pay off the altar boys before they slash some tires." He smiled vaguely in their direction and turned away, promptly bumping into a pleasant-looking young man. "Oh, excuse me. I'm sorry."

"That's okay. I was in your way." When Jon was about to go on, the man laughed. "You don't remember me, do you? I'm Verne Cirilo."

"Verne?" Jon laughed. "You've grown since I last saw you. How old were we then? About five?"

"That old?" Verne shook his head. "I remember thinking that I'd never find another friend after you moved. Until I met the three kids that moved into your old apartment," he added.

They both laughed, then Verne sobered up. "Hey, I was sorry to hear about your dad."

"Thanks." Jon shrugged. "So what are you doing with yourself now? Weren't we both planning on being cowboys when I moved?"

"I'm a cop. First district traffic," he said. "How about you?"

"I work with my father." He stopped and then continued awkwardly. "That is, I'm in the family business now."

Verne nodded. "Sam did all right for himself."

"Yeah, he didn't do too bad."

"I mean he was real cool. He had friends everywhere. Business, city hall . . . the outfit." Verne finished the sentence by nodding at the elderly gentleman who had introduced himself to Jon as Lou Alexander.

Jon blinked in surprise. "Outfit? You mean that old guy?"

Verne laughed heartily. "They don't all wear gorilla suits, you know. Yeah, my dad told me that there was a group of guys here from the old neighborhood who were real tight. Kept in close touch no matter where they went. Lou, your dad, a bunch of others."

Jon stared dumbly at Lou as he pretended to pull a coin from a little girl's ear. The old man gave the little girl the coin and she shyly curtsied. Jon's eyes lost their sharp focus and took in the entire crowd. This was some neighborhood. It gave the city its politicians, its laborers, its police, its executives. Born here, they left by separate paths, only to have them all terminate at Our Lady of Pompeii and Queen of Heaven. A thought nagged at Jon. Did those paths really stay separate until the end?

"We were supposed to have a meeting yesterday morning. Where were you?" Jon asked.

Guy looked coldly across his desk at him. There were shadows under his eyes and his face was strained, but he appeared cool and in control. Little wimp, Guy thought, he sure can put on a good act. Pretending like he's got some power around here. To keep from snickering out loud, Guy pulled at his cigar and stared out the door at Mrs. Flores typing diligently.

"I'm only going to ask you one more time, Ramsey. Where were you yesterday?"

Guy was angered by Jon's aggressive tone, and clenched his fists. His lips tightened momentarily, but he quickly gained control of himself. A scornful smile covered his face. "What's this 'one more time' stuff?"

Jon did not blink an eye or raise his voice. "Answer my questions or get out."

Guy's eyes narrowed. How he'd like to be the one to put this jerk in his place! "What'd your mother put in your pablum this morning, Junior?"

"I'd prefer that you don't mention my mother."

He was really asking for it! With difficulty, Guy reminded himself of Lou's instructions. He had to keep his mouth shut. Looking out the door at Mrs. Flores, he took another pull at his cigar. Ah, what was the difference. Let Junior have his fun. It wouldn't be long before he learned the facts of life.

He let his face relax into a sneering smile as he looked back at Morici. "So who wants to know where I was yesterday?"

"I do." Staring impassively at Guy, Jon went on. "You were at the funeral this morning and saw us bury my father."

Guy just shrugged. "You're breaking my heart, Junior, but it's a tough world out there."

"You don't understand, Ramsey. My father died and left a will."

"So?" Guy grunted impatiently. He was getting more irritated by the minute. This fool was nothing. He was a wimpy little kid that would fold at the first sign of work, yet he, Guy Ramsey, the real power in this place, was supposed to sit here and take this! Not for much longer, that was certain.

"My mother and I are the owners of the company," Jon pointed out coldly. "You work for me now, Ramsey."

"Like hell I do," Guy snarled, his anger suddenly exploding.

The slight smile on Jon's lips did not reach his eyes. "I don't know where you went to school but, in my book, owners hire and fire."

Guy had to erase that superior look from Jon's face. Nothing else mattered but those gloating eyes and that mocking smile. "You're not the only owner," Guy informed him. He watched for the look of shocked disbelief.

Jon's scornful gaze did not even flicker, but Guy felt a sudden chill creep along the back of his neck as the words echoed back to him. Oh Lord, he had been ordered to keep his mouth shut, and he had blown it. He had been given direct orders and he had forgotten them. He could hear Lou's cold voice asking him if he understood what "obey" meant, and he could almost feel Chuckie's huge hands on him.

The sudden silence in the air added to his fear and he automatically looked out the door toward the bullpen. Why was it so quiet? What the hell was going on out there? Mrs. Flores had stopped her typing and was staring straight at him, her dark eyes like two chunks of coal. The chill along the back of his neck deepened and he looked toward Jon, forcing away his uneasiness. He wondered if there was any chance Jon hadn't understood. He had always thought Junior wasn't too bright.

"Who are the other owners?"

Guy's mouth went dry with fear.

"Who are the other owners, Ramsey?" The voice was quiet. No shouting. No urgency.

Guy tried to swallow the painful lump in his throat. "It's . . . it's a privately held conglomerate. They're into a lotta things."

"What is the name of this private conglomerate?"

Guy took a deep breath. What did he do now? Dear God, why couldn't Junior have a heart attack just like his old man?

"I want to know the name of the conglomerate and the names of the principal owners."

Guy licked his lips and tried to swallow again. He was such a high-and-mighty wimp. Just wait until he met the owners. He wouldn't be playing the boss then. No, sir, he'd be groveling just like his old man did.

"Actually, the partners have been wanting to meet you. They've been planning on it." Guy hoped he sounded braver than he felt.

"When?"

"I was gonna talk to them today anyway. I'll check."

"Do that."

Jon left and Guy brought out his bottle of scotch. It was not until he drank the second tumbler that he was able to ease the painful lump in his throat. It was okay. Morici wouldn't say anything to Lou, and if he did, Guy could say his father told him. Sure, that was it.

Happily Guy poured himself a third drink. What was he so worried about? He had this in control.

"Mr. Ramsey. Oh, Mr. Ramsey."

Guy jumped at the sound of Mrs. Flores's voice and spilled some of the scotch on his hand. "Jesus Christ! What do you want?"

"There's a phone call for you, sir. And the young lady seems rather insistent."

"Can't you see I'm in conference?"

Mrs. Flores ignored the empty room. "She insists on talking to you right now, sir."

"Do I have to do everything around here?" He angrily grabbed the phone. "Ramsey here."

"Mr. Ramsey. This is Patsy."

"Patsy? Patsy who? I don't know no Patsy."

"I'm Donny's woman."

"Oh?" Guy was really irritated now. Why was that crazy biker having his girlfriend call him at work? He had been given orders not to contact Guy here. Well, this little slipup just cost Donny half the money Guy owed him.

"What do you want, Patsy?" He reached for the drink on his credenza.

"Donny's dead."

"What?" The rest of the drink spilled as the glass crashed to the floor.

"Dead, you dirty creep! He's dead." The girl took a deep breath and stifled a sob. "The cops found him in the trunk of his car this morning. He was naked and all beat up and burned all over."

What was she calling him for? He glanced around the room suspiciously as if he expected to see tape recorders getting his every word. "Look, Patsy—" He stopped and swallowed hard. The sinking feeling in his stomach got worse and his hands began to tremble.

"Somebody was mad at him about something. Do you know who?" Patsy asked.

Guy could feel the sweat form rivulets down his back. Oh, dear God. How could they know? So the Demons' contract with the partners did not allow free-lancing. He was paying Donny good money. Donny wouldn't have squealed. "No, Patsy. I don't know." There was a long silence; then Guy continued. "Honest, I really don't know."

"Well, I just want the money that you owe Donny."

"Money?" Guy croaked.

"Yeah, don't play cute with me. Donny told me that he was doing a little job for you and that you still owed him two big ones."

And who else did Donny tell?

"I need the money and I need it bad."

This was the time to get out, Guy realized. Cut all ties

and pray for the best. "Hey, look Patsy, I'm sorry about Donny and all that, but—"

"Don't try to weasel out of it," she screamed at him. "You owed it to Donny and now you owe it to me. You'd better pay up or I'll tell the whole world what Donny was doing for you. I'll call you back at three o'clock." She hung up.

Guy stared at the instrument as if it were a snake. What the hell was going on?

All of a sudden, he jumped up and moved rapidly out of his office. The pressure was unbearable.

"Oh, Mr. Ramsey, sir. You have a call holding on your other line."

"Jesus Christ, lady. Am I the only one that can do anything around here? I'm going to the men's room."

Mrs. Flores ignored the startled looks from the others in the bullpen and shot a steely glance into his eyes. "You had better take this call right now. The party is not accustomed to waiting."

Guy obeyed Mrs. Flores's directive. In a dull stupor, he went back into his office and picked up the phone. "Guy Ramsey."

"We didn't want Junior upset."

Guy licked his lips.

"Well, Lou, with his father dying—"

"We had discussed it, Ramsey."

"Yes, sir. I know. It's just that—"

"We gotta talk, Ramsey."

"Sure thing, Lou. I'm open all afternoon. Do you want me to come to the usual place?"

"No, you just stay where you're at. I'll send Chuckie and Marvin to pick you up. It'll be sometime after three o'clock. Chuckie's gotta take his kid to the dentist. These goddamn working wives. You always gotta work around them. Ain't like the old days."

"Yeah, you're right, Lou. I'm looking forward to our talk. We have a lot to talk about."

"Yeah, sure."

"Good-bye, Lou." Guy spoke to the dead line. So, that fat old bastard did it again. Ran whining to Lou. He'd think—

Guy froze. Morici was dead. He couldn't have called Lou, but somebody did. He rose to his feet, licking his lips nervously as he went to the door. Somebody out there was watching his every move. Watching and reporting back to Lou.

He found Mrs. Flores' eyes on him, and straightened up automatically, forcing the fear and worry from his manners as he sauntered over to her desk. He had to get out of the place, but neatly, not in a panic-stricken run. He'd make some excuses to the old broad so she'd front for him.

Good old Mrs. Flores. The perfect secretary. Brains enough to do her job, but not enough to think. It would be hours before Lou found out he'd gone.

Guy waited impatiently as she dealt with a medium sized man with longish grey-blond hair and tinted glasses who had stopped at her desk.

"Guenther Weiland, ma'am. City building inspector. Okay if I look around?" the man asked, showing her an identification card.

"Oh, certainly, Mr. Weiland. Would you like anyone to accompany you?"

He shook his head and went off toward the warehouse.

Guy watched him walk away with a frown. With his luck today, he'd probably get a barrelful of building citations for the old firetrap.

"Yes, Mr. Ramsey. What can I do for you?"

He turned back to his secretary. "I have to talk to Rudy out in the warehouse. I'll probably be there awhile."

"Very good, sir. I'll take your calls."

Guy walked through the warehouse without speaking to anyone. He jumped down onto the street from the loading dock and walked for three blocks before he found a cab. He told the driver just to drive around, while he leaned back and stared moodily out the window. He had to stop the trembling, he thought, and figure this out. There had to be a way. He'd make things right with the bosses and buy himself a little safety.

Melanie pulled away from the tall blonde man's embrace. "Damn," she muttered with an irritated glance toward her intercom. "I wonder who that can be."

The man followed her as she left the bed and went down the hall. She slapped the button impatiently. "Yeah?"

"Hey, babe. Open up."

"Uh-oh," she whispered, then turned to glance apologetically toward the man. He was so gorgeous, too, she thought sadly as her eyes traveled over the chest just rippling with muscles. They followed the trail of hair downward. Oh, what she was going to miss!

"Sorry, Lance," she said, and tossed her hair over her shoulder. "My old man's here."

Even his frown was magnificent. "I thought you said you weren't married."

She glided across the floor toward him, her naked body rosy with longing for his touch. Her right hand ran lightly across his chest and over his shoulder, pulling him closer to her. "Hey, sugar. Don't be mad. Why don't you go down to that bar on the corner and have a drink? I'll get rid of him and meet you there."

Lance frowned, but when her left hand found his flat stomach and her fingertips began their explorations, his look became more receptive. "Okay, doll, but don't make me wait too long."

That wasn't likely, she thought as she hurried him into the bedroom. It wasn't every day that she met up with such a gorgeous hunk who also happened to be the manager of Loop Import Motors. She had just wandered into the showroom to price that Jaguar XL and there he was—a perfectly delightful way to get the price within reach.

While Lance pulled on his worn jeans, she found his shoes and socks. She shoved them into his hands and tossed his shirt on top of them.

"He rarely comes during the day," Melanie said, her voice a soft purr. "He'll have to be getting back to work real soon, anyway."

She jumped at a sudden pounding on the door and picked up her own jeans. Carrying them and a T-shirt in one hand, she grabbed Lance with the other and tugged him toward the kitchen.

"Order me a rum and Coke, and I promise I'll be there before the ice melts," she said. After a quick kiss on his lips, she shoved him, still half-undressed, out the door. The pounding came again.

"Melanie."

She frowned and pulled her jeans on as she glanced around the kitchen. No trace of him there. She slipped her shirt over her head and hurried into the living room. Nothing there either.

She shook her hair loose and took a deep, calming

breath. Mr. Ramsey had better be mighty good since he had wrecked all her plans for the afternoon. She pulled open the door.

"Hi, darling," Guy said. "What took you so long?" He pulled her into his embrace and kissed her roughly.

Melanie shrugged herself free and walked toward the sofa. "I was cleaning the bathroom." She turned around to discover that he had a suitcase in his hand. What was he doing? Moving in?

He brought the suitcase over to the sofa and sat down, keeping it close to his feet. "Come on over and show me how much you love me," he said, patting the seat next to him.

"What's in the suitcase?" she asked. She sat down, ignoring his sudden addiction to loverlike phrases. His hand kept clenching and unclenching nervously. "You're wound tight as a drum. What'd you do, rob a bank?"

Guy's laugh was forced but she pretended not to notice as he put the suitcase onto the coffee table. "This here's just a little severance pay," he quipped. He flipped open the clasps, then pushed back the top. The suitcase was filled with money.

"Oh, Lord," Melanie breathed. She reached forward and reverently picked up one bundle. It was all hundreds, she saw, and had to contain at least five thousand dollars. That Jaguar was so close she could smell it. "There must be a couple hundred thousand here. Where did you get all this?"

Guy looked pleased with himself as he took the bundle from her hands and put it back into the suitcase. Then he closed it. "I told you. It's severance pay."

"What are you talking about?" Melanie demanded. "Did you quit Mid-America? They wouldn't give you that kind of money."

"Why not? I ran the place for years. Now that old Morici's dead, I don't want to hang around anymore."

Guy leaned back in the sofa, putting his hands behind his head. His eyes looked glazed, and Melanie wondered if he was on some drugs or had just had too much to drink. "So you just took all that money and left. Don't you think they'll notice it's missing?"

"Not a chance," he laughed, and then leaned forward to slip his hands underneath her shirt. "Even if they do, we'll be long gone and they'll never find us. It's time we blew this town, and now we can go in style."

"Where to?" Melanie asked quickly, her excitement mounting at the thought of all that money. She was vaguely aware of his hands on her and knew that he expected a response, so she let her hands tug at his shirt. "How about Vegas? Or Rome? Or Rio?" Lord, the places she would see! Who needed old Lance now?

"Hey, we belong together. You'd never let me down like those others!" Guy breathed in her ear. He pressed her body down on the sofa, his mouth hot and demanding as it covered hers.

She moaned softly for effect but her mind was racing ahead. Rio would be her choice, although they didn't have to settle on just one spot. They could see them all.

Suddenly Guy was on his feet and pulled her up. "Come on, baby. I'm loaded and set to go."

She followed him into the bedroom and tossed her clothes onto the floor. Usually, he would be all over her before she had time to lie down, but he wasn't this time. His hands were gentle as they caressed, seeking to enhance her pleasure rather than his own.

Melanie was surprised, then suspicious. What was going on? He enroll in Masters and Johnson's? Why was he the great, considerate lover all of a sudden?

She tried not to let her feelings show, and instead thought about the suitcase of money in the other room. It was a more powerful aphrodisiac than any caress, so that her body was more than ready for him, even if her mind was far away.

The last thing she wanted was some parasite clinging to her, spouting phrases of undying love. She liked her men strong and able to take care of themselves and her. That was what had first attracted her to Guy, his strength and feeling of power. Now, he seemed to be turning into a milquetoast wimp like Alan or Steve. She was no mother, ready to soothe and comfort. Hell! What would she get out of that kind of arrangement?

Afterward, Guy lay back, his body covered with sweat and his eyes closed. "God, you don't know how long I've wanted to get away. It's going to be great. Just the two of us."

Melanie lay on her side. Her right hand was tickling the hairs on his chest as she eyed him suspiciously. "Where we going first, sugar? How about Rio?"

"Rio?" He opened one eye and laughed at her. "I want to get away from all this shit, not get into more of it."

Melanie's hand stopped its tickling. "So where then?"

His eyes were closed again. "Someplace quiet and out of the way. Maybe find a secluded house along the coast in Mexico. Someplace where we can go for weeks without seeing another human being. Hell, we don't need anybody else anyway."

Melanie's face grew tight. It had taken her nineteen years to get out of Niles, and he wanted to imprison her in someplace even worse. With just their love to keep them warm, no doubt.

Guy settled himself into the bed more comfortably. "I got just one job to do before I go. I'm going to settle it tonight. Then I'll come back here for you and my little suitcase and we'll be gone." He yawned loudly, and she smelled the onions that he'd had for lunch. "Wake me up when dinner's ready."

"Sure, honey," she purred, and slid away from him. "Only I'll have to run to the grocery store and get something nice. So's we can celebrate."

"Okay," he said, already half-asleep. "Make it good. We ain't eating hot dogs ever again."

Melanie nodded her head as she reached for her clothes. She sure wasn't ever eating hot dogs again. Not with that little bank account sitting in her living room. Neither was she going to stay around and play housekeeper for some wimp.

She turned away in disgust from the sight of Guy's body. Something must have happened to turn him into such a creep, but she didn't care what it was. Let him whine to his mommy about it. She was going after better game, and was due some severance pay.

Her smile was excited as she glanced at the clock on her dresser. It was only a half hour since Lance had left. With luck, he'd still be at the bar and they could go get her car. Then, after dinner tonight, when Guy went off to do his job, she'd go also. But in her new Jaguar and with that load of money in the trunk.

Guy had been a good beginning, but with that suitcase she would have gotten everything out of him that she could. It was time to look for someone new.

# CHAPTER TWENTY-SIX

Toni knotted the thread and clipped the end off. Then she folded the gray woolen skirt and piled it with the others that she had mended. The end of September seemed early to be getting all her winter clothes out, but the weather had turned so cool it felt more like the middle of November. While freezing at Sam's funeral that morning, she had promised herself that she would mend her winter suits and get them to the cleaners.

The thought of the funeral brought an array of images to her mind that she preferred to avoid, so she turned with determination to the television and the ten o'clock news. As she checked the buttons on a long-sleeved white blouse, she listened avidly to the midweek report from the Bears' practice.

Maybe she'd start watching the football games on Sunday afternoons, she thought. It would help kill time on the weekends, plus give her something to talk about at work. Some of those new client sessions had been pretty trying so far. She was discovering once again that it wasn't enough to be a good accountant representing a good firm: she had to prove that she was one of the boys also. A little football knowledge might help.

She hoped something would, for she didn't seem to have that same drive and determination she had had. It was hard to continue pretending enthusiasm for her new assignment, and now she was discouraged. The job wasn't as exciting as it had once been.

She was probably just tired, both physically and emotionally, she told herself as she tightened two of the buttons on the blouse. As she tossed it into the laundry pile, the doorbell rang. She stopped, momentarily frozen with fear. It was true that the obscene phone calls had stopped and so had the notes. And she no longer felt as if she was being followed each time she went out, but not enough time had elapsed to let her relax. She walked slowly over to the intercom and pushed the button.

"Toni? It's me. Jon."

Her fear vanished, but she did not relax as she pushed the button to release the inside door. What could he want?

She glanced down at her blue jeans and knitted cotton pullover. She looked terrible, she thought, wiping her sweaty palms on the sides of her legs. Maybe she should go change. She could put on something a little dressier, or something a little more revealing. No, that would be dumb. There wasn't even time to clean up the living room, and she'd hardly have been sitting around sewing dressed in a strapless gown. He probably wanted something earth-shattering, like his key back.

Still, when his knock sounded on the door, she couldn't help but feel a glimmer of hope. He had loved her once; surely the argument they had had wasn't enough to erase all those feelings. Even when she had been angry at him, her love hadn't changed. Of course, he hadn't attacked her father the way he thought she had attacked his. She wiped her hands off again and pulled open the door.

"Hi," she said, and stood aside. "Come on in."

He was still dressed in the charcoal gray suit he had worn to the funeral, but the tie was missing and the top button of his shirt was open. The shadows of weariness under his eyes seemed to accentuate their coldness. His frown was hardly necessary to tell her that this was not going to be the loving scene she had hoped for.

"Why don't you sit down?" she said, waving him into the living room. She followed and hurried over to move the pile of clothes onto the dining room table. "Can I get you a drink? Some coffee maybe?"

He shook his head and sat down on the edge of the sofa. It was obvious that he would rather be somewhere else.

Toni tried to smile to bolster her own confidence and turned off the television before she sat down. It had sounded so loud and intrusive, but without it, the room was deathly still. She coughed nervously while Jon stared down at his hands.

"My mother appreciated your help these last few days," he said with a quick glance up at her.

"I felt I owed it to you."

He frowned uncomfortably and rose to his feet. His right hand rubbed the back of his neck as he stopped before the window and stared out at the lights below. His shoulders seemed hunched from tension; his stance bespoke weariness.

She longed to go over to him and take him in her arms. She could soothe away his worries if he would let her. They could talk things out while lying in each other's arms. Then slowly, as they forgot everything but themselves, they would make love. It would be perfect because they needed each other so, and they finally would have realized that their love was most important.

Jon turned to face her suddenly. "It's that damn mess at Mid-America," he said.

She felt her cheeks redden from her thoughts, but did not look away. "I'm not on that account anymore."

He nodded and came back to the sofa. "I know, but you still have more information about it than me. Ramsey is up to no good, I'm convinced of that much at least. I tried to talk to him today but got nowhere fast. He did admit that there were partners in the business, but he wouldn't tell me who they were."

"I don't know who they are either," she said gently. "Melanie was the one who told me they existed. Maybe you should ask her."

Jon shook his head quickly. "No, that's not that important right now. I just want to know what's actually going on there. Even if it implicates my father," he added.

There was a moment of awkward silence. Toni didn't know what he was asking of her. "I really don't know any more than I already told you," she finally said. "Just little things here and there."

"Maybe not, but you could help me find out." He had risen to his feet again, and began to pace the floor nervously.

"You see, I've got to know the truth. I meant to have it out with my father Friday night but never got the chance, although he probably would have just denied everything. Over the last few days I've done some hard thinking, though, and I have to admit that there were a lot of strange things going on there that I never questioned. Never even thought to question. Guy won't talk and my father can't. So that means I sit patiently and wait for someone to clue me in or I find out for myself." He stopped pacing and looked at her. "I've never been the patient type."

Toni forced a smile on her face. "I appreciate what you're saying, but I'm not sure why you are so determined. Your father's dead. Whatever he did is dead also."

"Is it?" Jon asked. "And even if it is, can I live with this doubt all my life? If my father was doing something illegal, I need to know. Maybe in time I can accept it, but I can't live with this doubt. Surely any truth would be better than my fears."

Toni sighed and stood up also. She had left a scissors on an end table and she put it back in her sewing box, carefully slipping it in next to the spools of thread. "Just what do you want me to do?"

Jon came up behind her. "I've looked all over that place and didn't find a thing, but I probably wouldn't know a good piece of information if it bit me in the ass. Ramsey had that place fairly well automated. All the data is in the computer, I'm sure of that."

She turned around to face him.

"If I could get the financial records out of the computer then you could figure them out," he told her quickly. "I have trouble reading our yearly financial statement. Accounting is Greek to me, but you could make sense of it. You could tell me what really is happening there."

Toni walked past him into the kitchen. The only time any spark of interest had come into his eyes was when he was talking about getting the records out of the computer. Her presence had meant nothing to him. Could she work closely with him, knowing that his feelings for her were dead? But since hers weren't, could she refuse him?

She poured herself a glass of water and drank about half of it. After she poured the rest into the sink, she turned back to him. "When did you want to do this sleuthing?"

"As soon as possible. Tonight, even."

"Tonight?" she repeated. Maybe that was better. Get it over with quickly rather than stew and fret for days about seeing him again.

"All right," she said, nodding slowly. "We might as well

get it over with. Give me time to make us a thermos of coffee and then we can go."

"I really appreciate it, Toni," he told her.

Yeah, she thought as she filled the coffee pot with water. She was the original Good Samaritan, ready to help all those in need. Or was she just jumping at the chance to spend a last few hours with Jon?

Jon was discouraged as he balanced the soda pop cans in one hand. They had been poring over files for the last few hours and were no closer to any kind of explanation. He stopped outside the computer room and stuck his small plastic CAS badge into a slot next to the door with the other. After reading the magnetic strip on the back, the door unlocked, then hissed closed behind him as he walked up the ramp into the room.

He looked across the room at Toni, his love and need for her rushing back in spite of his uncertainty over the past few days. She was gorgeous even in her blue jeans and no makeup. The bulky sweater she had pulled over her shirt might have camouflaged her tempting figure but it didn't blunt the edge of his desire. His memory played back scene after vivid scene of their love, and it was all he could do to keep from taking her into his arms.

The exhausted hunch of her shoulders as she sat before the computer terminal reminded him of the reason they were there and he pushed his own feelings away. She had come to help him find Guy's schemes, not for any other reason. And as much as he'd like to keep her with him longer, maybe they should give up on their search. If something funny was going on, it was well hidden. They hadn't found a trace of anything suspicious.

He went over to where Toni sat. "There was still some coffee in the pot, but I figured after brewing all day it's probably good for patching potholes. I got some Pepsi instead."

She shrugged. "I guess I should have brought my whole pot of coffee instead of just a thermosful."

"This has caffeine in it too, you know."

She nodded as she turned back to the console.

Jon looked at the dejection on her face and felt it himself. "This is stupid," he said suddenly. "I don't know what I expected to find here. Guy has had this operation running for years. Why should I be able to figure it out in a few hours?"

Toni said nothing. She pushed a few buttons and a new list appeared on the screen.

"Why don't we pack it in? It's almost two."

She made no response to that either.

"That's two A.M., not P.M.," he prodded.

To his surprise, she turned on him angrily. "If you want to quit, go ahead. I know that creep Ramsey was up to something and I'm going to get him if it's the last thing I do."

Her final statement was emphasized by the banging of her fist on the terminal stand. Then her determination melted into a look of embarrassment.

"My father was a big boy, Toni. If he was mixed up in some dirt, I'm sure he walked in with his eyes open."

"I'm sorry, Jon," she whispered.

Jon shrugged. "I loved him, Toni, but I'm past the stage of wanting a cover-up. Now I just want the truth."

She silently turned back to the computer terminal and idly paged through the information stored in its data bank. She didn't look too interested in what she was seeing.

The silence made Jon nervous as it dragged on. He glanced at the changing array of figures on the screen and then around the room, but there was nothing for him to do. "All of Mrs. Flores's plants are gone," he told her suddenly.

Toni grunted an unintelligible reply.

"She always takes such good care of them. I suppose she took them home."

Another grunt.

"Those plants are like her children. I wonder why she would take them home."

Toni glared at him. "What are you babbling about? How the hell should I know why her plants are gone? Maybe she just took them for a walk."

Her brief spark of irritation faded away, leaving her looking exhausted. He should never have dragged her over here in the middle of the night, he told himself. What was this big rush to know the truth? He could have waited until the weekend, anyway. They could have had the place to themselves during the day when they were relatively alert.

"I take it we're not getting anywhere," he sighed.

"I don't know about 'we,' but I do know I'm not getting anywhere," she snapped.

Jon spread his hands in a helpless gesture. "I told you accounting was Greek to me."

Toni nodded her head, then leaned back in the chair. She closed her eyes and rubbed her temples. "Yeah, I know," she said softly. "I'm sorry. I'm just mad at myself. There's got to be some clue here."

She opened her eyes to look at him. "I've been through the general ledger, the A/P file, the A/R file, the—"

He held up his hands quickly. "Hey, I know I sound dumb, but you have to go slow for me. The A/P file is the people we owe money to and A/R is the people who owe us money."

"Yes." Toni stood up and stretched. "I've gone through everything. Mid-America's books are all in balance. Nothing is out of whack."

"Do you want any of the source documents?"

"No." She shook her head and picked up one of the cans of pop. "We'd have to check the documents in detail against the computer files, and even with a whole crew of people it would take days to do that."

Jon shook his head. "Right now all I want is a hint of what's going on."

They stared at each other for a moment in silence. Then Jon took the pop can from her and pulled it open.

"I could have done that," she said with a frown.

"I had to prove I was good for something," he joked tiredly. "Don't want you to think I'm totally worthless. So far all I've done is point out that the inventory and sales figures on the general ledger sheets were too big to be believed."

She took the can from him; her eyes seemed unable to meet his. "I really didn't mean to snap at you," she said. "I'm just tired and frustrated."

Jon said nothing for a moment. He was frustrated, too, but not quite the same way. Having her this close to him in the relative coziness of the deserted warehouse was driving him crazy. He looked over at a stack of bound computer printouts. "What's that? A printout of the A/P files?"

"No. That's the ADMAS documentation."

"Was that 'add mess' or 'add mass'?"

Toni's glare was very mild. "My, what a comedian! You ought to be on the stage."

"Yeah, I know, and the next one leaves in thirty minutes."

He was glad to see the slight smile in her eyes as she turned back to the bound printouts. "ADMAS stands for Advanced Distribution Management Accounting System. It's a good accounting package for small firms like Mid-America. A lot of my customers use it because it's flexible and covers almost every situation that would come up."

A light went on in Jon's head. "Every situation, or almost every situation?"

"Almost," Toni mumbled, and sat back down.

"What do they do for the exceptional situations?"

She rubbed her eyes and yawned. "Most of my accounts say the hell with it and don't do anything."

"Come on, Toni, I'm serious." He felt a stab of guilt at the hurt look on her face. Damn it, she was doing her best. He didn't have to be such a bully. "I'm sorry, kid."

She smiled slightly. "That's all right. These programs have exits so you can leave their routines and go into ones that you've added for your own special needs."

"That's it. That's got to be it."

Toni just stared at him, looking like she was trying to get him into focus. He moved over and put a hand on her shoulder. "Do you know if this system comes with a machine language listing?"

"Yes, they're one of the few software houses that do," she replied uncertainly.

"Good." Jon clapped his hands. "Go find those listings and I'm going to do a quick study on this little monster and figure out how it works."

Toni got up, but moved slowly. "I thought you said you didn't know anything about this."

"I said I didn't know anything about accounting, but I am an engineer. We study how the machines work, not just how to use them." He pulled a *Principles of Operation* manual from the bookrack and was quickly lost inside.

After ten minutes of quiet study he turned to Toni. "Okay, kid, let's load the A/P data entry program into the machine."

Toni did as she was instructed. "Now what?"

Jon was figuring intently on a piece of paper. "Just a minute. I have to figure where this program was loaded in the machine. I haven't done this for a while so I'm a little slow at hexadecimal arithmetic."

When he finished, he went to the operator's console. He fiddled with the keys and soon had a string of letters and numbers on his display screen.

Toni was leaning over his shoulder and, seeing the data on his display, asked, "What's all that garbage?"

"This is the A/P data entry program translated into machine language. Each of these two-character sets represents one machine character. See, the numbers all start with F. So F1 is one, F2 is two, and so forth. A1 is the letter A, etc."

He heard her grunt behind him and went on. "You don't have to understand it, just read that machine language listing to me while I try and cross-match it to the program listing."

Toni looked dubiously at him. "Why are we doing all this?"

"Just trust me and read," he said.

Toni began. "A3, BA, D7, E5—"

"Did you say D or E?"

"E, E, E like in, in . . . Ellsworth."

"It gets hard to tell a D from an E or a P after a while. Why don't you give the letters names, like 'dog' for D, 'easy' for E, okay?"

"All righty. Here we go. Annabella one; Desdemona five; F, F . . . Fanny nine."

"Fanny nine?" He shot a quick glance at her.

"You don't like my names?"

Jon raised his hands in mock surrender. "They're beautiful. Just keep on going."

Toni droned on as Jon matched up the alphanumeric characters she was reading with parts of the machine-coded program on the screen before him. It was boring work and they soon felt more tired than they had thought possible. Suddenly Jon frowned. There was a discrepancy.

"Fanny, Fanny, Fanny, Fanny—"

"Hold it," Jon ordered.

"What's the matter, are you getting excited?"

He ignored her remark. "That string of single Fs probably means that the computer is supposed to jump over this part. Check the program listing and see where we're at."

Toni checked the listing. "It looks like that should be one of those user exits."

"Okay. And did Mid-America take that exit and add a program of their own or did they bypass it?"

Toni checked the listing again. "According to this, they bypassed it."

"All right. Now go to the end of your program listing. The number after the last instruction tells the amount of memory space the program uses. See it?" As Toni turned the papers, Jon's fingers tensed over the keyboard. This was it, he sensed. This had to be how Ramsey was working his scheme.

"Yeah, here is is," Toni said, and read off a number.

"Great," he mumbled, jotting it down on a paper next to him. He added a constant to it, then divided by sixteen. "Hang on a minute; I've got to convert this number to hex."

"Do you know what you're doing?" Toni asked him suspiciously.

He nodded his head.

"I'm glad, 'cause I sure don't."

He had been right, Jon thought, as his fingers flew over the keyboard. He checked the number on the screen against the number Toni had given him and nodded with satisfaction. The machine said that this program was using forty-five thousand more positions of memory than Toni's listing had given. There was a lot more to this program than they were able to read. Hidden somewhere in the machine must be the instructions to change certain amounts. But why were they there?

He frowned at the screen, his fingers still. Inflated expenses and sales figures, ghost salesmen, and silent partners. How did they all fit together? he wondered. What was the purpose of Ramsey's scheme? He thought of his father's reluctance to let him into the workings of the business and Ramsey's superior attitude. It was almost as if Ramsey ran a separate company whose profits and expenses were added on to Mid-America's. He even had his own separate work force.

Jon's frown deepened as everything became clear suddenly. That was just what Ramsey was doing. Not for himself, though. For the partners. He threw his pencil down, feeling disgusted rather than elated. He may have caught Ramsey, but he hadn't worked alone. His father had to have known all that was going on. Known and approved.

"Well, that's that," he said. "We've found it."

Toni stared at the screen and then back at him. "Found what?"

Jon sighed and pulled his thoughts together. She deserved an explanation, after all. Even if it made him feel dirty to tell of his family's involvement. "We found the key. Someone's patched into the computer programs and added extra instructions. That's why the figures on the bills don't always match the printout. The operator just enters what's on the bill, but on certain accounts the computer has instructions to double or triple the amount. Without the operator's knowledge."

She looked as if she could not believe it. "But the books all balance out."

"The computer balances the inflated figures. The only ones who might catch the errors would be the data entry operators since they know what amount they entered. But they never see this kind of profit-and-loss information, so whoever set this up was safe. That is, until they ran into a good auditor," Jon added.

Toni blushed slightly, but said nothing.

Jon began to pick up the materials they had used. Now that he knew what was going on, he had no desire to hang around any longer. He hadn't quite told her everything, but she would figure the rest out just as he had. And when she did, she would be disgusted with him and his whole family. He couldn't even blame her, though. What decent person wants to be involved with a crook? Or the son of a crook? "Might as well get out of here."

"Hey, not so fast," Toni protested. "I want to know why Guy did it. Were the profits so high that he tried to cut their taxes by inflating their expenses?"

Jon shook his head with a harsh laugh. "Hardly." He hesitated a moment, then plunged on. "My father was just running a washing machine for the outfit."

"Washing machine?" Toni rubbed her eyes. "Either I'm getting dumber by the day or I'm very tired. I don't understand."

Jon found it hard to look at her and played with the buttons on the display terminal for a few moments. In silence, he watched the letters scroll by in a blur before he began to explain. "Organized crime pulls in millions of dollars from gambling, prostitution, and its other activities. Since Uncle Sam doesn't approve of those occupations, they invest in a legitimate business. Their money is funneled through that company by increasing the sales and expenses on paper. More money in, more money out, but profits are carefully kept at an average level so as not to attract a lot of attention. Their workers are even listed on the company's payroll so they qualify for social security, group health insurance, pension plans, things like that."

"The ghost salesmen," Toni murmured.

He nodded. "Once the money comes out of the washing machine, it can be invested in other legitimate businesses, and the partners are seen as respectable members of the business community. All because of a nice little washing machine."

He stared in silence at the computer screen for a long moment. When he finally turned toward Toni, he saw that she looked astonished.

"How did you know all this just from checking that one file?" she asked.

"Everything just suddenly fell into place." He shrugged and got to his feet.

"Do you want to check the accounts receivable? Maybe you're wrong, and they won't be inflated also."

He shook his head. "What's the point? We both saw the general ledger sheet before. That inventory figure was way out of line and it would take us two or three years to reach that six-month sales figure. No, I just have to face facts. This great company that my father was so proud of was nothing more than a front for the mob. What was it that the *Tribune* had in the obituary? Outstanding civic leader?" He turned away from her suddenly.

"Jon, I'm sorry," she murmured. "I never dreamed that your father was involved when all this started."

He nodded. He was sick to his stomach with the anger and hurt raging through him. He wanted to strike out and, at the same time, crawl away and hide in shame. His vision was blured by tears and he could not face her yet, but he took a deep breath and forced himself to respond. "You did your job, that was all. You did exactly what you were supposed to do: call the facts the way you see them."

He felt so stupid. All that talk about the truth: All he wanted was the truth, no matter what it was. He could learn to live with whatever his father had done. What a load of crap! He hadn't wanted the truth; he had wanted to know it was all a misunderstanding. Or that there was a simple, honest reason for the discrepancies Toni had found. He had wanted his image of his father to remain unblemished.

Well, now he knew, now he had the truth. The uncertainty was gone, but the truth sure wasn't any better. He understood about Toni, also, and that hurt most of all. His anger and pain found an outlet as he turned to face her.

"At least I know now why you refused to marry me," he said. It came out more sticken than bitter. "I mean, I can understand your not wanting to get hooked up to someone working for the mob. I probably wouldn't either, if I was in your shoes."

"What are you talking about?" she cried softly, taking a step closer. She shook her head slowly. "What I suspected about your father had nothing to do with that."

He just watched her silently, seeing the emotions dance across her face but unable to feel anything beyond the pain. She touched his arm gently, but he still said nothing.

"Your father's actions don't change you any more than Melanie's actions change me."

A voice deep inside him told him to reach out to her, but he could not move. He saw the tears in her eyes and heard the longing in her voice, but there was nothing he could do. He was locked in his prison of pain and unable to touch anyone.

Her hand reached out to caress his cheek. Her touch was gentle and soft, and brought back a flood of memories. "Jon, I love you. What we found here tonight hasn't done anything to that. You're very important to me and always will be."

That invisible wall that was holding him back seemed to crack and suddenly Toni was in his arms. God, he needed her so. Not just her love, but her warmth and her strength. He tightened his hold on her, burying his face in her mussed cascade of hair. Just the scent of it took him back to their moments of love. The feelings of security and peace flowed through him. Maybe things were not as bad as they had seemed.

Guy smiled to himself as he drove past the Mid-America parking lot. His white Cadillac was still where he had parked it Wednesday morning. Only eighteen hours ago, but it seemed like years. He was sure a spotter was lying on the seat of one of those cars parked in the street, waiting for him to come. Well, whoever it was could stare up into his rearview mirror forever. Guy Ramsey wasn't so dumb that he'd risk his life for that car.

He laughed and swung his rented car around the corner and headed for the truck bay. Those jerks were probably so busy watching the Caddy, they'd never see him sneak in the building. He turned into the alley, scraping the bottom of the car as he bounced in and out of a pothole.

Good thing this was just a rented piece of junk, he thought. He had turned off his lights to avoid being seen, and discovered another pothole. The car swerved and scraped the brick wall of a neighboring building.

He laughed to himself. "Anybody that sees this old clunker parked in the alley will think it's just an abandoned pile of tin."

It had been pretty clever to rent the 1977 Plymouth at one of those cut-rate used-car rental joints, but that wasn't all he had done. If he was going to drive a clunker, he had to look like one himself, so he had gone to a Goodwill store and bought some old work clothes. A faded denim jacket covered up the frayed plaid shirt. And the jeans, well, he just hoped he wouldn't catch anything from wearing them. He looked just like a typical working stiff. Hell, Melanie wouldn't recognize him if she was paid to do it, and that broad would do anything for a buck.

He pulled the car up to the side door and killed the motor. Before he eased himself out of the car, he pulled a tattered Cubs hat over his head. That was the finishing touch to his disguise and completed the picture of the dumb clod.

He left the car and stood silently, leaning against the wall for several minutes. There were no new sounds in the street and certainly no sign of anyone coming into the alley. The spotters had probably looked right at him as he drove by, he thought, suppressing a chuckle.

Convinced that he wasn't being watched, Guy slid along

the wall to the door and stuck in his key. The door was so rarely used that it didn't want to open.

"Come on, open," he muttered. A solid slam with his shoulder pushed it open and he slipped quickly through. "Damn old building." He rubbed his shoulder. "Ought to be condemned."

The door had let him in near the utility room where the furnace and air-conditioning equipment were located. He took a few quiet steps further inside, then stood still, just looking over the dimly lit warehouse and listening. Nothing out of the ordinary, he thought with a shake of his head. Just the usual creaks of an old building and the scampering of rats.

He went back to the door and braced it open with a large can of cleaning fluid. Then he hurried out to the car, unloading the five-gallon cans of gasoline from the trunk and lining them up inside the warehouse. There were seven cans in all, and he could not help smiling at them. When this dump caught, Mrs. O'Leary's cow was gonna look like a piker.

Guy moved the can holding open the door and closed it quietly, then went down the hallway into the office area. He looked around his office and sat at his desk for the last time. A lump of anger rose in his throat as he gazed at the familiar surroundings.

Stupid idiots. This was the best little washing machine in all of Dunkirk Industries, but their guts had gone with age. A few minor problems and they hit the panic button.

He leaned back in his chair and closed his eyes. Once this was over, he'd move out of the country for a while and wait for things to blow over. In a few years, some of those old birds would have died off. The young blood waiting to take their place was a lot tougher. Once they were in charge, Guy'd get a hero's welcome.

He got up. Mexico wouldn't be so bad. After all, he had plenty of money, and Melanie for fun. And once he got there, he'd set up some scams of his own. Yeah, things would be fine. Guy Ramsey was one tough son of a bitch.

He left his office, closing the door behind him gently. If it hadn't been for that damn accountant, this old washing machine would still be going. That was the one thing that was bothering him: he had to run, while she'd be walking around free and clear. Well, he'd remember her. Someday his chance would come.

He crossed the bullpen and went down the hall to the computer room. He had to turn that damn halon gas off or it would release as soon as the fire alarm sounded. The computer technicians claimed it would smother any blaze in five to ten seconds and that would leave the data pertaining to this operation unharmed. He certainly didn't need that kind of disaster. Mexico wouldn't be far enough away to keep his ass safe.

He pulled his CAS card out of his wallet and noticed that the lights were on in the computer room. He ought to make a stop at that damn operator's house and kick him for forgetting to turn out the lights. The door hissed outward to let him into the room.

Just inside the door, Guy stopped short, staring for a long moment at the two people in the room. Surprised in each other's arms, they just stared back at him.

"Well, well, well," he said with a smile. "Isn't this a pleasant little surprise?"

He walked closer to them. The sudden terror in Toni's eyes increased the warm, pleasurable feeling that flowed through his body. He wasn't going to leave anything unfinished; he would get them both. That was going to be one fine vacation in Mexico. "What are you kiddies doing? Putting in a little overtime?"

"What the hell are you doing here, Ramsey?" Jon demanded, moving in between him and Toni.

Guy snickered and drew a pistol from his belt. If Morici wanted to play hero that was fine with him. "Just slow down, sonny boy. This is a .357 magnum. I can put a bullet through you that'll make a hole in your back bigger than your fist." A twinge of regret pulled at Guy's heart. If he had more time and a .22-caliber pistol, he could put a small bullet in Jon's stomach and watch him die slowly.

Jon stopped moving. "You might as well give it up, Ramsey."

Toni moved to his side and slipped her hand in his. "We know how your laundering operation works."

Guy smiled. "Pretty neat, huh?"

"It's all over, Ramsey."

Jon's voice was cold and angry, but Guy ignored him. Keeping the gun pointed at them, he moved over to the switch that controlled the release of the halon gas as a fire extinguisher and turned it off.

Toni tried a more persuasive tone. "Sam's dead, Guy. Put that gun away. You wouldn't want to add murder to the list of things that you've done."

He stared at her in disbelief, then burst into hard laughter. "My first hit was over ten years ago. It was a sixteen-year-old runaway. I bought the bitch a meal and rented a room so she could shower up. Then the little hunk didn't want to put out."

He laughed at the look of horror that crossed Toni's face. "As much as I'd like to stay and chat, I've got things to do, kiddies. So come along." He waved his gun, indicating that they should go ahead of him.

Jon stopped near the door and turned to face him. "Ramsey, you've got me. Let Toni go."

"Aw, aren't we the gallant one?"

"She hasn't done anything to you."

Guy felt his face grew hot. "Like hell she hasn't. If it wasn't for her this old washing machine would still be spinning along."

"It was just a matter of time, Ramsey. If Toni hadn't found the discrepancies, someone else would have."

Guy could feel the sweat of anger break out on his upper lip. "Shut up. That bitch was lucky. Lucky, but dumb. I only wish I had the time to give her what she deserves." He gestured impatiently. "Come on, get out in the warehouse. And take that purse with you," he added. "I don't want nothing left around."

They silently preceded him. The aisles were dimly lit by the lights that were left on for the watchman service, and Guy could see the anxious looks they exchanged. His delight increased.

He had had such terrible luck all day that he had never expected such a bonanza at night. If only he had more time, he could really have fun!

Jon stopped suddenly and turned to face him. "Ramsey, for God's sake. Don't do this."

Guy chuckled again and gestured with the gun. "Damn, I'd love to make you beg and crawl, but I just haven't got time. Business before pleasure, I always say. Move it."

Instead of resuming his walk, Jon lunged toward him. Instinctively, Guy sent the gun crashing to his head, and

311

laughed as Jon went down in a heap at his feet. Considering the little time he had, this was still going to be fun.

He looked up at Toni. Her face had gone completely white as she stared at the still form on the floor. "You animal!" she hissed at him, dropping onto her knees next to the unconscious form.

The gun still firmly in his hand, he reached down and let his hand slide along her soft cheek. "I love you too, babe. If I just had the time, I'd show you how much. But I don't, so let's go. Bring Junior along."

She stared up at him. "I can't carry him."

"Drag him."

She shook her head, tears in her eyes. "He's hurt."

Even now she thought she could fight him! "Drag him, or I'll shoot him right here."

Toni got to her feet and strained at Jon's body. The tears streamed down her face, increasing the erotic pleasure Guy was getting. His crotch felt tight and he smiled with regret. If he only had a little more time, this would really have been an evening to remember, but by morning he planned to be far from Chicago.

With a silent sigh, he put the pistol back in his belt. "Stop dogging it and pull. I don't have all night." He reached down and grabbed Jon's legs and dragged him toward a small shedlike storeroom near the far side of the warehouse.

Toni hurried after him, trying to hold Jon's head up off the floor. "You're hurting him," she screamed, crying bitterly all the while. "Damn it, you're hurting him some more."

Guy glared at her with hate. "Stop your caterwauling and carry your share. For all you know, he's dead already."

Guy reached the storeroom and pulled the door open. He heaved Jon's body in and gestured with a slight bow. "You next."

She hesitated slightly, so he pulled out his pistol again. "Move it, bitch. Now!"

As Toni went past, he grabbed her purse and pulled the zipper. He tossed her wallet and a handkerchief into the room, then several pens and a small box of aspirin. Nothing in there that could stop him, he thought, and tossed the purse in after them.

"Good night, sweetheart," he laughed as he slammed the door shut and locked it. "Who knows, maybe lover boy will wake up and heat you up."

Guy let loose a hearty laugh as he moved away from the storeroom. What a day! It was his worst day and it was his best day. If only he had more time!

"What in the world is this?" Guenther muttered aloud as he pulled his car up behind the parked Plymouth. The streets around the old warehouse had been deserted. What was this piece of junk doing in the alley?

He turned off the motor of his own car, a rented four-year-old Chevy, and silently got out. A heavy, industrial-type flashlight was in his right hand as he crept along the wall toward the car.

It was probably nothing more than a couple of early-morning lovers, but he was taking no chances. He was a professional and took great pride in his reputation. Every job was done right, and if he was a little overly cautious, it was only because he had seen too many people get tripped up by overlooking minor details.

There was no one in the car. He flashed the light onto the front seat and then the back. No lovers, no coats, books, magazines, not even any cigarette wrappers on the floor. Why was another rented used car parked here? He clicked off the flashlight and frowned at the car in the darkness. He didn't like the feel of that.

He walked slowly to the front of the car. It was a crisp autumn morning, but the hood was only slightly cool to his touch. The car had been parked here less than an hour. Where was the driver?

Guenther moved back into the shelter of the wall and glanced around the alleyway. Was there another mercury messenger in the area? There were a lot of old warehouses around and it was not impossible that another building needed to be disposed of tonight. Not impossible, but certainly unlikely. When Sammy scheduled these things he was very careful. He'd never schedule two in the same area on the same night.

Guenther lightly slapped his left palm with his flashlight as he thought. Something was wrong here, he sensed. Should he abort?

After a moment, Guenther made up his mind and moved

toward the side door of Mid-America. Sammy had said this disposition had to be accomplished tonight. If there was a problem he would just have to take care of it. Professionals did good jobs even under adverse circumstances. Using the key he had been furnished, Guenther unlocked the door and pushed it open.

"Jesus Christ," he muttered, stopping just inside the door. More than half a dozen gasoline cans were lined up. Someone else was there tonight, but he sure wasn't a mercury messenger.

Thoroughly disgusted by the lack of professionalism that he saw in front of him, Guenther moved further into the building and let the door close softly behind him. There wasn't an insurance company in the world that would pay off on a torching with the smell of gasoline all over the place.

What the hell is some damn amateur doing here? Guenther peered down the shadowy recesses of the warehouse. Occasional lights were on along the aisles of equipment, but he saw no one moving. Well, first things first. He had to get rid of that amateur before he screwed up the job. He just hoped that the intruder hadn't started splashing around that gasoline. There'd be no way he could dispose of the place tonight if it already stank like a filling station.

A sound caught his ears and Guenther ducked down behind some cans of cleaning fluid. Crouching quietly, he listened. As the sound became clearer, he could not believe his ears. Some fool was whistling. What was this? One of Snow White's dwarves, whistling while he worked?

The man came into view around a corner. He was dressed sloppily in work clothes that were obviously not his own. Denim stretched to fit and took on the shape of the body it was covering. Those pants had been stretched to cover someone with a bit more ass and less thigh. Besides, if he could afford a gold watch like the one Guenther could see on his wrist, he wouldn't choose a discount-house brand of jeans. Details, details. They always pointed out the amateur.

Still whistling merrily, the man walked past Guenther and straight to the cans of gasoline. He muttered something to himself and burst into happy little giggles.

Guenther went into action as the man bent over to pick

up one of the cans. With a quick, silent movement, Guenther brought the butt of his flashlight down sharply on the base of the man's skull. There was a slight snapping sound and then he fell.

"That must have been Happy," Guenther muttered as he glanced around. "Let's hope that he left Dopey and the others at home." The scampering of the rats was his only answer.

Guenther quickly checked his flashlight, relieved to find it still worked. He always bought quality merchandise and was rarely disappointed in it.

He stepped over the man, not bothering to look at him. That snapping sound as he fell had told him he was dead. Sharp to the base of the skull, that was how he had been taught in the Green Berets. Do it right and there was no need to check. The sound told him all he needed to know.

Guenther shook his head resignedly as he went over to the furnace room. His son was eighteen now, in his last year of high school. Guenther had been trying to convince him to join the army and learn a trade, as he had done. Jobs had been scarce back then, too, so he had enlisted and became a demolitions expert. But no, this kid wanted to be a lawyer. Kids. They wanted glamour. They didn't want to even hear that a tradesman could do well.

Guenther was certainly proof of that. He had applied himself and worked hard over the years. Now, in his middle age, he was a moderately wealthy man.

He sighed as he carried a ladder over to a wall near the furnace. Sons never listened to their fathers. They had to learn on their own.

Guenther replaced the battery in the dusty smoke detector with a dead one of his own. Then he moved the ladder over so that he could reach the huge wooden support beam that ran across the furnace room. It was not often that he found such an ideal spot to start the fire, but he had seen in his inspection yesterday that the wiring of the furnace was frayed and old. Keying the starter off the furnace was perfect.

He took a cigar-sized cylinder out of his pocket, shaking his head appreciatively. Only a few years ago, a similar starter was the size of a cigar box. *Time* magazine had said the diminutive microchip was going to revolutionize American society, and they were right as far as his work went. Smaller and much more dependable. Thirteen fires in the last two years and not one was questioned.

He placed the cylinder on a rafter near some hanging electrical wires. By pressing a button at one end of the cigar, he started a timer in one of the microchips. In exactly twenty minutes, another microchip would produce an electrical pulse that would ignite a chemical that, in turn, would melt and spread across the old wooden beam. When the chemical ignited it would produce a fire covering about four square feet in area and would maintain a temperature of eight hundred to a thousand degrees Fahrenheit for at least five minutes. The furnace room would be an inferno in another five.

Guenther replaced the ladder and closed the furnace room door behind him. There was a fire wall, he noticed, but it was crumbling and broken away. Contrary to insurance and state safety regulations, there also were several drums of cleaning fluid stored near the furnace room. The whole place would be an inferno in less than forty minutes. He could see another job well done.

He hurried back to the door, and frowned down at the body lying there. "Goddamn amateur," he muttered as he hoisted it over his shoulder and carried it out to his car. Then he carried out the cans of gasoline.

He had hoped to get this job over with quickly and get back home, he thought with irritation as he drove to a pay phone a few miles away. He was supposed to pick up Laura's new car around nine in the morning, and he wanted a few hours' sleep before he went on to work.

He called Sammy, and waited as Sammy called someone else, but all in all, the whole thing was settled rather quickly. He was given an address to drive to, and an extra twenty thou was going to be added to the fee for his extra work. That was the advantage of doing quality work, he thought, as he drove west on the Eisenhower Expressway. His customers knew his worth, and were willing to pay extra for it.

# CHAPTER TWENTY-SEVEN

As soon as the storeroom door was closed, the light went out and Toni was left in darkness. She heard the click of the lock being turned and Guy's laugh, the sound fading as he moved away.

"Guy! Come back here!" she screamed, and pounded her fist against the door. It was thick and solid and she wondered if he could even hear her on the other side. If he did, he made no audible reply. She fumbled in the darkness for the doorknob, but it did not turn.

"Oh, damn," she whispered, fighting back tears of fright. "What do we do now?"

She turned around, and with her arms outstretched, she inched across the room. "Jon?" she called, as she moved in the direction where he lay. Her arm banged into something heavy, and she heard the sound of metal hitting the floor.

"Oh, Lord," she whispered under her breath, and then got down on her hands and knees. Feeling carefully before she moved, she crawled about until she touched Jon's hand. It seemed cold and lifeless and she held her breath. What had that maniac done?

"Jon? Jon?" Her voice called his name with love as her hands touched his face with gentleness. She searched for any wetness that might be blood, but found none. He remained still.

If only Guy had left the light on, she thought, and then sat back with a start. Her purse! She had a tiny flashlight on her keychain.

She crawled back to the door where Guy had tossed her purse. She didn't remember his taking out her keys, so the flashlight must still be inside the bag.

Her fingers touched something soft and furry as she crawled and she pulled her hand away. It was just dust, she told herself, ignoring the scratching noises in the wall. She found her purse with relief and unzipped the key pocket. There was the flashlight.

The beam was weak, and the light would stay on only as long as the button was pressed, but it did throw a faint circle of light across the room. She tossed her wallet and other things into her purse and slipped it over her shoulder. Then she hurried back to Jon's side. In the dim light, she could see his eyes were still closed.

Her fingers trembled as she searched for the pulse in his neck. It was beating strongly, and that relieved her somewhat. Guy must not have hit him that hard. She loosened his shirt collar, and wished she had some water to splash on his face. She shone the light onto the shelves near her. The huge shadows distorted things, but even when she looked closer there were only equipment manuals and dusty spare parts. When the light reflected a pair of yellow eyes staring at her from the rear of one shelf, she turned the light back to Jon.

They couldn't just wait here for Guy to return. Who knew what plans he had for them? But she'd never be able to move Jon by herself. She had to wake him up.

She leaned forward and patted his cheek sharply, keeping the flashlight shining on his face. "Jon, please wake up," she cried. A note of panic had crept into her voice as she heard muted sounds from the warehouse outside the door. "Please, Jon. We've got to get out of here."

His eyes still did not open, and she sat back on her heels, letting go of the flashlight button as she tried to decide what to do. Her brain seemed foggy and useless. If only it weren't way past midnight, she might be able to think more clearly, she told herself. Or if she had had a decent night's sleep in the last five days.

Why had she even agreed to come? She had thought Sam was mixed up in something shady. Why hadn't she talked Jon out of his stupid sleuthing mission?

Hysteria would not help, she scolded, trying to get a firm grip on herself. She was not ready to die or to lose Jon again. The past five days had been bad enough; she was not going through that again. All she had to do was keep her wits about her and figure a way out of this mess.

She turned the flashlight on again. The first order of business was to wake up Sleeping Beauty.

Her sarcasm toughened her enough to give Jon a vigorous shake. "For God's sake, Jon. Wake up. This isn't the time for a nap."

His eyelids fluttered briefly. Although they did not stay open, Toni felt like shouting with relief. She'd better wait until they were safely out of there, she cautioned herself.

"Come on, Jon. If you don't keep those eyes open, I'll slug you myself," she threatened.

Slowly, as if the movement was against his will, the eyes opened and he stared dully up at her. The blankness was soon replaced by a frown as he shielded his eyes from the light. She turned it off.

"What happened?" he asked. In the darkness, she helped him get up into a sitting position, leaning against the shelves for support.

"You decided to play Sleeping Beauty to my Prince Charming."

"I thought Prince Charming woke Sleeping Beauty up with a kiss, not a slug."

"I was getting desperate," she admitted, her voice breaking.

Even in the darkness Jon was able to find her and pull her into his embrace. It felt so good to be snuggled against his chest, she could almost convince herself that she was safe as long his arms stayed tightly around her.

"Was that a light in my eyes a minute ago, or just your radiant beauty?" he teased.

She pressed the button and the shelves across the room appeared. "No, it was a real honest-to-goodness light. It was on my keychain." She let it go off again.

"Why are we in the dark, then?"

"Conserving the batteries," she pointed out, and snuggled deeper into his arms.

"Sounds wise. So tell me, what'd I miss?"

She hated to talk and admit their predicament. "Not much. We're locked in, and Guy left laughing."

"Sounds like him," he muttered. He brushed the hair from her forehead and leaned down to kiss it. "Are you okay?"

"Now that you've joined the living again, yeah." She put her arms around his waist.

"So what's our plan?"

"My plan was to get you awake so you could plan the rest."

His hold tightened slightly, but his voice was not the least bit loverlike. "What is this room? Are we locked in?"

She pulled away from him with a frown that she knew he could not see. "No, we're not locked in; he just wanted to give us some privacy."

"Dumb question, huh?"

She shrugged, and remembered that he couldn't see that either. "I tried the door and it's too thick to beat down with our fists, and the lock is defintely locked." She turned the flashlight onto the shelves next to him. "It looks like this is some kind of old storeroom, for obsolete equipment, maybe."

"Yes, I know where that is. Surrounded by the warehouse, and no windows. Great." He sighed. "Well, let's use your light to take a look at the door then."

She got to her feet first and helped him stand up. "How's that feel? Are you dizzy?" When he didn't answer, she turned the light back on. He was holding on to the shelf for support. His eyes were closed. "Maybe you'd better sit down again."

"If you point me in the right direction, maybe I can ram the door open with my head as I fall over."

"Oh Lord." She took hold of his arm. "Sit back down."

He opened his eyes. "No, I'm okay. How long was I out?"

She helped him take a step toward the door. It was hard to keep the flashlight on and support him. "I don't know. Maybe about ten or fifteen minutes."

They reached the door and Jon sagged against it. He had his eyes closed, and even in the dim light she could see that he was pale.

"What now?" she asked.

Jon opened his eyes slowly but did not straighten up. He reached over and tried the doorknob. It did not turn, and he grinned slightly at her. "I had to try."

She nodded. "If the hinges were on this side, we could try to take them out, but they're not. And the door's just too thick to break down." She turned around and flashed the light around the room again. "There's nothing here to use as a battering ram anyway."

"Except for me," he sighed.

"But we can't just sit here and wait for Guy to come back," she went on as if he had not spoken. "He's bound to have something awful planned for us."

Some of the terror she felt must have crept into her voice, for Jon reached over and pulled her into his arms.

"I'm sorry, darling," he murmured into her hair. "I know that I got you into this mess and I'll do my damnedest to get you out."

She nodded, her head against his chest so he could feel her movement.

His hand came up to caress the back of her neck and soothe the fear from her. "Once I get rid of this dizziness, I'll think of something, I promise. And then we'll be okay— we've got to be. I've been such a jerk these last few days, I have to have a chance to prove that I really do love you."

"I know you do," she whispered.

"Yeah, but I haven't shown it lately."

She smiled to herself. "I guess I really shouldn't complain. The last time I got locked in a room I was by myself, and at least this time I have you."

"You've been locked up before? Boy, you accountants sure lead a wild life," he teased. "So how'd you get out that time?"

"That was just in a john," she pointed out. "And a busboy finally got me out— My God!" She jerked away from him. "I forgot," she said, the flashlight shining into her purse as she searched through it. The wallet was tossed onto the floor, her handkerchief, her keys. "Here it is!"

"Here's what?"

She pulled a small plastic pouch from the bottom of her purse. "It's a tool kit. Don't you remember? I'm sure I told you about the time I was locked in the john at that French restaurant. I started carrying a little tool kit in my purse after that."

"Yeah, but—"

"And I know how to take doorknobs off!"

Without wasting any more time, she handed the flashlight to him and dropped to her knees. "Try to keep the light on the knob, will you?"

"I'm trying," he said, although the beam wavered slightly.

She looked up at him with concern. "Are you sure you're all right? You could sit down."

"And have you carry me out?" he scoffed. "No, thanks. Just get on with my rescue."

Toni shrugged and went back to her study of the doorknob. It was an old brass one, but it looked the same as every other one she had seen. She took the small screwdriver from the tool kit and fit it into the first screw. Pressing hard, she turned.

"Damn!"

"What's wrong?" Jon asked quickly.

Toni sat back on her heels. "The screwdriver bent. Didn't budge the screw an inch, either."

Jon said nothing, and she leaned forward to try again. The tools were small, she knew, but they were supposed to be strong. It must just be that the screws were stuck from all the years since the knob had been installed.

She stuck the bent screwdriver into the slot again and tried to turn it. She wasn't sure but she thought it moved slightly.

"What happened?" Jon asked.

"Nothing." She fit it in again, and turned with all her might. The tool did not bend any more, but neither did the screw move. Her fingers just slipped around the handle.

"Damn! Damn! Damn!"

Jon asked no questions, thankfully, as she fit the screwdriver in again. The same thing happened. Her fingers could not get a tight enough grip on the tool to do anything.

"Want me to try?" Jon offered.

"If my fingers are too big, I doubt that yours will be any better," she snapped.

"Yeah, right," he said quickly.

"Sorry," she sighed.

He reached down and patted her cheek. "Do you know how much I love you?"

She shook her head, tears suddenly blurring her vision again. The next thing she'd know, she'd have to go to the bathroom!

Stiffening her spine mentally, she took out the small pliers. She fitted the screwdriver into the slot and held the handle with the pliers instead. The screw moved slightly!

It seemed to take ages, but slowly, ever so slowly, the screw began to move. She had to hold the handle with the pliers but push against the screw at the same time. Her fingers were getting scratched and sore, but she barely noticed as the first screw came out and she started on the second. They would get out!

"It sure has been quiet out there," Jon noted suddenly.

"Maybe he left."

"Sure." Jon's sarcasm reflected her unspoken feelings. It would be too much to hope for. Guy would not leave with them still locked in the room able to tell the whole story. It might be quiet out there, but he would be back.

They both were silent as she coaxed the last screw out. It dropped to the floor with a loud noise. Then she wiggled the knob free of the surrounding bracket.

"Can you do it?" Jon breathed.

She didn't answer but moved the flashlight and his hand into a different position. After a few minutes of fiddling, there was a small clank outside the door as the other knob fell.

"My God, you did it!" Jon cried happily.

"I don't know," she said worriedly as she played with the latch release still left in the door. She stopped and listened for a moment. "Something sounds funny out there."

"Funny in what way?" Jon asked. He bent down to peer over her shoulder. "Do you think Guy is back?"

She shook her head and kept trying to turn the latch with the tools. She could not explain to him what she meant, but she knew something was wrong out in the warehouse. There was a tension in the air, and she felt a sense of urgency. Suddenly, the latch turned.

She had been leaning against the door when it became unlocked, and she fell forward, pushing the door open.

"Oh my God!" she breathed, staring into the warehouse from where she landed on her hands and knees. Through the open spaces in the shelves she could see flames. An eerie glow lit the building, illuminating the billows of smoke that gathered near the ceiling. The building was on fire!

"Come on," Jon cried, not paralyzed by the sight as she had been. He grabbed her arm and jerked her to her feet. Holding tight to her, he pulled her from the room and into one of the main aisles of the warehouse.

Jon stopped and Toni glanced around them. A few aisles away from them she could see the flames licking at the wooden beams. As she watched in horror, the beam caught and the flames raced across the wood high over their heads. There was a loud crash somewhere off to their right and waves of hot air pushed at them.

"The loading dock is the closest," Jon told her, and pulled her around the outside of the storage room, but they could go no farther. The furnace room was ablaze and it had spread to the piles of boxes stored in the loading area awaiting delivery. There was no escape that way.

"Let's try the office door," Jon shouted to her.

The roar of the fire practically drowned out his words as he pointed in another direction. Toni nodded, too terrified to do anything but obey. She had never been back in the warehouse before and had no idea where any doors were located.

Holding tightly to each other's hand, they raced down the main aisle and then turned into another, smaller one. Sparks from the burning beams fell around them: onto the floor and shelves, and onto them. Two aisles away, she saw a box burst into flames; then it spread to another and another until the fire seemed to be racing them toward the door.

The heat was so intense that everything seemed to be on fire. The floor felt hot right through her shoes, and she tightened her hold on Jon's hand. Even the air was becoming unbearable; each breath was a struggle that seared her lungs. She couldn't even cry, for the air had dried her eyes and skin. They felt ready to crackle and burn like the dry wooden beams.

Above the noise of the fire they heard a series of muffled explosions. Something ahead of them had caught fire. As they watched, the shelves at the far end of the aisle went up like torches. That way was blocked.

Jon turned and nodded behind her. "We'll have to try for the far end of the warehouse," he told her, leaning close to her ear. "We can break some windows to get out."

Toni nodded and they hurried back down the way they had just come. Thin plastic dishes that they had passed only moments earlier were now twisted and deformed from the heat. Shiny aluminum utensils reflected the flames all around them, giving the illusion of tiny flames dancing on each shelf. Plastic bottles of soap were sagging drunkenly, the liquid seeping out from melted seams and running onto the floor. But the tall, anonymous boxes were the worst to pass. What explosive terror was hidden inside them? Toni wondered, expecting each one they passed to burst into flames.

She tried to concentrate on Jon as he ran ahead of her. He knew the building, and would get them out. She loved him and trusted him, but would that do any good when up against a maniac like Guy? But he had planned for them to die in that tiny room, she reminded herself; he might not have covered every possible escape.

From behind them came the sound of something falling, and a shower of sparks flew by. A box from Combined Locks Paper Products caught fire and Toni fought the urge to burst into laughter. Maybe she should have gone up to Wisconsin after all. They probably didn't try to incinerate their accountants up there.

Jon seemed to sense her near-hysteria and pulled her along even faster. They rounded the corner and were back in the main aisle, running past the small storage room that was to have been their funeral pyre. Smoke was pouring out of the door as fire ate up the far wall that Jon had been resting against.

Toni looked away, forcing herself to notice that the fire seemed to be concentrated mostly in the office end of the building. The far end was still in shadow, although as they raced toward it, so did the fire.

With each step they took, the glow increased. The beams overhead were outlined by the flames that were eating them up. The air was not cooler as she had hoped, either. Even though they were farther from the center of the fire, it was still stifling and hard to breathe. The pressure seemed to be building, and she thought Jon must have sensed it also, for his hold on her hand tightened convulsively.

They raced down the center aisle of the warehouse. Toni glanced ahead, looking for some side aisle that would take them to the windows. She knew they were off to their left, for she had seen them past the loading dock and overlooking the parking lot. Surely somewhere up here they would have to head toward them.

A huge explosion nearly knocked the two of them over. The air seemed to change and grow less intense.

"The windows," Jon shouted to her. "They blew out."

Even as he spoke, there was a roar as the fire swept

down the shelves and toward the inflow of air. Toni turned toward Jon, her eyes issuing a mute appeal. How would they ever get out? He put his arms around her and held her close as he put his mouth near to her ear.

"There's still a way," he said. "But we have to get across the building. Over to the other corner." He pointed toward the far side of the building, away from the windows.

The shelves to their left were catching fire, and Jon glanced quickly at the shelves on their right. He ran a few feet back and pulled some boxes off to clear a space. Then he gestured for Toni to crawl through.

The shelves were metal and hot to the touch, but she hurried through into the next aisle. Even before Jon was across also, she was looking for a way over to the next aisle. She found a space that held a large coffee urn. It was heavy, but with Jon's help, they were able to move it aside. She crawled through, Jon close behind her.

The next aisle was harder, and they had to go closer to the flames to find some equipment they could move. It seemed that everything there was huge: warming tables, deep-frying units, even rolling serving trays.

Suddenly, Jon beckoned to her. When she came close, he hoisted her up to the second shelf, about five feet off the ground. It was empty on their side, and contained only tiny, red plastic booster chairs on the other. She crawled across and pushed the little chairs onto the floor. Then she jumped down, Jon following closely.

They were at the far wall, and Toni had no idea where they were going. The fire made the room as bright as day, but there were no doors or windows in that corner. Jon pushed past her and hurried down toward the corner. She rushed after him, but there was nothing there. Nothing but a pile of dusty old equipment.

Toni glanced behind her. The first shelf they had crawled across was burning and the second had a few boxes on the top that were catching fire. It was only a matter of minutes before the fire consumed the whole building, them included. What was Jon thinking of? How could they escape the fire by hiding in a corner?

He was busily moving the pile of equipment, and she went to help. The old pieces were already hot from the fire, but he only wanted to lug them a few feet.

trembling hand and pointed it the other way. "It shouldn't be too far to the river."

She clung to him, stumbling slightly over the filth that lay on the floor. They passed something particularly putrid smelling and a wave of nausea rose in her throat. She clamped her jaws down tightly, and held her breath as long as she could. They would be out of there soon; they had to be.

The sound of rats moving around them distracted her. Several brushed against her leg and she fought hard not to scream. "Where have they all come from?" she asked Jon.

"Upstairs. They're trying to escape the fire too, and probably have burrows all through this area."

One huge rat appeared in a hole high in the wall only a few feet ahead of her. As she watched, it raced down and hurried into the shadows before them. She shivered, but concentrated on where they were going. Which was worse, she asked herself, rats or the fire?

The tunnel was probably three hundred feet long, but it seemed like several miles. They reached the end suddenly. There, in the flashlight's circle of light, was a solid wooden wall. While they watched, two rats scurried out a hole near the bottom.

"Well, that's the way out, if we can fit," Toni sighed. She was ready to cry again, and angry at herself for it. Just because she was exhausted and terrified didn't mean that she had to behave like an idiot.

"I doubt that a door that's been near the water for sixty years is going to put up much of a fuss," Jon told her. "This time, you hold the flashlight."

She took it from him and pointed it toward the edge that he was inspecting. After checking it out, he leaned one hand against the side wall and kicked at the wooden door with his foot. The side he struck fell outward, leaving a black gaping hole.

The fresh air rushing in seemed wonderful to Toni. It was cold and damp and smelly, but wonderful. She took a deep breath and turned to look at Jon. He was grinning at her and held his arms open. She ran into them, hugging him and crying at the same time.

"Did we really do it?" she cried. "Are we okay now?"

He swung her in his arms and laughed. "Sure, just a short swim and we're home free."

She froze and looked up into his smiling face. "Jon, I can't swim."

He just shook his head, his smile never leaving. "Can you walk?" he asked, and led her over to the door. There was a narrow walkway along the river's edge. "All we have to do is walk along that until we reach a bridge. We ought to be able to climb up to the road there."

Jon pushed open the barricade and they slipped out. The walkway was about eighteen inches wide and just barely above the level of the water. At their backs was a corrugated metal wall that reached up to the street, at least ten feet above her head, maybe more.

"We'll be out of here real soon," Jon promised. "In half an hour, you'll be tucked safely in bed."

"I think I'd rather be tucked safely in a shower," she said, trying to joke. A rat raced out of the opening right after her and sped across her feet. She froze for a moment, then let her breath out slowly.

Jon tugged on her hand and nodded down the walkway. Together they made their way along the narrow path. Ten, fifteen minutes passed before they finally saw the bridge right before them.

"There it is," Jon reassured her. "Just over the fence and down the street to the car."

Toni was too tired to do anything but follow. She knew this was just a bad dream and that she was bound to wake up soon. She just hoped it would be before she had to meet another rat.

"Mr. Samuels . . . Mr. Samuels," the doctor spoke louder.

Jon turned from the window with a start. He had forgotten the name he had given the hospital. "I'm sorry, doctor. I guess I'm a little tired. How is T— How is my wife?"

"I've given her a sedative and she's waiting to go up to her room right now. We also gave her a tetanus shot as a precautionary measure because of that gash on her leg. Those cuts and scratches will have to be watched to make sure they don't get infected."

"Thanks a lot, doctor." Jon nodded his head. "Will she be all right?"

"She seemed close to hysteria, and exhausted, but I think she will be. I'm sure all she needs is some rest, but I

am glad that you agreed to leave her here for observation."
The doctor turned, ready to leave.

"Can I see her before she goes up to her room?" Jon asked quickly.

The doctor nodded. "She may be groggy, though, from the sedative," he pointed out, then turned and left.

Jon went into the small examining room where Toni was lying. She looked up from the cart she was on as she heard his footsteps.

"Jon, I don't want to stay here," she protested. She reached out and grabbed his hand, clinging to it tightly. "There isn't any reason for me to stay. I'm fine."

He saw the terror still lurking in her eyes, and could feel a tremor in her hand. "Hey, it's only overnight," he said lightly.

"Why didn't you give them our real names? What's going on? Why can't I stay with you?"

He sighed. With him was the last place she should be right now. "Look, Toni, it seemed like a good idea not to use our own names. Safer and all—"

"Safer from what?" she asked, glancing around them nervously. No one else was in the room and she turned back to him. "The place is gone. We escaped. It's over."

Was it, though? "Sure it is," he lied. "And I've got big plans for us. Once you get rested up—" He stopped suddenly and fought back the knot of fear. "Toni, I'm so sorry for all the dumb things I've done in the past few days."

She frowned at him. "Aren't we past the point of apologizing for everything? We both were pretty stubborn."

"I just wanted to be sure that you knew how much I love you," he said with as much of a smile as he could manage.

Her frown deepened. "What are you going to do?" she demanded, trying to raise herself up. She leaned on her right elbow for support, but fell back weakly. "Jon, don't do it. I can tell you've got another dumb idea, but don't do it. Your father's dead. Mid-America is gone. Let's just forget it all."

Would Guy forget that they knew what was going on? Would his partners be able to forget that they had escaped?

"Jon, please." Her voice was becoming panicky and he sought to reassure her.

331

"Hey, all I've got planned is a shower and some sleep," he said. "I'll be back in a few hours."

An orderly came into the room. "Mrs. Samuels?"

Jon nodded. "Right here."

"Jon!" Toni pleaded.

He smiled and leaned down to kiss her. "Take care of yourself," he whispered. "I love you." He squeezed her hand briefly and the man pushed the cart from the room.

Jon followed them out slowly. His right hand was in his pocket, fingering Lou Alexander's business card.

"You want to order breakfast now, sir?"

Jon looked up from the ice water he had been staring into. "Not right yet, thanks. I have some guests coming."

"Sure, honey." The waitress nodded, chewing her gum rapidly. "But you'd better order something, even if it ain't but a cup of coffee. Shorty sez, this ain't no Greyhound depot. You gotta order something soon or you're out on your ass."

Jon glanced over at Shorty, a large man in a white T-shirt working behind the grill. "Tell him I'll order in a few minutes. I'm sure they'll be here soon."

She leaned closer to him. "Hey, honey, I'll stand you a cup of coffee myself if you need it."

He smiled. "Thanks anyway, but I really am waiting for some guests."

"Hey, Crystal. Order up," Shorty hollered from the grill.

She winked at Jon as she moved away. "Just whistle if you want anything, honey."

Jon's eyes followed her absently as she walked over to the grill. Lou said he would be here. He wouldn't talk to Jon over the phone, but he had promised to meet him at this restaurant for breakfast.

Jon looked nervously at his watch again. The whole thing had gone far enough and was going to be settled that day, one way or another. Toni was everything to him. Her safety was more important than anything else and he was going to make sure she was protected. After all, Mid-America and all its records were gone. There was no need to pursue her any longer. If Lou wanted anyone they could take him.

Jon glanced up and saw three men enter the restaurant.

They looked around and then the short white-haired man came toward him. The grandfatherly Lou Alexander.

He took the thin black cigar from his lips and stretched out his right hand to Jon. His eyes sparkled with friendliness.

Jesus Christ, Jon thought, Lou was probably going to have him killed and he was giving him this long-lost-friend bit.

"Jon, it's good to see you again."

Jon rose from his seat and took Lou's hand in his own. "Good morning, Mr. Alexander."

"Sorry we're late, Jon. Chuckie had to work late last night and he wasn't moving too fast this morning."

Jon glanced at Lou's two companions. One was a dark-haired young man with hard brown eyes. The other, Chuckie, caused a peculiar shiver in Jon's stomach. He was an average-sized man with average features, except for his eyes. They were dark gray and totally lacking in any emotion.

"Chuckie, you and Marvin go have some breakfast."

"Sure, Mister A," the man said. He gazed around the room and then chose a table that had a clear view of the restaurant and street outside. He and Marvin sat down.

"Mr. Alexander," Jon began. "I—"

Lou held up his hand. "You haven't had breakf[ast] you? Never start the day on an empty stomach, waved the waitress over. "And call me Lou. E[veryone] does."

Even those he was about to kill? Jon wondered[. He or]dered pancakes and played with them as he waited [for Lou] to finish his bacon and eggs.

"You don't like pancakes, Jon?"

Jon shrugged as he stared at his plate. "I'm not particularly hungry today."

"Shame," Lou said, sipping at his coffee. "Why is it that these hillbilly joints make the best coffee?"

Jon just stared at him. Why was he playing this game?

Lou unwrapped a fresh cigar. "Life is peaks and valleys, Jon. Savor the peaks and endure the valleys." He worked at getting his cigar to draw properly; then he looked up at Jon. "What can I do for you, my son?"

Jon tasted bitter anger flowing into his mouth. "My father is dead."

"You lost a father. I lost an old friend. I do for his what

he would do for mine." The smoke slowly rose from his nose and mouth. "Now what can I do for you?" he asked gently.

Jon hardly knew where to begin, but he was tired of this dumb cat-and-mouse game they had played for the last half hour. "You can be honest for a change."

Lou's eyes turned rather cold, but Jon did not care. "You told me at my father's funeral . . ." God, was that only yesterday? "You said Toni's run of bad luck was over, but then you sent Guy Ramsey after us. Why are you playing games with us?"

Lou held his hand up to stop Jon. "For the moment, I will ignore your lack of trust in me. Please explain about Mr. Ramsey."

He seemed genuinely puzzled and that confused Jon. Was this just another trick? "Toni and I went to Mid-America last night."

Lou nodded. "And had the misfortune to meet with Mr. Ramsey?" he finished for him. "Might I ask how you escaped his wrath?"

"He locked us in a storeroom, and we managed to get out before the fire burned the whole building."

"And your Toni, is she all right also?" Lou asked.

Jon nodded slowly. The hospital did not seem quite so safe any longer. "I sent her out of town," he said. "I'm to let her know when it's safe to come back."

Lou sighed. "It seems you have reason to mistrust me, Jon. But rest assured, your Toni is safe now. I do not go back on my word. Mr. Ramsey did a bit on his own lately, but he won't trouble you any longer."

"How can you be so sure?"

Lou took a drag on his cigar before answering. "He had the terrible misfortune to have an accident last night."

Jon frowned.

"An automobile accident. Such a pity. He left a wife and two small children, but they will be taken care of. His wife is young. Who knows? She may marry again."

Jon was thoroughly confused.

"He's dead? But—"

"I only hope that you won't hold his actions against me. He was going through a difficult time near the end, but life will go on. That's the way of the world."

Jon didn't know what to say. Were they really safe? He

looked up at the soft gentle face that framed the rock-hard eyes. No, not really. One of the soldiers was dead, but the army was still at the walls.

"What do you want to do, Jon?"

"Do?"

"Yes, what do you want to do with your life?"

Jon could feel the heat of anger crawling up the back of his neck. "I know what I don't want to do. I don't want to be like my father."

The smile turned down and the mouth grew hard to match the eyes. "Your father did the best he could to take care of his family."

Try as he as he could, Jon could still feel his anger growing and his control slipping. "He worked hand and glove with the mob." His voice was rising and growing angrier.

More of Lou's face turned to stone. He raised his hand to quiet Jon. "Your father entered into some business dealings with old friends."

Jon's face twisted with a bitter smile. "Business? Sure, just like selling insurance or groceries."

Lou drew on the black cigar. "You're an intelligent man, Jon. You went to graduate business school, right?"

"Yeah."

"Isn't it the duty of business to meet the demands of its customers?"

Jon looked with hate at the little man in front of him. He had an insane urge to throttle him. He was the one that led his father down the road to ruin.

As Jon would not answer, Lou spoke again. "None of our customers buy with a gun at their heads."

Even though he didn't want to admit it, Jon knew that the same phrase probably applied to his father. No one had held a gun at his head. The carrot usually worked better than the stick anyway.

"They buy because they want to, Jon."

"Your products are not good for the public."

He saw a sardonic smile come to Lou's lips. Lou looked down at his cigar. "Is tobacco good for the consumer?"

Jon merely shrugged, refusing to answer.

Lou let the smoke escape slowly. Then he looked up from the tip of his cigar to stare out the window. "Sons don't seem to want to follow in their fathers' footsteps anymore.

I have two sons. One is a professor at Notre Dame and the other coaches at a high school in Milwaukee." He shook his head resignedly. "I think it all started with all the rebelliousness we had in the sixties."

Staring out the window, he seemed to be speaking more to himself than to Jon. "I have a daughter that wants to go into the business, though." He turned back to Jon with a laugh. "Do you think the government would get off my back if I opened up my executive ranks to women?"

Jon did not know what to say.

"I have other minorities, but no women." Lou stood up abruptly. "Well, the sun is starting its climb and there is a lot I have to do today."

He turned toward the two men at the table by the wall. "Chuckie," he called quietly, nodding toward the cashier.

He turned back to Jon. "Not too many sons want to follow in their fathers' footsteps anymore." He smiled sadly and shrugged his shoulders. "But, if that is the way of the world, then we fathers must adapt."

He reached down to shake Jon's hand. "Good luck, my son." He started to walk away, but turned back. "Take care of your lady, Jon. Frances says that she's very nice."

Jon sat still as Lou and his henchmen left. He stared out the window for a long while, almost unbelieving that things were really over and they were safe.

"You need anything else, sir?"

Jon looked up at the waitress and smiled tiredly. "No, thank you. I've got everything I'll ever need right now."

Toni was awake and watching the door. It seemed like it was hours since breakfast, but she knew it was still early. She was too worried to relax, though. Where was Jon? Was he at home resting or out on some other crazy scheme?

Each time a nurse came in, she smiled and chatted pleasantly for fear that they would give her another sedative. She was determined that she was not going to spend the day in a drugged sleep. When Jon came back, she was going to be awake.

She turned to stare out the nearby window. The other woman in the room had turned on the television and Toni tried to ignore its blare. Where was Jon now? If only she could believe that he was safe. She closed her eyes briefly.

The last few days had been such a waste. Five days of love lost because of stupid pride and misunderstandings. How tragic!

"Hi, lover."

Toni's eyes flew open. Jon was standing at the side of her bed. He had showered and changed his clothes, but there were tiny lines of exhaustion around his eyes.

"Jon?" she whispered.

He smiled and reached down to embrace her.

Safe within his arms, she was able to ask him the question in her heart. "Is it all over?"

"Are you kidding?" he laughed. "We're just beginning."

# CHAPTER TWENTY-EIGHT

Toni opened her eyes to find Spike sitting right in front of her, leisurely taking a bath in a patch of sunlight. The rest of the bed was empty.

"Where's Jon?" she asked him.

He blinked at her, and then went back to his washing.

"So don't tell me." She shrugged and rolled over onto her back, stretching her arms over her head.

It was Sunday morning, four days since the fire and she was finally starting to feel alive again. Hours of dreamless sleep had refreshed her. The scratches on her hands had disappeared and the ache in her arm from the tetanus shot was almost gone. Best of all, the emptiness in her heart had fled with help from Jon.

She slid a little further under the covers, enjoying the feel of the smooth sheets against her skin as she thought about the night before. They had made love and talked, made love and talked, and then made love some more until they had fallen asleep entangled in each other's arms. No nightmares had dared to disturb her.

Rolling back over on her side, Toni closed her eyes. She was no longer afraid of loving Jon, for everything else had faded into insignificance. The problem was convincing him of that fact, and that she didn't blame him for anything that had happened.

"Hey, you're not going back to sleep again, are you?"

Toni blinked suddenly and sat up. Jon was standing at the foot of the bed with a tray in his hands. Spike was gone and the patch of sunlight had moved.

"What's that?" she asked.

He carried the tray over and placed it on her lap. "It was going to be breakfast in bed, but now it's more like a late lunch. Each time I came up to take your order, you were asleep. Finally, I decided to choose the menu myself."

"Looks great," she told him with a smile. Bacon and eggs, toast, coffee, and juice. Pineapple-orange juice, she discovered.

"So what's the occasion, and why are you dressed when I'm not?" she asked when she finished the juice.

He pulled a small packet from his back pocket and tossed it next to her as he sat down on the end of the bed. "I went and got yesterday's mail out of your box so there'd be no reason for you to leave today either."

"How about clothes?" she pointed out, and picked up the mail.

"Who needs clothes?" He had already shrugged out of his shirt.

Toni tossed aside an ad from Saks Fifth Avenue and two bills, and opened a letter. "Good Lord!" she exclaimed as she quickly read it. "Melanie's in Las Vegas!"

"So that's why you couldn't reach her."

She nodded and glanced at the envelope. It was postmarked late Thursday from St. Louis. Melanie didn't have a car that she knew of, but Toni couldn't imagine her taking a bus.

"So what does she say?" Jon tossed his shoes near a chair.

"Nothing much. Just that she had enough of Chicago and was trying her luck in Vegas. Oh, and that she'd prefer it if I didn't let Guy know." Toni looked up with a frown. "She must have gone before Wednesday night."

"She always did have the timing down pat."

"Hmm." Toni put her mail aside and drank some of her coffee.

"Speaking of timing," Jon went on, "what'd you think about my idea last night?"

"Which idea?" she asked innocently.

He made a threatening movement toward her, then stood up and slipped his jeans off. "About my new business. There are a lot of terrific old buildings in Chicago that are just waiting for a great renovator like myself."

"And you need a CPA to count them for you?"

He draped the jeans over the back of the chair and frowned at her. "Come on, Toni. Be serious. You said yesterday you weren't happy with your job. It would be the perfect solution. You could run the business side while I handled the actual construction."

She shrugged with a teasing smile. "Oh, I'll admit it sounds tempting, but there are a few details that need to be ironed out."

"Such as?"

Her eyes ran over him as he stood next to the bed, and her breath quickened as her own body responded to the sight of his, but she could not resist teasing him further. "Like the matter of this name," she said, exaggerating her displeasure. "Morici and James?"

He took the tray off the bed and put it on the floor. "I suppose you'd prefer James and Morici?" His eyes had narrowed thoughtfully.

"Well, that's one possibility," she admitted. He leaned over her and her body tingled in anticipation. "But there are others."

"Like what?" His hands came down on either side of her body, pinning her down beneath the blanket.

"How about James and Associates?"

His hands moved, the right one whipping the blanket back so that her naked body lay next to him. "And I'm the 'Associates'?"

His hands roamed over her soft skin, exploring the territory with gentleness and passion. Moving with delicious slowness, they slid over her breasts, teasing the tips until they longed for more, and then past her flat stomach to her thighs and the softness between her legs.

Toni's arms reached up to capture his head and bring his lips down to meet hers. They tasted of coffee and pineapple-orange juice and love as he devoured the sweetness of her mouth. His tongue slid over her lips, playing the tempter as it left her unfulfilled and drew away.

"Hey," she protested softly. But then his lips found her breasts and sent waves of uncontrolled desire echoing through her.

As she shivered with passion, he lifted his head. A playful gleam was in his eye. "And what other suggestions did you have?"

She pushed him over onto his back and lay across his body. Her hands took control, caressing and tormenting him. His chest, his stomach, his legs. Every place but where he wanted her hands to be. She kissed his mouth, playing with his tongue and his lips, sending shivers of longing through his body that only made her increase her attack.

When his breath was coming as hard and fast as hers, she pushed back from him slightly. "Actually, you've mocked my ideas so, I don't think I should tell you any of my others."

He flipped her over so that he was on top once more. "Who cares?" he murmured, his lips along her neck. Kissing, tasting her. "We can call our business anything you want as long as we conduct all of our business meetings right here."

His mouth was on hers again, fastened tightly as their bodies lay alongside each other. Her arms wound around his neck and she pulled him closer and closer. The feel of him against her was driving her wild with desire. She was consumed by her need for him. The scent of his body, the taste of his skin, the sound of his breathing were all that she knew and all that she wanted. Just to be one with him would be heaven enough. There was no thought beyond the immediate and no sound but the murmurs of love.

Later, when they lay in each other's arms, Jon brushed the hair back from Toni's face. "We never did get that matter of the name settled, did we?"

She lay against his chest and stirred unwillingly. "If I remember correctly, you agreed to anything."

He groaned. "Take advantage of a man when he's down, would you?"

She just laughed and moved to kiss him slowly. "Actually, I was thinking more in the line of Morici and Morici," she told him.

He frowned for a moment; then it slowly turned into an uncertain smile. "Do you mean it, Toni? Are you sure?"

She laughed. "What's this, cold feet or a retraction?"

"No, it's neither," he said quickly. "I just want to know for sure what you're saying."

She shook her head with a fond smile. "I'm saying that I love you. That I want to marry you. That I can't imagine a life without you in it. I can stay at the accounting firm or I can go with you in your business; that seems a minor point as long as I always have you to come home to."

"Oh, Toni," he groaned, and shifted his weight so he

could kiss her lips. His words were lost amid the murmurs of passion and the whispers of love.

Spike edged silently into the room. The tray was still on the floor where Jon had left it. The scent of the bacon pulled him closer and closer. He stopped at an unexpected noise from the bed and waited, but no one challenged his right to the food, so he went on.

At the edge of the tray he leaned over and grasped the last slice of the bacon in his teeth. He pulled it gently away, then sped down the stairs to the patch of sunlight on the living room floor where he had eaten the rest. It was a good day, a marvelous one, in fact. Three slices of bacon and a soft, warm place to sleep. He wondered, did he dare go back up and eat the eggs, too?

# IT'S A NEW AVON ROMANCE LOVE IT!

### A GENTLE FEUDING
### 87155-6/$3.95
### Johanna Lindsey

A passionate saga set in the wilds of Scotland, in which a willful young woman is torn between tempestuous love and hate for the powerful lord of an enemy clan.

### WILD BELLS TO THE WILD SKY
### 84343-9/$6.95
### Laurie McBain    Trade Paperback

This is the spellbinding story of a ravishing young beauty and a sun-bronzed sea captain who are drawn into perilous adventure and intrigue in the court of Queen Elizabeth I.

### FOR HONOR'S LADY
### 85480-5/$3.95
### Rosanne Kohake

As the sounds of the Revolutionary War echo throughout the colonies, the beautiful, feisty daughter of a British loyalist and a bold American patriot must overcome danger and treachery before they are gloriously united in love.

### DECEIVE NOT MY HEART
### 86033-3/$3.95
### Shirlee Busbee

In New Orleans at the onset of the 19th century, a beautiful young heiress is tricked into marrying a dashing Mississippi planter's look-alike cousin—a rakish fortune hunter. But deceipt cannot separate the two who are destined to be together, and their love triumphs over all obstacles.

---

Buy these books at your local bookstore or use this coupon for ordering:

Avon Books, Dept BP, Box 767, Rte 2, Dresden, TN 38225
Please send me the book(s) I have checked above. I am enclosing $_____ (please add $1.00 to cover postage and handling for each book ordered to a maximum of three dollars). Send check or money order—no cash or C.O.D.'s please. Prices and numbers are subject to change without notice. Please allow six to eight weeks for delivery.

Name _____

Address _____

City _____ State/Zip _____

Love It! 5-84

This is the special design logo that will call your attention to Avon authors who show exceptional promise in the romance area. Each month a new novel—either historical or contemporary—will be featured.

**THE AVON ROMANCE**

### HEART SONGS Laurel Winslow
**Coming in April**                                                **85365-5/$2.50**
Set against the breathtaking beauty of the canyons and deserts of Arizona, this is the passionate story of a young gallery owner who agrees to pose for a world-famous artist to find that he captures not only her portrait but her heart.

### WILDSTAR Linda Ladd
**Coming in May**                                                **87171-8/$2.75**
The majestic Rockies and the old West of the 1800's are the setting for this sizzling story of a beautiful white girl raised by Indians and the virile frontiersman who kidnaps her back from the Cheyenne.

### NOW & AGAIN Joan Cassity
**Coming in June**                                             **87353-2/$2.95**
When her father dies, a beautiful young woman inherits his failing landscape company and finds herself torn between the fast-paced world of business and the devouring attentions of a dynamic real estate tycoon.

### FLEUR DE LIS Dorothy E. Taylor
**Coming in July**                                             **87619-1/$2.95**
The spellbinding story of a young beauty who, fleeing France in the turmoil of revolution, loses her memory and finds herself married to a dashing sea captain who is determined to win her heart and unlock the secret of her mysterious past.

**A GALLANT PASSION** Helene M. Lehr      86074-0/$2.95
**CHINA ROSE** Marsha Canham              85985-8/$2.95
**BOLD CONQUEST** Virginia Henley         84830-9/$2.95
**FOREVER, MY LOVE** Jean Nash            84780-9/$2.95

Look for THE AVON ROMANCE wherever paperbacks are sold, or order directly from the publisher. Include $1.00 per copy for postage and handling: allow 6-8 weeks for delivery. Avon Books, Dept BP Box 767, Rte 2, Dresden, TN 38225.

Avon Rom 5-84

# VELVET GLOVE

**An exciting series of contemporary novels of love with a dangerous stranger.**

*Starting in July*

**THE VENUS SHOE Carla Neggers**  87999-9/$2.25
Working on an exclusive estate, Artemis Pendleton becomes embroiled in a thirteen-year-old murder, a million dollar jewel heist, and with a mysterious Boston publisher who ultimately claims her heart.

**CAPTURED IMAGES Laurel Winslow**  87700-7/$2.25
Successful photographer Carolyn Daniels moves to a quiet New England town to complete a new book of her work, but her peace is interrupted by mysterious threats and a handsome stranger who moves in next door.

**LOVE'S SUSPECT Betty Henrichs**  88013-X/$2.25
A secret long buried rises to threaten Whitney Wakefield who longs to put the past behind her. Only the man she loves has the power to save—or destroy her.

**DANGEROUS ENCHANTMENT Jean Hager**  88252-3/$2.25
When Rachel Drake moves to a small town in Florida, she falls in love with the town's most handsome bachelor. Then she discovers he'd been suspected of murder, and suddenly she's running scared when another body turns up on the beach.

**THE WILDFIRE TRACE Cathy Gillen Thacker**  88620-4/$2.25
Dr. Maggie Connelly and attorney Jeff Rawlins fall in love while involved in a struggle to help a ten-year-old boy regain his memory and discover the truth about his mother's death.

**IN THE DEAD OF THE NIGHT Rachel Scott**  88278-7/$2.25
When attorney Julia Leighton is assigned to investigate the alleged illegal importing of cattle from Mexico by a local rancher, the last thing she expects is to fall in love with him.

**AVON PAPERBACKS**

Buy these books at your local bookstore or use this coupon for ordering:

Avon Books, Dept BP, Box 767, Rte 2, Dresden, TN 38225
Please send me the book(s) I have checked above. I am enclosing $_____
(please add $1.00 to cover postage and handling for each book ordered to a maximum of three dollars). *Send check or money order*—no cash or C.O.D.'s please. Prices and numbers are subject to change without notice. Please allow six to eight weeks for delivery.

Name _____

Address _____

City _____ State/Zip _____

Velvet Glove 5-84